There Is a Time for Everything under Heaven

There Is a Time for Everything under Heaven

A Time to Hate and a Time to Love

Richard Waltner

iUniverse, Inc.
Bloomington

There Is a Time for Everything under Heaven
A Time to Hate and a Time to Love

iUniverse books may be ordered through booksellers or by contacting:

iUniverse
1663 Liberty Drive
Bloomington, IN 47403
www.iuniverse.com
1-800-Authors (1-800-288-4677)

ISBN: 978-1-4502-8414-1 (sc)
ISBN: 978-1-4502-8416-5 (dj)
ISBN: 978-1-4502-8415-8 (ebk)

Printed in the United States of America

iUniverse rev. date: 02/09/2011

Contents

≡ ·╟╟· ≡

Chapter One

≡ ⑈ ≡

T hey met when he passed the counter where she had just finished making a purchase. She turned quickly, they collided, and the small bag he was carrying flew out of his hand. When it hit the floor the bottle of shaving lotion inside broke, splattering its contents around the area. As they both knelt on the floor to retrieve the soggy bag, she said,

"I'm so sorry, that was clumsy of me."

"It's OK," he replied, "it was only a small bottle of shaving lotion, it can easily be replaced. Both raised their heads and their eyes met at the same time. For a moment they looked at each other's face. What an attractive girl. He thought. What a nice looking man, she thought.

"Please let me replace the shaving lotion," she said.

"No, no, that's not necessary, but I'll tell you what you can do."

She hesitated for a moment then asked,

"And what would that be?"

"We are right next to a coffee shop; would you have a cup of coffee with me?"

She looked at her watch, and then at him again for a moment, and said,

"Sure, I guess that's the least I can do."

They walked across the hall, entered the coffee shop and found an empty table. He pulled out a chair and helped seat her. She thought

1

to herself that was nice I didn't think men did that anymore. He interrupted her thoughts asking,

"Can I get you anything to eat?"

"No thank you, just a cup of coffee."

She was approximately 5 feet 6 inches tall, of slender build with a very shapely figure. Her dark hair was pulled back and bound with a rubber band close to the back of her head, it was shoulder length. Her attractive face was clear and without blemishes. She was a very expensive call girl who catered only to wealthy men. He was 6 feet tall, with a very muscular well shaped figure. He had broad shoulders and narrow hips. His hair was also dark with an occasional wave. Unlike many men who were wearing their hair short, his was not; however, he was well groomed. Other than for an attractive mustache, he was clean shaven. He was a marital and sex therapist and had recently opened an office.

When he returned with the coffee he was smiling and said,

"I didn't know if you use cream, sugar or both, so I brought both."

She was charmed by his smile. It was so friendly and it came to him so easily.

"I like mine black," she said.

"I like mine with a little of both," was his response. He sat down and then said,

"Well, we might as well get acquainted. My name is Robert Sloan. My friend's call me Rob and I hope you will do likewise. I'm a marital and sex therapist and I have recently started my practice. Marital therapy has been around for a long time, however sexual therapy is a relatively new field. There are many people who need the help of a well trained therapist with their marital and sexual problems."

"Two friends of mine, we met in college, share a small building we had divided into offices. All of us are counselors and we decided to start our practices together. Zack Kettering is a child therapist and Ken Jones is a financial advisor and counselor. We each have our own office, Ken and Zack have secretaries, however I have not yet arrived at the point financially where I can afford one."

"When you do, I suppose she will be middle aged and with much experience."

"No, she will be young and pretty and able to handle the intimate details of a couple's relationship that are a necessary part of record keeping. That means I have to keep the records and do the computer work which doesn't leave me much free time."

"I was born and raised in a small town in south eastern South Dakota. After high school graduation, I enrolled at the University of South Dakota in Vermillion where I earned my Master's degree. I went directly to the University of Utah where I received my doctors' degree"

"You are a doctor?"

"For what it's worth, yes I am."

"What do you mean for what it's worth?"

"There are times when I am called on to talk about my college years I get the feeling there are those who think that I'm bragging."

"I would say that getting a doctor's degree is something to brag about."

Rob smiled.

"As I mentioned, there are many people who need help with their relationships, however, the idea has not yet sunk in that it is OK to get help when a relationship begins to flounder. With the high divorce rate as it is, more and more people are seeking help rather than ending the marriage or continuing to live in a relationship that is less than satisfying, especially sexually satisfying."

"I love my work and when I know I have helped, really helped a couple or an individual, I find it very satisfying."

My, she thought, he sure is open. I think I could tell him a thing or two about satisfying sexual relationships. For having met just a short time ago he certainly is open about himself and his profession. Because of his demeanor and attire I thought he was in the professions. This was supposed to be nothing more than having coffee together, but it's turning out to be far more than that. I wonder how much I can tell him about myself.

While he spoke, she looked him over. What a handsome man he is. He has such a friendly smile and it comes so easy to him. He is so disarmingly charming. I wish I had more customers like him. I'll bet it would be great having sex with him. Maybe I'll try to seduce him. On the other hand most likely he has a strong sense of morals and ethics and seducing him would not be easy if even possible. Oh well, it was a fun thought.

She wasn't surprised to hear that he was a therapist. There was something about his dress and demeanor that said professional. She wrinkled her brow, and then said,

"I didn't know there were such people as sex therapists. What do you do, help people get connected sexually?" Then she laughed.

Rob smiled and thought, what a pleasant laugh she has, then he said,

"Well, I guess I can say that is one of the things I do."

The moment the words were out of her mouth she regretted having said them.

"I'm sorry, I meant no offense."

"You don't have to apologize. I think what you said is very appropriate for those couples who aren't getting it together sexually."

Who am I to cast dispersions on anyone's profession, she thought. Rob told me what his profession is. Me, on the other hand I can't even tell him what my profession is.

"Well, other than filling in the small details of my life that is about it."

"Hardly," she said, "I know there is much more than that."

"Yes, but I don't think you would be interested in the minutia.

"How do you know?"

Rob flashed his smile again.

"I guess it's my turn. My name is Heidi Faust, and right now I'm between jobs, just not doing much of anything."

"Heidi is such a pretty name for such a pretty girl," Robert said.

"Be careful Rob, flattery will get you every where."

Both laughed.

"Please call me Rob. Where are you from Heidi?"

"My parental home is in Iowa" she replied. In fact I have been to Vermillion, a number of times. During my senior year I even considered enrolling in the University of South Dakota, however I wanted to get farther away from home."

"Your family life wasn't very good?"

"My family life was wonderful with both a loving mother and father and three brothers who were very protective of me. As a matter of fact, almost too much so. I'm the youngest. My home town is close to Sioux City. Where about in South Dakota did you live?"

"In a small town about 35 miles from Yankton. Do you know where Yankton is?"

"Of course, as with Vermillion I have been there a number of times. What an irony, on more than one occasion we were separated by just a few miles. If I had attended the University in Vermillion, who knows, we might have met during our college years."

"Gosh Heidi, that sure would have been great."

"I decided to attend the University of Washington. It was tough and expensive, but finally I received my masters degree."

"You have a master's degree?"

"Yes."

"Are you planning to get a doctors degree?"

"Heavens no, a masters is enough for what I do and further college is too expensive."

"How did you happen to get to Tacoma?"

"I pursued an ad in a local paper. A company was looking for a business administrator. I was eager to get out of Seattle, so the offer seemed tailor made for me. So, here I am. Like you there is much minutia which you wouldn't be interested in."

"And like you Heidi, how do you know?"

Neither was in a hurry to leave so they continued visiting, talking about their respective homes, some childhood anecdotes, some of their likes and dislikes, just small things. He asked her,

"When did you finish college, Heidi?"

"I finished my bachelor's degree two years ago in spring. I received my masters at the end of the fall semester."

"So," Rob said, "that makes us about the same age. I'm almost 26." Heidi laughed; "I'm 23."

"What do you know about that?" Rob responded. "Here we are two people who have just met, you are from Iowa and I am from just across the border in South Dakota. You have a bachelor's degree and I have just a bit more college and now we discover we are very close together in age. Is that a coincidence or what?"

They visited for another half hour when Heidi looked at her watch and said,

"My goodness, do you know we have been visiting for over two hours. I must be going. I want you to know that I really enjoyed our visit, and Rob, we did talk about minutia."

"Two hours," Rob replied, "has it been that long? I also enjoyed our visit Heidi, I enjoyed it very much. I don't want to seem too forward, but sometimes a fellow has to be when he meets a pretty girl. Would you have dinner with me one of these early evenings?"

She hesitated. Would it be wise to continue the relationship? She had already lied about her profession, how many more lies would she have to tell. At the same time how could she refuse him? Rob broke the silence.

"As pretty as you are, I'm sure you are either engaged or going steady. I should have asked you before I asked for a date."

"I am neither Rob, I'm as free as a bird."

She enjoyed their time together; he was such a polite man and such a good conversationalist. One date with him would be OK; she would guard what she said very carefully.

"You aren't being forward, I would like that very much Rob."

"Alright, let's check our calendars."

They got out their pocket calendars and both had the coming Sunday evening free.

"Is Sunday evening too soon for you Heidi?"

"No, that would be fine."

"OK," Rob said, "I know of a little out of the way Italian Restaurant, that serves up some mighty good food. Do you like Italian dishes?"

"I love them," responded Heidi."

"Alright, that's settled," Rob replied. "Until Sunday evening then, you take care of yourself."

"I will, she said, and you too."

With that said they turned to go their separate ways.

"Whoa," Rob said, "I need your address and phone number, and I'll give you mine."

They exchanged phone numbers and addresses and then went their separate ways. As she headed for her car, Heidi thought, my gosh, here I'm a call girl, and he is a therapist. Well, that doesn't mean we can't have a good time together. He doesn't have to know I'm a call girl. I'm going to have to make sure my car is in the garage otherwise Rob can't help wondering how a girl between jobs can afford such a fancy car.

Chapter Two

≡ ·||· ≡

As Sunday evening approached Heidi 's excitement increased. She said to herself. My gosh, I feel like a high school girl again going out on my first date. Why not, it's been years since I had a real date, and who could be better to have it with than Rob. I know I'm going to enjoy it.

She was glad she had told her manager that she was taking a couple of weeks off. The timing couldn't have been better. She needed a break from her business that was beginning to wear more and more on her.

The date was a complete success. Rob picked a restaurant that had a nice decor, nothing fancy, and the food was excellent. It certainly wasn't the kind of eating place she had become accustomed to. Often, when a customer paid for an afternoon and night with her, he took her out for dinner to expensive eating places. With Rob it was different. Because of his limited income he could not afford to take her to a fancy restaurant.

She said to herself, what do I care how fancy the restaurant is, I'll be getting back to them soon enough. Further, I want to enjoy the date with Rob. Most likely it will be our first and last date.

But that's not the way it turned out. Although they were miles apart so far as professions went they seemed very compatible in most other areas. They both liked good music, they both liked outdoor activities. Rob enjoyed hiking, back packing and camping. Heidi especially enjoyed hiking in the mountains. The only camping she had done was back in Iowa. Her father loved to fish and often the family would camp for a few days at a nearby lake while he and her brothers fished.

Rob spoke so favorably about packing food, clothing and his cameras into the mountains, setting up camp and then hiking, taking pictures by the dozens that the idea intrigued her. He spoke of places he went to often and talked much about his cameras and how they worked. She had wanted to get into photography, but never got around to buying a camera. She thought maybe some week end she would give it a try. But the hiking part was a joy for both of them.

They visited about experiences they had in high school, about past dates they had, about their infatuations that seemed always to be short lived. Rob told her that was a big problem young people faced, how to distinguish infatuation from true love. His premarital counseling almost always involved young couples. He had put together a list of questions the couple was to go over together. Some of the questions were pretty touchy and some involved discussing very intimate issues. He told her if a couple could get through the list without a lot of conflict it might very well be indicative of a love relationship. He commented on how much he enjoyed pre marital counseling.

Being raised in S.E.S.D., Rob was an ardent hunter. She could see the pleasure reflected in his eyes when he spoke of his love for pheasant hunting. Her dad and brothers were also pheasant hunters and James, her youngest brother in particular, enjoyed hunting white tail deer. She often accompanied her dad on his pheasant hunts and though she wanted to also hunt, her dad never got around to buying her a shotgun that would be adequate, but not punishing.

When Rob asked her what her hobbies were, she told him she really didn't have many hobbies. Photography intrigued her and that buying a camera was on her list of priorities.

"Heidi," Rob said, "That is one hobby of mine of which I could give you a lot of instruction."

He talked about single lens reflex cameras, about pixels and a number of other things about which she knew nothing. It was late when Rob stopped in front of her house. It was well lit up by street lights. Rob commented on the house saying,

"Rent must really cost you a bundle."

She answered by saying,

"Living in a nice house is one extravagance I allow myself."

Damn, she thought, another lie, but how can I tell him I own the house. How can I tell him about the other extravagancies that I have?

He was curious about her car he wanted to know what kind it was, what kind of mileage she got, about maintenance and other things men would know and be curious about. He was just like her brothers when it came to cars, talking about things that had no meaning to her.

She told him it was a small Ford that gave her very good gas mileage. Another lie, but how could she tell him she owned a Jaguar. Well, not to worry since this was just a get acquainted date. Soon she would forget about Rob and he would forget about her.

Each time she lied she remembered her dad's words, Be honest and don't lie for if you do, they will eventually catch up with you. When she thought about her mother and dad, her throat tightened up on her. She was neglecting them totally. Sure, as a call girl she was making lots of money but in other respects it was a real drag. She ignored her parents. She wanted to find a man she could love, a man she would have children with.

So long as she remained a call girl, those were only dreams. And even if she quit the business and fell in love, how could she go on living a lie for the rest of her life? Being a call girl, no man would be interested in marriage with her.

Rob got out of his Chrysler, walked around the front to the passenger side and opened Heidi's door for her.

"Rob, you didn't have to do that."

"Oh yes I did and I am also going to walk you to the door. Remember our Midwestern customs? A fellow always walked his girl to the door."

"That was the Midwest Rob and a few years ago."

"Do you object if I walk you to your door?"

"Of course not, I think it's very romantic."

When they got to the door, Rob said,

"Heidi, I had a wonderful time this evening, not once did we run out of things to talk about. Earlier both of us said the other would not be interested in minutia of our lives. That is what we have been talking about all evening. You seemed so relaxed and I know I was, like we have been dating for quite some time."

"Rob, it was a wonderful evening for me too. I don't date very often"

"A pretty girl like you and you don't date?"

"Men out here are not like South Dakota and Iowa men."

Another lie, she didn't date because she had no desire to. She had plenty of men around her most of the time.

"Heidi, can we do this again, would you accept another date with me?"

She was going to make up some excuse why she couldn't, but instead said, "I'd love to Rob."

"Great," Rob said, "I have your phone number and I will be calling you in a day or two."

"I'll be waiting for your call. Good night Rob."

"Good night Heidi and thank you again for a wonderful evening."

There wasn't much sleep for either that night, Rob couldn't get his mind off Heidi and Heidi couldn't get her mind off of Rob. Something was stirring inside Heidi that she had not felt before, and she liked it.

Although it was only a first date, Rob wondered if he could be feeling the first stirrings of love. My gosh man, he said to himself, Heidi is a very attractive and shapely girl, what am I feeling? Could it be nothing more than infatuation? He concluded it had to be more than that. He would be able to tell more after their next date.

It was only a few evenings later that Rob and Heidi had dinner and then went to a concert. This time when Rob walked Heidi to the door. they stood for a moment looking into each others eyes then Rob gathered

Heidi up in his arms and kissed her. Immediately she yielded to his kiss. It was a long kiss and when they broke, both were breathing heavily.

"Wow Heidi, you do things to me that I have not experienced before."

Heidi relied,

"I was going to say the same thing Rob."

"Heidi, I believe I have fallen in love with you. I know this is only our second date, but I'm not going to hesitate to tell you. I considered infatuation, but the feelings I have for you go way beyond that. Further, I am no longer a high school Junior."

Heidi was silent for a moment and then replied,

"Rob, I too believe I have fallen in love with you. After our initial meeting at the mall I had stirrings inside of me which I had not experienced. I know this is only our second date, but those feelings have grown as I spend time with you. I too have concluded that I have fallen in love for the first time."

Again that night there was little sleep, both were feeling the first pangs of love. This caused Heidi no little consternation knowing that as their love intensified the time would come when she would have to tell Rob the truth, that she was a call girl. And the relationship did intensify rapidly. Their get togethers were more and more frequent and soon they were spending most of their spare time together.

Being a good cook, Heidi often prepared dinner for them. Rob cooked for himself and when he had Heidi over, it was a fun time as she told him what he did wrong in preparing various foods. One evening it was so bad that when they sat down to eat, and ate a spoonful of this and that, they looked across the table at each other and started laughing. Rob folded his napkin, placed it beside his plate and said,

"Come on sweetheart, we're going out for dinner."

Heidi had informed Paul at the agency that she would not be returning, that she had fallen in love with a wonderful guy and it wouldn't be too long before there would be an engagement.

Paul was glad for Heidi. He said to her,

"If you recall, from very early on I told you that you didn't belong in this business."

"I know you did Paul and I believe it is that that made you such a dear friend. Paul there is one thing facing me that has me scared. Soon I'm going to have to tell Rob I was a call girl and I'm so fearful he will drop me like a hot potato."

"Heidi, if Rob truly loves you, somehow, in some way he will accept your past. I wouldn't worry about it too much."

"Thank you for the encouragement Paul, you always seem to come through for me when I need you."

One evening after they had eaten out Rob said to Heidi,

"OK Heidi Girl, what you would like to do this evening?"

"Are you serious Rob? Do you want me to pick the entertainment?"

"I sure do Sweetheart. There must be something you would like to do. It dawned on me the other evening that I'm the one who always makes the decision regarding our activities after dinner."

"Rob, we have been to several concerts and I like classical music, I really do, but I also love jazz. This evening there's a jazz concert which I would like to attend. I know you're not much of a jazz fan, but one concert isn't going to kill you."

"Heidi, if you want to attend a jazz concert then that is what we are going to do."

"Are you sure?"

"Sure as shootin, as we say in the Midwest. Just tell me where it is and we will be on our way."

"It isn't far from here and I'll direct you to the front door. We have a half hour before it begins so we don't have to be in too big a rush."

"OK let's go,"

Heidi was correct, Rob didn't like jazz, however this evening was an exception. It wasn't the music that caught his attention, it was Heidi. There were a number of performing artists. Once the music got going so did Heidi. In fact she got carried away, clapping, shouting and stamping her feet thoroughly enjoying herself.

Rob asked her,

"Are you familiar with the music of these various artists?"

"I sure am and this isn't the first time I've attended a jazz concert. In fact I go rather often. Are you enjoying yourself?"

"Not the music as much I enjoy watching you, you really get carried away."

"I know I do, but that's what it's all about. One goes to a jazz concert to get carried away."

On the drive to Heidi's house she turned to Rob and said,

"Rob, you really are a good sport. I thought you'd be sitting in your seat with a scowl on your face."

"Why should I Heidi? Towards the end of the concert I was beginning to get into the swing of things."

"I'm glad to hear that. Maybe we can attend other jazz concerts."

"When there is a jazz concert in town let me know and we'll be there."

Although it was late, they stopped at a fast food restaurant for a cup of coffee. As they were visiting Heidi said to Rob,

"We've been going together for a few months now. There is no further need for me to tell you I love you and I know you love me."

"I love you Heidi, very much so."

"I know Rob, but in the time we have known each other not once have you attempted to be physical with me. We kiss, hug and hold each other, but that's all the farther it gets. Don't you find me sexually appealing?"

"Aw Heidi, my desire for you is so strong that at times I find myself shaking."

"Then why don't you do something about it?"

"I want to Heidi, but I'm just a bit conflicted about us having sex just yet. I need a bit more time."

"What for?"

"To get things squared away in my head. Please don't be angry with me, it won't be too much longer."

"I won't get angry Rob, only I want to have sex with you real bad. To put it mildly, I'm really hard up. So please don't make me wait much longer. I don't understand why you are conflicted. After all you are not a virgin"

"And that's why I'm conflicted. I had it impressed on me that sex is for married couples."

Heidi thought to herself, the time has come for me to tell Rob that I was a call girl. I can't hold off much longer. I dread the thought of it.

This time when Rob walked Heidi to the door they kissed and didn't seem to be able to get out of the embrace.

"Are you sure you aren't ready now, Rob? I can feel you shaking."

"My body tells me, Rob do it, but my mind needs just a bit more time."

"I'm not going to put pressure on you, but please keep my needs in mind."

"I will Sweetheart, you can be sure of that. I'll be calling you in the morning so we can decide on what we are going to do next."

"I'll be waiting for your call. Good night sweetheart."

"Good night darling."

Chapter Three

≡ ·||· ≡

The next morning when he called Heidi, they made plans to spend Saturday in the mountains at one of Rob's favorite haunts, a place he called Vista Point. Both loved the mountains. It made no difference to Heidi where they went so long as she and Rob could be together.

It was fall, the foliage on the hill sides was changing colors as was the aspen groves. Though not much as yet, the mountains did have a mantel of fresh snow. All in all, it made for a very picturesque setting.

Robert pulled into Heidi's drive way at 7:30. a.m. He wanted to be at Vista Point early when the light on the mountains was just right. The sky was a deep blue color.

Rob was always in hopes that he would see Rainier bathed in a beautiful rose color. It was called alpenglow and Rob was ever hopeful that someday he would get the opportunity to photograph Mt. Rainier bathed in alpenglow.

They would be too late for any alpenglow if indeed there had been alpenglow that morning. Rob couldn't have hoped for better conditions for making pictures. Though an amateur, he was a pretty good photographer and amateur or not, he loved photography.

Heidi had decided that she could no longer keep the truth from Rob. This is the day she would tell him that she had been a call girl. She feared the worst, that the information would destroy their relationship.

She had not anticipated falling in love with Rob nor could she have imagined how wonderful being in love could be. The idea of losing him tore her apart inside. However, she could not keep it from him any longer. Sooner or later they would run into one of her customers. That would be far worse than telling him when they were alone.

Heidi was dressed in shorts and a sleeveless blouse. Her hair was in a ponytail with a kerchief on her head. Robert knocked twice and then opened the door.

"Heidi," he called,

"I'll be with you in a second Rob. I just finished brewing a pot of coffee. Have yourself a cup."

Since Rob was in a hurry, he went back to his car to retrieve his travel cup having decided to drink it on the way. Heidi came out of her bedroom. To Rob she looked great. Rob whistled loudly and said, "Gosh Heidi, you look sexy this morning. I can't guarantee I'll be able to keep my hands off you."

"Well I hope not Rob, I dressed for you and you alone. You had better find me sexy looking."

He noticed that Heidi appeared to be troubled. After they had driven for fifteen minutes Heidi had spoken only a few words.

"What's wrong Sweetheart? It's obvious to me that something is bothering you."

"I'm OK Hon. I guess I'm still not fully awake."

That didn't satisfy him, however he decided not to pursue it. Sooner or later she would open up. Another half hour on the road and they reached their destination. Heidi looked around for a sign.

"Rob there must be a sign here some place identifying this place as Vista Point."

"No sign Heidi, it's a name I gave the place because of all the vistas of Mt. Rainier there are from here. Rob retrieved his camera and tripod from the trunk of his Chrysler. Heidi asked,

"Rob, when are you going to get me a camera so I can join you. You said you would."

"I'm glad you said something Heidi, we'll go shopping some evening this week, however, if you want to join me that would be great.

"No thanks, this time I'll just walk around here and enjoy the beauty of Vista Point."

At the moment Heidi was too nervous and anxious to enjoy anything. Rob disappeared down one of the trails. When he returned in about 30 minutes, he had a big smile on his face and said to Heidi,

"I got some great pictures Sweetheart. Another 20 minutes and it would have been too late."

"I'm glad Rob, I wouldn't want to be responsible for you missing out on some great pictures"

How she enjoyed these outings with Rob. He was always so cheerful. As he was putting his camera and tripod into the car Heidi called out to him,

"Rob, when you finish please come over here to the table."

Now he would find out what was bothering her. Rob walked over to the table, sat down beside her and put his arm around her pulling her close to himself.

"Rob," she said, "I have something I must tell you that I greatly fear will destroy our relationship."

Robert furrowed his brow and asked;

"What in the world are you talking about?"

She looked at him with tears streaming down her cheeks.

"What in the world is the matter Heidi?"

"Rob, before we met I was a very expensive call girl, a prostitute." There was a shocked silence.

"Wha—what," Rob blurted out, "A high class call girl? You have to be kidding me."

"No Rob I'm not kidding you. I'm telling you the truth." Now she thought, our relationship is over.

Rob was silent. He stood up, jammed his hands into his pockets and turned from Heidi. He stood there silently for a minute then he said to Heidi in a broken voice.

"I have to be by myself for a while Heidi."

He walked a distance down a trail that led to the east, found a fallen tree and sat down. He lowered his head into his hands and soon sobs were wracking his body. It was if his world had come to an end. The girl he loved, a prostitute? What was he going to do?

After he had been sitting for 30 minutes, he said in a quiet voice,

"Lord, what am I going to do?"

Suddenly he had the answer. He felt it, he sensed it. It was as if a voice was speaking to him,

"Love her Rob, love Heidi."

Rob raised his head, looked out over the valley and said out loud,

"What am I doing here? I love Heidi, prostitute or not. I love her. Here I left her alone feeling sorry for myself, not giving any thought to how she must be feeling. She must feel awfully lonely there by herself. Poor Heidi, what must be going through her mind? Maybe she has walked off the trail. She could easily get lost."

He started running, all the while calling,

"Heidi, Heidi."

And then he picked up speed. Soon he saw the rear end of his car, however, it was hiding the picnic table. Once again he called,

"Heidi."

This time there was an answer;

"Rob, Rob, what's wrong?"

Then he saw Heidi running toward him. In a moment both stopped within a few feet of each other. Heidi was the first to speak,

"Oh Rob, you've been crying. Why did you call me?"

"I was afraid you would start down one of the trails and that you might get lost."

Heidi was looking at him. Rob took one step forward and took Heidi into his arms. He just held her close. Heidi could feel that he was still sobbing.

"Rob, what's wrong?"

He moved back a step and took Heidi's face into his hands and kissed her long and passionately.

"Heidi, Heidi, how I love you. Come into my arms again."

Heidi moved into Rob's arms, put her arms around him and lay her head against his chest.

"Do you really love me Rob after what I told you?"

"Yes, I really love you. I love you so very much."

Then it was Heidi who was weeping.

"I thought for sure when you walked away you were walking out of my life, that you never wanted to see me again."

"If I was, when you heard me calling you, I was running back into your life. I never want to leave you out of my sight."

"Are you sure Rob?"

"I have never been so sure about anything."

"But how can you still love me knowing I was a prostitute, knowing I have been intimate with many men?"

"Divine intervention Heidi, Divine intervention."

"I'm afraid I don't understand."

"Some day I'll tell you."

Rob pulled his handkerchief out of his pocket, wiped the tears from Heidi's cheeks, brushed a few stray hairs aside, cupped her face in his hands and again they kissed. Heidi spoke up,

"Rob, I was a prostitute, doesn't that make a difference to you? Many men have used my body to satisfy their sexual cravings."

"That is now behind us Heidi. Somehow we will deal with it, but one thing is for sure, it isn't going to drive us apart. We will let the past go as much as possible and concentrate on the present and the future."

"Are you serious Rob?"

"I have never been more serious in my life Heidi"

"Kiss me again Rob, please kiss me again."

Rob bent down to Heidi's upraised face and kissed her softly.

"Sweetheart, what matters is that I love you and you love me."

"I can't put into words how much I love you Rob. I couldn't live a lie any longer. I just had to tell you about my past."

"That took courage Heidi, great courage. That alone tells me how much you love me. Let's sit down, I believe both of us need to get off our feet for awhile."

Rob slid to the far end of the bench. Heidi stretched out and lay her head in Rob's lap. They looked into each other's eyes. Rob stroked her hair and smiled down at her. After remaining in this position for awhile, Rob said,

"Now Miss Heidi, I'm hungry. Let's have some of that lunch you fixed for us."

"Come to think of it," replied Heidi, "I'm hungry too."

Chapter Four

$$\Longrightarrow \cdot\|\cdot \Longleftarrow$$

After lunch they strolled hand in hand down one of the trails that led from the parking lot. It was a beautiful day just made for lovers. They frequently stopped to embrace and kiss. They came to a bench the Forest Service had built and sat down. Heidi looked at Rob and said,

"Rob, I know you have many questions and there is nothing to be gained by avoiding them. Can we take time to talk?"

"Of course we can Heidi, we are in no hurry, but do you think we should be dealing with them now?"

"Now is just as good a time as any."

"Well, I guess we can make a start. You want to guess what my first question is?"

"I don't have to guess, I know what your first question is. You want to know how many men I have had sex with, right?"

"You're right Heidi, I hesitated asking you because deep down I don't think I want to know."

"Maybe so Rob, but sooner or later you are going to ask. So I sat down and did some figuring. There are 52 weeks in a year. On average, I serviced three customers a week. That would make a total of 159 customers."

"What," said Rob, "You had sex with 159 men a year?"

"No Rob I didn't. Each month I would have to take off a week due to menstruation. So from 159 subtract 84. In addition I would take a 30 day vacation each year. That means there were four weeks when I had no customers so subtract another 12 customers. That means I had sex with 72 customers a year or a total of right around 216 customers in the years I was a call girl. Although it was a rule of mine not to have sex with more than one man an evening, there were a few times when a frequent customer would bring along a paying friend and when that happened I serviced two men in one evening. That happened only rarely. However, I would guess that happened about 10 times, so, it would be necessary to add to our 216, oh I would say another 10. So, now with that adjustment, instead of 216, over the span of three years, I had 226 customers. My gosh Rob, I really never gave much thought to figures, but over a span of three years I had sex with approximately 226 men."

There was a long period of silence, finally Heidi said,

"Rob, have you nothing to say?"

"I, I'm trying to let it sink in Heidi. Wow, you have had sex with 226 men. You were a regular screwing machine weren't you?"

"Well, that's rather crude, but if you want to put it that way, yes I was a screwing machine. I spent a lot of time having sex. Do you know street walkers, some at least, have sex with 800 plus customers a year. Why at 226 that makes me almost a neophyte."

Again Rob was silent.

"I shouldn't have said that and I'm sorry. It has no bearing on our situation. I know in your eyes 226 is a very large number. Rob I was a prostitute and a prostitute's business is to service men sexually. We are dealing with the first of your questions and you are having real difficulty with it. Please think of what I say as being in the context of my being a prostitute. I know there are things about me you are going to have difficulty with. Please remember Rob, a prostitute. I love you Rob and I'm not going to let you go."

Rob, was silent. Then he looked at Heidi and with a weak smile on his face said,

"Heidi girl, whatever you tell me isn't going to affect my love for you. I told you I love you, and that comes from the bottom of my heart. Had you told me you had sex with 500 men I would still love you. But 226 men, that just doesn't seem possible. It's darn hard for me to swallow."

"I know it is Rob, if you told me you had sex with 226 women in three years, I too would be shocked."

Rob looked at Heidi, smiled and said,

"For you that's possible Heidi, but for a man, I think it would be stretching it a bit far. A man would have to be a sexual athlete to establish that kind of a record. There may be a few, of course. In addition, most men wouldn't find the time or 230 women."

Again Rob was silent, obviously deep in thought. Then he raised his head, looked at Heidi and said,

"So, when you and I have sex, I will be no more than number 227, way back at the end of the line. To you I will mean nothing more than number 227."

"No Rob, you are wrong, granted that 226 is a big figure, not once did I have sex with a man I loved. Most were strangers to me and I was a stranger to them. For me it was just a physical act and for them it was just the same. There were return customers of course, but most I never saw again. Did I strike up a friendship with some of my return customers? Yes, I did, but that is all it was, a friendship and nothing more."

"Heidi, from what you've said, it appears to me most if not all of the men you serviced did little more than engage in vaginal masturbation. You didn't know them and they didn't know you. They did their thing and then left your house. You just said it was strictly a physical act and nothing more."

Heidi wrinkled her brow and said,

"Vaginal masturbation, how did you happen to come up with that description. Did you read it somewhere or is it original with you?"

"It seemed like good terminology for what you and your customers were doing. I don't know if it's original with me or not, undoubtedly someone has used the very words before I did. I used it in a paper I wrote and presented at a sex therapy conference. I got a good response from what one therapist called a neologism."

"What on earth does that mean?"

"A new word or phrase?"

"Original or not, I never thought of having sex with men whose names I didn't know, men who didn't know me as vaginal masturbation. I believe you're so right, they came to me strictly for sexual release when if they wanted to, they could have taken care of their sexual needs themselves. If they did, however, there would be no need for prostitutes. Vaginal masturbation, I like that."

"Does it bother you that your customers, most of them I would guess, did not see you as a whole person?"

"Are you saying they viewed me as a vagina and little more?"

"I'm afraid so Heidi."

"Often when I had sex with a customer and when he left I felt lonely. Do you suppose that's why?"

"Could very well be Heidi."

"What a lousy business I was in. I worked hard trying to convince myself that I enjoyed what I was doing and was happy. Rob, this may sound kind of crazy, but for me it will be like having sex for the first time. Why? Because it will be the first time I will be having sex with someone I love. I believe for me that's going to be a whole new experience."

"Hardly a whole new experience Heidi."

"Physically no, but emotionally yes."

"That may make sense to you Heidi, but it just doesn't register with me."

"Rob, you can't hold me responsible for something I did before we met and try as I may, there is no way I can erase what I'm telling you."

Rob was silent. Heidi started sobbing,

"Please Rob, don't leave me, this is the first time I have been in love and it feels so good. And I don't want to go back to being a prostitute."

While Heidi was crying silently, Rob looked over at her and his heart melted.

"No Heidi, no, I don't want to break off our relationship. I have no intention of leaving you. I love you girl and for me this is also the first time I've been in love and as with you it feels so good. I guess I'm wondering just how you and I can have a meaningful sexual relationship."

"Rob, I'm a woman and no one knows a woman's heart like a woman. You have no idea just how much I want to have sex with you. I can hardly wait. I, I'm afraid I just don't understand why you are making me wait."

"Right now I'm afraid I'll disappoint you Heidi and I don't want to do that."

"Disappoint me, why?"

"Undoubtedly some if not many of the men you had sex with were, well as men say it, are well endowed, and not only that they had considerable experience."

"Yes Rob, if you want to use that language, a good number are well endowed. Now Rob, I'm not just saying this to make you feel better, but are me size really doesn't make that much difference. For some of the girls it does."

"With three customers a week you had to be sensitized to size."

"Yes, of course I was."

"Well, how do you know I'll meet your expectations?"

"Rob, you haven't been hearing me."

"One more thing before we move on. You're not a very big girl, you have a darn nice figure, but you're so petite. Surely you encountered men who were just too big for you." Heidi was silent then said,

"That's true Rob, there weren't many, but there were a few who just had to flaunt the size of their penis. I knew I would have trouble with them. I asked them to please be careful lest they hurt me. Some men were very careful, but others were not. They would jam their penis into me so hard that indeed they hurt me. On one occasion when I was bleeding I had an exam. Dr Samson, my gynecologist said my cervix was eroded and that I must stop doing what I was doing if I didn't want to be in real trouble. She said young women who have sex with many men, especially uncircumcised men, run the risk of developing cervical cancer. Well I was only 22 and women of that age don't develop cancer so I kept at it. Just before I met you I saw Dr. Samson again. She really scolded me since the condition of my cervix had not improved and if anything was even a bit worse. She said, Heidi, I warn you, either stop what you're doing or you are going to be in serious trouble. My advice to you is to find a nice young man, have sex and have it with him only. No more of this entertaining three different men a week. I smiled, Dr. Samson said, Heidi, I'm serious, If you continue with what you're doing, prepare yourself for the worst. That scared me, but I still intended to go back to work after my two month break. The luxury that was mine was just too good to give up."

"Heidi, do you mean that even after that stern warning you were going to continue business as usual?"

"I was Rob, then I met you, I haven't had sex now for many weeks. I am hopeful that healing is taking place."

There was a long period of silence, then Heidi said,

"Rob, do you think it's possible that our meeting was more than coincidental? It was just after Dr. Samson's dire warning that we met. Had we not met, I would be prostituting myself right now and most likely my condition would be worsening. I have found that nice young man and I just know you will be gentle with me."

"You don't have to worry, Heidi, I'm not one of those exceptional men and even if I were, I would do nothing to hurt you."

"With a smile on her face, Heidi said, "Rob, don't be so sure that you aren't one of those exceptional men."

"Heidi Sweetheart, put that thought out of your mind. I am not one of those exceptional men. You know Heidi it very well may be that our chance meeting was not coincidental. Just a short time ago I told you about my decision to keep our relationship alive, that I loved you too much to give you up and that my decision was the result of Divine intervention. Heidi, I do believe we were meant to meet. I needed a girl to love, you needed a man to love and it happened shortly after Dr. Swanson gave you that dire warning."

"Rob Darling, that is so fascinating. You must tell me what Divine intervention means."

"I will Heidi, rest assured I will." Rob was silent and then frowned.

"What is it Rob?"

"A thought just came to my mind. It is possible you entertained an occasional sadist, one who can't reach his sexual highs unless he inflicts pain on you. It's when you wince or cry out that he reaches his high."

Heidi looked at Rob and just kept looking at him. Finally Rob asked,

"What's wrong Sweetheart, did I say something wrong?"

"No, no, I was just wondering from where you get all your smarts."

"A therapist, any therapist who works with people's minds is in a way a psychologist. Then there are some things he just has to learn. In addition, he learns much from working with his clients."

"Maybe so, but I'm amazed because I think you're right. I never had a single man apologize for hurting me. Rob, what an awful business I was in. Rob may I ask you a question?"

"Of course Heidi."

"Why are so many men concerned about the size of their penis? At times it seems that no man is satisfied with what he has. I constantly hear apologies about size."

"Heidi Girl, for many men the penis is symbolic of, a reflection of their masculinity. I would venture to say that a majority of men would be most happy if their penis was larger."

"But why? It isn't an issue with women at least not most of them. I know a few girls who think the bigger the better but they are in a minority. For most of us we wonder what the big deal is with men who worry about the size of their penis. How did they get this way?"

"When you tell a man that the size and shape of his penis is OK, I would venture to say that most don't believe you." "

"Why not and how does this get started in the first place?"

Often a group of boys will compare their penises however, since they are pre-pubescent, this is no big deal since they are all about the same size."

"Doesn't this embarrass them?"

"Naw, why should it, they're kids. Most often it has it's origin in the high school locker room. As a rule many boys shower together, boys all the way from freshmen to seniors, so making comparisons is easy. If a boy, let's say a boy who is just a bit behind in his development finds himself woefully lacking so far as size is concerned, this can be embarrassing and humiliating. If he is teased about his small penis this may make it much worse. It may very well be the case that he comes to see himself as inadequate. Worst of all, this can last him a life time even though when he reaches maturity he is normal in size, as normal as can be. You said penis size is not an issue with most women. This may be so, but women exacerbate, add to and perpetuate the problem."

"How."

"A recent ad on TV featured a scantily clad, very attractive young blonde. She sits on a stool and crosses her legs. The first words out of her mouth are, Men, size really does make a difference. This ad alone will blow many men away. Then there are ads that are not so directly blatant, but the insinuation is the same, size makes a difference. Heidi, billions of dollars are spent every year on gadgets, pills, creams, ointments, etc., all are said to increase the size of the penis both in length and diameter. They are all worthless. It is next to impossible to improve on what nature has decreed. Does this sound like men who are satisfied with what their genes have given them?"

"Poor men."

"Yes, poor men."

Heidi was silent for a moment then asked quizzically,

"Are you one of these men?"

"Not one to spend his money on quackery, but yes I have some anxieties."

"Are you concerned that you won't satisfy me?"

"Yes, I have some concerns."

"Rob, I'm amazed, you're a therapist. Look at what you have just told me and yet you are concerned?"

"Heidi, I'm a man first and then a therapist."

"Do girls go through the same thing?"

"Come on Heidi, what do you think?"

"That was a dumb question, wasn't it?"

"Adolescent girls have nothing to compare. They may examine each other's genitals, but most likely to satisfy curiosity and not to make comparisons, at least not comparisons that will make a difference to them. Some girls may examine each others genitals to make comparisons. Maybe when they reach pubescence they compare breast size but I doubt very much that that is problematic, at least in most cases."

"Heidi, you have had sex with approximately 226 men. You had to make comparisons, you had to become aware of size differences and you tell me that size never made a difference to you?"

Heidi was silent then she spoke up,

"What you say is true but, Rob, please don't worry, don't be anxious. I know you will be more than adequate for me regardless of size. You know what makes the difference? I love you, all of you."

"I'm anxious about it Heidi."

"That Mr. Rob is your fault, not mine."

"I know I shouldn't feel this way, but remember man first and then therapist."

Heidi looked at Rob, her eyes swept over his body.

"I'll remember it, but just the thought of seeing you naked excites me. You are built so well. I see the muscles in your neck and your biceps bulging in your shirt. I see your big chest and I'm raring to go. You may have anxieties and concerns, I have none."

There were a few moments of silence then Rob said,

"Well Heidi is your question answered?"

Heidi looked at Rob and laughed,

"What was the question anyway? Oh yes I remember, it had something to do with men's concerns over the size of their penis."

"Rob, can I ask you a personal question?"

"Of course you can Heidi."

"When you entered high school, were you under developed or precocious?"

Rob laughed heartily,

"Far from under developed. I was very precocious. I had long sideburns, I had whiskers on my face and I shaved daily. I had hair all over my body. In the comparison department I fared very well."

"See, I told you so," chimed in Heidi. Rob smiled and said,

"You know I was so hairy that the basketball coach refused to let me play unless I shaved and got a haircut. I was never put on the floor."

"What a mean thing for him to do."

"Heidi, he was an all around S.O.B."

Heidi looked up at Rob dreamily and said,

"Kiss me Rob, kiss me." Rob kissed Heidi passionately with the desired result.

"Rob, I'm so darn hard up that we just have to find a place where we can have sex. Do you realize it has been months since I last had sex?"

"I know Heidi Girl, but this just isn't the place. There are too many cars coming and going. It would do neither of us good to get arrested on a disorderly conduct charge."

"Alright Rob" Heidi said, "But when we get back to the house we are going to have sex. Excuses will do you no good. I want to have sex with you so bad. You're the one and only man Dr. Swanson told me to find and have sex with. You are that man, I found you,"

Rob was silent, then said,

"Alright Heidi, I've fought it long enough. I'm sitting here shaking in anticipation of having sex with you. You won't get any more arguments from me."

"Heidi, it's such a beautiful day, what say we walk one more trail and then it's off to find a place to eat."

"I'm fully in favor of it Rob."

"Let me grab my camera and we will be on our way."

"You and you're camera Rob, I think you like it more than you do me."

"I love you Heidi and that's a lot more than like. Further we are talking about two entirely unrelated things. I love you, I'm intrigued by photography, it's my hobby, and of course I can't pursue my hobby without a camera or two. There is no way you and my cameras can be compared." Heidi laughed.

"Rob, I was only joking don't be so serious."

"I know you were joking, but I wanted to make the distinction between you and photography."

"You did so very well, Rob. You know I would like to get interested in photography, would you help me?"

"Of course I will Heidi I would love to help you. First we have to get you a camera. As I said earlier, some evening this week we are going shopping to get you a good camera. No fooling around with a cheapie or a camera very limited in what it can do."

They strolled hand in hand down one more trail. After a short distance Rob said,

"Heidi, let's sit in the grass. I have a burning question that I just have to ask."

"Fire away Rob, it makes no difference what time we eat."

"How did you happen to become a call girl?"

"I was in college and always broke. Even though dad sent me money each month it was never enough. Even with my part time job at a fast food restaurant it still was not enough. I was slipping further and further into debt. A good friend of mine seemed always to have money, lots of money and I knew she didn't have a job, at least I didn't think she did. One day I asked her if her parents were wealthy. She said, heavens no. Then from where do you get all your money? She told me she was a call girl and rolling in money. I asked her what is a call girl? She answered, A prostitute who sells her body for money and for a call girl, lots of money. Then she said to me, Heidi why don't you give it a try. You're a very attractive girl with a good figure. Men will pay plenty to spend an evening or night with you. I told her I just couldn't do that, it would go against my moral principles and would be a betrayal of the very things I stood for. When ever I complained about finances she would say, Heidi, you don't have to be so poor. I started thinking about it, in fact it occupied too much of my thinking and interfered with my studies so I decided to give it a try."

"Nancy put me in touch with an agency. Soon after I steeled myself and drove to the agency. There was a nice young man behind the desk, his name is Paul. I told him I wanted to give being a call girl a try. His answer surprised me. You really don't, he said. You are so young and pretty, the last thing you want to do is degrade yourself by having sex with every Tom, Dick and Harry looking to have sex with a pretty girl. I told him that I only wanted to give it a try. Again he said, Don't, I have heard that from other girls but once they get hooked on their new found wealth they can't quit. I told him I had a very strong resolve and if I didn't care for it I would quit, but if I liked it I would stay at it at least until I was out of college. Then he asked me my name. I told him. He said, 'Heidi, please listen to me, I have been sitting behind this desk for a couple of years, believe me this is not the life for you, it is not the life for any girl. Please take my advice, turn around, walk out of the door and don't come back. Have you thought about your future? Don't you want to get married some day, have children and raise a family?' I replied by saying that I guess that is a dream every girl has at one time or another. I can wait for that."

"Paul replied, Have you thought about the kind of man who would marry a prostitute? I replied, that's not on my mind now Paul, sorry, but I'm going to give it a try. Then he gave up on me. He took a few pictures of me, pictures I was not proud of. Paul said, I'll tell you one thing Heidi, you sure turn me on. I think one of these days I'll give you a call and be one of your customers. I said do that Paul and it will be on the house."

"Paul asked, 'By the way, do you want to go by a name other than Heidi?' I replied, that's just my first name and using it is OK with me.

What do other girls do? He replied, 'Some keep their first name and others take on a different name. The choice is yours."

"The first encounter was the worst. I still wasn't convinced I should be doing this. Just the thought of charging money for men to use my body was repulsive to me. I told him to take it easy, but that seemed like an invitation for him to get rough. When he left I must have cried for half an hour. At that point I felt I had made a big mistake. The guy was a real bum and hurt me, however, when I received the money for putting up with him I concluded I could put up with a little pain for that kind of money. I told Paul about it and he promised me he would do his best to screen men before sending them to me. Nancy was so right. If I kept this up I would be rolling in money. Paul did a good job, succeeding men were much different, at least most of them were. They were gentle and considerate and I began responding to them. And that, Rob, is how I got started as a call girl. My plans to quit once I graduated went out the window and I kept at it until we met."

"Did you have any regrets?"

"At first yes, what I was doing was a total contradiction of myself. But like so many things the more I did it the less guilty I felt until I was comfortable selling my body. I enjoyed it most of the time and as I have said, I liked all the money and what it could buy."

"Were you orgasmic with your customers?"

"Most of the time, yes. I climax very easily Rob."

"Damn, that tears me up inside. You are mine giving you sexual pleasure is my responsibility. It didn't belong to 226 different men. For all purposes I have lost that responsibility. I really have nothing to give you. Now what are you going to do when you have sex with only one man, the same one over and over? Your orgasms will all be the same they will become routine and predictable. How soon will it be before you yearn for variety?"

"I don't believe ever Rob. I just know every orgasm with you will be wonderful. I will be held in your arms because you love me and not to just to hang on."

Again Rob was silent, it continued for some time. Finally Heidi spoke up,

"Rob, what is it? Why are you so quiet?"

"Heidi, I'm struggling with so many different emotions that right now I have nothing to say. You are mine and yet you are not. You belong to 226 men who were able to satisfy your sexual needs in most exciting ways. Tell me, how do I deal with that?"

"I don't know Rob, but what you just said is ridiculous. If our relationship is to continue you are going to have to deal with it and do so quickly. I knew you had questions, I knew some would be hard for me to answer and some answers would be difficult for you to handle."

"I still believe it is much better to get it all out in the open rather than having questions nagging in the back of your mind. I'm afraid that would destroy our relationship."

"If our relationship is to continue," asked Rob? "Are you now having some doubts?"

"No Rob, surely you understand what I'm saying? I have done my best to put your worries and anxieties to rest. It looks as if I have failed. If anything I have made them worse."

"I don't know Heidi, I really don't know, but what I do know is that I don't want to end our relationship. I love you too much."

"And I don't either Rob, but we must get things reconciled."

"We will Heidi and that's a promise. Some therapist I'm turning out to be, I can't even deal with my own relationship problems."

"Rob, don't get angry with me, but you are not acting very mature about this."

"I'm acting extremely immature Heidi and that's what bothers me. Enough questions for awhile Heidi, its time we found a restaurant and ate."

In silence they walked back to the car and left for a restaurant. As they were descending the overlook, Rob said to Heidi,

"I'm not going to be able to afford the kinds of restaurants you are used to frequenting, Heidi. You were in the business three years, and most of your customers were wealthy men. You must be quite well to do financially, you must be used to eating in some of the swankiest restaurants in the area. I'm a lowly therapist there is no way I can compete with your wealthy customers. I'm afraid the places I can afford to take you to are going to be pretty mundane."

Heidi was quiet for a while and then said,

"Yes Rob, you are right. I got used to living high and yes I have a healthy bank account. However, it's no longer mine, it's ours. The places you have taken me are not mundane. It's being with you that's important to me not how swanky a restaurant is. And Mr. Sloan, you are not a lowly therapist, yours is a very dignified profession. I'm going to get a job and with both incomes we will get along nicely. And Rob, there is something I have to tell you, something I have been keeping from you. Inside the garage is a Jaguar, it's one of my extravagances and now it's ours. You will love driving it. Maybe I should have told you earlier, but I was waiting for the right time. I don't know if this was it, but now you know."

"Heidi, your bank account, Jaguar and house are yours, not ours."

"Ours Rob, they are ours."

"Heidi, how can you be so generous, so selfless. I appreciate your generosity, but for now at least I prefer that you keep all three in your name."

"Alright Rob for now but only for now."

Heidi turned to Rob and asked.

"It will be some time before we find a restaurant, do you have one more question that won't require a long drawn out answer?"

"I think we have dealt with enough questions today but I have one that will require a short answer. How would you feel if I told you I had sex with 226 different women?"

"I wouldn't exactly feel like a happy camper. Now I don't know of course, but I don't think I would make a big issue out of it."

"Is that what I've done, made a big issue out of it? Heidi, using your own words, this is question and answer time. You shouldn't be surprised by or angered with my responses. What really bothers me is how you are responding. First you said you enjoy sex and I assume it was sex with your customers then you say you were orgasmic with most of your customers, with many different men. Are you going to find me as exciting and as appealing as those 226 men? If you should get bored with me you will begin to yearn for the days you were a call girl. Right now I feel so damn insecure."

"Rob we've been through this before. I don't know how to alleviate your anxiety and insecurity. I wish I did but in all honesty I no longer know what to tell you. I've done my very best to put those worries to rest. I don't want to tell you lies, don't you want me to be honest with you? If it helps, I promise you, hear this, Rob, I promise you I will never be a call girl again."

"Rob, we really aren't getting anywhere. I suggest that after we've had dinner and you drop me off at my house that we not see each other for two weeks"

"What, you don't mean that?"

"I do Rob,"

"But I don't want to be separated from you for so long."

"And I don't want to be separated from you for that long, but I really think it would be best. I know we can handle it because we love each other so very much. It will give you an opportunity to get things untangled in your mind and it will give me an opportunity to do my best to try to understand your feelings and to get things untangled in my mind."

"I don't like the idea, Heidi."

"Neither do I, but it's for the best."

With downcast eyes, Rob said,

"Heidi, is this the beginning of the end of our relationship. Are you fed up with me because I'm having some trouble dealing with your three years of prostitution? Couldn't you anticipate this? Two weeks, that's half a month."

"No Rob, no, that's the furthest thing from my mind. Don't you believe me when I tell you I am very much in love with you? I just think it would be best for both of us. Look at it as a test of the strength of our relationship."

"I don't need to test it, but what can I say? Alright Heidi, if you think that would benefit both of us, a separation for two weeks is what it will be. There will be no more questions today, but that doesn't mean I have no more questions."

"I'm sure you have more questions Rob, and eventually we will get to all of them. Ok, the hour is getting late and remember you are taking me out for dinner."

"I haven't forgotten Heidi."

"Rob, I also think it's best if we postpone having sex until the two weeks are over."

"Heidi, not when I've finally decided I'm more than ready for us to have sex. Just a short time ago you said you were darn horny."

"Right now I'm not very horny at all."

"Heidi, what's happening to us? I don't like the idea of a separation and now you show no interest in me sexually."

"That's not what I said Rob. Aren't you acting a bit childish about this? I just think a two week postponement would be best."

With a wane smile Rob replied,

"Childish, is that what I am, childish because I love you and I don't want a two week separation."

"Oh Rob, I shouldn't have said that. I guess I've gotten just a bit exasperated from our struggles with your questions. You are mine and I want very much for us to have sex, all I'm asking is that we wait until the two weeks are over."

Rob gave a big sigh,

"OK Heidi, if that's what you want so be it."

When they stopped for dinner, uncharacteristic of them there was very little conversation. Both were worried about the coming separation and what it would mean for their relationship.

When they got to Heidi's house, she fixed a pot of coffee and they visited and spoke of their love for each other. When it was time for Rob to return to his apartment, it was with misgivings that he kissed Heidi goodbye. However, she yielded to his kiss as she always did and returned it with fervor. Both were assured they were very much in love.

"Two weeks is going to be a long time for me Sweetheart, no kissing, no holding."

"And Darling it's going to be a long time for me too."

With a smile on her face she continued,

"I have every reason to believe we will both survive. And Rob, that means no phone calls."

"Why? Isn't it enough that we won't be seeing each other?"

"If we're going to do this right, for two weeks we must cut off all contact with each other."

"Well, I don't like it one bit, but as I said, two weeks it will be."

Heidi, during the two weeks we're separated, I'm going to start looking for a secretary. I just can't handle the work load alone anymore. It's wearing me out and it takes time away from the two us. I don't think I can compete with the going salary for secretaries, but I have to try. Further it will take my mind off our two week separation. Who knows, at the end of two weeks I just might have a secretary."

"Rob, I have wanted to say something about your heavy work load and yes, about the fact that even though we are together it takes time away from visiting with each other. I wish you the best of luck and I'll be pulling for you, however, don't forget the two weeks are to give us both time to reflect on our relationship."

"How could I ever forget that Heidi?"

They kissed once more then Rob said,

"That is going to have to last me for the next two weeks."

"And me too," said Heidi.

Chapter Five

≒ ·|||· ≒

Heidi was the first to feel the pain of separation. At least Rob had his therapy, but there wasn't much for her to do around the house. She went shopping a few times, however she bought little since there was nothing she really wanted or needed.

She took one day to drive to Vista Point not only because she loved the view, but also because she wanted to rekindle the memories. She sat at the table for awhile. The first memory to leap into her mind was that of her fear she would lose Rob once she told him she was a call girl. How she wept when Rob walked away from her. She was sure that when he came back he would say, Heidi, it's over. Suddenly she heard him calling her name and then they were embracing and Rob was telling her of his love for her and that so far as there relationship was concerned, the past made no difference. Tears came to her eyes.

How she wanted Rob to be holding and kissing her right now. How did she ever come up with the stupid idea that they should separate for two weeks? Next she walked down the trail in the direction Rob had gone. There was only one fallen tree across the trail, it had to be the one Rob sat on. He must have had a real struggle with himself. First she had been lying to him about her non-existing job and then she told him she was a call girl. She looked down that beautiful valley and could see Rob weeping and asking God what he should do, get out of the relationship or stay. Again tears came to her eyes.

"Darn", she said out loud, "I wish I wouldn't be so emotional. That's something I inherited from dad."

When she thought about her dad a sense of guilt almost over whelmed her. If he knew what his little girl had turned into, he would be heartbroken. He was so sure she would make a real place for herself in life. He had helped her with tuition, but he certainly didn't help her so she could become a call girl. Heidi, Heidi she thought, that will forever remain a dark cloud over your Life. And yet Rob loves you. How many men, even if they fell in love with a call girl would remain in the relationship. Rob is one of a kind. I really wasn't very understanding when I answered his questions the other day. I don't know why but I resented them and yet I encouraged him to do so. He is not through questioning me yet.

"Heidi," she said out loud, "No more resentment when Rob asks you questions."

She remembered his answer when she asked him how he could still love her knowing she was a call girl. divine intervention is what he said. She must remember to ask him what that means.

She sat quietly for another hour going over her years as a call girl, recalling many of the experiences. Then she spoke out loud,

"Heidi, you certainly had some good times in the business, you met interesting men, you had good as well as bad sex. You had good friends. Am I willing to give all of that up for Rob? Then there were the happy five, Sally, Judy, Liz, Betty and myself."

She thought about their weekly breakfasts together. It was always a fun time. It was a time to talk about customers who were different, had different sexual desires etc. She never said too much about her customers feeling it would violate their trust. They talked about the number of men they serviced who were married. They all found this hard to grasp. Why would a man spend so much money on a call girl when he had all the sex he wanted at home? The reality was many of these men had no sex at home. Then why did they stay in the marriage? It was she, who said,

"Because, in spite of being deprived of sex from their wives, they must have still loved them. After all, as important as sex is, there is more to marriage than sex. Remember girls, our lives are sex that is all we do and that is about all we know."

There was agreement on that, there was also agreement they would never marry. After hearing so many sob stories, marriage was the last thing they wanted. Again speaking out loud she said,

"You know Heidi, perhaps you should ditch all this being in love business and return to the agency and get back together again with the girls."

She thought of what she said earlier to Rob, that because of her sympathy and understanding she not only provided many men with sex, but was also sympathetic to their plights and gave them much encouragement. Like Rob, she was a kind of therapist.

She said "Maybe that's what I should do. I can give Paul a call and in a short time I will be entertaining customers again."

The more she thought about it the better she liked the idea. The thought was very disquieting, but after all, that is what the separation was all about, to give both of them a chance to decide once and for all if they wanted to continue their relationship. If she wanted out of it Rob would have to accept her decision.

What if Rob told her that in the best interests of them both it would be best to break off their relationship. Now the thoughts she had about returning to the agency frightened her. She loved Rob too much, there is no way continuing as a call girl could ever compensate for Rob's love for her and her love for Rob. Rob provided her with the one thing she felt was really missing in her life, the most important thing missing in her life, unconditional love.

For a moment it felt as if an icy hand gripped her heart. She had her cell phone in the car and wanted to call Rob, just to hear his voice, but the separation was her idea. She just had to go through with it as stupid as it was.

Just as quickly as the idea of being a call girl again entered her thoughts, it left them. There is no way she would give up Rob, not for the world. Her answers to his questions hurt him, made him anxious, confused him, but he loved her and nothing about her past was going to change that.

Heidi looked down the valley for another 10 minutes, gave a big sigh, stood up and walked back to her Jaguar. She wouldn't have that if she had not been a call girl neither would she have her house. Those were all material things and in no way could compensate for a warm loving body. Her love for Rob was only growing through the long separation. There was no question in her mind what she was going to do.

After looking around Vista Point one more time, she got into her car and started for home. She would stop at the little restaurant where she and Rob had a cup of coffee and if it was empty sit at the same booth. It was empty and she had a cup of coffee. Instead of sitting across from her, Rob had sat next to her. Just the thought of it gave her a warm Feeling. When she arrived home she again had to fight off the temptation to call Rob.

"Well, she said out loud, only one week left."

Rob had his therapy to do so his days weren't all that bad. It was the evenings that made him yearn for Heidi. He did not like the loneliness.

Chapter Six

≡ ⊣⊢ ≡

As soon as Rob got to his office the next morning he called two local newspapers and placed an ad stating he was looking for someone with secretarial experience. He reasoned that during the separation from Heidi would be just as good a time as any to start looking for a secretary. He stated clearly that he needed someone with considerable experience. His work load had become too heavy and he feared it would interfere with his therapy. In addition to bringing work home in order to get his notes into the computer he was usually in his office at 7:00 a.m. What concerned him was that the salary he was prepared to offer would not be enough to entice anyone to accept his offer. He looked over his financial resources carefully, however he could not go beyond the figure he had settled on. Answering calls and interviewing a potential secretary might help to keep his mind off how much he missed Heidi. Well Rob, he said to himself, I guess during our separation is as good a time as any to place the ad. Nothing will be gained by waiting. Whatever the out come of the separation you have to have a secretary.

Two days later he was receiving calls from interested parties. He was surprised at the number of callers who lost interest when he told them they would be working for a sex and marital therapist. He got responses like a sex therapist, whatever that is, I don't believe I'm interested. What's wrong with people, why do they reject me because I'm a sex therapist? Do they believe I'm some kind of a pervert.

In all, he interviewed three women in his office. One was young and quite attractive, however it didn't take him long to conclude she was a bit scatter brained and would not work out. The other two women were older, both had considerable secretarial experience but felt he was asking too much from a secretary. Also, they were dubious about someone who would pry into the private sex lives of couples. He tried to tell them that that is precisely why they come to him for therapy, that therapy can't be performed unless the therapist does pry into their private affairs including their sexual relationship. It was to no avail,

Rob was about ready to pull his ad when he received a phone call from a party who showed interest in the position. He said to her,

"Before we go any farther, I must tell you I am a sex and marital therapist."

"So," she said, "Is that supposed to make a difference to me?"

"I hope not, the women I have interviewed, when they found out I was a sex and marital therapist got up and walked out on me."

"I had a job," she said, "But I no longer found it interesting, I need a change. My name is Lorraine Stevens and I'm 26 years old. I am a whiz with a computer, love to interact with people and am actually interested in both marriage and sexual problems. I am happily married and I must tell you that one of the reasons I quit my job is because my former employer was constantly making passes at me."

"Why didn't you report him?"

"Naw, he really is harmless. Other than for the passes and sexual innuendoes he was a good employer. He's a man and isn't it hard for men not to make passes at attractive women? You're the therapist you should know. Let me be quick to say that I'm not saying I'm attractive, my husband says I am."

"Yes, being a man," Rob chuckled, "I can say that it is hard not to make passes at attractive women. However, let me be quick to say that so far I haven't done that."

"You might do it in the future?"

"Who can say?"

This time it was Lorraine who laughed.

"You sound like a good sport, Lorraine."

"I hope I am. Let me continue. I'm happily married and Ted, my husband, is currently a deputy sheriff with the county.

"Lorraine, I hope you don't mind me calling you Lorraine?"

"Not at all. Let's see, your name is Dr. Robert Sloan, correct?"

"You can drop the doctor, please call me Rob."

"I like your attitude Rob. Now the tough question, what would my salary be?"

"I almost hate to tell you. You appear to be just the kind of girl I'm looking for."

"How about the kind of woman you're looking for."

"My apologies, girl sounds young and woman sounds old and you certainly are not old. I'll try to watch my language. Well there is no sense in being hesitant."

With that he gave Lorraine the figure which was the maximum amount he felt he could pay. For a moment Lorraine was quiet, then said,

"That is a bit less than I was making."

"I'm sorry Lorraine, I would like to offer you more, but it's been a relatively short time since I opened my office. My business is growing and in the not too distant future I am hopeful I can offer you more. Before you make a decision, let me tell you what your responsibilities will be. You will be a receptionist, operate a computer, keep and file records, maintain the strictest of confidentiality, answer the phone, make appointments and above all, be able to make a good cup of coffee."

With that said, Lorraine burst out laughing.

"Of course, the most important would be the coffee. Well, for your information I make a very good cup of coffee. Before I give you an answer, I would like to meet you and I'm sure you would like to meet me."

"Very much so Lorraine. When would it suit you to come to my office?"

"How about tomorrow?"

They picked an hour convenient to both and then said their goodbyes.

When Lorraine entered Rob's outer office he about did a double take. If it weren't for facial differences he would be looking at Heidi. She was Heidi' height, same shapely figure, same color hair worn the same way and if he had to guess he believed she and Heidi would weigh about the same. Lorraine, of course noticed Rob staring at her and asked,

"Is something wrong?"

"No, no," answered Rob, "Lorraine, other than facial differences you and my Heidi, my girl friend, could be twins. Heidi is a very attractive girl and your husband is absolutely, right, you are a very attractive girl---, I mean young woman."

Lorraine broke out laughing,

"Rob," she said, "if you want to call me a girl, go right ahead. I like that better than woman anyway."

Rob found himself hoping that Lorraine would be impressed enough that she would take the position.

"Please sit down Lorraine. Could I get you a cup of coffee?"

"Please do, I didn't have time to drink a second cup this morning."

Rob filled two cups and gave one to Lorraine. She took one sip and frowned,

"You need to have someone give you lessons on how to make coffee. This tastes awful."

First Rob smiled then broke out laughing. In a moment Lorraine joined him.

"I agree with you whole heartedly Lorraine. You did say you can make good coffee?"

"Only the best."

Rob couldn't help but look at Lorraine which, of course, she took note of.

"Rob, do you and your girl friend—"

"Heidi, Lorraine."

"Do you and Heidi have a good relationship?"

"The very best, why do you ask?"

"Then I won't have to worry about you making passes at me."

Rob narrowed his eyes, looked at Lorraine and said,

"I can't guarantee you, but I will try my darndest not to make passes at you."

"Well then, I'm out of here," Lorraine said as she turned toward the door.

She quickly turned around and smiling faced Rob.

"I know you're not serious."

"Lorraine, I'm a jokester and I'm afraid you are going to have to get used to that. Of course I'm not serious, but you can't blame me if I look at you rather longingly from time to time."

"That I can take."

Rob showed Lorraine his files, the appointment book, the little room with running water and where the coffee is made, and then took her into his inner office.

"You can't make coffee, but you certainly have an attractive office, it's so neat and clean. Are the pictures ones you have taken?"

"I'm afraid I'll have to take the blame," Rob answered.

"They are very good. Photography must be a hobby of yours."

"It is Lorraine, I enjoy photography very much."

"Anyone who can take pictures like these can't be all that bad. I'm about convinced I can trust you," she said with a cocked eye.

"Aww, Lorraine, really I'm all good, there isn't a bad streak in me."

"We'll see."

"Lorraine, I'm hoping you will be willing to assume the housekeeping details in the two offices."

"Whoa, aren't you getting ahead of yourself? I have not yet taken the job."

"My apologies, I am getting ahead of myself."

"Should I take the job, the housekeeping would not be a problem, but I may have some suggestions on how to make your office even more attractive and maybe arranged a bit differently to make your client's more comfortable. For one thing, their backs shouldn't be to your best pictures. They should be able to look up and see them."

"Lorraine, you are an aggressive girl and I like that. If you like what you have heard and seen and if you can accept the salary offered the job is yours."

"I like what I've seen and heard, and I'm going to enjoy working for such a good looking guy. I'll take it."

Rob blushed and replied,

"Average, but not so good looking."

"I said good looking. Keep in mind that attractive girls can readily spot handsome men."

"We should make a pretty good team, a very attractive young woman and a relatively handsome guy", replied Rob.

"Now you've got it."

"When do I start?"

"The sooner the better."

"How about day after tomorrow, which would be Thursday? since I've already quit my job I believe I can swing it. I'm really looking forward to this job."

"I can almost say you'll love it. I don't believe you'll find working with me hard at all."

"Working with you?"

"Yes, working with me. We will be working as a team."

"Rob, in addition to being very handsome, your manners, demeanor and levity are what a girl likes to see in a boss."

"Not boss Lorraine, employer. I do not boss."

"Let me say," replied Lorraine, "I can't promise that I won't make passes at you."

"Any time you feel like it, go right ahead. That would be an ego booster for me. I'll warn my Heidi in advance."

"I'm looking forward to meeting your Sweetheart especially since we resemble each other."

"I'll see that you two get to meet just as soon as you're able to start."

It took only a couple days before Lorraine and Rob became good friends. As Lorraine said,

"I don't think of you as my boss, but rather as my employer."

It was only a short time before Lorraine and Rob became each others confidant.

One afternoon after he had seen his last client, he asked Loarraine to come into his office.

"Well Rob, how is the seperation going?"

"Not good of course." He replied "You have been a great help as I wait out the days. Lorraine, can we talk about something very personal?"

"Well I guess it depends."

"Oh forget it."

"I shouldn't have said that, it's important enough for you to bring it up, I should have said, of course."

"Are you sure?"

"I'm sure Rob. You and I have discussed and talked about a number of personal and intimate things already."

"Yes we have but, but I have done most of the talking. Come to think of it Lorraine, I don't think you have brought up any personal, intimate issues."

"Your right Rob, I haven't. I'll have to change that, won't I."

"Lorraine, I am no teenager and yet I have had little sexual experience.

One was with a girl while in high school. We were both neophytes and it didn't turn out very good for either of us. The other was with a woman who was about ten years older than I. When she first had me over I couldn't get an erection. I was so humiliated and sure she would taunt me and tell my friends at work. Instead she was very understanding, and told me not to worry about it and that we would try it again.."

"The next time I visited her I had no problem. She was quite experienced and all I can say is that it was ecstatic. I had no idea that sex could be that pleasurable. I liked her and she liked me. She was very attractive, and had dark hair and as you know, just the color I love on a woman. And a body, wow, I never knew a woman could be so beautiful with her clothes off. She said we could have sex anytime, but I never took her up on the offer. I was too conflicted about it. I wonder what she thought? Looking back I could kick myself. Oh yes, she was not married. I wondered why, she was so attractive? Had I been 10 years older I could easily have fallen in love with her."

Rob was silent for a moment then a smile crossed his face.

"Now I wish I had gone back many times. We worked together at the same place. Missed opportunities Lorraine missed opportunities. That was about eight years ago and that's the extent of my experience."

"Lorraine, there's something you should know. Before Heidi and I met, she was an expensive call girl."

Rob was quiet giving Lorraine time to allow what he had told her to sink in. After a while she said, " Heidi, a call girl?" To say I'm a bit shocked would be an understatement. Did you know that from the start of your relationship?"

"No Lorraine. I had fallen in love with Heidi and even though she had been a prostitute, I couldn't give up that love. Further, Heidi loves me. Well, we are very much in love and when you are very much in love you don't give up that easily. About two weeks ago we sat down and did some figuring. Now this is our secret Lorraine, but Heidi has had sex with about 226 men."

"Come again," Lorraine said in complete surprise. "Two hundred plus men?"

"Yes, and I have had sex with only two women. I'm afraid I feel woefully inadequate."

"That means you and Heidi have not yet had sex."

"Not yet Lorraine and it's because of me, of course, not Heidi. Here's a girl who regularly had sex three times a week and suddenly she is cut off from it. I know she is chomping at the bit and darn it, so am I."

"You are still conflicted, right?"

"Right. I was brought up to believe sex is a wonderful thing but to be reserved for a husband and wife. Darn it, I know it's a wonderful thing. I've experience it."

"What about now?"

"I'm more than ready for it Lorraine, but I am largely inexperienced and Heidi, well what can I say besides she is greatly experienced. I feel inadequate, I'm anxious that I will be a complete disappointment to her. I fear I won't be able to satisfy her and if that happens I'll be a complete wreck."

"Rob my experience was much like yours. I too had sex two times before Ted and I were married and both were big disappointments. The guys were interested in only their own satisfaction and the heck with me. I thought to myself, well if this is all there is to it forget it. Ted on the other hand had a good deal of experience, not like Heidi of course, but he certainly was not ignorant. I knew Ted had great expectations and I feared I would be a big disappointment to him. We talked about and I told him how I felt. You know what he said? I'm glad you are inexperienced. I love you and if there is something you need to learn I will be a patient teacher. And you know Rob he was Ted and I have a wonderful sex relationship. Heidi knows where you are coming from, I'm sure your fears and anxieties are unfounded."

"Heidi has said the same thing. Lorraine, I think I'm letting my ego get in the way."

"I think you're right. One more thing Rob, women are much more understanding about a man's ego and as a rule are more patient." She waited and a smile played across her face."

"And may I add are much more long suffering. You just told me the older woman with whom you had sex with was very understanding and actually tried to build up your ego. Would you like me to be your teacher?"

"Lorraine, why do you tempt me so? You're so darn pretty, you have such a great figure and above all, you exude sexuality. And now you ask me if I would like to have you as my teacher. You're darn right I would, but I also know that's out of the question."

Then a smile crossed Rob's face,

"But thanks so much for the offer."

Lorraine smiled and said,

"But we can talk about anything can't we? Now take it from your teacher, stop worrying. I know what I'm talking about and I have had just a bit more experience than you have."

"You know Lorraine, you are the perfect office wife. How could I be so lucky in getting you as my secretary?"

"Rob, is it suddenly getting warm in here or is it me?"

Nope it's not you, I have about reached the boiling point."

"Well," said Lorraine, "I must be going. I need to get outside in order to cool off. By the way Rob thank you for all the compliments."

"You know me Lorraine they are given in all sincerity. Lucky you, when you get home you have a husband waiting for you. I, all I have is an empty apartment."

"You certainly can go to Heidi's house and spend the evening or the night with her."

"No I can't Lorraine, Heidi and I are about at the end of a two week separation. Heidi thought it would be best if we stayed away from each other for two weeks in order to get things straightened out in our heads."

"That doesn't sound like a bad idea Rob. It sound to me like Heidi has a pretty smart head on her shoulders."

"She does Lorraine, Heidi has a masters degree in business administration."

"She does. and she turns to prostitution?"

"Lorraine, Heidi was rolling in money. The love of money got the best of her."

"How much longer do you have until your two week separation is over?"

"Two more days Lorraine just two more days."

"It's almost over Rob. Two hundred and twenty six men, my gosh, I wonder what it would be like to have sex with 226 men?"

"Well, as pretty as you are, you certainly would have no trouble being taken on by an agency. Have Heidi give you Paul's number."

"Who is Paul?"

"A very good friend of Heidi's who did all he could to talk her out of being a call girl. Better yet, ask Heidi about it."

"Now Dr. Sloan, don't you temp me. I'm darn curious, but I certainly won't give prostitution a try, but I'm going to ask Heidi about it. Good bye for now and stop worrying. I have a hunch in a few days you will show up here and tell me it went great."

"Goodbye Lorraine"

On the morning of the fourteenth day, Heidi called Rob before he had gotten out of bed.

"It's over Rob, the two weeks are over. I'm dying to see you. The past two weeks have not been easy ones."

"Sweetheart, they haven't been easy for me either, just the opposite. They have been damn hard for me."

"Rob, you must not swear. I'm fixing a big supper for this evening. When will you be over?"

"If it's at all possible, I'll try to get away from the office by four. If not it will be about five. Four or five when I get there I'll be at your door."

"Whatever, when you leave your office Rob, hurry. Oh by the way, did you find a secretary?"

"The very best Heidi and she took the job just a few days after we started our two week separation. We have become the best of friends."

It was four when Rob arrived at Heidi's house. She was waiting for him at the door. He grabbed her and kissed her. It was a long kiss and when they broke the embrace both were breathing heavily.

"Is supper ready yet?"

"No why do you ask?"

"Because lady, I'm going to take you into the bedroom and rape you."

"Oh you are, are you? It's going to be just the other way around. It is I who will be raping you."

Rob picked Heidi up and carried her into the bedroom. He tore off his clothes while Heidi tore off hers. A quick shower and then they jumped into bed. By the time they were through showering, both were so aroused they could hardly contain themselves.

Heidi said, "Well big boy, I see you have a mighty erection and you were the worry wart."

In a very short order Heidi had an orgasm followed by a second a few minutes later.

"Now Mr. Rob, I'm going to focus all my attention on you. You are going to feel things you never dreamed it was possible for a woman to do."

And she was right in a very short time Rob had his climax. Afterward they just lay in each other's arms.

"Well Rob, didn't I tell you there was no reason for you to worry? Did I act as if you were inadequate and that you could not satisfy me?"

"I'm sorry Heidi, you were right all along. I'm afraid I had no confidence in myself and little in you."

"Were you a failure? Certainly you are not impotent. Rob sweetheart, what made the difference?"

"It was Lorraine who made the difference Heidi. We had a talk about my worries and anxieties. She made sure the conversation was super charged with eroticism. She couldn't wait to get home to Ted and I couldn't wait to get to your house."

"Thank you Lorraine, thank you so very much," Heidi said.

"And Lorraine dear girl, that goes second for me too."

As they lay in bed, Heidi asked Rob if he had come to any decisions during the two weeks they were separated.

"Yes," replied Rob, "That I love you so very much and that I don't want a separation like this again."

"My being a call girl made no difference?"

"What call girl, I never heard anything about a call girl?"

"Oh Rob, You're a silly guy. I'm just so happy that your love for me has grown."

"And Heidi, did you come to any decisions?"

"Rob I thought about what it would mean to me if I became a call girl again, but every time I did, my love for you blotted out the thoughts. The two weeks of separation were unbearable. On the first day I wanted to call you and I had a real struggle to keep from doing so. Each day got worse. Rob sweetheart, I love you so very much. I too do not want another separation."

Rob pulled Heidi close, kissed her passionately and in a moment they were making love again. After they finished Heidi said,

"Now I have a dinner to finish. I want it to be near perfect."

"Do you mean that's more important than having sex again," Rob said with a smile,

"We can get to that later, but right now, finishing dinner is priority number one."

As they were eating Heidi said,

"Now tell me a bit more about Lorraine."

"She is a very attractive young woman, about your age and has an outgoing personality that doesn't stop. She is a darn good sport and a pleasure to have around. Before she left the interview we were joking and having fun with each other. The roles she will have to carry out didn't bother her one bit. One thing I insisted upon is that she be able to make a good cup of coffee. She thought mine tasted horrible."

"And she was right."

"Heidi if it weren't for facial differences you and Lorraine could be twins, same color hair worn the same way, very pretty and with a figure much like yours."

"How do you know that?"

"Well, she dresses much like you do. Her outfit was pretty skimpy. She covers herself well, but dresses in such way as to bring out her best assets."

"You seem to really be taken with her. Do you think you'll be able to behave yourself"?

"Heidi come now."

"Is she married?"

"Very happily so, her husband's name is Ted, Ted Stevens."

"I'm glad to hear that."

"I feel fortunate to have a secretary like Lorraine. A number of other women called, one was young the rest were middle aged. I interviewed three. The young woman just wouldn't work out. The two older women had considerable experience, but walked out as soon as they heard I was a sex therapist?"

"Why?"

"I really don't know why. One said she thought it was an invasion of privacy for me to be asking people about their sexual relationships. Maybe she thought I was some kind of pervert."

"But that's what sexual therapy is all about."

"I tried to tell them that but they didn't buy it. One more thing about Lorraine, she is anxious to meet you."

"And I am anxious to meet her."

Chapter Seven

≡ ⑉ ≡

In a relatively short time Heidi and Lorraine became good friends and had lunch together a time or two. Lorraine asked Heidi,

"When do the two of you plan to get married?"

"Soon I hope, however, he has not given me a diamond yet so he hasn't asked me to marry him. I know a diamond will be coming though."

Rob and Lorraine worked as a team and as his business continued to grow he was able to increase Lorraine's salary to the point where he was competitive with what most agencies paid their secretaries. In fact, he went beyond what was the norm. At one time she told him he was paying her too much.

"No way Lorraine you are worth every cent I pay you and more."

He told Heidi,

"In greeting clients as they come through the door, Lorraine is gracious, polite, outgoing and easily strikes up a conversation and keeps it going until I am ready for them. She and I can discuss about anything."

Heidi asked,

"You don't discuss things with her before we do first, do you?"

"Personal items no, items that pertain to business yes."

"So long as the personal items are discussed by us first so far as I'm concerned Lorraine, being your confidant, is no problem for me."

"And Heidi I am her confidant though she is a bit more reluctant to talk about personal things than I am. I guess that comes from my counseling where most of the time it is personal things that are at issue. It doesn't hurt to get an objective opinion on some issues."

"Isn't that an invasion of privacy," asked Heidi.

"Hardly since she puts into the computer all the notes and comments I make as the therapy session progresses."

"You're right I guess I forgot about that, but I certainly understand why Lorraine has to keep everything she reads in the strictest of confidence."

"On a more personal level I value her advice. When it comes to getting you a gift for example, as a woman she knows what appeals to women. And when you and I take off for a few days I can leave knowing the office is in good hands. About the only thing she can't do around the office is the therapeutic work."

Heidi found it difficult to find a job primarily because she could not put together a vita or resume. Since she had not had employment other than a call girl. There was no one who could give her a recommendation. She was getting discouraged when a small ad in one of the papers caught her attention. A realtor was looking for someone who would primarily take people to show them the house or property in which they were interested. The ad said nothing about a resume. She thought to herself, I'm sure it won't do me any good, but it won't hurt to call the number and make inquiries.

The man who placed the ad was a Mr. James Simpson. He told Heidi that whoever he hired had to have an out going personality and be able to interact with people in a friendly fashion.

"Mr. Simpson I believe I can say that I will charm your customers. I have an outgoing personality, I am friendly and most at ease when interacting with people. And yes, I can drive a car or a van and have been doing so since I was 10 years old. I have lived in the Tacoma area for 5-1/2 years and know my way around the metropolitan area."

Mr. Simpson asked her to come to his office for an interview.

Heidi walked into his office and introduced herself.

"My name is Heidi Faust"

"Heidi, I like that name. My name is James Simpson. Please sit down."

When she sat in front of his desk the first thing he said was,

"Please join me for a cup of coffee."

Mr. Simpson returned with coffee for Heidi. Heidi thanked him, took a swallow and frowned.

"Something wrong Heidi?"

"Yes Mr. Simpson, your coffee is awful."

Mr. Simpson broke out laughing and said,

"You know Heidi I have never learned how to make a good cup of coffee."

"That Mr. Simpson is a problem most men have. If you hire me I can assure you, you will be drinking the best coffee in town."

"That in itself is just about reason enough for me to give you the job."

"I can do a lot more than make a good cup of coffee. My boy friend tells me I'm an excellent cook."

"That means you would bring cookies, breads and other baked goods to the office."

"If that is what you would like me to do, yes."

Heidi found him to be a congenial, friendly and fatherly figure and liked him from the moment they started to talk.

"May I ask how old you are Heidi?"

"Mr. Simpson you may ask, but that doesn't mean I'm going to tell you." Heidi replied with a smile. "I'm almost 24."

"Are you married?"

"Not yet, but I hope to be soon."

"That means you have a fiancé, right?"

"Not quite yet, but I'm expecting a diamond any day. It seems Rob has a tendency to procrastinate on most things."

"I assume Rob is your soon to be fiancé."

"Yes he is Mr. Simpson and he's a wonderful man whom I love very much."

"I'm glad to hear that Heidi. Do you and Rob plan to stay around here for awhile?"

"We do, Rob is a sexual and marital therapist who opened his business not too long ago. His business is growing rapidly which makes both of us happy. In fact his work load has gotten so heavy that it was only a short while ago he was able to hire a secretary."

"A sex therapist, I wish there were those kinds of therapists around when Doris and I first married. It might have saved us a lot of frustration."

"You'll find I'm an easy man to work for Heidi. I've made my fortune and selling real estate is kind of a hobby of mine and something I do to keep busy. I like you Heidi, I like your cheerful disposition and the ease with which you josh around with me. And you certainly are right you seem completely relaxed as we visit."

Heidi could hardly tell him that came from three years of interacting with men as a call girl.

"And Heidi, if I may say so, you certainly are an attractive young woman."

"Mr. Simpson, you should know that flattery will get you everywhere."

"Heidi if you want it the job is yours."

"Before I say I'll take it, I have a question for you."

"Fire away Heidi."

Heidi narrowed her eyes, cocked her head slightly and with a frown on her face asked,

"You're not a wolf are you? Am I going to have to guard against you making passes at me?"

First Mr. Simpson looked puzzled and then broke out laughing,

"Heidi, I believe there is a bit of a wolf in every man. I've been around long enough that I believe I can say no man ever gives up on attractive women, looking at them or otherwise. How can a man help but admire a pretty girl and though the temptation might be to make a pass at you rest assured it won't happen."

Heidi threw her head back and laughed,

"I know it won't Mr. Simpson, I just thought I had to throw that in for the sake of a bit of levity. If you are pleased with me Mr. Simpson, I would be most happy to take the job."

"Pleased with you Heidi, you are going to be a bright bulb around here."

"One thing more Heidi, when it's just you and I around the office it's James, not Mr. Simpson. That is much too formal."

"Alright, James it will be and you will call me Heidi, agreed?"

"Agreed Heidi."

"Oh, I have another question for you Heidi. Are you a native Washingtonian"

"No James, I was born and raised on a farm in North Western Iowa."

"Are you serious?"

"Why yes I am."

"Heidi, I was born and raised near Omaha. I joined the Navy to see the world as it is said, however, I spent most of my time at Bremerton. I liked it so much out here that I decided it is here that I wanted to live. What brought you out to Washington?"

"It was the University of Washington. I received both a bachelors and masters degree in Business Administration. If I had it to do over I would have majored in the Social Sciences. I don't like being cooped up in an office. As a child and teen aged girl I spent most of my time outdoors. That is one reason that I jumped at the opportunity to apply for the job you were advertising."

"Sometimes we make mistakes like that. From what little I know about you I think the Social Sciences would have been a good choice. You may spend a day or two in the office a week, but primarily you will be out and about ferrying customers to houses and parcels of land."

"That sounds so good."

"Was your home anywhere near Omaha?"

"Yes quite near, a little town south of Sioux City."

"What a coincidence. Let me tell you something that is even more coincidental. Rob was born and raised in a small town 35 miles from Yankton, SD."

"Heidi, you have to be pulling my leg."

"No James, the three of us were born and raised in contiguous states. Do you know where Yankton is?"

"Oh sure, I have been there on numerous occasions. Heidi, this is most interesting. The three of us are going to have to get together and talk about the good old Midwest. Doris, my wife is from Bremerton."

Heidi and James got along almost like father and daughter. She loved her work, especially taking people around the Tacoma area and interacting with them. She had a special knack for putting people at ease. That was something else that came from her call girl days. And best of all the sales began to increase markedly. Heidi felt good about what she was doing and good about herself. Her self esteem seemed to be growing daily.

One morning James said,

"Heidi, business has picked up considerably since you started working for me. Customers frequently comment on your pleasant disposition and what a pleasure it is to do business with such a pretty girl. As of now I'm raising your salary and commission."

Heidi was elated.

"Thank you James that makes me feel so good."

"You don't have to thank me Heidi, you've earned it."

Chapter Eight

≡ ⋅ǁǀ⋅ ≡

H eidi swung her legs onto the floor and said,
"Are you ready for breakfast?"

"I sure am, in fact, I'm very hungry."

"Are you surprised?" asked Heidi? Laughing Rob replied,

"Not one bit. Would you like to go out for breakfast Heidi?"

"If it's OK with you I'll fix breakfast and we'll eat here."

"Suites me fine," replied Rob.

"Anyway," said Heidi, "There is something I would like to talk to you about"

"OK," said Rob "We'll talk."

Rob put on the coffee while Heidi fixed eggs and bacon. Reaching into the freezer, Heidi took out a package filled with sweet rolls. Rob looked at them and asked,

"Did you make these?"

"Sure did," replied Heidi.

"When and how did you learn to cook?"

"As a child I would stand on a stool and help mother as she cooked. With every dish she would teach me step by step. We never had much money and there were six mouths to feed. I have three brothers all older than I am. When mom found a job and went to work the cooking was turned over to me. I would come right home from school and go to work on the evening meal."

"Do you like to cook Sweetheart?"

"I love to cook, cooking is one thing I can do well."

"I know of another thing you can do well."

"Rob, would you please get your mind off sex just for a little while, Heidi said laughingly.

"Rob, I don't want to bring up the past, but may I remind you that the main reason I became a call girl is because I couldn't recall ever having enough money and college was putting me deeper and deeper in debt to the point I couldn't even afford the essentials."

"I understand," replied Rob.

"OK Rob, let's eat."

With that Heidi brought the eggs, bacon and sweet rolls to the table. Rob started to eat, looked up at Heidi and said,

"Heidi, this is delicious. Wow! You really can cook."

"Thank you Rob," Heidi said smiling.

As they were eating Rob said,

"OK Sweetheart what is it you want to talk about?"

Heidi laid down her fork, looked at Rob and said,

"I want you to move in with me. We have known each other for about six months and for the last five or close to it, we have spent all of our non-working hours together."

"Do you really mean that Heidi?"

"I certainly do. The only concern I have is that we would be living together out of wedlock and you might have scruples about that."

Rob thought for a moment then said,

"A week ago I would have said yes, I do, but now Heidi I'm ready to do so."

"Further," said Heidi, "with your stronger than strong libido how could you ever make it if I weren't close by to answer your every beck and call?"

"I wouldn't make it," laughed Rob. "I'll pay my share of rent and everything else."

"Rob, have you forgotten this is our house and it's paid for in full."

"I don't feel right about this Heidi."

"Well start feeling right about it right now. No house payments, no car payments. We are in the clear. And by the way, soon we'll take our Jaguar convertible out for a drive."

Rob was quiet for a moment and then said,

"Alright Heidi, I'm eager to move in with you and I won't argue about the rest."

"Oh Rob Darling, I'm so glad, I don't want to be separated from you again not even for a little while. I am a new person and I am living a new life, one that I thought would never be possible for me."

"Sweetheart we are both living new lives and like you, I never thought it would be possible for me."

"We have the whole day," said Heidi, "Let's move your things over here today."

"OK there's no reason why we can't. I really don't have that much to move. My apartment was furnished so all I have to move are my personal affects."

"Good, let's get dressed and get going."

"Heidi," Said Rob, "Aren't you forgetting something? There is something we need to do first."

Heidi turned to Rob and with a smile on her face said,

"Rob, you're not serious."

Rob broke out laughing then said,

"For once I'm kidding, but that's only for now."

"Understood," said Heidi.

By mid afternoon Rob's personal effects were moved. Heidi had two dressers so Rob used one. Her closet was a large walk in closet and there was plenty of room for Rob's clothing. Rob was a hunter and had several guns. Heidi looked around and said,

"That closet there in the hall is about empty, put your guns in there."

With that out of the way Heidi said to Rob,

"We haven't eaten since 10:00 this morning and I'm hungry. I'll throw something together for us and we'll eat."

"Sounds great, we've been so busy I forgot all about food."

Heidi looked at Rob then walked over to him put her arms around his neck and kissed him.

"Rob Darling, I'm so happy. I didn't know what happiness was until we met. You know I kind of fell for you that morning six months back when I bumped into you at the department store. I was only going to take a few sips from my cup and then excuse myself. Your demeanor was so disarming, you seemed so genuine and you were, I should say you are very handsome to boot. The more we visited the more I wanted to visit."

"It was meant to be Heidi. By the time we left the restaurant I really didn't want you to walk off. I had to ask you for that first date. I didn't know how to keep you from slipping away from me. And then when you accepted I couldn't believe my good fortune. How quickly our relationship developed, how quickly we fell in love. Seems we never had an argument about anything. Oh there were some tough times when you told me you were a call girl and when we got to the questions, but I feel we resolved both quite well. And now we are living together like husband and wife."

"Oh Rob, that sounds so good. We must not wait too long before we make it just that, husband and wife."

They moved into each others arms and just held each other tightly.

After their mid afternoon lunch Rob said to Heidi,

"What say we go into the living room and sit on the couch, it is now I who has something to say?"

"OK," said Heidi, "let's go. Now what is it of importance that is on your mind?"

"Now that we will be living together we have to think about how the ordinary tasks of living together are going to be divided up. We want to be fair and both satisfied with the division of labor. Above all we both want to be satisfied with the roles each of us is going to assume. We want to avoid a power struggle in our relationship. I can tell you that a power struggle between husband and wife is often the cause for marital disruption and divorce. I have been thinking about this. Let me share it with you."

"The cars will be my responsibility. If something serious develops it will be my responsibility to see that they are fixed. I will mow the lawn and shovel the sidewalks should they need it. We will work on our finances together. So far as finances are concerned, we need to agree on how we are going to bank. Now both of us have our separate accounts. We can merge them or keep them separate. Either is OK with me but it's something we need to agree on."

"Rob, what do you think if we would keep them separate until we are married and then merge them? It would be a bit awkward having two different names on our check blanks."

"Good point Heidi, but that doesn't mean we can't share if that should become necessary. Whatever, we need to work on our finances together. And remember, nothing is carved in stone. If the arrangement doesn't seem to be working out we can make some changes."

Then it was Heidi's turn.

"Cooking, keeping the kitchen and house clean will be my responsibility as will putting together a grocery list each week. I would be most happy if we can go shopping together."

"I would like that Heidi."

"Also doing the laundry will be my responsibility. And since I'm working I will appreciate any help you can give me with these daily and weekly chores."

"I'll be happy to, but as you know I'm not much of a cook."

"Heaven forbid, that will be my responsibility and mine alone."

"Rob, I didn't know that each of these can be a power issue."

"Believe me Heidi they often are. My father had to be in charge of everything and I mean everything. Before my parents were married mother held many responsible jobs. She left home at 16 so she worked on her own for nine years. They were 25 when they married. Dad had to be in charge of everything. He even did the grocery shopping and kept mother in the dark about their finances. I suppose he considered finances his and only his responsibility. I know mother resented this very much and there is no doubt it affected their relationship. Mother is a strong woman and so far as her leaving dad that is out of the question."

"What you just said about your parents helps me to understand the need to divide the power in our relationship. Being single it had never dawned on me that a married couple had to have some consensus on what each was responsible for."

"If one of us feels we are getting dumped on too much then it is that individual's responsibility to bring it up so it can be resolved. It sounds so easy since we haven't even had a chance to share the many roles in our relationship. Again nothing is carved in stone. I am flexible and I know that you are too. Of course when a baby comes along all of what we have talked about will have to be renegotiated."

Heidi's face lit up, she turned her head and looked at Rob.

"Oh Rob, just to hear you talk about a baby gets me all excited."

"I'm glad it does Sweetheart, however it will be awhile before we can take that step."

"I know Rob, but please know I look forward to having your child."

"Our child Heidi, our child."

As they worked at assuming the many roles that marriage entails there were a few glitches, however, they were resolved without conflict. Once Heidi said,

"Each time you help me with the laundry, I have to tell you all over again how to do it. Can't you catch on?"

Rob could have blown up, instead he said with patience,

"Show me one more time Heidi and I'll try my best to remember. I am not doing this grudgingly, I want to help you."

"I know Rob and I shouldn't let my impatience get in the way."

One evening a number of weeks after they started living together Heidi was in bed waiting for Rob. He made it clear that he was ready for sex again like he was last evening and the one before that.

"Rob, Honey, so help me you are going to burn yourself out."

With a hearty laugh Rob replied,

"No way Sweetheart, no way."

Narrowing his eyes he said,

"Is it possible that it is you who is burning out?"

"Rob, are you serious after being a call girl for three years?"

"Well, you seem to be the one complaining about frequency."

"Darling you have to know that I only have your best interests at heart."

"Well, if that's the case let's dispense with the chatter and get to the activity."

"Come ahead big boy, I can still run circles around you."

Rob, cocked his head, narrowed his eyes and said,

"I'm not so sure about that. Heidi do you remember Karen and Richard Fenton's song, 'We're Only Just Beginning?'"

"Of course I do, however, we certainly haven't only just began we've been at it for fully six weeks."

"That's exactly what I'm telling you."

"OK Boss, whatever you say. I'm only kidding Rob. You don't know how much satisfaction it gives me to give you pleasure. It makes me feel so good. Further Mr. Rob I have a strong libido which also needs satisfaction often."

"So I've noticed Miss Heidi. It wouldn't be any fun and not nearly as satisfying if I couldn't give you pleasure."

As Rob undressed Heidi took note of how powerfully built he was. His biceps bulged, the muscles stuck out in his chest as they did in his thighs.

"Rob, you really are a fine specimen of a man."

"Well, I was wondering when you would get around to recognizing that Miss Heidi."

"Now enough about my physique, I think you are just stalling. It's time for action."

"Come ahead big boy, I'm waiting."

Chapter Nine

$$=\!\!\!\!|\!|\!|\!\cdot=$$

Rob had been thinking about getting Heidi a diamond for some time. The time had arrived, however he felt intimidated when he thought of the size he would be able to afford. Heidi had jewelry, although she was not much of a fancier of it so she didn't have many pieces. She did have a beautiful diamond laced necklace and a few rings one with a beautiful ruby in the center and small diamonds clustered around it. Heidi told him they were gifts from customers. Instead of hoops in her ears she wore studs almost exclusively. Rob would stand at Heidi's dresser looking at the pieces of jewelry and wonder how she would react to a rather small diamond, the best he could afford. Well, he said to himself, she's just going to have to like it.

Since Lorraine was his confidant he could tell her about his anxieties.

"Rob, what you forget is that it isn't the size of the diamond that matters to a girl, it comes from your heart because you love Heidi and that's what matters. Whatever you decide on I'm sure Heidi will be overwhelmed, if not by the diamond itself then by the fact you want her as your wife."

"How do you know Lorraine?"

"Heidi and I have become good friends. Several times when we have had lunch together she asked me if I thought you would ever ask her to marry you given her background and all. I assured her that your love for her was so deep that when it came time, her background would make no difference. I'm glad you have decided the time has arrived. Even Heidi can become impatient."

"Rob, can I ask you a question and I'm sure this is something you and Heidi have talked about. Heidi, like I, is not a big girl, she is really petite. Every time I look at her I wonder how could such a small girl handle customers who, who one might think were much too large for her?"

"Yes Lorraine we have talked about this. As unlikely as it seems, she had trouble with very few customers. Beyond that, I don't know how she did it."

"Can I get very personal?"

"Lorraine you're my confidant and I'm yours although as I said earlier sometimes I wonder if you see me that way."

A bit surprised Lorraine asked,

"Why Rob, why do you say that?"

"I believe I take you into my confidence very often, but I don't think you see me as one you can really trust."

"Rob, that really hurts."

"I'm sorry Lorraine, but I want you to think of how often you share something intimate with me."

Lorraine was quiet for a spell.

"I guess you're right Rob, I really don't share much with you. I guess it's just because I don't have much to share. Can you accept that?"

"Do I have a choice?"

"Rob, I want you to know I trust you implicitly. You know as well as I there are times when we work in a very sexually charged atmosphere, times when I am highly aroused and times when you are highly aroused. I have never had to tell you to lay off."

"Lay off, is that the way you put it?"

"Only, because at the moment I can't think of putting it any other way."

Rob smiled and said,

"OK Lorraine, I hear you. Now you were about to ask me a very personal question, what is it?"

"I've changed my mind Rob. What I was going to ask is really none of my business, I'm sorry I even gave it a thought."

"I know what you were going to ask Lorraine." Rob said with a smile. "You see, that's how well I know you. Sexually Heidi and I are very compatible. I don't mind telling you I worried about size for some time and even with repeated assurances from Heidi I still wasn't sure. Heidi told me numerous times not to worry there would be no problem and you know what, she was right. I recall her telling me, see, wasn't I right? That Heidi is quite a girl Lorraine, and even given her past I feel very fortunate to have her. Her love for me has never wavered."

"How did you know what my question was Rob?"

"Because I know you. Now, back to the diamond, although Heidi doesn't have many pieces of jewelry, she is used to expensive items. Repeat customers treated her very well. A ring from me is going to look pretty cheap sitting beside what she already has."

"Rob, a moment ago I told you what the meaning of a diamond is to a girl. I don't believe making comparisons will even cross her mind. Regardless of how many rings she has she will have only one from you and that's what's going to count."

"How do you know?"

"Because I'm a woman Rob. When you were a teenager and beyond I think you should have done a lot more dating. It's obvious you don't know much about girls."

"Lorraine, I work with women every day."

"It's not the same Rob. This is Heidi and she is the girl you love. You know Rob, you have many anxieties. Maybe it's time you saw a shrink."

After having said that, Lorraine broke out in laughter. Rob joined her.

"A shrink seeing a shrink now that would be something wouldn't it? You know we aren't getting very far with this ring business. I'll show it to you after I buy it and you can give me your honest opinion."

"I'll go you one farther, if you want me to I would be more than willing to go with you when you pick out the diamond."

"Would you Lorraine? I would appreciate that. Schedule appointments accordingly and when it seems like a light day, we'll take off an afternoon. But don't wait too long, as you said Heidi could get impatient."

Lorraine looked at the schedule and said,

"Friday is already light why don't I just keep it that way."

"Good idea."

Lorraine liked jewelry, however her choices were not extravagant. She and Rob went directly to the jewelry store where she made most of her purchases. The owner walked up to them and said,

"Well if it isn't that beautiful young woman again. Why is it that after a man has made his choice for a mate he runs into all kinds of beautiful women?"

"Thank you for the compliment Tim however, as you can see, I'm wearing both a diamond and a wedding band."

"Do you think I haven't noticed that before? It's not every day a girl as beautiful as you comes into the store."

With a sly smile Lorraine said,

"If my memory serves me correctly, you sold both to Ted."

"Indeed I did. I didn't offend you by calling you beautiful, did I?"

"Of course not, what woman would be offended when someone calls her beautiful even when she may not be."

"You can drop that even when she may not be."

Looking at Rob he said,

"She is beautiful isn't she?"

"She sure is. If she weren't I would never have picked her as my secretary."

"You mean you get to see her every day?"

"I sure do."

"You lucky dog you."

"You know Lorraine you're a darn good sport. Some women would be offended by a compliment like I gave you and might even level a sexual harassment charge against me."

"Not I Tim, I'll take your compliments any day."

"Now with compliments out of the way, what can I do for you today Lorraine?"

"Rob wants to buy a diamond for the love of his life. As his secretary I can tell you he can't afford anything in the very expensive range."

"Rob," he said, "What's the limit?"

"I'm afraid it will have to be $750.00"

"I can assure you that for $750.00 you can get the love of your life a very beautiful diamond and it will be considerably larger than a pin head."

"If it's not I'm out of here," Rob replied with a smile.

Tim who was the owner turned to Lorraine and said,

"Lorraine, I'm going to consider you the customer. I am going to bring out a couple of trays priced somewhat higher than $750.00, but for you they will be no more than $750.00."

Rob was dazzled by the rings that lay before him. Lorraine said,

"Rob these are beautiful rings, I believe we will be able to pick the right one for Heidi."

Tim said,

"Heidi, is that your girl friends name? I love the name Heidi."

"Yes," replied Rob, "A lovely name for a beautiful young woman."

"Well then," said Tim, "Let's get to it."

Rob wanted a ring that would compliment Heidi's small hand. First he picked up one then put it down. Then he picked up another and also put it down. He scanned the trays and then saw what he wanted, a combination yellow and black gold ring. The black in the ring fairly made the beauty of the diamond stand out.

"Lorraine, Tim, what do you think of this one?"

Lorraine said,

"It's beautiful Rob if I were Heidi I would be thrilled to receive this ring."

Tim chimed in,

"You have made a very good choice Rob. When I set the trays down that is the one I had my eye on."

"Good and well," Rob said, "This ring it will be."

Tim asked him if he knew Heidi's ring size.

"No I don't, but I did bring one of her rings that fit her perfectly."

"That's even better," said Tim.

"Make it this size and Heidi and I will soon be engaged."

"Can you give me at least 24 hours to size it?" asked Tim.

"I just don't know, 24 hours seems like a long time," replied Rob.

"Tell you what," said Tim with a twinkle in his eye, "Give it to her the way it is and after you do so she can bring it in and I'll size it."

Rob laughed,

"Twenty-four hours will be just fine Tim and if you need more time, a day or two longer won't hurt."

"It will be ready for you tomorrow at this time."

"Thank you Tim, thank you Lorraine, I'm glad I didn't set out on this venture alone. It's such a beautiful ring I may have to buy a cheap one for Heidi and I'll wear this one around my neck."

"You had better not," piped up Lorraine.

Rob reached out and shook Tim's hand.

"I saw the price tag on the ring Tim. I don't want you to be shorting yourself."

"I won't be Rob, I'm just glad I could be of help. Further, if you had not come in I wouldn't have had the opportunity to lay my eyes on this beautiful young woman again."

As they left the store, Rob said to Lorraine,

"Well Lorraine, I think we made a good choice, what do you think?"

"Rob, I wish you were giving that ring to me, but as you can tell I already have a couple of rings on my left ring finger."

"Aw shucks," said Rob, "I guess I'm just not at the right place at the right time."

Lorraine replied,

"I could leave my rings home, you could slip it on my finger and we could have a ball for one day. How would that be?"

"Great," said Rob, "Which day?"

"One day in 2050, would that be, OK?"

"Aw heck," said Rob, I knew there was a catch somewhere. You're just so darn sexy Lorraine."

"Easy Rob, you already have a girl who knows much more about satisfying a man than I do."

"Oh," said Rob, "I don't know about that, you've had a lot more experience than I have."

"Yes, and that's because I'm married."

Rob smiled,

"Lorraine you're such a good sport, I don't know what I would do without you."

"Well, so long as you have a practice you won't have to do without me."

On the drive home Rob wracked his brain trying to decide where, when and how to give Heidi the ring.

"Of course," he yelled out, "At our favorite overlook, Vista Point, where Heidi told me she was a call girl. That is where we expressed our love for each other after Heidi's revelation and that is where we overcame the first obstacle to our relationship. Now is the time."

The ring would be ready Wednesday afternoon. The following Saturday would be ideal if the weather cooperated.

When he got home Heidi had supper waiting.

"Surprise," she said, "We eat early this evening."

"Great," replied Rob. "Heidi, how would you like to spend Saturday at Vista Point, our favorite place to view Mt. Rainier?"

"I'd love to go there Rob, I need to get out for a day."

"OK, Saturday it will be."

Rob picked up the ring on Wednesday. As he looked at it he said to Tim,

"My gosh, I didn't realize Heidi's hands were so small."

He shook his head and then said to himself, I still don't know how Heidi could handle customers of every size and shape.

He didn't want to think about it so pushed it out of his mind.

Thursday and Friday were busy days for Rob. He didn't have much time to think about rings, engagements, etc. But Friday evening the excitement hit him. He was going to have to keep his cool if he didn't want to broadcast his excitement.

Saturday morning Heidi packed a lunch. It was early fall and the weather was cool, however, a sweater or light jacket would be sufficient to keep comfortable. It was early when they set out for Vista Point. Rob wanted to stop for breakfast at the quaint little restaurant where they had eaten a time or two. It wasn't out of the way and the food was good.

When he pulled into the parking lot Heidi was surprised since she had packed a big lunch that would suffice for both breakfast and the noon lunch.

"Well Heidi Girl, I just want to take you out for breakfast this morning."

"How thoughtful of you Rob, I like this little restaurant."

As they ate breakfast Heidi said,

"Vista Point will always hold a special place in my heart. I was sure my life would fall apart and my heart would break. Instead it came together in a way I could never have dreamed of and my heart soared to new heights."

"Heidi, have you ever thought about writing poetry, at times you can be very poetic."

Rob gave a big sigh and continued,

"It will always hold a special place for me also Heidi. I had some very bad moments there, but I also realized just how much I love you."

After breakfast they set out again.

"Heidi, you don't mind if I stop to take a few pictures, do you?"

"Rob, you have taken pictures from every angle from here to Vista Point. How many of each do you need?"

"Gosh Heidi, each day presents new opportunities. It sounds as if you would just as soon I not stop."

"Rob Sweetheart, you stop just as often as you want I was only teasing you."

"There are times when I don't know if you are having fun with me or not."

"Rob, you know I'm a tease. Would you sooner I not do so?"

"Never Heidi, I'd miss your teasing. It just takes me a couple seconds to sort it out at times."

Rob slid from behind the wheel, leaned over and gave Heidi a kiss.

"How wonderful it is to be out today," said Heidi, "It's so beautiful."

Ahhh, Heidi's happy, that's good, thought Rob.

When they pulled into the parking space at Vista Point, Heidi jumped out of the car and ran to the picnic table. She called to Rob,

"Rob, the picnic table is still here."

Rob walked over to the table and already there were tears in Heidi's eyes.

"Oh Rob, that table holds such bitter-sweet memories for me. It was here I thought I lost you and it was here you gave me your unconditional love. I was so relieved, so happy and I have been happy ever since."

Rob said,

"We'll have to eat at the table when we have lunch. Now I want you to come with me. Do you remember after you told me you were a call girl I said I had to be alone for awhile?"

"How could I ever forget that Rob, I thought you were walking out of my life. I was heart broken."

Hand in hand they walked to the fallen tree on which both Rob and Heidi had sat. They were facing a long, narrow canyon with trees from bottom to top.

"Let's sit Heidi."

They sat and Heidi linked her arm through Rob's.

"Do you recall when I came racing back to you and you asked me how I could love you knowing you were a call girl?"

"Yes, of course I do. Then you said, Divine intervention Heidi, Divine intervention. I asked you what that meant and you told me you would explain later. Well Rob, It's now later. What did you mean?"

Rob leaned over and kissed Heidi's waiting lips.

"I was sitting here praying, asking God what I should do and it came to me Heidi, it came to me. Love her Rob, love her."

"Are you saying God spoke to you?"

"In a way, yes Heidi. I sensed it, I got my answer. It was then I came running back to you calling your name."

"Rob, you told me that regardless of my background you loved me, you loved me very much and you took me in your arms and you kissed me and just held me. We both were shedding tears."

"Yes Heidi, I don't know if I said it then, but I say it now, when I gave you my heart I gave it to you for keeps. Heidi, he said as he took his handkerchief out of his pocket,

"Dry your tears."

"Does my crying bother you?"

"Bother me, heavens no I love to see you cry when you're happy."

Heidi looked out over the valley to snow capped peaks in she distance.

"How beautiful," she said, "How utterly beautiful."

While she was gazing down the valley Rob took the ring from his pocket. He reached over and took Heidi's left hand. He slipped the ring on her finger, a perfect fit, and asked,

"Heidi I love you and I want you forever. Will you marry me?"

Heidi looked at the ring in disbelief and said nothing. Again she began to weep, bawl really, making no effort to quiet her sobs.

"Rob, it's beautiful, are you sure it's for me?"

"Positive," said Rob.

"You know I will marry you, of course I will marry you. I have been yearning for you to ask me, however, I came to believe because of my background you would be satisfied with the status quo."

"No Heidi, I will be satisfied only when you are my wife. About the ring, I'm sorry Darling that is the best I could do."

"The best you could do, what do you mean? It's the most beautiful ring I have ever seen. Oh thank you Rob, thank you. I will wear it always and Rob, that's a promise."

"I certainly am expecting you to, Heidi."

"Did you pick it yourself?"

"No Heidi, I had the help of a woman who knows what women like in jewelry. Lorraine helped me and there was also some help from the jeweler."

"Dear Lorraine, she is a wonderful secretary and a wonderful person, isn't she?

"She is tops Heidi, the very best."

"Now I know why you wanted to spend the day at Vista Point. I had no idea I would hear a proposal coming from you and would receive such a beautiful ring. Take me in your arms and kiss me."

Rob cupped Heidi's face in his hands, kissed her long and passionately and pulled her tightly to his chest.

"Rob. This has to be the happiest day of my life. You know what I would like you to do? I would like to have you make love to me right here and now."

"There is nothing I would rather do than to make love to you right now, however I fear we might get a bit of frostbite on our rear ends."

"Oh you," Heidi said. "Alright, if not right now then just as soon as we get home."

"As soon as we get home, that's a promise Heidi."

"Rob, let's go back to the picnic table and walk the trail we walked when you came back to me and took me in your arms."

"Aw Heidi, you're just an old romantic, aren't you?"

"You bet your boots I am. Give me your hand and let's go."

"I'll do that Heidi."

They started down the trail arm in arm, stopping every few minutes to kiss and just hold each other.

"Rob Darling, It's been a perfect day, just perfect."

"It has been Heidi and I'm a very happy man. Now the next step is for us to get married."

"I agree and let's do so quickly."

"It can't be too soon for me."

Again they started down the familiar trail, slowly, with Heidi's head resting on Rob's shoulder and her arm around his waist.

Chapter Ten

= ⅢⅠ =

Weeks after Heidi had received her diamond she was still floating on cloud nine. It was a Wednesday evening Rob arrived home at his usual time. Heidi met him at the door, they kissed, embraced and Rob asked,

"What are we having for supper?"

"Nothing here at home," Heidi responded. "This evening I'm taking you out for dinner. We are going to one of the places customers used to take me. It's a rather ritzy place called the 9th Hole Dining Club and it's expensive, but this is a treat from me to you, we have a reservation."

"You don't have to do that Heidi. With your cooking every meal is a treat for me."

"Thank you Rob, but this will be something different. I know I don't have to, but I want to. I've been looking forward to this for a week."

"OK," said Rob," "I'm looking forward to it too. I'll take a quick shower, shave and put on my new slacks and sports jacket, something more fitting for, as you say, a ritzy place."

As they drove to the restaurant Heidi was a bundle of anticipation.

"I know you're going to like this place Rob, the food is outstanding."

"Aren't you afraid it's going to revive some memories that you would just as soon forget?"

"Yes it might, but that's OK since the events took place in my other life."

When they entered the restaurant Rob looked around and said to Heidi,

"This sure is a ritzy place. I'm surprised you didn't have to pay a cover charge."

"Since when does one have to pay a cover charge to eat at a restaurant? Further this is not a restaurant in the usual sense of the term it's more of a private club."

"If that's so, then how were you able to make a reservation?"

"Because," said Heidi, "I'm a life member. One of my frequent customers with whom I came here often bought me the membership."

"It appears some of your customers treated you very well."

"They did Rob remember most of them are wealthy."

After they were seated and given menus, Rob opened his and gave a low whistle.

"Heidi, have you looked at the prices on this menu, they're atrocious."

"Yes Rob, I have looked at the prices, remember I have been here before, a number of times. I know the food and service is expensive and I agree they are as you say atrocious, but tonight we're going to be atrocious. This is my treat to you."

"I don't know if I can enjoy my meal knowing how much it's going to cost you."

"You had better enjoy it. It will cost me at least the profit from the sale of three homes." Heidi said laughingly.

"Are you sure only three?" replied Rob with a smile.

"Well we're here we have our menus I've made a selection so let's dine in luxury."

"I'm just funning with you Heidi. I'm really looking forward to the evening. I notice there is a stage, what kind of entertainment is provided?"

"Sometimes it's an orchestra and sometimes dancing girls. That you would like since in the past at least, they have been scantily dressed."

"What do you mean by scantily dressed?"

"They wear nothing but pasties and a G-string."

"Wow," said Rob, "let's get the show on the road."

"I figured that would get a rise out of you."

"I assume there is nothing wrong with that since you brought me here?"

"Nothing at all Rob, I just want you to enjoy yourself."

As they were eating and visiting a man walked up to their table and said,

"Heidi, I thought it was you. Where have you been? I've been trying to book you for months. Every time I call I get the same answer, she is not available. Well, you apparently are available for this guy."

"Joe this guy, as you call him, just happens to be my fiancé. I'm no longer in the business and haven't been for at least six months."

"Your fiancé, that's a good one, does he know what kind of business you were in?"

Heidi looked at Rob. His face was white and the muscles in his face were twitching.

"Hey fellow in case you don't know, your engaged to a high priced whore."

In an instant Rob was on his feet.

"What did you call Heidi?"

"I just said what she did, that's all"

Rob first grabbed him by the front of his shirt, cocked his fist and said,

"Why you lousy S.O.B., I'm going to rearrange your face."

He was about to hit the man when Heidi yelled,

"Rob, Rob, don't please don't hit him. What will be gained if you do?"

Rob released his grip somewhat and said to Joe,

"Apologize to Heidi and be quick about it or I'll beat your face so you won't be recognized."

"Sure, sure," he said. "I'm sorry Heidi I apologize for what I said. That was damn crude of me. I guess I realized we would never be together again and I was just striking out at you. You haven't forgotten that I declared my love for you once, have you? The name I called you is the most insulting name a man can call a woman. I'm sorry, please forgive me."

Heidi looked at Rob's face which was beginning to relax.

"I forgive you Joe, but what you said is very difficult for me to forgive, however you have my forgiveness. Joe, I had many customers who declared their love for me. Some were joking and like you some were serious. I'm sorry if you feel hurt, but that's really neither my fault nor my problem. Now leave and never approach me again."

By this time the manager had come to their table and wanted to know what the trouble was.

Rob spoke up,

"Would you please escort this crude character to the door, he just insulted my fiancé and I'm still shaking with anger. I'm not a violent man, but please get his face out of here."

"Joe, what the hell is the matter with you that you would insult a man's fiancé? I never had you pegged as that kind of guy."

"I'm sorry Harry I guess I just lost my cool, I once was in love with this man's fiancé."

"That's no excuse to be rude and crude Joe."

"I know that now Harry."

"Joe, I'm going to ask you to leave and please do so without any further comment."

Rob released his grip on Joe's shirt and Joe quickly walked away.

The manager said to Heidi and Rob,

"I'm sorry this unfortunate incident happened. You have my apology. I can't recall another time when something like this happened."

Heidi responded,

"You and your establishment had nothing to do with it Harry. In no way do Rob and I hold you responsible."

"Thank you ma'am," Harry replied, "This evening your meals are on the house."

"That's not necessary," said Heidi, "In no way do I hold you responsible."

"Responsible or not, your meals are on the house."

"That's very kind and considerate of you, but not necessary. Thank you for your generosity."

"You are most welcome. When you have finished your meals I'm going to have a bottle of my best wine brought to your table. That also is on the house. Maybe it will help you to forget about Joe, just a little."

Harry left and Heidi broke into deep sobs.

"Oh Rob, I'm so sorry, I didn't want you to hear anything like that."

"Listen Sweetheart, you will recall that we discussed this very thing happening. I have nothing but admiration for you. You handled this whole situation very well. If you hadn't spoken up when you did I would have hit him and hit him hard. Now dry your tears and forget it. What he said had no effect on me other than to make me very angry."

Through her tears Heidi smiled and said,

"That, my muscle man, was very obvious."

Rob pulled his chair beside Heidi and put his arm around her.

"Don't cry sweetheart, that guy isn't worth crying about. I believe he was jealous and hurt that he would not see you again. Did the two of you get along well?"

"Yes," said Heidi, "I wasn't only his call girl, but in a way we were friends. He once told me he loved me. It appears I'm paying quite a price for being a call girl. I'm so sorry Rob I would have given anything if this wouldn't have happened."

"Now you listen to me, I love you, do you hear? I love you."

"I know Rob and I love you too and your understanding."

"Now let's forget about it. Only four of us know about this and I have a hunch Joe is going to keep it to himself."

Heidi looked at Rob and said,

"Rob Sweetheart, I don't feel much like eating lets go home."

"No Heidi, we have meals to finish and this is something you have planned and looked forward to and we are not going to throw it all to the wind. Further," He said with a broad smile on his face, "We are going to get a bottle of the club's best wine. Surely we can't pass that by. And Heidi Girl, what about the dancers? You wouldn't want me to miss out on them, would you?"

Heidi thought for a minute then a smile broke out on her face,

"OK, since you put it that way we'll stay."

"Good girl."

Although the incident with Joe put somewhat of a damper on their visiting, visit they did and as Heidi said it would be, the food was delicious.

"I can understand just a wee bit why the dinners are so expensive. This food is delicious."

"I thought you would like it, that's why we came here regardless of the cost which as it turns out, costs me nothing."

When their table was cleared, a waiter brought them a bottle of wine, pulled the cork and said,

"Let me remind you that the meals and the wine are given to you with the compliments of the house."

"You and Harry are very kind," replied Heidi, "Thank you so much."

"You are most welcome. You mentioned Harry's name, do you know him?"

"Yes I do, I have been here a number of times before this, you perhaps don't remember."

"Ma'am, I'm sorry, there are so many people that come and go that there are very few I remember."

Rob poured Heidi a glass of wine and then filled his glass.

"Isn't that a lot of wine for you to be drinking?"

"Yes it is and there is more from where this came."

"Rob, you don't intend for us to drink the whole bottle, do you?"

"I sure do Miss Heidi, now let's get with it."

It wasn't too long before a bit of levity and joking was introduced into their visiting. And they stayed until the bottle was empty. Heidi looked at Rob and said,

"Darling, do you think you are capable of driving?"

"If we had to drive through heavy traffic, no, however since that is not the case I think I can make it."

"What if we get stopped by the police?"

"I'll just have to make darn sure that doesn't happen."

Heidi looked at Rob and broke out laughing.

"Wouldn't that look good in the paper? Marital and sex therapist along with his ex call girl fiancé were ticketed for drunk driving."

Rob broke out laughing.

"I'm afraid both of us would have a lot of explaining to do."

"Rob, you don't look too inebriated to me."

"Don't you mean drunk, Heidi?"

"Inebriated sounds better."

"Rob, are you aware you called Joe an S.O.B? This is the first time I have heard you use those words."

"Yes Heidi, I'm not proud of it, but I did call Joe an S.O.B. and I have no regrets, he had it coming."

"I guess he did, but promise me you won't make a habit of it."

"How about once a day, would that be too often?"

"Oh you. Rob, would you mind if we didn't stay for the dancing girls, I'm tired, my mind is foggy and I'd like to go home."

"Sweetheart, it will break my heart if we don't stay for the girls, however, since you are tired and your mind is foggy and why not, given all the wine you drank, we will go on home."

On the slow and careful drive home Heidi was first quiet and then started weeping. Try as he may Rob could not comfort her.

"Sweetheart, there were a few rough moments, but look at the great time we had."

"I know Rob that should be first and foremost in my mind however, I just can't get Joe's words to you out of my mind."

"It's behind us Sweetheart, we can't go back and undo what has been done. I'm just thinking of the good time we had, your excitement over planning this evening, the good food and of course, the vintage wine. Do you think I'm weaving a bit with my driving?"

"Heidi was silent for a moment and then chuckled and said,

"Yes Rob, I do believe you are, however, right now I'm a poor one to judge your driving. I can't even see straight much less drive a car."

"We don't have much farther to go and so far we haven't run into a patrol car. I think we might make it."

"We had better. I can see that headline you mentioned. How would I ever explain it to Mr. Simpson?"

"And me, how would I ever explain an arrest to Lorraine and to my patients. Ah ha, there are the lights to the house, we're home. Whew, what a relief it is."

Rob walked to the passenger side of the car picked Heidi out of her seat, carried her to the front door, held her with one arm, opened the door and carried her to the bed. He knelt by her side and stroked her forehead.

"Thanks for a wonderful evening Sweetheart." He looked her in her face and said, "I sure like it when you wear your beautiful hair in a pony tail. It makes you look younger."

Heidi rose up on her elbows, stared at Rob and said,

"Rob Darling, I'm really not that old. I'm just two years behind you and I certainly don't consider you old"

"Well, the pony tail just makes you look younger."

"OK, have it your way, the pony tail makes me look younger."

Heidi rolled to her right side, raised up on one elbow and said,

"I'm so sorry Rob I wanted so much to save you from embarrassment like that."

"Sweetheart, I was not embarrassed, only angry and my heart went out to you. I wish I could have shielded you from Joe and his thoughtless remarks. You did a wonderful thing by asking me not to strike him."

"And you did a wonderful thing Rob by not striking Joe. You are not a violent person, just the opposite. Had you hit Joe, right now you would be wringing your hands and asking yourself, why did I do it, I hit him so hard?"

"You know me pretty well Heidi, don't you?"

"I had better after all we've been together quite a few months now. Rob, please don't get me wrong, but I feel kind of sorry for Joe. I know how I would feel if you rebuffed my love for you."

"I understand Sweetheart."

Rob pulled his handkerchief from his pocket and wiped the tears from Heidi's eyes. Heidi smiled and said,

"You and your ever present handkerchief. Between the two of us there have been many tears haven't there?"

"There have been Sweetheart, there surely have been."

Rob helped Heidi undress then pulled the covers over her. Then he undressed and climbed into bed. He pulled Heidi close, leaned over and kissed her.

"Rob Sweetheart, what would I do without you? I just can't imagine you not being by my side offering your support and words that always comfort me."

"You know Heidi, what happened this evening is but a dim memory."

"Rob Sweetheart, it's a dim memory for me too and you know why?"

"No why?"

"Because, we're both so damn drunk."

Both broke out in almost uncontrollable laughter. When it subsided they cuddled and soon both were sleeping.

Chapter Eleven

═ ╹╽╻ ═

The first anniversary of Robs and Heidi's meeting at Phillips Department Store was rapidly approaching. They had been living together for approximately seven months and engaged for four. One evening both were in the living room reading. Heidi put down her book and said,

"Rob, can we visit for a while?"

"Of course we can sweetheart. Come over here and sit beside me."

Heidi moved to the couch and sat beside Rob.

"Now, what is it you would like to visit about?"

"Do you realize it has been four months since you gave me a diamond?"

"Has it been that long?"

"Yes, as a rule the next step is marriage and though I have brought it up a time or two, you have said nothing about a wedding? Don't you want to marry me?"

"Heidi, how can you even ask a question like that? Of course I want to marry you."

"Well then let's get with it let's talk a bout a wedding."

"OK let's talk. I want to be married by a minister," Said Rob.

"It really doesn't make that much difference to me, I certainly do not object to being married by a minister. As you know organized religion doesn't mean much to me."

"Heidi that is something you said you would be willing to work on with me. I don't like it that you have no use for religion. In fact it causes me concern."

"Why, are you afraid I'm going to go to hell?"

Rob winced and Heidi caught it.

"You don't have to be sarcastic Heidi."

"Rob, I'm so sorry, that was very unkind of me to say. I didn't mean to hurt you. All around I guess I'm just not a good person. Perhaps we shouldn't be talking about a wedding."

"That is nonsense Heidi it has nothing to do with our marriage. I'm trying my best to understand where you are coming from. I guess I just find it difficult to believe you have no use for religious beliefs."

"What beliefs I had I gave them up when I was in college. A number of professors convinced me that the only thing that is real is that which is proven by science that which is measurable and revealed to us by our senses."

"There are a lot of things that can't be measured. My love for you is an example. I can tell you I love you, there may be some biological changes that take place when I feel love for you, however, it cannot be proved that those changes are because I love you. Other emotions can evoke the same changes. When we are up at Vista point and I look out at the beauty before me, to me at least, I know there is a God. What I am looking at most likely took millions of years to be completed, long before man inhabited the globe. The beauties of nature are there for us to enjoy. I believe God intended it to be so. What I'm looking at is a product of his creation and not something that just happened by chance. Can I prove it? Of course not, but I don't have to prove it. I believe it and accept it on faith."

"I don't know what faith is."

"Aren't you the one who said that our meeting was more than a mere coincidence? Didn't Dr. Swanson tell you in so many words that unless you change your sexual ways you could develop cervical cancer? And what happened, we met, we fell in love and you left the life of a call girl. When you told me you were a call girl and I left you for a time and then came running back to you, took you in my arms and told you I loved you, you asked me how it could be that I still loved you. I said it was due to Divine intervention. You wanted to know what that meant and I said I will tell you later. Well it's later."

"Rob, are you implying that God brought us together and sustained your love for me?"

"Yes Heidi, I am. You can't accept that?"

"Right now I don't know what I believe or can accept. Now, can we get on with our wedding plans?"

There was a moment of silence. Heidi looked at Rob and could see by his expression that he felt hurt.

"I'm sorry Rob that was like me saying end of discussion. I didn't mean it to sound that way it's just that I'm anxious to get on with our wedding plans. When we talk about religion we go off in different directions and that's my fault, not yours. I guess I should start attending church with you. I might learn something."

"Alright Heidi, but this conversation is not over. My concern about you remains."

"I'm sure it isn't Sweetheart."

"We have agreed we will be married by a minister. Do you have someone in mind?"

"Since I have been attending the community church not far from here I'll ask Reverend Dunn if he will marry us."

"Alright, Reverend Dunn it will be. Would you like to ask a few friends to attend?"

"I would Heidi. I want Lorraine and Ted to be there as well as Zack and Ken and their wives, how about you?"

"I am going to ask James and his wife and Paul and his wife to attend."

"How about your call girl friends, are there a couple you would like to invite?"

"Rob, you have to be kidding, the last people I want at our wedding are call girl friends. Until we are married I don't want any of them to know anything about our wedding."

"Can you trust Paul not to mention it to your friends?"

"Rob, Paul is one of my dearest friends. I trust him implicitly."

"OK, we have the invite list made up."

"I believe it's called the guest list, Rob."

"Whatever."

"Do you think we could take our small wedding party to the 9th Hole Dinner Club.? As you know, I am a member so we would have no trouble making a reservation."

"You mean you want to return to the place where we had trouble with Joe?"

"I'm willing to take that risk, Rob. I don't believe lightening strikes in the same place twice."

"That my dear girl is faith. We're not talking about lightening Heidi, its two people acquainted with each other bumping into one another."

"So you don't think my idea is any good?"

"I think it's a great idea Sweetheart. We'll do it, but have you given thought to what dinner for seven couples is going to cost? You did look at the menu when we had dinner at the club, didn't you?"

"Seven couples, I thought six."

"We certainly have to ask Reverend Dunn and his wife to be our guests."

"I forgot about them Rob."

"Yes, it will be costly, but if we're careful with our spending the next couple of weeks I think we can do it."

Heidi thought to herself, If I were still a call girl five, six, seven hundred dollars would be nothing. I made that and more in one evening. Heidi, get those thoughts out of your head you're not a call girl any longer, your planning your wedding.

"I have an idea how we can cover it. The cost of the reception can include my birthday present and Christmas present, and I'll even give up eating out for a few weeks."

"You really want to go to the club don't you?"

"Very much so."

"And you have no concerns about running into another ex-customer?"

"None Rob. What do you think it will cost?"

"Five, six hundred dollars and maybe more."

"That much?"

"At least that much, but Sweetheart we are going to get married only once. We'll make it."

Heidi laid her head on Rob's shoulder, looked up at him and said,

"Thank you Sweetheart, thank you very much."

Rob handed Heidi the calendar and said,

"Now Heidi Girl, pick the date."

"Can I?"

"Of course you can."

Heidi looked at the calendar and said,

"In three weeks it will be one year since we bumped into each other in Phillips Department Store. Wouldn't it be nice to be married on the anniversary date of our initial meeting?"

"Let's see, it was in mid-March, about the first day of spring, right? Do you think you can wait that long?"

"No, but I will."

"Alright, I'll ask Lorraine and my two colleagues and Reverend Dunn. You call Paul and James and invite them."

"The wedding will be on March 16 that is the anniversary date of our collision at Phillips. It will be on the 16th if it suits Reverend Dunn."

"You remember the date Rob?"

"How could I forget, it was the day you came into my life."

"Thank you Rob, I didn't think setting a date and working out a plan would go so smoothly."

"Why not Sweetheart, don't we see eye to eye on most things?"

"We do, don't we Darling."

"Sunday I'll talk to Reverend Dunn. Say, there is no reason you can't go to church with me. I'd like you to meet Reverend Dunn. In fact I have a strong hunch he would want to meet you before marrying us."

"You're going to get me to go to church one way or another, aren't you?"

"It was just an idea. I have a hunch Reverend Dunn would like to know what the bride to be looks like."

"Rob, I ---."

Heidi stopped in mid sentence, hesitated a moment and then continued,

"I'll be happy to go with you Rob."

"Good Heidi, I'd feel honored to have you accompany me."

"Now one more thing," Heidi said, "What are we going to wear? I know one thing for sure, for me it isn't going to be white."

"I guess you're right, white wouldn't be too appropriate given what it signifies."

"Given what it signifies I should wear black. I'll find something that will look real nice."

Rob said,

"And I have what I want I won't need to buy anything."

"You have so many nice jackets and slacks and I know you don't like to wear suits. OK, so that's settled."

On Sunday Heidi put on a chic outfit that Rob liked her to wear. It was a bit short, but Rob didn't think it would raise any eyebrows. As they entered the church Heidi whispered to Rob,

"It's been quite a few years since I last set foot in a church. I feel almost like a hypocrite."

Rob whispered back,

"Forget about hypocrisy and try to get something out of the service."

After the service Heidi said to Rob,

"I certainly have a lot of questions to ask you."

"Good," replied Rob. "Let's hang back so I can talk to Reverend Dunn."

They waited until the church was cleared then started out the door. Reverend Dunn was standing where he had been greeting parishioners. Rob stepped forward and introduced himself.

"Your face is familiar young man, but until now I don't believe we have met."

"Reverend Dunn, I want you to meet my fiancée, Heidi Faust."

Heidi extended her hand and Reverend Dunn took it.

"I hope you don't mind if I tell you that you are a very attractive young woman?"

"Not at all," replied Heidi, "And thank you for the compliment. I believe most people appreciate compliments."

"I would hope so, but it's gotten to the place where a man isn't sure he can compliment an attractive young woman without running the risk of facing a harassment charge."

"It's unfortunate Reverend Dunn, but I fear you are right."

"Reverend Dunn, Heidi and I are ready to be married and we would like you to marry us, would you do that?"

"Have you picked a date?" "

"Yes, March 16."

"If my calendar is clear it would be an honor. Come with me to my office and I will check my schedule."

Heidi and Rob accompanied Reverend Dunn. He took out his schedule book and scanned the month of March.

"Sunday the 16th would be fine so long as it's in the afternoon or evening."

"We were thinking about five o'clock. It will be a small wedding. If all invited guests are free and show up there will be 14 of us including Heidi and I."

"Five o'clock would be fine."

"Reverend Dunn, Heidi and I want you and your wife to be our dinner guests following the ceremony. Now there may be one catch which we hope will prove not to be a problem for you. The dinner will be held at the 9th Hole Dinner Club. It is a very nice eating place, it serves delicious food, but it also serves alcoholic beverages."

"Young man that will not be a problem. There aren't too many eating places one can pick these days that doesn't serve alcoholic beverages"

"And Reverend Dunn, we plan to toast our marriage with champaign. You and your wife don't have to join us."

"Why not, I like a little champaign and so does Louise. The marriage of such an attractive couple would be amiss without a little champaign. May I ask how long you two have known each other?"

"On the 16th it will be just one year since we met."

"It appears you two have known each other long enough to make your marriage work."

"We had better Reverend Dunn," spoke up Heidi, "Rob is a marital and sex therapist. He spends his days helping couples to keep their marriages together. He better be able to keep ours together."

Reverend Dunn broke into a hearty laugh.

"Rob, may I call you Rob?"

"Nothing but, Reverend Dunn."

"I often have couples come to me for counseling and they bring with them problems that I cannot adequately deal with. If you want to give me your card, when I have such a problem I can refer them to you."

"Thank you Reverend Dunn, I would appreciate that very much."

"Rob, may I ask you a question?"

"Of course you may."

"How did you come to combine marital therapy with sexual therapy?"

Heidi broke out laughing and Rob joined her.

"I'm not laughing at your question Reverend, but that is exactly the same question Heidi asked me shortly after we met. I think I can sum it up for you by saying where there is a marital problem there is a sexual problem and where there is a sexual problem there is a marital problem. They go hand in hand and I can't treat one without treating the other. There are exceptions of course but what I have said is generally the case."

"Ahhh," said reverend Dunn, "How right you are."

"I don't suppose you will need a rehearsal?"

"Both of our families are in the Midwest, it's too far for them to drive. Lorraine, my secretary will accompany Heidi down the aisle. I will step out and take her hand in mine and then you can marry us. Nothing like the couple wanting to get married telling the reverend what he is supposed to do, is there?"

"Quite the contrary, I'm glad you know exactly how and what you want to do. Oh yes, you will have rings?"

"Yes sir, we have the rings."

"Alright, it's agreed, I'll see you at four thirty on Sunday afternoon March 16th. Oh by the way, since there will be but a handful of people present we will hold the ceremony in the chapel."

"Great idea," replied Rob. "I have a hunch we would feel pretty lonely in the sanctuary."

The small group gathered at the church at four thirty on the afternoon of March 16. Introductions were made. Rob and Heidi were glad to meet Paul's wife who was an attractive and out going young woman.

When Rob shook Ted's hand he said,

"Ted, through Lorraine I know you."

"And Rob, through Lorraine I know you. All we had to do was meet and shake hands. How come it's taken this long to meet each other?"

"It's due to negligence Ted."

Reverend Dunn, a most friendly and congenial man endeared all the guests to him.

Everything went according to plans, what plans there were, except Heidi didn't expect to break down in tears during the brief ceremony. She looked up at Reverend Dunn and said,

"I assure you they are tears of joy."

After Reverend Dunn pronounced them husband and wife he said,

"Rob, you may now kiss your bride."

"It will be a pleasure Reverend Dunn."

Rob looked at Heidi's face for a few moments then said,

"I love you Sweetheart." Heidi replied,

"And I love you Darling."

Then they kissed.

The dinner at the 9th Hole Dinner Club went very well. The atmosphere was right for a wedding party, the food was delicious and the champaign was on the house. Everyone was in a visiting mood. When Paul was asked what line of work he was in he had his answer well rehearsed.

"I work for an agency that helps young women find employment. This is particularly true of girls who are in college, badly in need of money and don't know how to begin looking for work."

No one pursued his response any further. Rob leaned over to Heidi and whispered in her ear,

"That Paul is one smart cookie, he couldn't have put it better and yet remain truthful."

Heidi whispered back,

"Didn't I tell you he was quite a guy?"

After the tables were cleared, the waiter brought a decorated cake, compliments of the house.

"My goodness," said Heidi, "What a pleasant surprise. I hadn't given any thought to a cake. I might have known that Harry wouldn't miss a beat." It was the first meeting for Rob and James. From the start they hit if off great. James said to Rob, "You are a fortunate man to have Heidi as your wife. She is a wonderful, young woman who everyday brings a rainbow of light to the office. In fact she is more like a daughter to me then an employee."

"Isn't it coincidental that the three of us were born and grew up in the tri states of Nebraska, Iowa and South Dakota? Rob, we must get together to talk about our Midwestern days."

"We will do that. James, we certainly will do that."

It was a happy group of people that left the club around midnight. Reverend Dunn made it a point to speak to Rob.

"Rob, I can't remember when I last had such an enjoyable evening. You and Heidi have wonderful friends."

When Heidi and Rob arrived home Rob walked around to Heidi's door, picked her up and carried her into the house.

"Well Mrs. Sloan, how does it feel to be Mrs. Robert Sloan?"

"Wonderful Rob Wonderful, why did we wait so long?"

"Oh I don't think it was too long, how about just the right length of time. Take it from the therapist if you will."

"Well my husband," Heidi said, "There is a tradition that on the wedding night a couple celebrates their marriage by engaging in sex. Shall we get with it?"

"My Dear, I'm more than ready, but how about a shower first, it got pretty warm in the club. I did quite a bit of sweating."

"That's because you are a husband for the first time. You have company however, I too did a lot of sweating and that's because for the first time I'm a wife."

As usual the sex was the best ever, but as Heidi said,

"It certainly wasn't a consummation of our marriage, at least not in the usual sense that consummation is used."

Chapter Twelve

Rob and Heidi had been married 2-1/2 years. Their love for each had only grown. Almost everything they did they did together. James had turned more of the real estate business over to Heidi while he and Doris traveled. Rob had reached a point with his therapy that clients were scheduled as much as two weeks in advance. Financially they were more than comfortable. One evening instead of going straight home they met at a restaurant close to home and ate a leisurely dinner.

It was about eight o'clock when they arrived home. Rob had ordered a book on new therapy techniques and was reading from it. Heidi was in the kitchen going over some recipes. When the phone rang Heidi picked it up.

"Hello is this Heidi Trent?"

Heidi had to think quickly. Trent was the fictitious last name she told Paul to use.

"It was Trent but no longer, I'm married."

"But you were Heidi Trent, Right?"

"That's right who are you?"

"Oh you wouldn't recognize my name, however, I know you. I was one of your regular customers when you were a call girl. I visited you quite frequently."

Heidi broke in,

"I had quite a few customers who visited me often. That still doesn't give me a clue to who you are."

"I told you I had fallen in love with you and asked you to marry me."

Heidi responded with,

"I had quite a few customers who told me they had fallen in love with me and proposed marriage. That still doesn't tell me who you are and why are you calling me anyway?"

"To tell you that your life is about over."

"What," said Heidi.

"I am still in love with you and still desire you. You were one of a kind in your business and now your husband has you all to himself and has you any time he wants you, and I see you only occasionally. Even if we met on the street you wouldn't recognize me after 3-1/2, years, but I recognize you and now I know what your name is. Since you are no longer a call girl and are now married I can no longer have sex with you. Well Lady, after 3-1/2 years I'm going to get my revenge. I'm going to kill you. You won't know when it's going to happen, it will be sudden and unexpected and when it happens your husband will feel just like I do, deprived of you. You have such a nice body and you know how to use it. You are so pretty and you went out of your way to please me."

Heidi broke in,

"Who are you anyway, how did you get my phone number?"

"Oh there are ways. Goodbye Heidi, you were so good at what you did and how I miss it. You and I just might have made a very good match. I'm going to miss seeing you from time to time."

Then he hung up.

"Rob," Heidi called out in a shaky voice, "Come here quick. I just had a phone call from someone who said he is going to kill me."

Looking at Heidi's pale face, Rob asked urgently,

"Kill you, who in the world was it?"

"I have no idea. All I know is he said he is a past customer of mine, he fell in love with me, asked me to marry him and I turned him down. Over the years I had quite a few men who told me they had fallen in love with me and even a few who proposed marriage, but with most it was just fun. Whoever this guy is and after all this time he said he is going to kill me for spurning him. What are we going to do?"

"I'll call the police, but since he has not shown himself or injured you I don't believe there is anything they can do."

Rob called the police, however as he surmised there was nothing they could do since no crime had been committed. Most likely he called from a pay phone so it would do no good to try to trace the call.

He was told,

"My advice to you would be to keep vigilant none the less. Do you have a permit to carry a concealed weapon? If so, I believe if I were you I would start carrying a handgun."

"Yes I have a permit and thank you for your advice. We will be as vigilant as we can be."

Heidi was frightened and Rob was very much concerned. What if it wasn't a crack call, how could they keep vigilant when they didn't know who to look for? The caller said Heidi's death would come suddenly.

"Well, at least I can arm myself," Rob said to Heidi. "I may not have time to get to my pistol if need be, but it wouldn't hurt to have it. I'd better get used to carrying it on my person."

Rob went into the bedroom and took his 9mm Berella out of the stand on his side of the bed. He had an in the waist band holster which concealed the weapon and yet made it readily accessible and indiscernible so long as he kept on a jacket or sweater. When he got to work he could put it in his desk drawer.

When he and Heidi went on their outings he carried it with him always. He reminded Heidi often of that.

"This part of Washington isn't like Iowa or South Dakota. Some characters out here would just as soon kill you as not."

Rob and Heidi belonged to a team that shot competitively with other teams in the area. If called upon to do so he could shoot his pistol with deadly accuracy. He practiced drawing it a few times and he did so rather clumsily.

Well, he thought, most likely I won't need it any way. Most likely it was just a crack call from a disgruntled ex-customer and was out to scare Heidi.

For the next week Rob drove Heidi to work and picked her up in the evening. She didn't want to drive to and from work alone nor did she want to be left alone. She felt quite confident the man would not strike while she was ferrying customers about the area.

The caller had frightened Heidi badly and put her on edge. Rob thought, If someone called and threatened my life and said death would come suddenly and without warning, I too would be uneasy and extra careful.

After the second week the tension and anxiety began to lessen and they became less cautious. Heidi now took her car to work. They took their evenings out, went to a movie, a concert and to dinner. They no longer talked about the phone call. They were once again back into the routine of things. Both had concluded that it indeed had been a crank call. If the caller had been serious he would have acted by now. It was good to get it off their minds.

A month had gone by and the phone call was forgotten. It was Saturday morning and time to get groceries for the week ahead. Rob decided to go with Heidi who was still just a bit hesitant about being alone. Shopping was a bit of an ordeal when Rob accompanied her. He either wanted to pick up items she did not need or he tried to discourage her from buying some items which she did need. None the less, it was fun shopping together. Heidi knew that Rob was just having fun with her.

With a cart full of groceries they went back to Rob's Chrysler and put the groceries into the trunk. When he finished, Rob was about to take the cart to one of the nearby stalls when something prompted him to look behind. What he saw horrified him. A man stepped from behind a car with a rifle in his hands. In a flash Rob realized the time had come. Thoughts raced through his head. There was no time for him to go for his pistol. Heidi was fully exposed. He yelled her name, jumped behind her and gave her a hard shove which knocked her into the car besides theirs and then fell to the concrete.

Suddenly Rob felt as if he were hit in the back with a sledge hammer. He did not hear the shot. The impact of the bullet spun him around and he fell against his car. He reached out for something to grab hold of then everything went into slow motion and though he dropped instantly to the concrete the sensation he felt was that he was slowly sliding down the side of the car. As he slid he could see a wide smear of blood staining the car door. He called out,

"Heidi, Heidi."

Heidi lifted his head into her lap. Blood was now trickling out the side of his mouth. Rob turned his head, looked up at Heidi, raised his left arm and stroked her cheek with the back of it. In a barely audible voice he said,

"Heidi my Sweetheart, I'm dying. Remember always that I love you." Heidi screamed.

"No Rob, don't die, you can't die. If you die I will too"

Rob's arm fell from Heidi's cheek and his head rolled to the side. Again Heidi screamed.

"You can't die Rob, Oh God Why?"

By this time a small crowd had gathered. She heard someone say that an ambulance and the police had been called and would arrive in a matter of minutes.

For the first time Heidi noticed the amount of blood flowing from Rob's chest. Blood was also seeping out of his back. Someone said,

"The bullet went clear through him he's bleeding from his back as well as his chest.

Heidi was now in full view of the gunman. He slowly raised his rifle and was about to put the crosshairs on her. The rifle never got to his shoulder. A store customer who had just gotten into his pickup witnessed the entire incident. Instantly he reached for a .45 automatic in his glove compartment, jumped out of his pickup, but was too late to prevent the first rifle shot. As the man raised his rifle again he leveled his .45 on him and fired. The man with the rifle staggered, but again attempted to raise his rifle. The man with the .45 fired again and kept firing until the gunman had collapsed onto the concrete.

Tucking his pistol into his waistband he ran to where Rob and Heidi were on the concrete.

"Stand aside," he said to the people gathered around Rob and Heidi. "I'm part of an EMT team."

The crowd made an opening. The man knelt by Rob's side next to Heidi and put two fingers on his carotid artery, moved them a bit and said,

"His pulse is very weak, but he is alive."

He looked at Heidi and said,

"My name is Alex."

Heidi sobbed,

"Mine is Heidi."

Someone tried to pull Heidi from Rob's body. Alex said sharply,

"Leave her alone."

In a very short time the ambulance pulled up to where the crowd was gathered. Alex stood up and called to the attendant,

"He has been on the concrete about five minutes, his pulse is very weak, but he is still breathing. He needs blood and he needs it badly. Rig up a stand and get blood flowing real fast."

In a few moments blood was flowing into Rob's body. The problem was it was flowing out about as fast as it was flowing in. The medic from the ambulance called emergency at the hospital and quickly explained the situation.

"If you have to, give him all the blood you have and get him over here as quickly as you can. We will be ready for him in surgery. It sounds as if we are going to have to open his chest and go to work on that damaged lung."

Heidi was standing next to the medic.

"Did I hear that he still has a pulse beat?"

"Yes he does, it's not very strong, but he's alive. Are you his wife?"

"Yes," she sobbed.

"What went on here anyway?" he asked.

Alex explained as succinctly as possible what had transpired.

"I strongly believe that Heidi's husband was not the target, but rather Heidi herself."

The medic turned to Heidi and asked,

"Why would anyone want to kill you?"

"He was a secret admirer and felt that if he couldn't have me neither could anyone else."

Alex spoke up,

"I'm afraid I had to kill the gunman in order to prevent him from killing Heidi. I believe he's dead, but it would be best if you checked him."

The medic ran over to the fallen man and quickly returned.

"You did a good job. He won't be ambushing any one again."

Rob was in the ambulance. The medic gave Heidi and Alex the name of the hospital to which Rob was being taken.

With sirens wailing a police cruiser pulled up, the officer jumped out and surveyed the scene. Then he asked,

"What happened here?"

Again Alex explained what had happened only this time he spoke in more detail.

"Is that guy over there dead?"

"I'm afraid he is. He was getting ready to shoot again when I hit him with my first round. When he tried to bring his rifle to his shoulder again I emptied the magazine into his upper torso."

Heidi sobbed,

"I was his target, not my husband."

The police officer extended his hand to Alex and said,

"I wish we had more citizens like you. If you had not acted as you did most likely this woman and her husband would both be dead."

Heidi said,

"Officer, my name is Heidi. It's my husband who was shot."

With tears flowing she continued,

"How I wish that the bullet had taken me and not Rob."

The police officer looked at Heidi and said,

"My name is Vic, please tell me why would anyone want to kill you?"

"He was a secret admirer, he called at our home and said he had fallen in love with me and if he couldn't have me then neither could my husband."

"You mean you knew the man?"

"No, apparently he had been stalking me for some time and had followed me at times as I walked the streets."

"How do you know this?"

"When he called I answered the phone and he told me he was going to kill me, it would be sudden and unexpected."

"If you were his target, why is it that your husband was shot?"

Alex spoke up.

"May I answer your question? Heidi is more than stressed out. Her husband was not the target. I witnessed the entire incident. Her husband turned just in time to see the gunman raise his rifle. He jumped behind her, gave her a shove which knocked her to the concrete and then the man fired."

"What you are saying is that he took the bullet intended for her."

"Yes."

Under his breath Vic uttered,

"Greater love has no man."

"I've heard that before from Rob," said Heidi, "But it didn't make much of an impression on me. Now I understand fully what it means. Rob was willing to die in my place."

"Heidi, there aren't many men who would do that. Your husband is an exceptional man. Did you notify the police about the phone call?"

"Yes, but they said there wasn't much they could do."

"That isn't exactly correct they could have put surveillance on you. If the man had been stalking you and was using the same car, they might have picked up on it."

Alex spoke up.

"I suppose I'm in very hot water for killing the gunman, however, under the circumstances I felt I had no choice."

"Are there witnesses?" Vic asked Alex.

"Quite a few, but with today's current attitudes I don't believe many would testify in my behalf. Some will say that the man was demented and shouldn't have been killed. To them it would have been OK if Heidi had died. That type doesn't give thought to the innocent victim."

"I know Alex and we have some men and women in the Department who feel the same way. I'm glad to say the preponderance would agree with you and me."

One woman spoke up,

"A good number of us will be more than willing to testify in behalf of this good man. My car was parked right next to his pickup and it happened just as he said it did. Had he not acted quickly either the wounded man or both he and his wife would be dead."

The officer turned to Alex and asked,"

What is your name?"

"Alex, Alex Popinsky."

"Alex, I don't believe you will have to worry about being in hot water. What you deserve is a medal for your bravery. The man could have turned his rifle on you."

"I was ready for that," responded Alex. "I am a man of deep spiritual convictions and faith and I have killed a man. That is going to be hard to live with."

"Alex, the commandment Thou Shall Not Kill, doesn't apply to what you did. This isn't the first time I've seen something like this happen. Since we have officers who have had to kill in the line of duty and since they feel the same guilt and remorse you do we asked a Jewish Rabbi what the commandment meant in the ancient Hebrew language. He said that in early Hebrew the translation meant Thou shall not commit murder. One thing you didn't do is murder the rifleman."

"That makes me feel some better. You know, when I first started carrying my gun in the glove box I often wondered if push came to shove, if something like this happened and I could save my life or that of someone else would I be able to act? I now know that I can."

When Rob was loaded into the ambulance Heidi was told to follow in her car. The medic gave her the name of the hospital, but she couldn't remember. She sobbed,

"I can't recall the name of the hospital to which Rob was taken. I don't believe I could drive now anyway."

Alex Spoke up,

"I heard the medic say where Rob was going to be taken. I'll take you to the hospital and you can get your car later."

"Oh thank you Alex," Heidi sobbed.

Vic said to Alex,

"I have to take your .45 as evidence until a coroner's inquest is held. You'll get it back just as soon as possible. I don't want you to be without it for long."

"Neither do I," replied Alex. "I'll be glad to get it back."

"Thanks for relinquishing it so readily," said Vic, "We'll be in touch. Undoubtedly your testimony will be needed."

Vic first walked over to the dead man, picked up his rifle then walked to his patrol car. As he left another ambulance pulled into the parking lot, loaded the dead man into the back and drove off.

Turning to Heidi Alex said,

"Quick Heidi, come with me. Let's go to the hospital."

Heidi followed him to his pickup. She saw the pool of blood in which the dead man had lain.

She said to her self, first Rob's and now the gun man's. Thank heavens his body is gone, if he was still lying here I might have recognized him. I'll never know who he was.

In a minute she and Alex were on their way to the hospital. When they arrived Rob was already in surgery. Alex turned to Heidi and said,

"I'm sorry Heidi, but I have to be going, my wife will be worrying about me. I'm sure Rob's shooting has been on TV and most likely my name will have been mentioned. What is your husband's full name?"

"It's Robert Sloan, Dr. Robert Sloan."

"Did you say a doctor?"

"Yes but a doctor of the social sciences. Rob is a therapist and not a medical doctor."

Heidi put her arms around Alex and hugged him.

"How can I ever thank you for saving my life and for giving me so much support?

"You can thank me by going into the little chapel over there."

Alex pointed to the chapel across the hall.

"Pray, pray like you never have before that your husband will survive and heal."

"But Alex, I don't know God, I haven't set foot inside a church since Rob and I were married."

"Heidi, you go into the chapel and make a real effort to get reacquainted with God. He is waiting for you and prayer may be your only hope for Robert."

"I'm afraid I've led a sordid life," Heidi said to Alex.

"In one way or another in God's eyes we all have, replied Alex."

"Alex, I'm so grateful to you for what you have done and said . I will go into the chapel and try very hard to pray for Rob. Do you really think God will listen to my pleas?"

"I know he will listen to them Heidi, but I don't know if he will answer them in the way you want him to. Only God knows that."

"Alex, I know your name since you mentioned it to Vic, but please give me your phone number and address. I will let you know how this all turns out. I'll give you mine. Let's keep in touch," Heidi said.

"And Heidi, I too will be praying for both you and Rob."

Heidi was standing next to a pay phone. She said to herself, I must call Lorraine and James. First she dialed Lorraine's number.

"Lorraine, is that you?"

"Heidi, I've been waiting for your call. I'm frantic, what happened and how is Rob?"

Very quickly Heidi told Lorraine what had happened.

"Rob is in very critical condition, at this point I don't know if he will survive."

"Oh Lord no Heidi. I'll stay in the office to answer phone calls and to inform his client's what happened. Then I'll close it down."

"No Lorraine, don't do that. Rob will be back. Somehow I just know he will be back.

"Are you sure you don't want me to close the office?"

"Keep it open and if Rob dies then we can decide what has to be done."

Sobbing Lorraine said,

"Rob dying, I just can't believe that. When I heard about the shooting over TV I thought it had to be another Robert Sloan. I want you to know that I will be praying for both you and Rob. It all seems to have happened so fast. I'll be in the office on Monday at the same time I usually arrive There are going to be phone calls from clients since I'm sure most everyone has heard about the shooting."

"Every thing happened so fast Lorraine that my head is reeling and I feel like I'm in a daze. I have to hang up Lorraine. I must call James."

Heidi dialed James' number, he picked up the phone and when he heard Heidi's voice, his first question was,

"How is Rob?" His second question was

"How are you"?

Again Heidi quickly explained to James what had transpired.

"Heidi, don't worry about getting back to the office, come when you feel you can."

After her phone calls, Heidi sat down and wept bitterly. A nurse came by and noticed. She asked Heidi what was wrong. Heidi said,

"My husband has been shot and is now in surgery. I have no idea how he is doing."

"I'll see if I can find out. What is your husband's name?"

"Sloan, Robert Sloan."

"Ill be back as quickly as I can."

In a few minutes the nurse was back,

"I'm afraid the news isn't very good Mrs. Sloan."

"Heidi please, my name is Heidi."

"The surgeon is doing everything possible to save your husband's life, however, the bullet damaged his right lung badly. Other tissue was damaged as were two ribs which had to be removed. The critical problem is that blood being infused into him runs out about as fast as it can be put in. Right now they are in his chest cavity trying desperately to repair his damaged lung in order to get the bleeding stopped. The amount of blood being used is more than usual with a wound like his."

Heidi broke down. She sobbed out,

"I'm going to lose Rob, is that what you are telling me?"

"I'm afraid so Heidi, but never give up hope. Have you tried praying for him?"

"Why does everyone tell me to pray?"

"Because prayer may be your only hope, Heidi."

"That's what Alex said."

"Rob, Rob please don't die. I can't go on without you, I won't go on without you. If you die I will join you."

"Heidi, you mustn't talk that way. There are wives who lose husbands every day in here. Somehow they manage to go on."

"Perhaps the difference is I don't want to go on."

"Heidi, I have to be going now, I'll keep you posted. Remember don't give up hope and pray that your husband will recover."

"His name is Rob," sobbed Heidi.

An icy chill swept over Heidi. She remembered what Reverend Dunn said in his sermon the day Rob asked him to marry them. His words screamed out at her.

"The wages of sin is death."

It was her sin that would be responsible for Rob's death.

"Oh God No," she sobbed in a whisper, "No, no, no, he is dying in my place. Rob, if you die I have no right to go on living. I promise you I will join you in death."

Heidi was left alone and that is one thing she disliked very much. She stood and walked to the chapel door. She said to herself,

If I go inside, how do I pray? Dad told me once that one prays just by talking to God. The prayer doesn't have to be fancy or eloquent, just tell God what it is you want.

She could do that, but she didn't know God. How could she pray to Him. She felt drawn to the chapel door. Once there she opened it and went inside. She was alone. She noticed how peaceful and quiet it was. Since the chapel was intended for patients and/or their families there were only a few pews. She walked to one in front and sat down.

The chaplain whose office was just across from the chapel saw Heidi enter.

Heidi began to pray.

"God," she said, "I don't know You and I doubt that You know me although Rob says You do. I'm just going to talk to You like I would to my dad. My Rob is lying at death's door. It seems the doctors can't save him, but several people have told me You can and that I must pray that You will do so. I don't know if this is a prayer or not and I hope I'm not doing it the wrong way. Please don't let Rob die. He is such a good man and never hurt anyone. God, that bullet that struck Rob was meant for me. He stepped behind me so he could take the bullet instead of me. See God that is how good a man Rob is. I must admit to You that I have led a sinful life. I used to be a call girl, a prostitute and maybe You have no use for prostitutes."

Heidi did not hear the chapel door open as she was talking to God. The chaplain quietly entered and sat in the back pew.

"I don't know when it was I stopped going to church and learning about You and believing in You. I used to go with my parents and then I just stopped. I guess I didn't believe all that stuff about You being invisible, that You hear and answer prayer that people don't really die only their physical body does. I guess I started going down hill from there."

"I wasn't a very good girl. I know I hurt my parents many times. I know that on more than one occasion dad even wept. I know that mom and dad prayed for me. If You tried to get to me I just wasn't receptive."

"I came out here to Washington to go to college. I was glad to get away from home. I wanted to be on my own. Dad called me his Little Girl. I'm not very tall You know. I love dad and mother too, but dad and I were the closest."

"When I arrived out here they wrote to me regularly, but I sent only a few letters home. They would call from time-to-time just to find out how I was doing. If they knew what I was doing I know it would have broken their hearts. Rob said You are just like our earthly father. You love us, You care for us and You want the best for us. If that's true and You hear me, my dad loved and cared very much for me. He only wanted the best for me."

"I'm not trying to hide anything from You God, I fell into sin. I knew what I was doing was wrong, but I did it anyway. Now my Rob is dying because of the sins I have committed. You know that's not right God, he shouldn't be dying because of what I did. Don't take him God, take me instead. Let him live."

"I had no real happiness until I met Rob and we were married. He is such a wonderful man, he accepted me and what I did and God, he loves me just like dad loves me only in a bit of a different way. I was the happiest girl in the world now I feel as if my world is ending."

"God, before I say goodbye, I want You to know Rob tried very hard to get me to know You. I just kept telling him I wasn't interested. He never got angry with me; he never blew up at me. All he did was love me."

Heidi stopped talking and broke down in heavy sobs. When she calmed down she continued,

"Oh yes God, I want You to know that I am a faithful wife to my Rob. I may have caused other men to stumble and fall, but I would never think of being unfaithful to Rob. Thank You so much God, I hope that You heard me."

"Well God, other than begging You to save Rob I guess that is all I have to say now except for one thing. I don't want to go on without Rob. I don't believe I will go on. I will do whatever I have to do to join him. Goodbye God."

Heidi had not heard the door to the chapel open. After she closed her prayer, the chaplain said,

"Go ahead and cry, I have all evening and night if necessary. When and if you need me I am Chaplain Clay Cunningham. I heard part of your prayer to God and it was a very good prayer. Miss, miss..."

"My name is Heidi Sloan, please call me Heidi."

"Mrs. Sloan there is no doubt in my mind that God heard your prayer. I'll tell you what Mrs. Sloan, if you call me Clay, I'll call you Heidi. I saw you enter the chapel Heidi, but I didn't see you come out. I decided to enter to see if I could be of any help."

"Clay do you really think God heard my prayer?"

"I know He did Heidi, but you must accept that God does not always answer prayer the way we want Him to."

"Are you telling me Rob will die?"

"No, no not at all, but we just don't know how God is going to answer prayer."

"Oh Clay," Heidi said, "I feel so helpless and so alone. My husband is in surgery and his chances for recovery are not good. He was shot when he jumped behind me and was struck by a bullet meant for me."

"Greater love has no man than he who lays down his life for his wife. That's paraphrasing a bit, but I'm sure you have heard that verse of scripture before."

"Yes a police officer quoted it. That's a wonderful way for you to put it Clay."

"The original is something Jesus said to his apostles when he was trying to tell them what the ultimate love is."

"Clay, I have been a sinful woman and that is why I prayed as I did. Although others told me God would here my prayer I really didn't believe it. But you know, I felt a kind of peace come over me as I prayed"

"That doesn't surprise me Heidi, I would say that is very likely an indication God heard you."

"Clay, I believe Rob's shooting was God's punishment on me for my sinful behavior."

"Heidi, please believe me God did not punish you by seeing to it that Rob was shot. That is not the way God operates."

"I hope you're right Clay. I love Rob, I love him more than myself. Rob is such a good man. I really believe God is saying "Heidi because of your sinfulness I am taking Rob from you."

"Heidi, you must stop thinking that way. The Bible says, All have sinned and come short of the glory of God. All those living and dead have sinned. If God doesn't forgive our sins then heaven is going to be an awful empty place. In your prayer you said something like you loved your dad and your dad loved you. And then you said Rob told you to see God as your father only He is your heavenly father. And you prayed as if you were talking to your dad."

"Clay, if I can't forgive myself for my sinful ways how can God forgive me?"

"You have to ask Him to Heidi, you have to ask Him to."

"I haven't done that because I don't believe God forgives a sinful woman like me. Further I don't have much time to do so."

"What do you mean Heidi?"

"Earlier I told God that if Rob dies I don't want to go on living."

"Heidi, I ask you not to think or talk that way. Should Rob die you wouldn't be the first woman who lost her husband by some senseless act of someone else, women who loved their husbands just as much as you love Rob."

"I know Clay, one of the nurses said the same thing and as sorry as I feel for those women they can't feel my pain."

"That may be right Heidi, but they feel pain like you do. You have to have faith that God will not let Rob die."

"I don't know what faith is Clay."

"Faith is the belief that something we are hoping for, something that is not yet seen, will happen. If you believe Rob will die then you don't have faith. Do you believe the sun will rise tomorrow?"

"Of course I do."

"Putting it simply, that Heidi is faith. Tomorrow is off in the distance and we really don't know for sure that it will rise tomorrow morning, but we believe it will, we have faith it will. If we didn't have faith that it will rise then we wouldn't make plans for tomorrow."

"So that is what faith is. It is right in front of my eyes because I believe the sun will rise tomorrow morning. So not knowing what the outcome of Rob's surgery will be, I should have faith, I should believe the outcome will be favorable. Then that is faith."

"It is Heidi, what you are hoping for, what you want to have happen is not yet known, but if you turn around and say, Rob will live, then you are showing faith."

"But what if he dies?"

"Earlier I told you that God does not always answer our prayers in the way we want him to. If you say, God you let me down, You didn't answer my prayer then you have given up on faith. Let me say again Heidi, when I came into the chapel I heard you ask God not to take Rob from you. If you believe Rob will die then you no longer hope for something not yet seen. So far as you know Rob is still living. Doesn't that give you enough reason to have faith?"

"That's easy for you to say, you're a man of the cloth."

"That has nothing to do with it Heidi, it's because I believe. Not in the sense we usually use the word, but believing as we use the word when we have faith."

Clay held up his Bible.

"This is what I believe and that requires a lot of faith."

"Anyway Clay, it's too late for me. I guess I can say I have gone too far down the road to hell."

"Well Heidi, if you have no faith and if you don't ask God to forgive you for past sins before you die, yes then you will go where you don't want to go."

"You believe then that there is still hope for me?"

"I sure do, but you have to act on it. What is Rob's standing with the Lord?"

"He has made peace with God and he has the kind of faith you have been talking about. He has tried to help me see the light, but my sinfulness always stands in the way."

"Only if you allow it to continue. Heidi, stay here I'm going to get you a copy of the Bible. I'm sure Rob has more than one, but I want you to have one you can call your own, a Bible that you can write notes in or pose questions in the margins, to write down doubts you have and what you understand and accept and what you don't understand."

Clay left leaving Heidi alone and Heidi prayed.

"Lord forgive me my disbelief, help me to believe. Help me to have faith. And Lord, I'm not giving up. I beg of You to heal Rob, don't let him die."

Again Heidi started sobbing.

"What's the use," she said, "The nurse said Rob was in critical condition. But when I say that I have no faith. It's all so confusing."

Clay returned with a leather bound Bible.

"Heidi, I'm giving this to you. It's a Bible I bought on a sale a few weeks ago. It caught my eye."

"Clay, I can't take your Bible from you."

"Heidi, do you know how many Bibles I have?"

"I suppose you have at least three or four."

"How about a dozen. There are many translations. Heidi, please listen to me. Your Bible will do you no good if you don't read it. Did you know that year after year the Bible exceeds the sale of all other books with given titles? At the same time it is perhaps the least read of books in people's libraries."

"I will Clay, I promise you I will."

"Now I'm going to leave you alone. Here is my card. If you should need me I am as near as a telephone. Remember Heidi, keep the faith."

Clay left and again Heidi was alone.

"I don't know how to pray God, really pray, but I'm going to talk some more."

Heidi spent another hour in the chapel telling God about all the joys and happiness in her life, what she believed to be the good and bad things in her life. When it came to her three years of prostitution, she discovered she could speak to God just as easily as she did on any other topic. When she finished she felt better.

"As Clay said, I must keep the faith."

Heidi left the chapel and walked back to the waiting room. In a short time the nurse she talked with earlier entered.

"I've been looking for you, I have good news. Rob seems to be rallying. The bleeding has slowed considerably, his breathing is more regular, his blood pressure is coming up and his temperature has started to drop. These are all positive signs. He is still in critical condition, but it appears he is out of danger."

Heidi could no longer control herself, this time she bawled. She said over and over,

"Thank You God thank You. My prayers have been answered."

The nurse sat down beside her and put her arm around Heidi's shoulders. "

Rob is better, have faith he will continue to improve."

Heidi was surprised that even the nurse encouraged faith.

"Have you been in the chapel praying?"

"I'm not much at praying, but I know God answered my prayers."

Did you meet Clay?"

"I did and what a wonderful man. He gave me so much encouragement."

"Around here we all love him."

"What's your name?" Heidi asked.

"It's Susan." Replied the nurse.

"Thank you, thank you Susan. For the first time since Rob was shot I have hope and I really have faith he will continue to improve and in not too many days he will be able to come home to me. Susan, God answered my prayers, me who is so unworthy."

In the next few weeks Heidi and Susan became good friends as did she and Clay.

When Rob was out of danger she called Lorraine to give her the good news. She could hear Lorraine weeping on the other end.

"God does answer prayer Heidi."

"I know that now Lorraine. Keep the office open."

She also called James who told her to stay with Rob until he had made considerable improvement.

"Let's see," she said, "There is one more phone call I have to make. Oh yes, to Alex."

When she called, Alex answered the phone.

"Alex this is Heidi. Rob is out of danger and though he will be a few weeks recovering, he's going to live."

"You went to the little chapel and prayed, didn't you?"

"I did Alex and it was the best thing I ever did. Thank you for the encouragement to do so."

"Heidi, never dismiss the potential of answered prayer."

"I won't Alex, I assure you I won't."

"And Heidi, please keep in touch. I'm so happy for you."

"I will Alex and that's a promise."

Chapter Thirteen

Heidi walked into Rob's room, he was waiting for her. After they kissed Rob held Heidi and said, "Heidi, I'm going nuts. I can't wait any longer, we just have to have sex it seems like the last time we did it was years ago."

"Rob, this is a hospital room."

"At this stage I don't care what it is. Would you at least take your clothes off for me?"

"Do you think I can get undressed and dressed before someone comes into check on you?"

"The next will be a blood draw and that will be in a half hour."

"OK Rob, for you I'll do anything, even in a hospital room."

Heidi was wearing a short skirt, blouse, skimpy panties and no bra. She dropped her skirt, slipped her blouse over her head and kicked off her briefs. She stood naked in front of Rob.

"Oh my gosh," he moaned, "You don't know how I've yearned to see you that way."

"Oh yes I do, after all, we've been together for 3-1/2 years and married for 2-1/2 years. She walked close to Rob and he ran his hands over her body. When he stroked her genitals she gasped.

"What's wrong?"

"Wrong, wrong, Rob I'm just as hard up as you are."

"Yes, but I'm lying here in bed almost naked. You see me in the buff nearly every day."

"Your right Rob and I haven't run my hands over you."

"Heidi, it's still 20 minutes before my blood draw, do you think you can slide in here beside me?"

"Rob, if I did and we got caught, it wouldn't bother me one bit, however, we don't know if you could take it. It might stress you too much."

"So what."

"So everything. I had better slip my clothes on before someone walks in."

"Oh no, don't do that."

"Rob, I have to. I just had an idea, let me ask Susan if there is any way we could have sex and if so if it would be too hard on you."

"It's worth a try Heidi."

Heidi stepped into the hall and almost bumped into the nurse headed for Rob's room for the blood draw.

"Is Susan on duty this morning?"

"Susan is at the desk."

Heidi went to the desk, Susan looked up and said,

"Hi Heidi, you sure look chipper this morning."

"Susan, believe me I feel chipper. Could we go somewhere where we can be alone?"

"Sure, follow me."

Susan led Heidi to a small room, one she had to open with a key. When they were in, she locked it.

"OK, what is so secret that we have to be alone?"

"I'll be blunt and come straight to the point Susan. Rob is climbing the wall, we need to have sex very badly. Has that ever been allowed between a husband and his wife in the hospital?"

Susan smiled and said,

"I had a hunch that is what you were going to ask. It has been allowed Heidi. We call it a conjugal visit. We have found that under certain circumstances when a man has sex with his wife, it sometimes speeds up his recovery. It certainly improves his outlook. However, I'll have to check with his doctor first. Will you be here for awhile?"

Heidi looked at her watch.

"In about 45 minutes I have to head out to my job."

"I'll get back to you just as quickly as possible."

In 10 minutes she was back.

"I called Rob's doctor and he said go ahead, but you will have to do all the work."

"Susan, believe me, I'm well practiced at that, however, there is hardly time now."

"How about this evening?"

"That would be better. Rob and I always cuddle after we have had sex, but how do we pull it off."

"I'll tell the night nurse what will be happening in Rob's room and to see that no one enters for an hour and a half. Would that be long enough?"

"Oh yes Susan, you are a darling."

"Well, I don't know about that but I am married and I believe I know how Rob is feeling about now. How about you ?"

"Susan, I'm just as hard up as Rob is."

"Why wouldn't you be, you've had to go without sex just as long as Rob. OK then this evening it will be."

Heidi laughed,

"It sounds more like we are plotting a murder rather than a tryst in a hospital room between a husband and his wife."

Susan joined in the laughter and then said,

"Enjoy."

"Enjoy, it will be ecstatic Susan. Thank you so very much."

After work, Heidi stopped at a fast food restaurant, had a burger, went home to take a shower and put on a pert little outfit Rob liked to see her in. When she got to Rob's room, the nurse in charge had a big smile on her face.

"Mrs. Sloan,"

"Heidi please,"

"Heidi, everything is arranged. Rob's room will be closed just as long as you need it to be. And Heidi, enjoy.?"

Heidi blushed, turned to the nurse and said,

"I usually don't blush, but this is something new for me."

"Don't worry, you won't be disturbed."

"Thank you so much," replied Heidi.

Heidi entered Rob's room. She hadn't told him his doctor said they could have sex so long as she did all the work. She closed the door and said,

"OK big boy, the time has arrived."

"For what?"

"For what you've been longing for."

"Heidi, please don't play games with me."

As Heidi was stripping off her clothes, she replied,

"No games Darling, this is the real thing."

In a moment she was in bed with Rob. He grabbed her and pulled her close and kissed her. She thought like he had never kissed her before. Soon Rob said,

"Sweetheart, I can't wait any longer. How are we going to do this?"

"I'm going to do all the work, you just lie back and enjoy it."

"Do you think you know how?"

"Rob, I was a call girl for three years, I learned every trick in the book."

Heidi climbed astride Rob and in a moment she climaxed. Rob had to hold on to her. When she relaxed he said,

"Not fair, I was supposed to be first."

"Sorry she said," When I have to come I have to come. Now It's your turn."

In a very brief time Rob climaxed. He looked up into Heidi's face and said,

"Heidi Girl, I do believe it was better than the first time."

"Aw come on Rob, you just have a poor memory," she joked.

"Thank you Heidi, thank you."

"Rob, you don't have to thank me. Do you want me to thank you every time I climax?"

"If I want to thank you I will. Will there be time for us to do it again."

"Well," said Heidi, "Did you feel any pain or discomfort in the area of your wound?"

"None Heidi, I feel absolutely invigorated."

Heidi laughed,

"That's exactly what Susan and I both were hoping for."

"Well, you can tell her, mission accomplished."

"Oh Rob, it's so good to hear you joking and to see you smiling again. Let's wait a little while, then we can do it again."

"How much time do we have?"

"As much as we need."

"That Susan, she's a sweetheart."

"She is Rob, believe me she is."

After they finished the second time they wrapped themselves in each others arms and soon were sleeping.

"Heidi awoke when the nurse tapped her on her shoulder.

"Heidi, it's time for some medications, for a blood draw and to check Rob's drain. Did it stay in place?"

"Everything's in place, it is as if Rob was given a shot of adrenalin," Heidi said as she looked at Rob who was sleeping soundly.

As she raised up, the sheet slipped down to her lap exposing her breasts. The nurse looked and said,

"I wish I had breasts as nice as yours."

"I'm sure you do," said Heidi.

"Well, my husband says they are nice, but they can't match yours."

"If your husband says they're nice, isn't that all that counts?"

The nurse smiled and said,

"You are very perceptive aren't you? You know when to say the right things."

Heidi smiled in return and said,

"I didn't say what I did to make you feel good, I said it because it's the truth. Don't you agree?"

"I sure do, you've made my evening."

"What time is it?" Asked Heidi.

"It's 10:00."

"Ten o'clock, my goodness, we've been sleeping for two hours.

"That's good, but now it's time for me to take over."

She smiled and Heidi laughed.

"If this becomes necessary again, just let Susan know."

Rob was now awake, Heidi stepped out of the bed and turned around to face Rob,

"Take a good look Sweetheart, you might not see me this way for a day or two."

"Awwww Heidi, Rob moaned. "Can't you climb back in bed with me?"

"Not tonight Rob, it's time for your nurse to take over."

The nurse said to Heidi,

"You two sure are uninhibited."

"Why not," replied Heidi, "There is nothing to be ashamed of about our bodies or about sex between two people who love each other."

"I wish I could feel that way."

"You can, just let go of those inhibitions."

"Maybe you can give me some lessons on how to do it," the nurse said with a smile.

"Any day, any day," Heidi said with a laugh.

Heidi bent over and kissed Rob.

"See you in the morning Darling."

"Thank you Sweetheart."

"Rob, you don't --."

"I know, I know, but I want to thank you anyway. This evening was some thing very, very special with us."

"Very special," replied Heidi with a smile.

As she walked out the door she waved to Rob who waved back.

Chapter Fourteen

By the middle of October Rob was anxious to get to the grass foot-hills to do some pheasant and grouse hunting, or what ever he might kick up. He was under strict orders from his doctor to avoid all strenuous activity.

"Stay on even ground as much as you can and don't go taking off on some mountain trail. Your wound is still healing. Whatever you do don't do any heavy lifting. If you do I fear the bleeding will start again."

The last thing Rob wanted to do was to short circuit the healing process. One thing for sure, he didn't want to end up in the hospital again.

Although Heidi's father and brothers were pheasant hunters, her father had not encouraged her to hunt. As a result she had never hunted and until she met Rob she had no desire to hunt.

Rob wanted Heidi along as his hunting companion. She agreed to go with him just to get an idea of what hunting upland game was all about. She did not have to be coaxed to go with Rob. Since he was shot she didn't want him out of her sight. Rob had told her that next year when they went hunting he would have her shooting a shotgun as well as a rifle. The idea didn't particularly excite her since she was thinking about ringing ears and a sore shoulder, but if Rob wanted her to learn how to shoot his rifles and shotgun as she had his pistol she would give it her best try. She needed no encouragement with Rob's pistol since she was more than proficient with it.

Not only had Heidi not hunted she had never fired a gun. Rob had told her the first thing she was going to learn to shoot was a rifle and then later a shotgun.

"Heidi, I want you to start carrying a pistol with you in your purse at all times Tacoma is a big city and being so close to Seattle it really isn't safe for a woman to be by herself or to go unarmed."

Again Heidi said,

"OK Rob, if that's what you want me to do but I'll need a small handgun first"

"That will be no problem Heidi."

Rob was a good instructor. Their first day at the range was a pleasant surprise for Heidi. Rob explained the mechanical aspects of his guns, both the revolver and automatic pistol, but not his long guns, that came later.

Rob started her with a .22 caliber rifle. He put hearing muffs over her head since she was sure the little gun would be loud and would cause her ears to ring. He also strapped on a shoulder protector so the butt of the gun would be resting on it and not against her bare shoulder. She closed her eyes the first time she pulled the trigger. Much to her surprise she felt nothing.

After that first shot she commenced shooting and as Rob expected she shot well, hitting the bulls eye a reasonable number of times.

At the next session Rob had Heidi shooting his 243. It was a caliber big enough to bag a deer and yet without the recoil of a larger caliber. It was, however, with the handguns that Heidi really shined, especially Rob's Berella 9mm automatic. In competition shooting she used Robs Berrella she wanted one and Rob promised to get her one. She had not yet shot Rob's shotgun.

Rob told her that would come later.,

"When you buy me a gun to carry in my purse, I want a 9mm like yours."

Rob was elated over how well Heidi shot.

"I knew you would do well, it seems that women are just naturals when it comes to shooting accuracy and do you want to know why?"

"Why?"

"Because women shoot for the sheer pleasure of it and not to compete with one another. Shooting well is not a macho thing with them."

Heidi reveled in Rob's praise.

"Why can't we get a shotgun for me so I can also shoot birds?"

"Becoming proficient with a shotgun isn't like shooting a pistol or rifle, it takes much practice. I want you to do a lot of shooting at clay birds. Before next year's season we will buy you a good 20 gauge over/ under shotgun, one much like mine. The 20 gauge is not punishing and is the ideal upland game gun."

"You're fooling with me, there are no such things as clay birds."

"You want to bet?"

"I know better than to bet with you."

"Do you remember the other day when we stopped at Cal's Sporting Goods Store and I bought a couple boxes of shells? We passed a shelf where there were boxes of small orange colored discs. You stopped and looked at them, I was waiting for you to ask me what they were, but you didn't. I was going to take you by those boxes again to explain what they were, however, I forgot. Those my dear Heidi Girl are clay birds."

"For heavens sake, couldn't some one come up with a better name for them?"

"I suppose, however, any shot gunner knows what clay birds are, there would be no sense in changing the name."

"OK, so now I know what clay birds are. I like the looks of your shotgun and will be glad when I have one of my own."

"Before we're through it appears you will have a new shotgun, a new rifle and a new handgun. No matter what I hunt, I will have a hunting partner."

"Wouldn't you sooner go with one of your men friends?"

"No Heidi Girl, with you at my side I would be the happiest."

"Rob Darling, I just love it when you call me Heidi Girl."

"Well if that's the case you will be hearing it more often."

It was early November before Heidi and Rob were able to take their much awaited weekend hunting trip. The place Rob had picked was a 2 hour drive from home. Ken suggested a place where, as he said,

"I've always gotten birds and the ground is very level. If you take it easy it shouldn't be a strain on you."

He also gave Rob and Heidi the use of his 4-wheel drive pickup.

Since they wanted to get an early start they spent Friday night in a motel close by the place they would be hunting. By daybreak they were in the field and ready to begin hunting. Heidi had packed a lunch which she carried in her day pack.

For the first week in November, the temperature was mild and the sky was a brilliant blue. In fact it was balmy. They had walked about a half mile when Heidi turned to Rob and said,

"Rob, did you tell anyone where we were going?"

"Not exactly, Ken suggested this area, he would have some idea where we were headed, however it covers quite a few miles of ground. Should something happen to us I would assume he would tell a search and rescue team about it. Did you tell anyone Heidi?"

"No Rob, I didn't either. I guess we should have told someone."

"We'll be OK," said Rob. We'll take our time and won't get too far from the pickup."

They walked slowly for an hour without kicking up either pheasant or grouse. After a short rest they started out again. Though they were walking slowly, they were getting further and further from the pickup.

Another ten minutes and Rob bagged a pheasant. Heidi was about overcome with excitement. After putting the bird into the back of his hunting vest they continued. A short time later a cackling rooster burst from the shrubbery in front of Heidi.

"Shoot Rob shoot," she shouted.

"Heidi, the bird was just a bit too far for a 20 gauge with field loads."

"You mean one can't shoot a shotgun like a rifle?"

"Precisely, with a 20 gauge and field loads the maximum range would be about 40 yards."

"I had no idea you would be so limited with your shotgun."

"Well now you know. Once we get you shooting clay birds you will see very quickly what I'm talking about."

After walking another 15 minutes Heidi said,

"Oh look Rob there's a cabin just inside the trees."

"I see it Heidi, most likely it belongs to a deer hunter or to a group of hunters who use it in the fall."

"Wouldn't it be nice if we had a cabin like that? If we did we could hunt, and spend the nights in the cabin. All we would have to do is dress, eat breakfast and be out in the field again."

"Who knows," replied Rob, "Maybe someday we can afford a cabin in the woods."

After walking a short distance further, a sharptail grouse got up in front of Rob. He shot and missed. There was silence for a moment when Heidi broke out laughing and said?

"Rob, you missed."

"I sure did Heidi, missing is all part of the hunt."

"I'll bet that if I would have had a shotgun I would have gotten it."

"Maybe so," replied Rob, "You were close enough to me that it would have been in range for you."

"Next fall I'll show you how to shot pheasants and grouse," Heidi said teasingly.

"Well, we'll just have to wait and see about that," Rob said with a laugh. "Let's go just a bit further and then lets eat lunch. After that I think we should start back to the pickup."

"So soon?"

"We've been hunting about 4 hours and it's just as far from here to the pickup as it was from the pickup to this spot. I don't want to overdo it. I promised my doctor I wouldn't. Let's go on for another 10 minutes, eat and then start back."

"OK Rob, I certainly don't want you to overdo it."

As they were eating the wind changed from the south west to the north and had a distinct chill to it. Rob turned around to face the north and said to Heidi,

"There's a large bank of clouds off to the north west. I don't like the way they look. We had better quickly finish our lunch and then start back to the pickup."

"Do we have to Rob? This is so much fun and it's exciting."

"We can hunt on the way back, Heidi. We may have passed up more birds than we flushed. Also, the season is still open for a few more weeks. If time permits we can come here again and give it another try, but right now we had better skedaddle out of here."

Rob stowed the remainder of the lunch into his day pack.

"Let's get going," he said to Heidi.

When they had gone a short distance Heidi asked,

"How far are we from the pickup Rob?

"I would guess 2 to 2 1/2 miles. Hopefully, no further."

Rob looked back and saw that the cloud bank was rapidly approaching.

"Heidi, we had better get a move on, those clouds look bad."

"And it's turning colder," replied Heidi.

They had gone about one half mile when the storm hit. The temperature plunged and snow began to fall. In addition, a brisk wind had come up. Soon visibility was very limited. They plodded on a bit further when Heidi said,

"Rob, I'm afraid. I didn't dress for this kind of weather and I'm cold."

Rob took off his hunting coat and began to help Heidi into it, however she protested and would not accept it.

"No "Rob", she said, "You'll freeze."

"Put it on Heidi. Hold out your arms and I'll help you slip into it."

Rob still had on a heavy vest and a heavy wool shirt, however, the wind cut right through them. "

Let's keep going Heidi, we still have a ways to go"

"We're going to get lost," Heidi said in a frightened voice."

"We'll be OK so long as we stay just inside the trees with the grass land to our left. Visibility is bad, but there is a line I can see that marks the boundary between the trees and the grass land."

The wind was steadily increasing and it was getting colder. After plodding on for another 15 minutes and making very little headways, Heidi shouted to Rob,

"I don't think I can go much further."

"You have to Heidi if we stop we'll freeze."

"I'm so tired I can hardly put one foot in front of the other."

"Heidi, you must keep going."

"Rob," she said shouting at the top of her voice, "You must be freezing, you're shaking."

"I'm not going to say we aren't in a bad fix," Rob shouted back to Heidi, "However, we have one chance and that is the cabin we passed earlier. We can't be far from it. Just keep going, one foot in front of the other."

Heidi stumbled and fell.

"You go ahead Rob and save yourself. I just can't go any farther."

"Heidi, if you can't get up I'm going to lie down beside you and we will both freeze. I am not going to leave you."

"I want to go on Rob, but I can't, I'm too cold and I'm exhausted. It feels good to just to lie here."

That sent a shudder through Rob. Heidi was starting to feel the symptoms of hypothermia.

"I'm going to pick you up Heidi, can you hold my shotgun?"

"Rob, your wound is not completely healed, you can't carry me."

"I'm going to carry you as far as I can. If I drop, at least we are together and we will die that way."

With Heidi in his arms Rob stumbled forward. He could feel his strength waning fast, he was freezing and the site of the surgery scar started hunting him badly.

"Well Lord, I guess this is it," he said, "At least I'm glad that Heidi and I are together." Almost immediately he sensed a response,

"Don't give up Rob, you can make it."

"What did you just say Rob?"

"Oh nothing just mumbling to myself."

Rob scanned the trees to his right hoping to see the cabin. Just when he felt he could go no further, he saw a dark object and knew at once it was the cabin.

"Heidi," he shouted, "It's the cabin."

Barely able to open her mouth, Heidi replied dreamily,

"Good Rob, Good."

Rob forced himself to make it to the cabin door then he remembered it was locked with a heavy padlock.

"Heidi, can you stand, just for a minute or two? I'll put you down and you hang on to me."

He put Heidi on her feet she put her arms around his waist and hung on teetering back and forth. Rob took the shotgun from Heidi's hands, held the barrel close to the lock and pulled the trigger. The lock bounced a jig but didn't open. He put his finger on the trigger again, put the barrel to the lock and pulled it. This time the lock sprung open. He quickly pushed the door open and with his right arm lifted Heidi and dragged her inside. He pulled the door shut behind him.

The cold remained, but at least they were out of the wind and blowing snow. He looked around, there was a rough hewn table and a couple of chairs surrounding it. He lowered Heidi into a chair then he looked around for the stove and there it was standing in one corner as it should have been. In addition there was wood stacked up on one side of it.

"Heidi," he chattered, "There is a wood stove and wood now if I can only find the matches."

That was no problem a box of matches was on a small shelf to the left of the stove. With hands about frozen he pulled out his knife and with difficultly cut a few strips of wood from a bare log. Next he looked for paper, any kind of paper, however he couldn't find any. Reaching into his pocket he pulled out his wallet, took out a number of bills, crushed and rolled them between his frozen hands. When he felt he had enough, he laid the small pile of paper on the bottom of the stove and picking up the shavings, stacked them in such a way that they made a small pyramid.

"Heidi," he said, "Do you think you can strike a match?"

"I'll try Rob."

Heidi's hands were also numb, however, she was able to strike a match but the head broke off.

"Take another and try again."

Again she struck the match and it ignited.

"Drop it in the center of the pyramid of sticks."

When she did, at first it looked as if the match would go out, however, one of the bills caught fire and then another and soon there was a fire large enough to ignite the shavings and twigs. As the fire gained momentum Rob fed it larger and larger branches. When he felt the fire would continue burning he laid a couple of wrist sized pieces of wood on the burning twigs and branches. Finally he felt it was time to lay on small logs about the size of his calfs. After that he believed there was little danger the fire would go out so long as they fed wood into the stove. He paid no attention to the size of the logs.

Heidi started weeping. Rob offered up a silent prayer, Thank you God, I think we'll make it now.

He looked over at Heidi, he couldn't tell if she was conscious or not.

"Heidi," he called, "I have a fire going and soon you should feel the heat."

Heidi raised her head and mumbled,

"Thank you Rob."

"Come over here," Rob said.

"I can't move." Replied Heidi."

Rob walked over to Heidi,

"Put your left hand around my waist, and raise yourself up. I'll pull your chair closer to the stove."

With great effort she got to her feet. With Rob's help she was able to make the few steps closer to the stove. Rob lowered her into the chair. In a few moments Heidi said,

"Rob, the heat feels so good. I was sure it was over for us. I was so cold I started to feel warm."

"You were becoming hypothermic Heidi and I wasn't far behind you."

"How did you ever find the cabin?"

"By the Grace of God, Heidi."

"We wouldn't have made it, would we?"

"No Heidi, we wouldn't have made it."

As she started to warm Heidi began to shiver.

"You're coming out of the hypothermic state," said Rob.

Heidi looked up at Rob with a weak smile on her face. Suddenly the smile vanished.

"Rob," she said with alarm in her voice, "You're bleeding from the incision in your chest."

"I know it Heidi and we have to stop it. I've lost too much blood already."

"It's because you picked me up and carried me, isn't it?"

"It's everything combined."

"No it isn't, picking me up and carrying me was too much of a strain."

"For whatever reason Heidi, you're going to have to help me. Take that bucket over there, open the door and fill it with snow."

Heidi filled the bucket with snow and brought it to Rob who was now sitting by the stove. His face wore a grimace of pain.

"Rob, you're hurting."

"It hurts like hell Heidi, but pain or no pain we must stop the bleeding. Help me get this vest and shirt off my right shoulder."

Rob held out his right arm and Heidi pulled on the sleeve. Rob let out a yell.

"I'm sorry Darling, I'm sorry," Heidi sobbed.

"Never mind my moans and groans. We must bare my chest. Pull the sleeve off my shoulder and arm."

Heidi got the shirt off, but not before Rob got woozy and almost passed out. She looked at her hands which were covered with blood. She started to sob uncontrollably.

"Not now, there is no time for tears. Make a snowball and press it against the part of the wound from which the blood is coming"

Heidi did as she was told and steeled herself against Rob's out bursts of pain. When the snowball melted she made another and pressed it tightly against Rob's wound. At last the bleeding slowed to just a trickle.

"Now what?" she asked.

"Heidi, we need a compress. In my day pack in the first aid kit are a number of 4 X 4 gauze squares. Take out a few, fold them and press them against the area from which the blood is coming."

"There is nothing with which I can tie the gauze to your chest."

"Look around there must be string or some kind of rope somewhere in here."

"Here's a piece of rope but it's filthy. It looks as if there is dried blood on it."

"It must have been used to hoist a deer for cooling," Rob replied. "Forget about the filth. Hold a small piece of wood against the 4 X 4s and wrap the rope around my chest being sure the rope presses the wood against the wound."

As Heidi wrapped the rope around Rob's chest he let out a yell. Heidi was afraid he was going to pass out. After some time she said to Rob,

"The bleeding has stopped. Be very still and try not to move your left arm."

"Can you drag the mattress over here? I have to lie down or I'm going to pass out."

Heidi pulled the dirty mattress off the make shift bed and drug it to the stove. Rob dropped to his knees and Heidi helped him to lie on his back. Suddenly Rob began to shake.

"I'm freezing Heidi. Aren't there some blankets in here?"

"There are several at the head of the bed, but they are covered with dirt and the droppings from some kind of animal."

"Forget that," said Rob through chattering teeth. "Bring them over here and cover me with them."

Heidi covered Rob who then became quiet. She didn't know if he had fallen asleep or passed out. She sat in her chair, buried her face in her hands and began weeping.

"Rob," she said, "You have suffered so much for me. What's to become of us? We didn't tell anyone where we were going. No one knows where to look for us."

Rob opened his eyes and said,

"Heidi, this storm can't last forever. Once it blows itself out I'm sure you can find the pickup and go for help."

"You mean leave you here alone, not a chance."

"But..."

"Forget it Rob, I'm not leaving you. A short while ago you refused to leave me and now you want me to leave you. Not a chance."

"What do you suggest," asked Rob.

"Right now, I'm going to crawl under those covers with you and get some sleep. I'll have to keep getting up in order to keep the fire going, but that is nothing."

When they awoke in the morning, Heidi said,

"The first thing I'm going to do is look around in here. Maybe somewhere there is a cache of canned or powdered foods. It would seem reasonable that who ever owns this cabin would leave a cache of food, dry foods such as rice, and oatmeal that would not be ruined by freezing temperatures. As soon as it gets light I'll start looking"

"That won't be long," answered Rob. "Have you looked at your watch lately? It's 6:30 a.m., and have you noticed that the wind seems to have died down? I think the storm has pretty well blown itself out. I wouldn't be surprised if we saw sunlight before too long."

Rob was correct, by 8:00 the wind had stopped blowing and the sky was clearing. Heidi noticed patches of blue sky. Immediately her spirits soared.

"We're going to make it Rob, were going to get back home."

In a weak voice Rob replied,

"Didn't I tell you we would?"

"How did you know?"

"Faith Heidi, faith."

"When we get out of here Rob you are going to have to tell me more about faith. Clay gave me a couple of good examples of it. I thought I knew what it was, but when I thought about it, it only left me more confused. When you were shot I believed I had discovered what faith is. Rob, I've slacked off in reading the Bible Clay gave me and so far as understanding what faith is, now I don't believe I have gained anything. In fact I fear I've even forgotten some of the things about faith that Clay talked about."

"Heidi, I've mentioned it to you before that faith, like anything you retain has to be nurtured. I believe its past time you go to church with me on a regular basis and that you set aside some time each day to read your Bible. After this experience and how at the last minute we found the cabin, I would think there would be no question in your mind that God had his hand in it."

"You are right Rob I am through fighting with my professors who convinced me that religion was just so much baloney. I am going to go to church with you and I hope we can study the Bible together."

"I'm glad to hear you say that Heidi.

"We could easily have frozen to death. couldn't we have?"

"We could have, yes, but it wasn't going to happen."

"You really believe that don't you?"

"Yes Heidi I really believe it. If the two experiences, my shooting and now this doesn't convince you that there is a God who watches over us I really don't know what more I can say or do."

"Rob, ever since my time in the hospital chapel and your miraculous survival I have believed there is a God, a God who does watch over us but you're right, I do nothing to nurture that belief. I believe it and that's all. I still feel I don't know God very well."

"We're going to change that Heidi, but you have to be willing to change."

"I am now Rob."

By noon the temperature had rebounded. Now Rob's spirits were soaring as well. Heidi started looking for a food cache, but without success. She was about to give up when she moved a rug to pull it closer to the door. Then she saw it, a trap door of sorts. She got down on her knees but couldn't get her fingers under the door and there was no handle or ring on it.

"Rob," she said , "I've found something, but I can't open the trap door."

Rob turned his head and could see the outline of the door.

"Get my emergency kit, inside is an all purpose tool. Bring it to me and I will open the screwdriver. You should be able to stick it between the door and the floor and by pushing down on it the door should open."

She did and it did. She found what she was looking for, cans of spam, chili, chicken, rice and oatmeal. There were other items as well. Rob smiled as Heidi called out the names.

"It looks like we are going to have a feast today. Most likely you will discover that the canned goods have not frozen since it was such a fast moving storm.

Heidi looked around and said,

"I can't find a can opener."

"Not a problem," replied Rob, "Bring me the all purpose tool and I'll have a can opener for you in a jiffy. If you have trouble opening the cans, bring them here and I'll see what I can do."

Heidi opened one of the make-shift cupboards and found a small set of steel cooking ware.

"I found some pieces of steel cooking ware but they are rusty."

"Don't fret about a little rust, open the door, grab a handful of snow and start scrubbing. The rust should be superficial and you should be able to remover the worst of it. A little iron in our diet isn't going to hurt."

"Rob Darling, I will soon have rice with canned chicken spread on the top. I'm going to get some snow, put it in the pan and boil the rice. It's going to take quite a bit of snow, but who cares, we have a whole outdoors full of it."

Heidi put the steel cooker on top the stove and filled it with snow, not once but several times. In a short time the water was boiling. Into this she poured the rice. She had trouble opening the can of chicken so Rob opened it for her.

Heidi opened the door to another cupboard and said,

"Oh My."

"What is it?" Rob asked.

"There is an enamel ware coffee pot here and there is coffee in the cache of food. Won't a cup of coffee taste good? I'll make some coffee and by the time it has boiled the rice should be ready."

"Move over rice," she said, as she put the coffee pot on the stove.

When the coffee boiled and when the rice was soft, Heidi took the can of chicken and spread it over the rice.

"Now Mr. Sloan, I am going to feed you and feed you well. You have to regain some of your strength before we try to walk out of here. We're going to have to spend a few days in the cabin, but who cares, we are alive, we are warm and we have food."

"God is good, isn't he Sweetheart."

"Yes Rob He is good."

And then they ate the first food in almost 24 hours.

"Darling," Heidi said, "Wasn't that the best food ever?"

"It sure was Sweetheart didn't I say we were going to have a feast?"

After they ate, Heidi stepped outside to look around. When she returned to the cabin she said,

"Darling, it's absolutely beautiful outside. The sky is a dark blue and the snow is pure white. It's so bright it hurts the eyes. And there is a large pile of chopped logs just a short ways from the cabin. It is actually balmy outside. That storm had to be a freak. It came so fast, got so cold and now in a relatively short time the temperature is almost balmy again. Once you have regained strength we shouldn't have any trouble finding our way back to the pickup."

"Rob, I've been thinking, Mr. Simpson will be wondering where I am and Lorraine will be wondering where you are. Before we show up they are going to be frantic and worst of all, they really don't know where to start looking for us. When you told Ken we were going to hunt in this general area, which could cover many, many miles it really didn't give him a clue where to start looking."

"Why in the world did we leave the cell phone in the pickup?"

"Because we certainly had no idea something like this would happen. Yes Sweetheart, there is going to be much anxiety with those we know, however, we will show up. I'm sure search and rescue teams are already looking for us."

"But where do they start Darling?"

"That's the problem Heidi, where do they start. You did a pretty good job of running down the things we have to be thankful for but you left out the most important."

"What is that Rob?"

"We have each other. For a time it appeared both of us would perish. We're alive, the bleeding has stopped and I agree with you, in a few days I will be strong enough for us to walk back to the pickup"

"We have each other, how right you are, how could I forget?"

"You didn't forget, you just didn't mention it. Heidi, once we are cleaned up I'm going to have to go to emergency and have my wound looked after. I'm concerned about an infection setting in with all the filth in here. I have no pain or discomfort in the area of the scar so I'm hopeful I'll get by without an infection."

"Is there anything I can do?"

"No, I think we had better leave well enough alone."

"Rob,"

"Yes Sweetheart,"

"I want you to know that this experience has not dampened my enthusiasm for hunting. I have a hunch you believe this would be it for me so far as hunting is concerned. No way, this has been some experience, one we will never forget and one we never want to repeat, but there is no reason it should haunt either of us. Before next fall I want that over and under shotgun you promised me, a 20 gauge wasn't it?"

"That's my girl," Rob replied." "Maybe we won't be able to make it back here again this year, but there is always another season."

"It does my heart good to hear you say that Rob, and your right, another trip back here this season is pretty much out of the picture, but there is always another season."

Rob felt it was best if he stayed on the mattress for the day while Heidi took short walks around the cabin. She never ventured so far that she couldn't see the cabin. It was just so good to be alive and to feel the warmth of the sun.

Once when she returned to the cabin, Rob said,

"Sweetheart, tomorrow morning you are going to have to help me get up. I need to exercise my muscles."

"You don't think that will be too soon, do you?"

"No," Rob replied, "Blood replaces itself rather quickly. Granted I lost quite a bit, but so long as you keep putting such good food in front of me I think I'll be OK. I believe my strength will return rather quickly."

On another occasion when Heidi returned to the cabin she said,

"Look Rob, when we walked into the cabin I was sure my hands and feet as well as my face were frost bitten. There is not a sign of frostbite and I can't see any sign of frostbite on your hands and face either."

"Did you expect to?" asked Rob.

"Of course," answered Heidi.

Rob looked at Heidi and said very gently,

"Oh ye of little faith."

"Yes," answered Heidi, "But that little faith has been bolstered by this experience. You are going to have to help me understand about faith."

"That's music to my ears," answered Rob.

The next couple of days were warm and balmy, except for the deep drifts the snow was melting rapidly. Rob alternated between walking for a brief time and lying back on the mattress. He was on the mattress and Heidi was at his head sitting with her legs tucked under her.

"You remember the first time I held your head in my lap?"

"How could I forget though my memory of events was very short. I thought it was all over for me."

"So did I," said Heidi. "I was never so frightened in my life and here we are in the same position once again. You're hurt, I'm OK and I'm nestling your head in my lap."

"Lean down Heidi, I want to kiss you."

"Rob, I haven't brushed my teeth in quite a few days. Are you sure you want to kiss me?"

"Bend down Heidi." The kiss was a long and passionate one.

"Why don't you crawl under the blankets with me so we can make love?"

"In the shape you're in? You can't be serious, but it also tells me your feeling better."

"When it comes to sex, I'm always serious, but I guess your right Sweetheart, however the desire is sure there." Heidi laughed and said,

"We can make up for it later."

"OK," said Rob, so long as it's a promise."

"It's a promise," responded Heidi.

"Isn't it interesting Heidi, a few days ago we about froze to death and we didn't know what shape I would be in because I lost so much blood and yet now, a few days later, sexual desire again presents itself. Heidi, I'm convinced, with all cultural trappings put aside, the first and primary objective of man and woman here on earth is to reproduce. How many times in the Old Testament did God tell the Hebrew people to reproduce, to replenish the earth?"

"Rob, you're quite a guy. Here we are in quite a predicament and what are you thinking about, sex?"

"It goes deeper than that Heidi and that is what I was trying to explain."

"I know Rob, it was no different when you were in the hospital. Does your mind ever slow down?"

"Yes, when you and I have sex."

"Rob, you're a silly guy, you and all you're theorizing. But you want to know something, I'm glad you're hard up because it tells me you are feeling better and getting better."

"Well Heidi, what about you, you're the other half of the equation?"

"I'm willing to bet you I'm just as hard up as you are. And this time I'm not afraid I'll lose my bet."

"It's so good we can have fun with each other as we are now. That's the joy of a good marriage, a good relationship shining through.

The next morning, their third in the cabin Heidi helped Rob to his feet. It was obvious he had made considerable progress. For their evening meal, what there was of it, he sat at the table with Heidi.

A variety of food was running low although there was plenty of rice, oatmeal and dried potatoes. Rob spoke up,

"Well Heidi, tomorrow we try walking out of here."

"No we aren't," said Heidi, "We're going to stay here one more day. We are not going to attempt to walk back to the pickup too soon. What would I do if you couldn't make it, if we were stuck between the cabin and the pickup?"

Rob was silent for a moment then responded,

"We would be in a pickle, wouldn't we? Let's see, if we remain here till the day after tomorrow, we will have spent five days in the cabin. You and I can say we really experienced cabin fever."

"I'm as anxious as you are to get out of here Rob, between keeping the fire going and watching over you I am getting kind of wearied. I don't know about you, but I'm not sleeping very well at night. I'm sure you've noticed how quickly it cools off in here once the fire begins to die."

"And I feel guilty that I can't be of any help."

"Don't feel guilty I would sooner have you rest than trying to carry a load of heavy wood. I'm tired, but I'll survive and with luck we will be sleeping in our own bed the evening of the day after tomorrow."

"We'll make it Sweetheart, I'm sure we will."

That night when the fire burned low, without disturbing Heidi it was Rob who got up and added more wood. It took some effort, but he made it. He crawled back under the blankets and pulled Heidi close to him. She mumbled something he couldn't understand. As he lay there he wondered if he would be able to make it back to the pickup day after tomorrow. Soon he was sleeping soundly.

Both awoke around 8:00. Heidi was the first to get up. She looked over what was left of the food, opened a can of powdered orange juice and poured some water in the steel Dutch oven. Next came the oatmeal. As she looked at it she said,

"You know Darling, not to complain, but I'm getting kind of tired of oatmeal. Once we're out of here it's going to be awhile before I fix it for breakfast."

She looked over at Rob who was propped up on an elbow and was resting his head in his hand.

"How long have you been lying there like that?"

"Since you got up."

"You've been watching me, haven't you?"

"Yup, I sure have."

"Learn any thing new?"

"Nope, nothing new, but it was a joy for me to watch you anyway."

"Now," Heidi said, "Let me help get you up and to the table. You're going to spend most of the day on your feet and if you do real well we will leave here tomorrow morning. One thing is sure we don't want to get caught in another storm."

"Tomorrow it is Heidi, tomorrow we walk back to the pickup."

"Darling," Heidi said, "One way or another I have to take a bath or shower soon. I'm getting pretty rank. If we can't leave tomorrow, I'm going to heat water, go to one of the corners and while you pour water over me I'll do the bet to clean myself up at least a little."

"Without any soap? Sweetheart, I don't exactly smell like a bed of roses either."

"Yes, but your not a woman and that makes a difference. A woman can go about three days without a bath or shower and that's about it."

"I don't think we had much of a choice Heidi."

"We didn't of course, but don't you mind feeling grungy."

"Not really."

"You men, you are really something."

"Sweetheart, by tomorrow evening we should be home then you can shower as long as you're heart desires."

"And it will be a long one, it will take a lot of water before I feel really clean. I can't wait."

Rob spent most of the day on his feet. He took short walks outside, returned to the cabin walked some more, went outside again and continued the routine most of the day. It seemed to drag by for both of them.

As they were eating supper, Rob commented on how his walking went.

"I don't think we will have any trouble getting back to the pickup."

"I thought you did real well today Sweetheart."

As darkness set in, they crawled under the blankets for what both hoped would be the last time.

"Are you sure you want me to sleep with you Rob?"

"Why do you ask?"

"I told you I smell pretty rank and I don't feel one bit clean."

"Well, if you prefer going outside and sleeping in a snow bank go ahead."

"I'm only thinking about your nose. I have always prided myself on being fastidious and clean. Without doubt that comes from my days as a call girl. I actually feel embarrassed over how unclean I am."

"Heidi Girl stop worrying about how you smell. I don't smell anything but my own B.O. and that I can tolerate."

"Alright, if you say so."

A can of spam and powdered orange juice made up their breakfast. Rob took out his hunting license and wrote on the back of it explaining the use of the cabin. He left his name, address and phone number informing the owner he would pay for the lock, the food they ate and the use of the cabin. He also wrote that if it were not for the cabin both he and Heidi would have perished in the storm.

He put the message on the table and a small piece of wood over it so a draft wouldn't blow it into some corner where it wouldn't be found.

It was 10:00 a.m. when they started out for the pickup. At first the going was slow, but gradually Rob began to feel stronger and then they picked up momentum. It was the deep snow banks he found difficult to navigate. They stopped and rested often.

After about an hour both were tiring when Rob called out,

"There it is, we made it, Thank God."

When they reached the pickup Heidi crawled in first then gave Rob her hand helping him to get inside. Once in, they sat back and looked at each other. Rob smiled and said,

"Mrs. Sloan you could use a little make up this morning."

"And Mr. Sloan you need to shave."

Heidi leaned over to Rob and they kissed.

"Well Darling, the Lord certainly was with us. For a time I believed our chance of survival was nil. We not only survived, but we did so in remarkably good shape"

Then his face lit up with a smile,

"Actually Darling, it was like a 2nd honeymoon, wasn't it?"

"Oh sure, just like a second honeymoon."

Then both broke out laughing. Rob looked at the dash and said,

"Now let's hope the pickup starts. Actually there is no reason it shouldn't. It hasn't been that long since we parked. Further, it's quite warm so thick oil should not be a problem. Keep your fingers crossed and say a little prayer Sweetheart."

Rob turned the key and immediately the engine sprang to life.

"Hooray," both of them shouted.

"Whew, what a relief. Let's thank our lucky stars it's a four wheel drive pickup. Snow drifts shouldn't give us any trouble."

Rob put the pickup into reverse, backed around and started for the main road. The road, trail really, had been outlined by the blowing snow and it was easy for Rob to stay on it. Snow banks were no problem just as he thought.

Then they were on the main road which had been largely cleared of snow. Rob shifted the pickup out of 4 wheel drive, slowly got out turned in the hubs and with Heidi's help got back in the pickup. Both were elated as they drove home and it didn't seem to take long. The 150 miles seemed to melt under the wheels and then they were home.

Rob said,

"Let's leave the shotgun and other gear in the pickup. I can bring it in later."

Arm in arm they walked to the front door, Heidi unlocked it and they stepped inside. Home never looked so good.

"Now, out of these filthy clothes and into the shower," said Heidi.

"While you shower I'll make a pot of coffee," Rob replied.

Heidi got into the shower, adjusted it to where it about burned her skin, lathered herself real good and just let it run over her for about 10 minutes. It not only drove the chill out of her body, but cleansed her as well. For the first time in almost a week, she felt clean, really clean. She got out of the shower, called Rob and started drying herself.

Rob walked into the bathroom, looked at Heidi naked in front of him and said,

"Heidi Girl, wrap up or I'll forget about taking a shower."

"Like heck I'll cover up," said Heidi. "Get into the shower I can smell you from here."

"Sorry," Rob said, "I'll flush that down the drain in a hurry."

When Rob finished with his short shower, Heidi had cups of steaming coffee on the table. Rob came into the kitchen in a clean pair of shorts which was all the pajamas he had.

"What," said Heidi, "Are you through already?"

"Sure," said Rob, "remember I'm not a woman."

"You got me there," said Heidi.

"And you will notice I even shaved."

She took a step to where Rob was standing and asked,

"Did you shave for me?"

"What do you think?"

She threw her arms around him and said,

"Darling you smell great and even if you didn't, I would kiss you anyway and I want you to know I appreciate it that you shaved for me."

Then they kissed. They sat at the table, warm and cozy drinking hot coffee, looking at each other and thanking their lucky stars they could be in their own kitchen drinking coffee. It seemed like a long time since they last did that.

"Heidi Darling, Rob said, 'I'm chomping at the bit."

"Do you think you're up to it Sweetheart?"

"So long as you take the initiative, I'm more than up to it."

"Let's go," she said. "I've had plenty of experience doing that."

"So I've noticed," said Rob,

"Don't remind me."

Their love making was slow and unhurried. Both felt it was the best ever. Afterward they lay looking at each other. Heidi started laughing,

"Rob Darling, it seems every time we have sex it's the best ever. How many times have we said that?"

"I couldn't begin to count the times," answered Rob. "But isn't it good that every time is the best ever?"

"It's wonderful," replied Heidi.

They didn't intend to do so, but both fell asleep in each other's arms.

Later they made their necessary phone calls. Lorraine was a nervous wreck. She thought both had probably frozen to death in the unpredicted storm.

"It's so good to hear your voice Rob. I kept making appointments. I had to believe that you would return to the office. You will be more than busy. When will you be coming in?"

"Just as soon as I can," replied Rob. "I was hoping you would continue to make appointments. I'm about ready to go to work."

"Rob, I'm not going to question you over the phone, but when you get back to the office you are going to have to tell me all about your ordeal."

"I will Lorraine you know I will if Heidi doesn't beat me to it."

"Rob I am so thankful that both Heidi and you are alright. I want you to know I prayed for you often."

"Thank you Lorraine and I want you to know that it was prayer that brought us through."

"Now may I speak to Heidi," asked Lorraine.

Heidi took the phone and of course had to tell Lorraine all about their adventure as she called it.

"We'll have to have lunch one of these early days. I'll fill you in on what I left out."

"I'm looking forward to it Heidi."

Heidi called Mr. Simpson. He too was certain some tragedy had befallen them.

"James, I'll be back in the office day after tomorrow. Will that be soon enough"?

"Hurry back Heidi, I'm dying for a cup of good coffee.

The next day Rob checked in at a same day care treatment center. His scar was again healing nicely and there was no sign of infection. With the filthy rope, blankets and all, he felt that was a miracle.

"Well," he told Heidi when he got home, "Sweetheart, everything about our ordeal was a miracle."

It was about two weeks later that Rob received a letter from a Walter Olson. It was his cabin that saved their lives. He was just glad that the cabin had been a life saver for them He also informed Rob that for the use of the cabin and food, he owned him nothing.

He informed Rob that a sudden severe storm like the one they survived happened only once in about every 10 years or so. Rob responded to his letter thanking him from the bottom of his and Heidi's hearts and sent him a check for $500.00.

"The check is just a small token of our appreciation not only for the life saving use of your cabin, but also for your generosity. Please do me the small favor of cashing it."

Chapter Fifteen

= ⫘ =

I t was the expected kind of winter in the Seattle-Tacoma areas, rain, clouds and gloom. Every once in awhile the monotony was punctuated by a few days of blue skies and warmer temperatures. Rob's recovery from his gunshot wound was progressing nicely though he still had to avoid over exerting himself.

During the second week in February Rob and Heidi had their evening out. While in the hunter's cabin the past fall they promised themselves that should they survive they would celebrate by spending an evening at the 9th Hole Dining Room. Neither of them complained about the cost. This time they could afford it though they felt a bit guilty spending so much to eat out when they had plenty of food at home and Heidi's superb cooking. Heidi said,

"Let's not let such thoughts spoil our evening. We owe it to ourselves."

As they ate they visited and reminisced.

"Rob, since last July it has been a trying time for both of us. First it was you being shot. I was never so frightened and discouraged in my life. I was sure I was going to lose you. You know, there was something I never changed my mind about. Had you died I would have joined you. There would have been no reason for me to go on."

"Heidi, you mustn't talk that way."

"I could never have been happy again Rob so why would I want to go on."

"Had I died, it would have been extremely difficult for you, but in time the pain would have lessened."

"It wouldn't have Rob and even if it would have, I would not have had time to wait that long."

"Put those thoughts out of your mind Sweetheart, I survived and here we are having a wonderful dinner just before the 4th anniversary of our meeting."

"Has it really been that long?"

"Four years Sweetheart four very fast years."

"Yes, and four of the happiest years of my life. And Rob, in just a short time we will have been married for three years. Just think for three years I have been Mrs. Doctor Robert Sloan, Sex and Marital Therapist. I have been so proud."

"How about Mrs. Robert Sloan?"

"No way, you may feel no pride in the fact you are a doctor, but I do."

"And so soon after you were shot we had that near death by freezing experience. How could we have had such anguish in just a few months?"

"I don't know Heidi, but I believe God had a message for us. For me it is, love her Rob and for you it is love him Heidi."

"You know I used to say, do you really think so Rob? No more. If it weren't for God watching over us neither of us would be sitting at this table enjoying such good food, such good visiting and most important of all, each other. Yes Rob, I believe I now know what faith is and what it means to trust in God thanks to you and Clay."

"I'm so glad to hear that Heidi, you no longer have to worry that when we die you will go in one direction and I in another."

"We're both going to the same place Rob, there is no question in my mind about that."

"I'm so glad to hear that Heidi."

"I know Rob, my stubbornness and refusal to look at any perspective other than the one I have held for quite a few years have caused you grief."

"Sometimes the Lord moves slowly, but he moves. And Heidi, since those dangerous experiences of last year I believe our love for each other has grown by leaps and bounds if that's possible."

"I agree with you Rob, how many couples have the kind of love for each other that you and I have?"

"I don't believe too many, Sweetheart. I can truthfully say I haven't seen too many in my practice. Heidi, there's something I must say, remember you have to nurture your faith and beliefs. You can lose them just as quickly as you gained them. Backsliding is an easy thing to do. For you as well as I, prayer should be a daily event. In fact it should be an event every time you feel you have something to share with God."

Rob looked around and waved to a waiter who then came to their table.

"Would you please bring us a bottle of your good semi sweet Italian wine?"

"Coming right up sir."

"Rob, we can't afford the wine."

"Tonight we are going to afford it."

"OK, and I'm going to enjoy it."

As they were sipping wine Heidi looked at Rob and said,

"Sweetheart, I have something to share with you."

"What is it Heidi Girl?" Heidi was quiet.

"Sweetheart, what is it?"

"Rob, I'm almost 27 years old, you will soon be 30. I want a baby Rob and I don't want to wait much longer."

Rob reached across the table and took Heidi's hands into his.

"Just a bit more time Sweetheart, just a bit more time and we will start a family."

"But Rob, you have been saying that for almost two years now."

"I know I have Heidi Girl, but you won't hear me saying it much longer. Let's just wait a few months longer."

"Rob, James told me he would give me a maternity leave. A couple of months after the baby is born I'll be able to go back to work."

"What would you say if I said I will try my darndest to get you pregnant this summer?"

"I'd say it's wonderful so long as you mean it."

"I do, you just keep reminding me."

"I could stop taking my pills without your knowledge."

Rob was silent.

"I guess you could Heidi."

"But I don't want to do that unless you force me to do so."

"This summer Sweetheart, this summer we will start making a baby."

"Alright Sweetheart, I'll take your word for it. The earlier in the summer the better.

When they crawled into bed Heidi snuggled against Rob and said, "Thank you for a wonderful evening Darling and thank you for agreeing to start working on having a family this summer. I'm excited about it already."

With a smile on his face Rob said,

"Should I say that the pleasure will all be mine?"

"That's what you think."

In a more serious tone Rob said,

"Heidi, I feel guilty, you shouldn't have to be thanking me for my willingness to start a family. I should have been much more attentive to your wants. You'll have that baby. In fact, if we are lucky you will have it in just about a year from now."

"Rob, there is one thing I have to do first. I must check with Dr. Swanson, my gynecologist, to make sure that my tubes were not infected when I had Chlamydia. If they were, then most likely we can forget all about starting a family."

"Good Lord Heidi, I certainly hope not."

"I'm keeping my fingers crossed Rob.

Rob turned his head and kissed Heidi.

"A baby is going to bring some changes to our ordered life, but I have every reason to believe we will survive them."

"We will Darling that I can promise."

Chapter Sixteen

Heidi got on the phone with Rob.

"Sweetheart," she said, "I'm going to take off work early this afternoon, run out to Phillips in the mall and do a little shopping. I'd like to get a new outfit. I know I have a closet full of clothes and I know I'm a clothe horse, but I just feel like I want to buy something."

"OK Sweetheart, pick something that will turn me on."

"Rob I have a closet full of skirts, skimpy blouses and short tight fitting shorts. You name it and I have it. All I have seems to turn you on. What works best for you is when I have nothing on."

Rob laughed and Heidi joined him.

"I'll be a little late in getting home so don't worry about me."

"OK, remember to get something that brings out your best qualities."

"Rob, there is nothing I can buy that will bring out my best qualities, at least not for you and if I could most likely I'd end up in jail."

"We'd better get off the phone Heidi or I won't be able to see my next client."

"Now wouldn't that just be too bad. I'll see you around seven."

While Heidi was browsing around Phillips she was reminded it was here she met Rob. That seemed like yesterday. She was so happy that time seemed to fly by. She found herself a chic little skirt with a colorful matching blouse.

She looked at herself in the mirror and said to herself, maybe it won't bring out my best qualities, but it will come darn close to it. Since Rob didn't like her to wear slacks or men's attire she had given up on them. Further, she did have, as Rob says, great assets so why not show them. She held up the outfit to look at it again and thought,

"At least it will be legal."

She hadn't worn an outfit like that in almost four years.

Heidi walked up to the counter to pay for her skirt and blouse and stood behind a petit blonde. She sure looks familiar from behind, Heidi thought. She reminds me of Sally.

Heidi stepped to the side so she could see her face. It was Sally.

"Sally," She cried out, "It's you."

Sally turned around and in a loud voice said,

"Heidi, Heidi,"

Then the two of them hugged.

"It's so good to see you Heidi."

"And it's so good to see you Sally."

"We haven't seen each other since you left the agency.

"How long has that been?" asked Sally.

"Almost four years, in fact this is where I met Rob."

"Who is Rob?"

"My husband, Sally. The most wonderful man in the world."

"So you fell into the marriage trap."

"What in the world do you mean Sally?"

Sally said,

"Let's go across the hall to the coffee shop and continue our conversation there."

After they got their coffee and seated themselves, Heidi asked,

"What did you mean when you said I fell into the marriage trap?"

"Haven't you noticed how life has become so routine, so predictable, so uninteresting? Day after day you get up, make breakfast, get dressed and then go off to work for eight hours and for a fixed salary to boot. I assume you have a job? Then when you get home you and your husband greet each other with a kiss. You eat clean away the dishes either read a book or watch TV and then go to Bed. Maybe you have sex and then it begins all over again,"

Heidi laughed.

"You have it all wrong Sally. Being that you aren't married, obviously you don't know what you're talking about. It's not like that at all and even if it is a settled routine, what's wrong with that? Being a call girl was also pretty much of a routine. Three times a week, the same thing over and over again."

"Yes, but each night or whenever, it was a new customer or an old one with whom you could visit with and joke around. There was excitement Heidi. Each evening you would ask yourself, what's he going to look like? What is he going to ask me to do? Is he average, above or below in the penis size department."

"Well, there may be some truth to that, but I certainly haven't found marriage to Rob boring, dull and routine as you put it. Sally, he is the most wonderful man in the world and I am deeply in love with him."

"Heidi, it is routine and boring, admit it. You just have to tell yourself those things, don't you? Why don't you chuck the marriage business and get back into the call girl business where there is real excitement and money, money Heidi, lots of it. Look at what being a call girl has enabled you to buy. I know Paul would take you back at the drop of a hat, or I should say at the drop of your panties"

Sally broke out laughing.

"That's pretty good, isn't it?"

"Sally, first of all you don't know what in the hell you're talking about and second, you are beginning to irritate me. I thought we could have a nice friendly visit, but no you start out by attacking my marriage. I'm through with the call girl business. I have a wonderful husband and I have my self esteem back again."

"Maybe, but I still think you are missing out."

"Are all of the girls we started with, The Happy Five we called ourselves still working for the agency or have some of them left?"

"Nope, they are all there and we still have our weekly get together. You should join us sometime. What a fun time we have. Seems that one or more of the girls has had an experience with a customer that is just hilarious. Come on Heidi, get back into the business."

"That's enough Sally, you stay with your prostitution and I'll stay with my marriage. Greet the girls, I must be on my way or Rob will start worrying about me."

"See, I was right, the routine of your marriage, Rob will worry."

"Go to hell Sally."

"My but you use strong words Heidi,"

"Only because you have brought them out in me. I hope we don't meet again for a long time."

Heidi got up and walked out of the mall. As she drove along she couldn't get what Sally had said out of her mind. Boring, routine, doing the same thing day after day. Maybe so, but she was happy with her marriage to Rob. Further, she would do nothing to hurt him.

Rob was waiting for her when she walked into the house. They kissed warmly.

"Well," asked Rob. "Did you find what you were looking for?"

"I sure did, let me run into the bedroom and I'll try it on for you."

When Heidi came out of the bedroom, Rob took one look and said,

"Wow. Sweetheart I believe dinner is going to have to wait this evening."

"Ah ha," said Heidi, "I thought the outfit would do that to you. OK big boy, come on, I don't want to keep you waiting."

After they finished making love, Heidi snuggled up against Rob and said,

"It's so good to be married and in love with you. That was wonderful Rob. Now let me fix a bite to eat and let's talk about our weekend. We are still going to Seaside, aren't we?"

"You bet we are. We have reservations in Astoria, remember?"

She loved the coast and when they went, Rob would say,

"Let's forget about expenses this weekend and just enjoy ourselves."

She even enjoyed the crowds in Seaside. That was a switch for her since ordinarily she avoided crowds. Each time they went to Seaside, there were so many people coming and going and all buying junk, and I am one of them. It brought a smile to her face.

Heidi wanted to take her Jaguar to Seaside and she wanted Rob to do the driving. She wanted to just sit back and enjoy the beauty of the rolling hills of the coastal range. Having lived a good share of her life in flat Iowa, she just loved the mountains. It was a love that she and Rob shared. She thought, there are so many things we share. We are so compatible

They left for Astoria after work on Friday evening. Rob told her not to fix dinner since they would eat at one of the reservation casinos. As she was admiring the scenery her visit with Sally popped into her mind.

The gall of that Sally, she thought. Criticizing my marriage and ridiculing me for being married. What does she know about either? To give up what I have by returning to the call girl business would be absurd. Sure the five of us had some good times together. The bond between us had been close. If I felt down I could count on the other four to bolster my feelings. Sure there were aspects of being a call girl that were fun and even satisfying, especially the money. No way, she said to herself, I'm through with that kind of life. Once again I would be a prostitute. Further, it would mean leaving Rob. I cannot forget that Rob loves me in spite of my past. How many men would marry a woman who had sex with close to 226 or more different men? And I promised Rob I would never return to that kind of life.

As usual the weekend on the coast was great. They went to bed when they wanted, got up when they wanted, ate when they wanted, made love when they wanted and even drove down the coast as far as they wanted.

When they started for home Sunday afternoon they agreed that it had been a great weekend. They would be ready for the work week ahead.

"Remember," Rob said as they were driving along, "Next week we go to Mt. St. Helens and Mt. Rainier."

She looked forward to the drives to the volcanoes and to taking pictures of both. She seemed to find new venues for pictures no matter how often they went. Because of her growing interest in photography, Rob had gotten her an 8 pixel single lens reflex digital camera. It was fun to see who took a better picture of a particular scene. Her reflex camera opened new photographic horizons. Rob's gift took her completely by surprise. She was sure he had forgotten his promise to get her a camera.

"Well," she thought, "That's my Rob."

The week went fast as they made plans to spend the weekend at the volcanoes. They would spend the night at Packwood. This would put them very close to Mt. Rainier and not too far from Mt. St. Helens. Rob's therapy business kept growing. His clients, who he helped, spread the word to their friends and of course advertising also helped.

Tacoma was growing and people were looking for small acreages not too far from the city. As a result Mr. Simpson's real estate business was also growing. Heidi liked her work. Often Mr. Simpson would send her to show a piece of property to a potential customer and with pride she noted she was a good sales person. She had to attribute some of that to the ease which with she entertained her customers when she was a call girl. That did not go unnoticed by Mr. Simpson. Since she started working for him she had received two salary increases. In fact more and more James was turning the business over to her. He and Doris frequently took trips leaving her in charge.

Taking care of the office business as well as ferrying people about the area kept her more than busy. Nonetheless, she felt a great deal of pride in her ability to sell property and to run the office. I have arrived, she said to herself. Between her and Rob their income was good. They talked about the time when they might be able to buy a small acreage close to Tacoma.

The weekend arrived and on Friday afternoon they left for Packwood.

Saturday was spent both at Sunrise and Paradise. It seemed to Rob he was always stopping so Heidi could take pictures. Rob asked Heidi,

"Now who is the one who always wants to stop to take pictures?"

On Sunday they left early for Mt. St. Helens. They drove on the north and east side of the volcano where the devastation of the eruption in 1980 was most noticeable. Rob said to Heidi,

"Just look around, the destructive power of nature is awesome. And to think this volcano was formed many thousands of years ago, maybe millions."

"Well," Heidi said, "We won't live long enough to see Mt. St. Helens heal itself."

"I guess not," replied Rob.

It was so good to spend weekends like this together. Heidi believed it strengthened their love for each other.

Monday morning it was back to work. Both were refreshed and eager to get going. By now Heidi had pretty well forgotten her unpleasant visit with Sally, however, it was during her lunch hour that the phone rang and Sally was on the other end.

First she apologized for antagonizing her when they had coffee in the mall.

"I hope you won't let that visit of ours affect your feelings for me."

"Well, you made me pretty mad. After all, who are you to tell me my marriage is dull and boring. You know nothing about it. The truth is, you know nothing about marriage."

"Heidi." she replied, do you mind if I respond to that?"

"Go ahead."

"I'm glad I know nothing about it. For me, in no way do I want to be tied down by a husband and marriage," "Heidi responded,

"I see this conversation is leading us nowhere. Don't bother me anymore."

She hung up on Sally.

For a few minutes she sat back and thought of the good times she had in the call girl business. This time it was a bit harder for her to put them out of her mind. In fact they kept creeping back in for the rest of the day. And the truth was the Happy Five, Sally, Betty, Liz, Judy and herself did have good times together.

By the end of the week she had pretty well pushed the call girl business out of her mind. From time to time though, it seeped back into her conscious awareness. When it did she started seeing it from a different perspective. This bothered her. She kept telling herself she was through with the call girl business for good.

That evening she got home before Rob. When he came in, as usual, the first thing he did was to take her into his arms, kiss her and tell her how much he loved her. For some reason the kiss didn't feel like it usually did. Rob sensed that Heidi seemed to be holding back a bit. Oh well, he thought she may just be tired and forgot about it.

The following Monday during her lunch break the phone rang and this time it was Liz who was on the phone.

"Heidi, how good it is to hear your voice. It's been so long."

"It's good to hear you too Liz. How's business?"

"It's booming Heidi, seems more and more conventions are being held in the Tacoma area. In fact if I wanted to I could have a customer every evening, seven days a week. That however, would be pushing it too hard. I don't know if I could hold up with that kind of a schedule. Also, we are now getting a larger percentage of the fee the customer has to pay. It's costing more to visit a call girl, Heidi."

"We have a good reputation, a reputation for having the most attractive girls in the area. Heidi, why don't you come back and be a member of the Happy Five once again? I'll bet you aren't making a fraction of the money you would make if you got back into the business. You're an attractive girl and have the kind of body men love. Isn't it kind of a shame to waste it on one man?"

"Waste it on one man, what do you mean? This one man is my husband. Sorry Liz, I have learned that money isn't everything. I have a husband who accepts my past and who loves me. Money can't buy that. I also have a good paying job."

"Heidi, let me ask you, how long will it be before you start tiring of your marriage and wishing you would be single again?"

"Never Liz, never. I have to go now Liz, my lunch hour is up."

"You know Heidi, you never had to say that when you were servicing customers. Oh, and one more thing, you aren't getting any younger and the customers like young girls."

"Goodbye Liz."

This time it was difficult for her to put out of her mind what Liz said. Liz was right, when she was a call girl, as a rule daytime hours were hers. There were times when a man would want to see her during the noon hour, but not often. And like it or not, she wasn't getting any younger. How long would it be before men no longer found her desirable?

Well, she said to herself that will never happen with Rob. None of the four girls were married so how did they know she would tire of her marriage? She loved Rob, she loved everything about him. She felt secure and financially they were very comfortable. They didn't need to make more money.

For the rest of the week the call from Liz bugged her. She spent more time in front of the bedroom mirror. Maybe her skin was getting a bit loose. Then she saw a single gray hair. Ah me, she thought, "I'm getting gray."

When Rob asked her what she wanted to do over the weekend, she said,

"Let's stay home for a change. Would that be OK with you?"

"Sure Sweetheart, I guess we both have enough to keep us busy."

Heidi had noticed that when she kissed Rob, when he held her, it just wasn't quite like it used to be. In fact, she wished he wouldn't kiss her so often. And though the frequency of sex had not decreased it just wasn't the same. She found herself faking orgasm more and more often.

The following Monday during her lunch hour it was Betty who called. Heidi asked her,

"Betty, has Sally put you up to this? First Sally, then Liz now you and next will be Judy. I made a mistake by giving her my work number."

Betty's message was the same as that of Liz and Sally. Come on back and start living again.

At first her gradual withdrawal from Rob bothered her, however. Rob had said nothing so she assumed he was not aware of the change taking place in her. More and more she thought about becoming a call girl once again.

She had talked to Sally, Betty and Liz and all had the same message for her, come on back. Business is booming and she could make scads of money. If she played it right she would eventually be able to buy that small acreage for herself. Anticipating what each new customer would be like was exciting to her. After all, it had been almost four years since she saw her last customer. In no way would the sexual variety become boring to her. Just thinking about it brought back a flood of memories. She wondered if men were coming up with new ideas of what they could do with their bodies. The more she thought about it, the more she continued her disengagement from Rob.

The change in Heidi did not go unnoticed by Rob. He tried to remember when he first became aware of a barely perceptible change in her. If he recalled correctly it was just before they spent the weekend on the coast. Everything about the weekend was great. They just plain had fun together. After Sunday, however, he could again feel the shift in Heidi's responses to him until, that is, they spent the weekend at Mt. Rainier and Mt. St. Helens. Then, just as when they were on the coast, it was a great weekend. It gave him satisfaction to see the pleasure Heidi was getting from her photography. She thanked him again and again for the digital camera which she said opened new vistas of photography for her.

On Monday, just as if on cue, he began to feel Heidi drawing away from him. When he kissed her she didn't want to stay in the embrace long, and when he hugged her he could feel her pulling away from him. Although the frequency of sex had not decreased, more and more he became aware that she was faking orgasms and if she thought she was fooling him she was badly mistaken.

As he thought about it, he realized it was just about three months back when he noticed the slightest change taking place in Heide. He had made up his mind to bring it up to her, but concluded it most likely was just a phase she was going through.

Then it dawned on him. Why didn't he think of it before since he often heard from clients that one or the other was doing about what Heidi was doing. She was seeing another man or maybe several men. After all, she knew what sexual variety was and she was a very sexual person.

The thought about floored him. His wife unfaithful? They loved each other, at least he loved her. Maybe she no longer loved him. What ever, he could see and feel his marriage unraveling before his eyes.

Rob was correct for it was just three months earlier that Heidi met Sally at the Mall and Sally had put pressure on her to return to the business of being a call girl again.

Heidi thought, But that couldn't have been what caused her to start cooling to Rob. Sally made me thoroughly disgusted. But she concluded it was not a mere coincidence, the two tied in too close together.

The following Monday it was Judy who called. Heidi asked her,

"Why has Sally put you up to this? I made a big mistake giving her my office number."

Judy's message was the same as that of Sally, and Betty, and Liz.

Come on back and start living again. We want you back. The Happy Four is just not like the Happy Five. Forget about marriage and your husband.

"But Judy, I have no reason to leave him."

"You're wrong Heidi, you have plenty of reasons. Maybe he has done nothing wrong, but you have your life to live."

From that point on her disengagement from Rob accelerated. She avoided his kisses and his embraces, started wearing a night gown and she stopped making herself available for sex. Still Rob said nothing which surprised her.

Once again it was Betty who called her. When she suggested she join them for lunch Saturday noon, she accepted without hesitation. She would give Rob some excuse that he would accept or so she thought.

Lorraine arrived at the office at her usual time. She noticed Rob's office door was open. She knocked gently on the door frame.

"Come in Lorraine and have a seat. Lorraine," he said with a heavy sigh, "My marriage has come unraveled. Apparently Heidi no longer loves me. We don't kiss, we don't hug. Sex, what is that? And we don't communicate. If we exchange a dozen words a day that would be a verbal marathon."

Lorraine sat in stunned silence.

"I knew something has been bothering you for sometime Rob, but your marriage coming apart, I'm shocked. What's been happening?"

"I have no idea, I can' think of anything I might have done or said to turn her so thoroughly against me. Three months ago we had two wonderful weekends, one on the coast and the other at Mt. Rainier and Mt. St. Helens. But as soon as the weekends were over, I could feel she was disengaging from me again. That has continued until now. We hardly look at each other."

"Rob, I just don't believe Heidi would do that. How many times has she told me she loves you and has never been happier in her life"

"Well, something has happened to both. I think I have it figured out Lorraine, another man or other men have come into her life. She was a call girl and used to different men and sexual variety, I'm one man and sex with me is sex with me only, there is none of that anymore."

"Rob, you really don't think it's another man?"

"Lorraine, you type up my notes from therapy sessions, doesn't the scenario I have just given you sound familiar?"

"I must admit that it does Rob."

Rob lowered his head and wept silently.

"It's over Lorraine, all I'm waiting for is for is Heidi's request for a divorce,"

"Oh no Rob not that."

"That Lorraine, and I'm really not sure why. What I just told you is a guess and I could be wrong. There is no way I can patch things up, she won't give me a chance.

"I'm so very sorry Rob I know how much you loved Heidi."

"Love Heidi, Lorraine. She may have fallen out of love with me, I still love her.

It was during the lunch get together that all of Heidi's friends put the pressure on her to leave her marriage and Rob and return to the agency to become a call girl again.

Heidi protested,

"But I just can't leave Rob without giving him some reason."

"Do you still love him?"

"I don't know."

"Are the two of you having sex?"

"No, and isn't that a damn irony. Here I am about to have sex with many different men and I won't even have it with my husband."

"What in the hell is wrong with you Heidi?" In spite of your outburst it sounds like you have reason enough to leave him."

"But, but how?"

"Haven't you heard of a divorce?"

"Divorce, I can't do that, I have no reason to take that kind of drastic action against Rob."

"You just gave two that are reason enough, no love and no sex."

"I didn't say I didn't love him, I said I don't know."

"Well if you don't know, you don't love him."

"When Rob and I fell in love I promised him I would never go back into the call girl business again"

"So you break a promise. So what?"

They were too convincing. Heidi gave up her defenses and decided she would leave Rob, however she had work to do before she was ready for customers.

"But what if Paul won't take me back?"

"That should be the least of your worries. "

"He'll take you back at the drop of a hat," Betty said.

"You were a real money maker for the agency."

Betty was not quite right as Heidi would soon find out.

"So," asked Sally, "How soon can you be back in business?"

"It will be awhile. First I have to give Rob more reason to accept our parting and then there is the matter of redecorating my house. I'm going to entertain my customers in my house."

"Didn't you just say you and Rob have not had sex in quite some time? Aren't you chomping at the bit?"

"No we haven't, but right now that's the farthest thing from my mind.

From that point on, Rob's and her relationship took a nose dive. Heidi was aware that Rob was withdrawing from her. He no longer made an effort to kiss or hug her. She had succeeded in killing that. In addition, his advances to have sex stopped quite some time ago. The night gown she wore spoke volumes to Rob. The time was about right.

Now, she thought, how do I break the news to Rob? He will be hurt of course, deeply hurt, but he'll get over it. He's young, good looking with a great physique. There are a lot of girls out there who he could choose from. For a moment she felt a pang of jealousy. She never anticipated saying something like that.

Before she told Rob, she would have to talk to Paul to make sure she did indeed have a job waiting for her.

She would also have to tell James she was leaving her job. She really didn't want to do that, she liked him and he treated her so well. After working for him for close to three years she was now an experienced realtor. She and James got along so well and she sold a lot of real estate for him, both homes and land. He told her it was because of her outgoing personality and the ease at which she could interact with people. She could hardly tell him that all of this was due to her interaction with her many customers. Her self esteem and respect had returned. Heidi, she said to herself, you have to be crazy to give up everything you have gained over the past four years, your love for Rob and his love for you, your self respect and esteem, your most satisfying job and a wonderful boss. And for what, to become a damn whore again. At that moment the last thing she wanted to do was to sell her body to strangers. Why oh why am I doing this? It's too late now, I have burned my bridges behind me.

She gave Paul a call and set up an appointment to meet with him. When she sat down and told Paul what she wanted to do, Paul was not the least bit enthused about it.

"Heidi, why in the world would you want to become a call girl again? You have a wonderful husband and a happy marriage. I know, remember I've met Rob. Many, many women would give an arm and a leg to have what you have."

"Paul, you mean I had a loving husband and a happy marriage. That's in the past now. It's not Rob's fault. He has done nothing to warrant my leaving him. It's a decision I came to on my own."

"Oh Yeah, you aren't being truthful Heidi. Sally, Betty, Liz and Judy put you up to this, didn't they?"

"Why do you ask Paul? Yes, initially it was Sally and then the other girls joined in."

"Heidi, can't you see the pattern here. I'll bet you dollars to donuts that they took after you because they envied you your happy marriage. No one in his mind would marry those sluts. Please Heidi, reconsider. Go back to Rob."

"That's no longer possible Paul. Further I thought you would be glad to have me back."

"Not at the price you're going to have to pay."

"I made a lot of money for the agency."

"You did Heidi, but I don't want to see you come back. The business isn't like it used to be. Drugs have now crept into the scene. You will be under pressure to use drugs to enhance your sexual feelings and activity. That can be darn dangerous Heidi. In addition more and more girls are being physically abused. Some nut case shoved his fist up one of the girl's vagina. He tore her vaginal walls and she had to be hospitalized. There is some question whether or not she will be able to have intercourse without experiencing pain. One more thing Heidi, you are one of the few girls who left the business and did something positive with her life.

"Paul, I've made up my mind."

"I'm so sorry Heidi. You realize you will fall into the category of a prostitute, a whore."

"Paul, that's crude."

"Maybe so Heidi, but it's the truth. You are going to have to watch yourself so you don't attract the attention of the police. One complaint from a neighbor and you could end up in the slammer."

"I have always been very careful."

"Have you told Rob yet?"

"No, that isn't going to be easy. It's really going to hurt him, but I have to tell him."

"And hurting him isn't reason enough for you to reconsider, the man who loves you and took you away from this sordid life. The man who gave you happiness like you never had before?"

"No, I'm sorry Paul."

"What a shame the lives of two good people ruined. I suppose you will be operating out of your house again. How long will it be before you are ready for your first customer?"

"It will be a couple of weeks Paul. I have to redecorate my house."

"So it looks more like a whore house, right?"

"Paul, you are a very dear friend, but I resent that. I also have to get Rob out of the house before I start with the decorating."

"You mean you're kicking Rob out of the house?"

"It's my house and I can't very well run my business with him hanging around."

"It's your house, not yours and Robs?"

"It's my house Paul."

"Well, I see it's no use trying to reason with you. Heidi, mark my word, you are going to come to regret what you are doing, regret it very much. I want to say one more thing, what happened to that sweet young kid from Iowa who walked in here about seven years ago looking for work.?"

"She has grown up Paul."

"No Heidi, she has become a mean bitch without a conscience."

"Paul, you're my friend."

"I am Heidi, but the truth is the truth. When you're ready for your first customer, give me a call."

Chapter Seventeen

Heidi was expecting Rob to say something. A few days after her meeting with Paul and after they had eaten in silence, Rob pushed back his chair.

Oh, oh, thought Heidi, Here it comes.

"Alright Heidi, this has gone on long enough. What in the hell is going on with you? You are no longer a wife. We have become two strangers sharing the same house and bed. Why in the hell we're sharing the same bed I'll never know. For damn sure nothing ever happens in it.

Heidi was shocked, kind, mild Rob, she had never heard him use such language.

"For the past 3-1/2 months you've been withdrawing from me and I don't know why. The last time we had a good time together was when we spent the weekend at Rainier and St. Helens."

"After that you didn't want to go anywhere with me. I would meet you at the door, your kisses were not kisses at all. Your hugs were meaningless and there was no cuddling what so ever. You put that stupid night gown on and we stopped having sex. Did you think I was so stupid that I didn't know the night gown was your signal to me that there would be no more sex? For the likes of me I couldn't figure out what was happening to you. Now the last two weeks have been intolerable. You treat me as if I were someone you despised."

"Rob, I do owe you an explanation. I'm going to be a call girl again."
Rob turned white.

"You don't mean that Heidi, you can't mean that."

"Every word of it, you yourself have been talking about how stale our marriage has become. Nothing happens,"

"Damn it, you made it that way."

"It's the same old routine day after day. There are times I could scream. You know I'm a person with strong sexual needs. In the past three months I have become more and more frustrated."

"No sex, hell woman you wouldn't let me touch you."

"That happens when a woman falls out of love."

"Falls out of love, is that what's been happening?"

"Yes Rob, I no longer love you so there is no desire to do the things you mentioned. By the way Rob, you will have to move out of the house just as soon as possible."

Rob smirked and shook his head

"So now you are kicking me out of your house. What else? Heidi, this all started three months ago, the day you called to tell me you were going shopping at Phillips. That was the beginning. What happened at Phillips?"

"I noticed all the people coming and going, they sounded excited and happy. They were on the go. I started thinking that our marriage, our relationship had become stale. Perhaps I needed a change. I had a standing offer to return to the agency, to go back in the business as a call girl again. At first I put the idea out of my head. It just kept knawing at me and the more it did the more it appealed to me. I thought it would be wise to let our relationship cool before telling you and I see that time has come. I'm going back Rob."

Rob was still cool.

"Surely you haven't forgotten the day you told me you were a call girl. We were at our favorite overlook. You told me, I went off by myself for a time and came to a quick decision that I loved you regardless of your past. You were so afraid I'd tell you our relationship was over. I remember telling you that if you had had sex with 500 men I'd still love you. My love for you was too deep to let you go. On that morning you promised me you would never be a call girl again,"

"Oh sure I remember, but that seems like 100 years ago. And promises can be broken. Just like that Rob."

"Just like that promises can be broken Heidi?"

"Heidi, do you remember when you took me out to dinner at Club 9, the time when Joe was so rude to you?"

Heidi thought, to defend my honor he would have knocked Joe clear across the room.

"We were both so drunk we didn't know if we could make it home. We did, you couldn't walk so I carried you to the bedroom, helped you undress and tucked you into bed. I mentioned that the happening with Joe was but a dim memory. You agreed and said, you know why, because we both were so damn drunk. We couldn't stop laughing. We had such a wonderful time that evening. When I was about to crawl into bed with you, you told me you couldn't imagine me not being by your side comforting you. You didn't mean that?"

"Oh Rob, I said a lot of things."

The moment the words were out of Heidi's mouth she regretted it, regretted it keenly. Why did I say that, she said to herself? We did have a wonderful time. We had many, many wonderful times. Rob loved me in spite of the fact I had been a call girl and he was constantly going out of his way to prove it to me. And now I treat him and everything we did together as if it were of no account. She finally saw what she was doing and wanted to undo it, but it was too late. She might as well put the finishing touches on their relationship.

"Have you forgotten when I was in the hospital after taking that bullet meant for you? It appeared I was going to die. You went into the little chapel and you told me you prayed, prayed like you never did before. You met Clay and Susan and both gave you the encouragement you needed. Later you told me that had I died, you would have taken your life."

Heidi was quiet

"Have you forgotten how hard up both of us were? After you talked to Susan, she made arrangements for us to have sex in my room. We both agreed that for whatever reason it was the best ever. We felt so close to each other. I not only survived, but we were having sex again. You had to do all the work, but you had plenty of experience at that."

Heidi responded,

"That was rather juvenile of us, wasn't it?"

"Juvenile, juvenile, what in the hell do you mean? Have you forgotten the good times we had on the coast and at the two volcanoes? How many times did we go to each and more than once because you wanted to take pictures. On the way home, you just had to eat at a reservation Casino. You loved those outings and they were always special for us."

"Those memories no longer mean anything to me."

"No longer mean anything to you?"

"No Rob they don't."

"And you putting on that silly nightgown. Do you think I was stupid, too stupid to get your message?"

"Rob, I did that so you wouldn't get aroused?"

"So I wouldn't get aroused. What kind of tricks do you pull with your customers to get them aroused? And yet, you put on a stupid night gown so I, your husband, wouldn't get aroused. Damn it, I can't believe what I'm hearing. You're giving yourself more credit than you deserve Heidi. By then I had lost all sexual desire for you."

Again Heidi was silent.

"You're just not going to listen to any reasoning are you?"

"Rob, can't you see our marriage is over."

"No I can't in spite of three months of estrangement and in spite of all the mean things you have been saying now, I still love you. You must still have a little love for me."

"Sorry Rob, but I don't"

"Heidi, it wasn't so long ago that we talked about having a baby, remember? It was when we had that wonderful night out and that wasn't long ago at all, that you told me you wanted a baby and scolded me a bit for putting it off so many times when you brought it up. Other than talking about having a baby we spent most of the evening declaring our love for each other. We were still doing so when we went to bed. My Lord woman, have you forgotten that wonderful evening?

"Sure I remember telling you I wanted a baby and I'm damn glad we didn't act on it. I guess we talked about our love for each other, but much of that has faded from my mind."

"Heidi, have you lost your mind. It is you who kept after me to have a baby. How could you possibly have forgotten our declaration of love for each other? That was just a couple of months ago."

"Rob. Can't you get it through your thick skull that this marriage is over?"

What a mean thing to say, she thought. I am now saying things I never intended to say. Yes, I wanted that baby very much, I wanted Rob's baby. To make my point I even swore.

"So, I almost lost my life in order to save yours. You were so sure I would die and you begged God to spare my life. You were not alone with your prayers, many were praying for both of us including Clay who without, I doubt you would have made it. And how about the mental agony we went through on your first hunting trip? You so enjoyed the hunt and were anxious to join me in bird hunting. We easily could have frozen to death and yet there was satisfaction in knowing that if we had to die we would die together. That's how much we loved each other. I was freezing yet I took off my jacket to give you just a bit more warmth. You could go no further. I hadn't been out of the hospital long and was to avoid straining myself. Yet I picked you up in spite of pain and carried you until we came to the cabin. We agreed that as difficult and painful as those days were, they only strengthened our love for each other. Don't those memories mean anything to you?"

"I remember Rob, but the memories don't carry the same significance for me as they do for you. And I must say you certainly do have a good memory."

"My Lord, I can't believe what I'm, hearing."

"Rob, you're a therapist, you know people fall in love and fall out of love. I have fallen out of love. Both of the deeds you have mentioned were very noble of you, but Rob that was a long time ago."

"There is no sense trying to reason with you any more Heidi Now more than three years later you tell me that nothing I have mentioned means anything to you."

"Well Rob, as I said, both were noble deeds, but to me it feels like they were a hundred years ago."

Oh God, Heidi said to herself, this can't be me speaking. I have become some kind of a monster. How can I hurt Rob so much? I keep telling him I no longer love him. That is a damn lie, I love him as much as ever and yet I have done about everything in my power to convince him that I no longer love him.

Heidi could see tears in Rob's eyes, but his voice was strong and resolute.

"One hundred years ago and it was noble of me, huh, that's all, just noble of me."

Heidi could see Rob's face change. He was grinding his teeth, his jaw muscles were flexing, he was clenching and unclenching his fists. The look on his face frightened her, it was a look of pure hatred.

"Noble of me, well I'll be damned, it was noble of me. Noble like anyone else would have taken that bullet. Like anyone else would have carried you ¼ of a mile while freezing and in constant pain. All right you two bit whore, you've been so damn smug and self righteous. You've had your say, now it's my turn. You two bit whore."

Oh, oh, Heidi said to herself, now it's really coming. Rob has gone off the deep end. He even called me a whore something he has never done before.

"I almost died for you twice. I gave you all the love I had within me. I loved you more than myself. I tried to be the very best husband a woman could ever have and all along I thought you loved me."

"Well Rob, what---"

"Shut up bitch, keep your damn mouth shut. You've said all you're going to say. Now you're going to listen to me. I couldn't understand why you were withdrawing from me. It hurt like hell. All your crazy behavior, I thought and hoped it was nothing but a phase you were going through. That's why I didn't say anything. Now I regret it, damn how I regret it. I'm not a violent man but now I believe I should have given you a good beating. All the while I was trying to rekindle our love you were conniving behind my back. You deliberately waited three months to tell me because you needed three months to kill my love for you. I may be naïve, but I'm not stupid Heidi. I should have guessed you were up to something no good."

"Rob. I …"

Rob took a step closer to Heidi and said,

"Damn it, how many times do I have to tell you to keep your mouth shut? Who in the hell put you up to this in the first place? I'll never believe you did the turn about by yourself. First you withheld your kisses, then your hugs and snuggling and you thought you could get by with it. You completely cut me off from sex and then you put on that stupid night gown. You have the gall to tell me it was to keep me from getting aroused. You give yourself too much credit lady. You could strip in front of me right now and I would be repulsed. Someone I hate is not going to turn me on. Was there ever any explanation from you? No, not a teensy weensy bit, hell no, not a word. Now you sit there and tell me, tell your husband who loved you so damn much, that it was noble of me to almost die for you. You have the gall to tell me it was noble and nothing more."

"You are so damn blind that you couldn't see it was an act of love, pure love. But no, it was noble of me. What the hell is wrong with you woman, noble, is that all I was? Damn you have a short memory. For almost four years I had nothing but love for you. If you had any love for me, any at all you would never have pulled the mean stunts you did."

Rob shook his head and chuckled,

"Maybe I'm the one who is stupid after all. You had no love for me woman, you just did a good job of play acting. Why in the hell couldn't I see through it? I know why, because love is blind. Well lady, you killed that love, you killed it all. I had a reservoir of love left for you earlier this evening but that has been drained. I have nothing but contempt for you. You have made me hate you."

"Had I known you were going to pull these tricks on me, had I only known, I would have let you take that bullet. It would have been a hell of lot better in more ways than one. But no, I had to be noble and step behind you. Noble is what I had to be, I didn't do it because I loved you I did it because I was noble. If that doesn't take the cake. Would you like me to take my shirt off so once more you can see the scar that runs from just below my neck to my abdomen? You should. That lady is a scar of a noble man. Come to think of it, you haven't seen me naked in a long time, I have a hunch you have forgotten what that scar looks like."

"You killed our marriage Heidi, just as sure as I'm standing here. You set out to kill our marriage and you succeeded, you also succeeded in turning my love for you into hatred. I loath you, I despise you. I don't know why you did it, but I don't believe for a moment it was entirely due to a burning desire to be a whore again."

Heidi was in a state of shock, she was scared to death. In almost four years of knowing Rob, not once did he ever use the word whore. She had never seen Rob like this. He was rambling, he was clenching and unclenching his fists. Maybe he's going to use that big fist to bust me in the face. He could kill me with it.

"It wouldn't surprise me one bit if you have been screwing someone behind my back After all, you had become accustomed to feeling a variety of cocks in you, three different ones a week if my memory serves me correctly. How dull, how boring, the same uninteresting cock for three years, Man that must have been hard for you to bear."

Rob suddenly spun around and stepped towards Heidi who by now was cowering and trying to protect her face with her arms. Rob looked around, started chuckling and shaking his head.

"And to think once upon a time we called this our love nest. Oh excuse me lady, not our love nest, your love nest. Oh damn, how could I be so blind. I ask how could I be so blind. Of course, I was blinded by love. I was also blind because it never dawned on me that you might be screwing some other man on the sly. After all, another man would have provided you with variety. Just a moment ago you told me that sex with me had become boring."

"If you have been cheating on me I hope his cock can do for you what mine failed to do. Ha, I trusted you too much. Rob suddenly spun around and stepped towards Heidi who was still cowering and covering her face with her arms. Rob looked around, started chuckling and shook his head."

Heidi opened her mouth. Rob yelled out,

"Don't say it bitch, I told you to keep your mouth shut. You had the floor before now I have it.

"Well now whore, since I can't began to satisfy you sexually, you will be able to screw from morning to night. I sure wish I could use the four letter word. I wonder why I can't because I sure want to. The word screwing just doesn't do justice to what you're going back to. You want to know something whore? I hope all those boy friends screw you to death. My, wouldn't that be a fitting end for a whore."

"You know that just might happen. If my clouded mind serves me correctly, you were told by your doctor to screw only one man lest you develop cervical cancer. You know the worst thing you could do is exactly what you are going back to, screwing three different men in one week, week after week, month after month. Then you will get a pain and you're doctor will tell you, Sorry Heidi, but I warned you. And you will say, I know doctor, but I just couldn't be satisfied screwing the same man over and over and over again."

"Well Heidi, I'll leave your whore house and will be moved out entirely by tomorrow evening. The sooner I'm out the sooner you can be whoring again. Call Paul and tell him to send you a customer now that that jerk of a husband is out of the way."

Rob's eyes narrowed and Heidi felt he was looking right through her. Again he shook his head.

"You turned my love for you into contempt. By the way, do you know what the word noble means? Look it up you might have the opportunity to use it on some other sucker."

"When I'm moved out of your house, I'll put your keys on the kitchen table. Look long and hard at those keys for they will represent a covenant between you and I, an agreement that this piss poor marriage is over for you."

Heidi was shocked into silence. Kind, gentle Rob had become a menacing animal. I hope his parting shot won't be a fist in my face. He is angry, he is irrational. He is always so careful to see that his language is correct. He is rambling, like a mad man. I made that kind, gentle man into the animal he has become. Oh God, what have I done, what have I done.

Heidi could hear Rob rummaging around in the bedroom, drawers being pulled out and shoved shut, closet door opening and then banging shut. Then there was silence and Heidi waited for Rob to come out. It was a full five minutes before he did so. He had a jacket, trousers, shirt, tie, under clothes, socks and a pair of shoes over his arms and in his hands. She could see that his face had mellowed considerably.

Rob stood for a moment looking at the floor then he turned and stepped towards Heidi. Again she threw up her arms.

"You don't have to do that Heidi, I'm sorry I frightened you, I never would have struck you, not in 100 years. And Heidi, I don't hate you, I have never hated anyone or anything in my life. You recall I once told you there was a very thin line between man the socialized animal and man the beast. What you just witnessed and heard was the beast in me. I am ashamed and shocked at what I said. And Heidi, forgive me for calling you a whore. I never thought that word would leave my lips, especially directed at my wife and you are still my wife"

"I will be moved out of here by tomorrow evening. Please do me the favor of not being present, I do not want to see or talk to you again.

And when you get those divorce papers drawn up, don't drop them off yourself. Have your lawyer or someone else do it."

Divorce, Heidi Thought, for some reason divorce has never crossed my mind. In all our time together I never once thought about it. Now Rob is anticipating that I will divorce him. And why not. Everything I just said is geared to a divorce. I suppose in time that will come, but not now. I am in no hurry to divorce Rob.

With that Rob turned slowly and walked out of the door and out of Heidi's life. Heidi called after him, however he either didn't hear her or chose to ignore her call.

Heidi was unable to move. She was paralyzed by a myriad of feelings. She was still frightened, she was aghast at what she had said to Rob, she wanted to tell him she loved him but couldn't. The only man she ever loved, she treated him like a piece of dirt. All of the memories he recalled she remembered keenly and what did she do, she made light of every one of them.

It wasn't that long ago that after having made love she told Rob she would like to have a baby. And how did she respond to Rob? I'm damn glad we didn't act on that. Every response to Rob was meant to hurt him. Why? So she could become a whore again. No, it had to be more than that. When she spoke to Rob it was as if it wasn't she who was speaking but someone else speaking through her.

She so thoroughly killed his love for her that he never wants to see or talk to her again. That means she will never again be held in his arms, never kissed by him, never have him make love to her again and never have him explain things to her that she just couldn't comprehend. He loved to do that and she loved to have him do it.

Heidi didn't weep, she wailed and she didn't care if the neighbors heard her. And yet, as badly as she had hurt him, before his tirade he said he still had a reservoir of love for her.

That was the only opportunity he gave her to tell him she was all wrong and she did love him, loved him very much. But no, she kept saying things that were meaner and meaner. She fell onto the couch. Saying out loud

"Oh God, what have I done, what have I done? Rob believed you brought us together. I too believe that but now it is I who has driven us apart. You can do only one thing, turn your back on me."

I am a useless, worthless piece of humanity taking a gift you so willingly gave me and destroying it in a terrible way. What hurts me the most is the nonchalant way I treated the memory of Rob almost dying in the hospital and of his bravery in carrying me to the little cabin. Oh those memories hurt so bad. How could I, oh my God, how could I? Rob was willing to die for me. I can never forget the sound of that awful bullet striking him in the back. He lay there dying and yet he mustered up enough strength to raise his arm and stroke my cheek with the back of his hand. He even was smiling when he said, Heidi, never forget that I love you. Those memories will haunt me to my dying days. I really don't want to go on living anymore.

What is left for me, nothing but prostitution. I have burned all my bridges behind me. Rob is gone, Lorraine, my good friend, Lorraine is gone, James is gone, Ken and Zack are gone, Clay is gone as is Rev. Dunn. I have severed myself from my family so they are gone too. What I fear the most has happened to me. I am alone. The only friend I have is Paul. I despise the four whores who put me up to this.

"There are things I must do before I start seeing customers again. I hate the thought of it, but they will have to wait. Right now I must get some sleep."

But there was no sleep for Heidi, not that night or the next or the next. It did not go well for Rob either. Once his anger subsided he thought about the things he had said to Heidi. He said to himself I completely lost my cool. I have never been so angry in my life. She purposely made me angry so it would be easier for me to give her up. It didn't work. In spite of everything, I still love her. My love for her is too deep to just drop it. The things I said to her, I called her a bitch and a whore. In our three years of marriage I was so careful not to use the word whore and yet I called her a whore over and over again. She was so frightened, I'm sure she thought I was going to hit her. I was angry enough to do it, but I would never strike Heidi, I would never strike any woman. Worst of all I told her that I hoped her customers would screw her to death, that it would be a fitting end for her. I told her I never wanted to see her again. With all that both of us said to each other, it is very unlikely we will see each other again.

Well it's over, all over. Now I'm tired and I'm going to bed.

As with Heidi, there was no sleep for him that night and very little for the nights that followed.

Rob moved fast and since it was a week end, by Saturday night he was moved out of Heidi's house. Before he left and after his outburst he told Heidi not to be around while he was going in and out of her house moving his belongings. She was nowhere to be seen.

Chapter Eighteen

≡ ·|||· ≡

Unable to sleep, at 4:00 AM Rob got up and went to his office. He was haunted by the things he had said to Heidi. How could he be so crude? How could he say such awful things to the girl he had loved beyond description? He wasn't some back alley bum. Yes she had said awful things to him, but that was no excuse for his behavior. Regardless he should have been able to keep his cool.

Most of what he had said he deeply regretted. Heidi must have thought he had lost his mind. As he sat alone in his office he shed tears from time to time. Both had burned bridges behind themselves. The thought that he would never see Heidi again cut deeply into his heart. The end happened so fast. He tried to reason with Heidi, but it was useless. Her mind was made up, she no longer loved him, her marriage was a drag and she was going to once again be a call girl.

Lorraine walked into the office on Monday morning. She noticed Rob's office door was open. She muttered

"I must have forgotten to close it,"

She walked over to close the door and then noticed Rob sitting at his desk with his face buried in his hands.

"Rob, what on earth are you doing here so early?"

"Please come in Lorraine and take the chair in front of my desk'

Lorraine said,

"Let me perk a pot of coffee first, I am sure you could use some."

In a few minutes Lorraine returned to Rob's office.

"Lorraine, it's all over, my happy marriage has come to an end."

"What on earth do you mean?"

"How many times in the past couple of months have you asked what's wrong? You were aware I was not my old self. I even told you I believed my happy marriage was unraveling. Heidi and I had it out last night, she told me she no longer loved me and I told her I hated her and thus ended our marriage. She kicked me out of her house, can you believe that?"

"What do you mean her house?"

"It is her house, it has been all along and I suppose that gives her the right to kick me out."

"But why Rob?"

"Hold on to the chair Lorraine, Heidi is going back into the business of being a call girl again."

Lorraine sat in dazed silence unable to speak for a moment.

"I, I don't believe it Rob."

"Believe it Lorraine. Our marriage has been unraveling for three months. First the kisses and hugs came to an end and then Heidi denied me sex. Lorraine, can you feature that, me, her husband, she denies me sex and yet she is ready to have sex with strangers three times a week so long as she remains a call girl. Is that incredible or what?"

"For Heidi our marriage has become dull and boring. Everything about me has become dull and boring. Our kisses and hugs no longer had meaning to her. Sex with me was just hum drum. She needs good sex, exciting sex and I am no longer able to provide it for her. She needs a change she said, life can't go on this way for her. She needs excitement in her life. She needs challenges."

"All the fond memories we built up over the past three years mean nothing to her. She wants out. I tried my best to talk her into giving our marriage another chance. It was all to no avail. She wants out, period. We were like two strangers sharing the same house."

"This was all deliberate. She believed all this denying would cause me to dislike her and it would be easier for me to leave."

"Do you dislike her Rob?"

"Friday night I told her I hated her. Yes Dr. Robert Sloan, sex and marital therapist told his wife that he hated her. But that's only the beginning of what I said Lorraine. I completely lost it. After she told me she was going to be a call girl again I tried to reason with her, but it was to no avail. I brought to her attention the wonderful marriage we had, the many good times we had. I brought up the fact I almost gave my life to save hers, that when I was freezing and we thought we were going to die, I gave her my jacket in hopes of making her just a bit warmer, that I picked her up and carried her to the cabin when I had strict orders not to strain myself in any way. She said, Oh Rob that was 100 years ago. Then the best she could do was to tell me in the most unconcerned way that it was noble of me to do those things. That's when I lost my cool Lorraine. Noble and nothing more. Those were not acts springing from the deep love I had for her. They were just noble."

Rob lowered his head, buried his face in his hands and wept. Lorraine kept quiet. When Rob raised his head, Lorraine said,

"I'm so sorry Rob, so very, very sorry. I knew that something was wrong. I noticed a change in you for quite some time. I wanted to say something, but figured it was none of my business."

"I wish you would have said something Lorraine, I didn't want to burden you with my problems, but it would have been better had I shared it with you."

"As bad as Heidi's nonchalant attitude was and as bad as the things she said to me were, the worst is the way I conducted myself. I was awful Lorraine. I yelled at her, called her a bitch, and a whore. I called my wife a whore. In the almost four years we have known each other, I never so much as mentioned the word whore. Oh God forgive me. I even told her that I hoped her customers would screw her to death."

With a sad smile Rob continued,

"I wanted to use the F word, but I couldn't bring myself to do so. Maybe worst of all was that I must have frightened her half to death. I could see fear written all over her face. And seeing that, I believe it incensed me even more. She was afraid I was going to hit her. At one point when I was shouting and stepped closer to her, she raised her arms and covered her face to protect it. Oh god Lorraine, I was terrible. My wife was cowering before me fearful that I would strike her."

"She tried to talk and I said, keep your damn mouth shut bitch. I said that more than once. I told her that all I had for her was love and she turned it against me and that it had been replaced with hatred for her. Lorraine, I said I hated her. I don't believe I have ever hated anyone or anything in my life, yet here I was screaming at my wife, the girl I loved so intently for almost four years, telling her I hated her."

Rob was silent for a long moment, then said,

"Lorraine, you know that there is but a thin veneer of socialization, of our humanness that separates us from the beast that dwells within. Rip off that veneer and the beast is exposed. For a time last evening, I was that beast, so much so that I even frightened myself. Heidi experienced and felt that beast."

"Rob, don't be too hard on your self. You said it earlier, Heidi deliberately provoked you. You are a man of patience, you are long suffering, what Heidi said must have been infuriating. Why is she going to be a call girl again?"

"She no longer loves me Lorraine and that being the case there is no longer reason to stay in the marriage."

"Rob, that doesn't sound at all like Heidi. As you know we are good friends, we have had good times shopping together, having lunch together visiting over the phone, etc. She couldn't tell me often enough how much she loved you. How many times did she tell me that she was so happy, that she didn't know life could hold so much happiness for her."

"I am convinced that Heidi didn't come to the decision to be a call girl again on her own. Something or someone got to her. It could be that a call girl friend encouraged her to come back into the business. I am speculating of course but all you have told me just doesn't sound like Heidi"

"You could be right Lorraine, but if so, she never mentioned anyone. You know what hurts me the most, though Heidi will start divorce proceedings, of that I am sure, she is still my wife. What hurts me so darn much is knowing that many faceless and nameless men are going to be using Heidi's body to satisfy their sexual lust and believe me from what Heidi has told me, some of the desires can be way out. Her body is mine Lorraine, We said as much when we took our marriage vows. It doesn't belong to anyone but me."

"I'm so sorry Rob, I can understand why just knowing that would tear you apart inside. Rob, let me get us coffee and then we can continue."

Lorraine filled two cups of coffee, sat again and said,

"Rob, I don't believe for one moment that Heidi has stopped loving you. Her telling me of her love for you was just too strong."

"But Lorraine, she told me she no longer loved me and believe me she said it with a straight face. She said, This marriage is over, I no longer love you."

"Forget about that, I'm a pretty good judge of people. Her love for you was and I am convinced still is genuine. One cannot give up a love like that overnight."

"How about in three months?"

"You know what I mean Rob."

"Then what is wrong with her?"

"I don't know what is wrong, but one thing I know is that girl still loves you."

Rob forced a weak smile and replied,

"She sure had a strange way of showing it,"

"Rob you are going to hear from Heidi again, I know you will. Don't ask me how I know, but you will hear from her again."

"Alright, Lorraine, let's assume she does get in touch with me, then what do I do?"

"You still love her, don't you Rob?"

"More than I can tell you Lorraine. When I gave my heart to Heidi it was for keeps."

"Do I have to tell you what you are going to do? You will find out what got into her when the two of you get together, and then she will reveal to you that her irrational behavior did not start with her."

"Lorraine how can I take her back knowing she again has had sex with many, many men?"

"I don't have an answer for you Rob, you will have to cross that bridge when the time is right. Rob, I just thought of something, remember when you told me that after Heidi told you she was a call girl you went off by yourself to make a decision. You said that as you sat on the fallen tree you literally shouted out, Lord, what shall I do? You said you almost got an immediate response telling you to love her. If that was God speaking to you, do you think he is going to go back on those words?"

"I never thought of that Lorraine and I don't have an answer to your question. Thank you Lorraine, thank you for listening to a broken hearted therapist."

"You know you don't have to thank me Rob, my door will always be open to you."

It was a couple of weeks after Heidi and Rob had their confrontation. For a time Rob felt it would be best if he closed down his therapy practice. He remained distraught especially over the way he had responded to Heidi's decision to become a call girl once again. He also felt anyone who behaved toward his wife the way he had to Heidi, was not in a position to be a therapist. He couldn't save his own marriage what right did he have trying to save the marriages of others? It was largely due to the sympathy and encouragement given to him by Lorraine that he continued his practice.

Chapter Nineteen

≈ ·|||· ≈

Rob had finished seeing clients for the day. The door to his office was open. Lorraine walked to it and gently knocked on the frame. Rob looked up.

"Do you have time to visit with me for awhile, Rob?"

"Of course I do Lorraine, you know that without asking. Come in, sit down and tell me what's on your mind."

"I'll get right to the point Rob, do you think it's wrong for a woman or a man as far as that goes, to desire to have sex with someone other than their spouse? I'm not talking about falling in love, just being physically attracted to him and desiring sex with him?"

"Is that a problem for you Lorraine?"

"Yes Rob and I think you know who the man is."

"I do?"

"Yes, he's sitting right in front of me."

Rob was quiet then said,

"You, you would like to have sex with me?"

"Very much so Rob. The other morning when you were hurting over the breakup with Heidi, I wanted to have sex with you real bad. I thought it would give you some comfort. You have been deprived for so long and I thought just the physical closeness of us engaging in sex might make you feel just a bit better."

"Lorraine, thank for your thoughtfulness. Your heart is certainly in the right place and I love you for it, but we couldn't do that for if we did you would be guilty of being unfaithful to Ted and if by chance I'm still married, I would be guilty of being unfaithful to Heidi. I'm afraid that would cause you much grief."

"I didn't say I would do it Rob, although I would like to, I just asked if you thought it was wrong for me to desire to have sex with you. You certainly have a heightened sense of conscience that you live by."

"That isn't it alone Lorraine. I care for you very much and I don't want you to be hurt."

Rob sensed that Lorraine's question was a most sincere one and was troubling her.

"Lorraine, again I'll give it my best shot. We can control our behavior, but we can't control our hormones. They know nothing about rules and regulations."

"Lorraine, you will understand what I am about to say. It is not wrong to be tempted, it is wrong to yield to that temptation. Many men desire sex with women other than their wives and many women desire sex with someone other than their husbands. It only becomes wrong when they give into the temptation. If you indeed desire to have sex with me it certainly doesn't mean you don't love Ted as much as ever. Am I right?"

"You're right Rob, it has nothing to do with my love for Ted. Again, as much as I would like to have sex with you I wouldn't, I'm just talking about the desire."

"Lorraine, you are a very attractive and sexual woman. I couldn't begin to guess how often I desire to have sex with you and that had nothing to do with my love for and desire to have sex with Heidi. Why wouldn't a man desire to have sex with a woman who is attractive and exudes sexuality? Just keep in mind that there is a big difference in desiring to do it and actually doing it."

"And Rob why shouldn't a woman desire to have sex with such a handsome, caring, compassionate and intelligent man? If I exude sexuality so do you."

"I know you're overdoing it Lorraine, but thank you for the compliments."

"Rob, I'm not overdoing it, I mean every word I said."

"I'll let you in on a trade secret Lorraine. Therapy can be very explosive. It isn't unusual for a woman who has had her self esteem damaged by her marriage, by her husband and by her own behavior to attempt to seduce the therapist. In an effort to do so, some go as far as to remove their clothes. In some cases it would be quite easy for the therapist to take advantage of the woman's vulnerability and have sex with her. It would also be highly unethical, immoral and maybe even illegal. It would in all likelihood put an end to therapy and cause even more serious problems for the woman."

"Are you saying this has gone on behind your closed door?"

"Yes Lorraine, a number of times."

"Don't you find it extremely difficult to behave yourself?"

Rob smiled and said,

"Behave myself, that's a good way of putting it Lorraine. Yes I do, but I would never take advantage of the opportunity,"

"My goodness," said Lorraine, "What else goes on behind closed doors?"

Rob smiled,

"I'm not through yet Lorraine, if you and I were to have sex, it would destroy the good relationship we have. Why? Because after sex our relationship would be on a different level, it would be difficult for us to continue as employer and employee."

"Yes," Lorraine said, "I can see where having sex could have a very negative affect on our relationship. So, we can look at the merchandise, but don't touch it."

"Ahhh Lorraine, well put. You know kiddo, you are one smart cookie."

"I'm glad you think so, but let me say you have been an excellent teacher and therapist. So what do we do when we desire sex with each other?"

"We don't keep it secret, we talk about it., we tease each other and most likely get aroused, but we don't touch the merchandise. You know Lorraine, I'm sure you have caught me looking at you hungrily more than once."

"I sure have and I assume you are undressing me with your eyes."

"My apologies Lorraine, I sure have been."

Lorraine was silent and then said,

"If a female client takes off her clothes for you I certainly wouldn't mind doing so, so long as it remains our secret. Would that be so bad?"

"Lorraine, please don't tempt me especially now since I can't go home and have sex in order to satisfy my burning desires. Keep in mind those women, and there really aren't that many, who strip in my office, are interested in seducing me not because they necessarily want to have sex with me, but rather to help alleviate guilt feelings or to have their self esteem restored by a man who finds them sexually desirable."

"Some of the women have been unfaithful to their husbands. They are being overwhelmed by feelings of guilt. Their reasoning in stripping is that if they can get the therapist to sin then their sin really isn't all that bad."

"Well, should I take them off or shouldn't I?"

"Lorraine, Lorraine, you don't know how badly I want to say yes, but that too would be pushing the envelope too far."

"Why?"

"Well, I really don't know why, it would be very intimate. And I fear that stripping would be only the beginning. I'm sure you can see that."

"Well, you can look, but you don't have to touch."

"Lorraine, I'm a man, the temptation would be too intense."

"You can control yourself with counselees why not with me."

"You want to take your clothes off for me, don't you?"

"Yes."

"Ahhh, Lorraine, you're a good girl. How could I be so lucky to get a secretary like you?"

"And Rob, how could I be so lucky to get a boss like you?" "Not boss Lorraine, employer. I would never boss you."

"Well, alright, I won't take my clothes off," Lorraine said with a smile, "But anytime you want me to, let me know."

"I will, you can rest assured I will. And Lorraine, I so much would like you to take your clothes off for me. It's an awful struggle for me to say no. Lorraine, are you as aroused as I am?"

"Yes."

"You're lucky, you have Ted to go home to and you can seduce him. I have nothing to go home to."

"Awww Rob, I'm so sorry."

"Well, it most likely would do me no good anyway."

"Rob I want so much to help you, but as you have so wonderfully pointed out, I can't."

"Now you have the spirit, you can't."

"Well Lorraine, it's time we went home. Ted will be wondering what's holding you up."

Both stood. Rob said,

"Stand right where you are Lorraine,"

Rob walked around his desk, stood in front of Lorraine, looked down into her eyes and with his hands brushed hair from the sides of her face. He put his hands on her shoulders, pulled her close and kissed her long and hard.

"I have wanted to do that for a long time. I hope I haven't offended you?"

"You haven't offended me Rob. I have wanted you to kiss me for a long time. I guess it's not as risky as taking off my clothes."

"How I wish you and I would have met before you met Ted and I met Heidi."

Lorraine smiled and said,

"Me too Rob, but it wasn't meant to be. Whew, do you know what that kiss did to my libido?"

"Yes I do Lorraine because it did the same to my libido. Now, hurry home, Ted is waiting for you,"

"Lucky me Rob."

"Yes Lorraine lucky you."

"Have you heard anything from Heidi?"

"Not a word Lorraine. When and if I do hear from her you will be the first one to know. In fact I have no doubt it will be through her lawyer."

"It might even be that she calls you and not me."

"You've given up all hope, haven't you?"

"I have Lorraine. I'm sure she has no desire to see a mad man again. Further, by now she will be busy entertaining men."

"Rob, Rob, you're too hard on yourself. Don't give up, woman's intuition you know. Goodbye Rob, see you in the morning and thank you ever so much for helping me with my question and for showing such wonderful restraint. I can now put that issue to rest. The desire will still manifest itself, but it isn't going to cause me anxiety."

"We certainly did much more than deal with my question, didn't we?"

"We certainly did Lorraine."

"Rob, you are a wonderful therapist and a man who has a lot of self control. I have no trouble in understanding why your business has grown so rapidly."

"Not so wonderful Lorraine, I couldn't even save my own marriage."

"That really bothers you, doesn't it?"

"Very much so."

"Let me say it one more time Rob, it isn't over yet. In a round about way your therapy might be instrumental in bringing Heidi back to you. Good evening Rob, I'll see you in the morning."

"Yes you will if I can get my libido to settle down. If I can't I'll give you a call. I had better stay home."

"Sorry Rob, you have a full schedule tomorrow. That should help you keep your mind off me."

"Nope, it won't."

"How about you?"

"I'm going to be swamped with work. And with Ted waiting for me at home, my libido will be satisfied at least for a little while."

"Good evening Lorraine."

Chapter Twenty

≡ ⫶⎪⫶ ≡

In the morning after a sleepless night, Heidi got up and went into the bathroom. She looked in the mirror and didn't like what she saw. She said to herself I look awful, I can't remember when I've looked so bad. I have dark circles under my eyes. That's a first for me. Well, there are cosmetics to take care of that. Rob said I always looked beautiful to him."

Her eyes filled with tears and she muttered,

"Rob, oh Rob, what have I done to us?"

After she showered she went to the closet to get an outfit for the day. When she opened the door the first thing she noticed was the empty space where Rob's shirts, jackets and slacks used to hang. She caught her breath. She looked down where his shoes used to be. Now there was just a big empty space. She really didn't want to, but she went to Rob's dresser and opened all the drawers.

"Empty," she said, "Just like my head."

There was nothing left of his under clothes, handkerchiefs, T-shirts etc. in the drawers. Nothing of Rob remained. She thought, Well Heidi, this is what you wanted and you got it. I'm going to get a cup of coffee, a pen and paper, sit at the table and make a list of things that need to be done before I'm ready for my first customer. Right now, I feel like it's something I have to do, not want to do.

She poured herself a cup of coffee, raised her cup and was looking at the place where Rob always sat. She put down the cup and thought she was going to cry. Rob should be having coffee with her, he should be teasing her and joking with her. She sobbed a few times.

Why was I so gullible, so stupid. I just can't understand it, I didn't have to listen to Sally and the other whores, I should have just said no and don't ever bother me again. She sobbed a few times. Instead, she was alone at the table and she didn't like it. Rob should be with her.

Heidi started on her list. She needed new living room drapes, erotic pictures to hang on the living and bed room walls. Why didn't she just hide the ones she had when she met Rob? Pictures weren't cheap. She would need to get a few x-rated videos. It irritated her that some of the men had to watch videos before they got aroused enough to have intercourse. Am I not sexy enough?

She had to buy a few cartons of condoms. Why? She thought, Why do I have to buy the condoms that should be the customer's responsibility. The problem was there were some men who would show up without a condom and then insisted that she go bare back. She didn't like that. It was from one such man she picked up Chlamydia. Just thinking about it made her feel unclean.

"Well", she said out loud, "It's an occupational hazard and I'll bear with it." And then there were lubricants and plenty of it. She often found condoms irritating and then painful if she wasn't well lubricated.

She would need a couple of very revealing outfits, the kind she could not wear on the streets. Finally the tile in the bathroom and shower had to be replaced. Oh yes, and liquor. That she was also expected to provide. She looked at the list and thought, that's going to cost a bundle. It's really going to put a strain on my bank account.

After she finished her list and coffee she sat and just thought. She had lied so much to her mother and dad, telling them about fake jobs she had, telling them about her new apartment and about all the nice young men she had been dating. Now it had been a long time since she had written. What must they think? What if she received a letter from her mother saying she and her dad were coming to Tacoma for a visit?

The thought made her shudder. Her dad especially had so much faith in her.

There's that word faith again. She thought, Rob used it a lot. From him I learned what it meant. Dad had faith, he believed she would find a good paying respectable job, that she would always conduct herself in a respectable manner and above all, she would never lie. He had so much confidence in her. Faith, the things that are hoped for, but not yet seen. So much faith he had in her. They had been so close.

Suddenly it was too much for Heidi. She ran to the bed, threw herself over it and shed hot tears. She couldn't stop crying and eventually cried herself to sleep.

When she awoke it took her a moment to get her bearings. The clock said 1:00 PM. She had gotten out of bed at 8:00 AM, how could it be 1:00 PM? Then she remembered the long talk she had with herself. Again she got up, splashed cold water over her face and dressed. What would she do today. She would start by buying the revealing outfits.

Yes, dad had great faith that I would always conduct myself in a respectable manner. Mom and dad would be shocked beyond words to know I destroyed my marriage of almost three years. She had never told them she and Rob were married.

In one of her mother's letters she had written,

"When are you coming home, we miss you so and it seems like we haven't seen you in years." It had been years, in fact the last time she saw them was at the airport when she left for Seattle. They deserved much better from her. My gosh, she thought, what kind of a person am I to neglect my wonderful parents like I have. When she answered her mother what she gave her was a lie.

I must push those thoughts out of my mind or I will become a complete wreck. It's bad enough the way it is.

Heidi put on a light jacket and drove to a restaurant for a late lunch. How would she ever explain the Jaguar to her parents? With lies of course. And Rob had such faith in her that she always told him the truth. She knew he never lied to her. He had said, Heidi, I don't believe you have ever lied to me. But she had, many times during the past four months.

Heidi, you are going to hell so you might as well go full bore. As Rob said, get yourself screwed to death. That would be a happy and pleasurable way for you to exit this life. Why not, why shouldn't she have sex with customers until she exhausted herself? Some of the experiences were darn good. It was great to be uninhibited. After all, I am lost, eternally lost anyway.

It was no fun eating alone. How she disliked loneliness. She looked around the restaurant and saw no one she knew. No one knew her either. I hate being alone she said to herself.

She noticed a couple of high school age boys looking at her and decided it was time to leave. When she got into her Jaguar she said to herself, first I'll go to the agency and then I'll pick up the skimpy garments. It's time I tell Paul that I'm coming back to work. I can't wait until the last minute.

She was glad to see Paul. She considered him her best friend.. Paul was never happy that she was a call girl. She sensed that he liked her, liked her very much.

When she walked in, Paul greeted her.

"Heidi, it's good to see you again. What's it been, about a month since you were here?"

"It's good to see you Paul. Yes it's been about a month since we had our talk."

"Heidi, I hope you have come to tell me you got that crazy idea of being a call girl again out of your head."

"No Paul, I'm here to tell you I'm about ready for my first customer. I'm coming back to work. Paul."

"Ahhh Heidi no, stop joking with me."

"It's no joke Paul. Four weeks ago I wasn't sure, now I am."

"You know it's unusual for us to hire a married woman."

"I'm aware of that Paul and I'm still married, but in name only. I just haven't had time to see a divorce lawyer."

"You're not serious Heidi. Has it gone that far that you are thinking about divorce?"

"I wouldn't be here Paul if I wasn't thinking about a divorce. Does that make sense?

Another lie, she said to herself. A divorce is one thing I have given no thought to and I wonder why.

"Paul, my marriage is over. Now, can we get back to business?"

"Their is no chance that you and Rob can reconcile your differences?"

"None."

"Alright Heidi, I'm not going to run the same arguments by you again. If you insist I'll put your name back on the roster. You're such a pretty girl Heidi, like the girl next door. You have already picked up one disease and that was minor. The next one may be far more serious. You will be playing Russian Roulette with your life."

"Paul!"

"OK Heidi when will you be ready for your first customer?"

"I hope no longer than a week, two at the most. I have a few items to pick up and I have been told the tile being replaced in the bath room and shower will soon be finished. I also have to tell Mr. Simpson that I will be leaving my job."

"You had a job?"

"Yes Paul a good job working for a very nice gentleman who treated me royally."

"And you're going to throw that to the wind also? Call me when you're ready Heidi and I'll schedule a customer for you."

"Paul, I want you to know that I really appreciate your efforts to dissuade me. I hope you will continue to be my friend."

"Always, Heidi."

As Heidi left the agency she wondered why she didn't feel glad that she was on the roster. She knew why, there was no sense denying it, she loved Rob and she knew that once she had sex with her first customer, for sure it would be all over with Rob. And Paul, dear Paul there was a lot of truth in what he said. He tried so hard to discourage her four weeks ago.

There was still plenty of time for her to pick up a couple of skimpy, revealing and erotic outfits. She would have to go to one of the larger porn shops for that. If there was time she could order a couple from the Playtime catalog, however, she would not have that much time. She picked up two very revealing outfits and decided she might as well be naked.

She was close to the mall and Phillips. She had a sudden urge to visit the place where she and Rob met. She walked into Phillips and to the counter where she collided with Rob. She felt an uncomfortable tightness in her throat. Here's where it all began, she said to herself.

Next she walked across the walkway to the small eatery where she and Rob had coffee. That hurt even worse for it was here she began to feel the first tinges of attraction to Rob, it was here she made a date with Rob, the first date she had in quite a few years. She wanted to weep, but felt this wasn't the place. She got a cup of coffee and carried it back to the table where she and Rob sat.

She watched people flowing by the open door. She noted some seemed happy and she envied them. Others with no smile on their faces seemed to be down or sad. She could join the ones who were down and sad.

She was deep in thought when she heard her name being called.

"Heidi, is it really you?"

She looked up and Juanita was standing by her side. She hadn't seen Juanita since she left the agency nearly 6 years ago. She wondered if Juanita still worked for the agency. She seemed to have aged since she last saw her.

"Juanita, it's so good to see you. It's been a long time."

"And it's good to see you Heidi."

Heidi stood and they hugged. Heidi asked her if she would join her for a cup of coffee? She would be glad to have coffee with her. She was tired and needed to rest. Juanita was Spanish American, strikingly attractive with her long black hair and slim figure. Customers had their preferences and often a Spanish American girl was requested. Some men believed that Spanish American women were the hottest women around.

"Juanita, it's been so long, we have to get caught up on what has been happening to each other."

"A lot has happened since we last saw each other Heidi. I married a wonderful, loving man. Jeremy is an auto mechanic and a darn good one. However, auto mechanics are not at the top of the income ladder. I wanted to get out of the call girl business so bad when we married, but the reality of our financial situation almost forced me to remain a call girl. I don't entertain as many men as I used to, just when we are in need of money and that seems like all the time"

"Paul has been very good to me allowing me to work just when I have to."

"That Paul is a peach isn't he Juanita?"

"He's a great guy Heidi. Being a call girl hurts Jeremy and myself very much. Can you see a husband kiss his wife good bye as she leaves the house to have sex with other men? Or, when he has to leave the house when I'm entertaining at home? I know he weeps often when I leave or he has to leave the house. I have no job skills Heidi, so I have to use what I do have to make money and that's my body. If I didn't have a husband like Jeremy the world would be a pretty bleak place for me."

"I must tell you Heidi, I took time off to have a baby, William Fernando Smith. That's quite a monicker for a little guy, isn't it? He's such a cute baby it really tears me apart when I have to leave him or when Jeremy takes him out of the house."

Juanita lowered her head and wept.

"I'm so sorry Juanita. Are you sure you have no skills you can market?"

"I was a good student, at the top of my class and I excelled in typing. I can really zip right along."

"Juanita, the key board of a computer is the same as on a typewriter. Couldn't you take evening courses to learn how to operate a computer?"

"Evenings off? That's when I work, when I entertain customers."

"It must be very difficult for both you and Jeremy."

"I love children Heidi, Jeremy and I wanted to have at least two more, but there will be no more."

"Why Juanita? If you and Jeremy want them, why don't you have them?"

"About six months ago I picked up gonorrhea from a customer. If he didn't have to use a condom he would pay me an extra $150.00, pay me and not the agency. That was too good to pass up. I ignored the symptoms until I could no longer do so. I had let it go too long and both of my tubes were infected. It's no longer possible for me to conceive. No more children Heidi. I'm told that for a call girl that's an occupational hazard."

"Yes," responded Heidi, "I guess it is."

Heidi thought of when she and Rob discussed having a baby neither felt they were ready. She was supposed to get pregnant sometime during the summer months. Boy, I'm glad the time wasn't right, she said to herself.

"Equally as bad, I infected Jeremy. He sought medical treatment as soon as he noticed a discharge and he is OK. He suffered no damage to his organs. That was before I knew I had the disease. Have you any idea how much it hurts to know you infected your husband? A lesser man would have left me. Jeremy will not have intercourse with me until three or four days after I have seen my last customer. I don't blame him, he feels I am not clean, but I miss the closeness and intimacy with him. You can imagine the cost of medical treatment for both of us, especially me. I don't know if we'll ever get it paid off."

"Now enough about me Heidi. I have been told that you have a wonderful husband and a wonderful marriage. I was also told that you are so happy since you quit as a call girl."

"I did have a wonderful husband and marriage, but that is behind me now."

"What do you mean Heidi?"

"I'm going back into the business Juanita. I'm going to be a call girl again."

Heidi hesitated for a moment then said,

"I'm about ready for my first customer. I gave up both my husband and my marriage."

"You can't mean that Heidi, going back into the business?" Have you lost you're mind? You gave up you're husband? Paul told me that he met him and he is such a nice and friendly guy."

"I'm going to be operating out of my house again and I couldn't very well have a husband hanging around the house."

"Heidi, listen, please listen, I have to be a call girl, but not you. Paul said you're husband is a professional man."

"Yes Juanita, he is a marital and sexual therapist."

"Couldn't he save his own marriage?"

"He didn't see it coming. I had been disengaging from him for almost three months,

He knew something was wrong with me, but would never have guessed I was going to be a call girl again. By the time I told him my mind was made up."

"Made up, just like that your mind was made up and you didn't give a damn what it would do to your husband, am I right?"

Again Heidi was quiet as she looked across the table at Juanita.

"Juanita, I have never heard you use a cuss word."

"Heidi, this time it is more than warranted. What a mean, dirty trick to play on the man who loves you."

Heidi sat in silence, turning her cup round and round.

"I imagine I have to say I played a dirty, mean trick on the man who loved me. I don't think he has any love left for me."

"And that doesn't bother you?"

"Yes it bothers me and the guilt trip you're laying on me doesn't help."

"Good, I'm glad it doesn't. Wake up Heidi and take a good look at what you are about to do."

"What I'm going to do is become a call girl again."

"Heidi, you're impossible, you are as stubborn as a mule."

"Did you say your husband is a therapist?"

"Yes, Rob and two other men own a counseling service. One is a child therapist and the other is a lawyer specializing in estate planning."

"Is your husband successful?"

"Yes, after a slow start he is now very successful."

"So you don't need the money a call girl like you makes, am I right."

"No, but I believe I need the excitement, the anticipation and the sex."

"Ah me Heidi, you're not being truthful. You're just telling yourself that. There is much excitement and anticipation in a good marriage. And the sex, is your husband, impotent?"

"Heavens no Juanita, he is a bundle of sexual energy."

"Then why oh why are you going back into the call girl business? Didn't you find the sex with your husband enjoyable and satisfying enough?"

"Well yes, I, I, Juanita, you are getting me all confused. Right now I really don't know why I'm going back into the business."

"Then stop this nonsense."

"I can't Juanita it's too late for that. I have nothing to go back to."

"I'm sure Paul told you that the business has changed. There are dangers and risks I don't believe you faced when you were a call girl."

"Yes, Paul tried to scare me with all kind of things. He said that customers were no longer reliable. They can get violent and abusive. Juanita, I don't and won't entertain such men." "

"How will you know and men are much stronger than women. If you don't give them what they want they can get pretty violent."

"Well, I can't worry about that."

Juanita turned from Heidi and shook her head.

"There's one more thing I want to say, then I must be going.

You are still married, right?"

"Yes I am."

"Do you realize that the first time you have sex with a customer you will be committing adultery? Were you married by a minister?"

"Yes, Rob wanted it that way."

"Then you took a vow before God that you would remain faithful to your husband. For me, my very life is a contradiction. Every time I have sex with a customer I'm committing adultery. I used to go to confession, asking for God's forgiveness. I no longer do that. One is supposed to repent of his or her sins. Heidi, that means, in affect, that you won't do it again. And yet I do it again and again and again. What good is confession? There are times I could scream. But you Heidi, you have not yet been unfaithful to Rob."

Heidi remained quiet.

"What frightens me is that Jeremy may tire of our arrangement and leave me. I don't think I could stand that, I love him too much. And yet, how could I blame him?"

Juanita buried her face in her hands and wept. After Juanita gained control of herself Heidi said,

"I guess I'm really not much concerned about committing adultery. I have long concluded that when I die I'm going straight to hell. So adultery is just another reason that is where I will be sent."

"I feel so sorry for you Heidi. Of course you are aware that if you do commit adultery and if you have any hopes of getting back together with your husband, you can forget it."

Juanita took a long look at Heidi and said,

"Heidi, I don't think I know you anymore. The Heidi I knew was a sweet, kind and sensitive young girl. Maybe that's what made you so popular with men. You aren't that way anymore. Well Heidi, I have to be going. I want to spend just as much time with Jeremy and my little boy as I can."

"If God still hears my prayers, I will pray for you. How soon will it be before you start up again?"

"In less than two weeks. A drunk has been installing tile in my bathroom and shower stall and he is not reliable, but he did promise me he would be finished in about a week. I give him two."

"Goodbye Heidi. Even though we have different takes on what you are about to do, lets keep in touch. You give me your phone number and I'll give you mine,"

Both stood and hugged. Juanita stood for a minute and then said to Heidi.

"Heidi, do you know what we are? We're whores."

"Juanita not you too."

"Yes Heidi, we can call ourselves prostitutes or call girls, but when all is said and done we are whores. There is one thing I remember from one of my English classes. In one of his plays Shakespeare said you can call a rose any name you want to, but it will still smell like a rose."

She turned and was on her way.

Heidi sat at the table staring at nothing. Both Paul and Juanita made so much sense in what they said. Yet here she was still trying to convince herself that being a call girl again is what she wanted to do, what she should do.

Well, she thought, in a day or two I will have forgotten what both of them said. Finally she broke from her reverie, walked to her car and started for home .As she drove towards home, Heidi was thoroughly confused. The closer I get to seeing my first customer, the more dubious I am about it, she said silently to herself, Juanita is so right, if I have any hopes of getting back together with Rob, that will be lost after I have sex with my first customer. For sure he won't want me.

When she got home she unlocked the door and stepped inside. The house seemed so unfriendly and cold. She looked at the walls where her pictures would soon be hanging.

Well Heidi, it will look just like a whore house and why not, it is a whore house. Just saying that was a bit unnerving to her.

The man putting up new tile was finished in a week. Heidi looked over her house. The bathroom and shower were attractive, the pictures hanging on the living and bedroom walls disgusted her, but in the past her customers liked them.

"Well," she said out loud, "I guess I'm ready for my first customer, but I'm really not ready. Everything is in place, but I don't know if I want to go through with it." Then she noticed the Bible Clay had given her lying on a lamp stand next to the couch.

She said to herself, It won't do to have the Bible in full view, I'll have to hide it or my customers might think I'm some kind of a religious freak. As she placed it behind a row of books, a wave of guilt swept over her. I promised Clay I would read and study it, however I haven't opened it for a long time. He would be so disappointed in me, maybe even hurt. Another broken promise. Oh well another broken promise so what, I live by broken promises. The truth be known, I'm a fallen woman in many ways. I'm more useless than ever. What ever faith Clay and Rob instilled in me is long gone. What little I have read from the Bible really hasn't helped me. I'm not being honest with myself. After Rob and I almost froze I as much as told Rob that it was by God's grace that we survived. I promised Rob I would read the Bible and go to church with him. I forgot that pretty quick after the incident.

Heidi wondered why Sally had not called. A short time ago she was so eager to see her back in the call girl business, but since she had made the break with Rob she hadn't heard a word, she had heard nothing from any of the girls. She remembered Sally's idiosyncrasies. She remembered that Sally envied others their happiness. She once said that it wasn't fair that while others were happy she had to content herself with being a whore. I really don't like the business Heidi, I'm tired of putting on a false front for so many jerks and many of them are just that, jerks. I'm tired of having my body used just to satisfy men's sexual desires. I have yet to have one customer treat me like a whole person. If there were something else I could do to make as much as I'm making as a call girl, I would do it in a moment.

Heidi remembered what Rob had told her. To your customers you are nothing more than a vagina. Sally felt the same way.

And yet she made no effort to find another job. She hadn't found relations with her customers as bad as Sally said she found hers and that was because of Paul. He picked very carefully the men she serviced.

Dear Paul, he did so much to look after her. If Paul had had the courage to date her and start a relationship with her, could they have married? She put the thought out of her mind.

Heidi thought about Sally's envy of other's happiness. Suddenly she felt as if an icy hand gripped her heart. Sally's primary interest was not that she return as a call girl, rather it was to destroy her love for Rob and her marriage. She had said, It's not fair, other's are happy and I have to content myself with these jerks who see in me nothing more than a sexual object.

None of my customers treat me as a whole person. Some of the guys come in as happy as a lark and even though they are being unfaithful to their wives, when they are through with me they return to those wives and continue their happy marriages.

So that was Sally's motive, to destroy her love for Rob and her marriage. She felt an inner rage building. All along her goal was to kill my love for Rob and to destroy my marriage and like a sucker I fell for it. I detest that woman, I despise that woman, I hate her like I have never hated anything in my life.

It was the very next day, as she was hanging erotica on her bedroom walls, Sally called.

"Well Heidi, did you get rid of that jerk of a husband of yours?"

Heidi came unglued.

"Damn you, don't you ever call my husband a jerk again, do you hear?"

"Tut, tut, tut, Heidi, let's keep that anger in check. Well Heidi, I succeeded in doing what I set out to do. I destroyed your marriage. I have a hunch that now you are just as miserable as I am. What do you think of that?"

"Sorry to disappoint you Sally, but I had already figured that out. What a viscous bitch you are."

"Now Sally it's my turn, listen to me and listen to me well. Sally old whore, I'm going to kill you. You destroyed my life and I'm going to destroy yours. Keep looking behind you for you never know when I'll be standing there."

"You wouldn't dare."

"Oh yes I would."

"I'll call the police and tell them what you told me."

"It won't do you any good since no crime has been committed, yet. I should know I've been there. Goodbye Sally and I hope you go to hell."

Heidi hung up the phone.

The next day Heidi went to Cal's gun store where Rob bought his reloading supplies Cal was behind the counter.

"Hi Heidi, I haven't seen you in a long time. How is that handsome husband of yours?"

"He's still my husband Cal, but we are no longer together."

"Awww, I'm so sorry to hear that. I told Julia, my wife, that if there is one marriage that is going to make it it's the marriage between Rob and Heidi."

"Rob can't be blamed for our breakup Cal it's all my fault. Rob had nothing to do with it."

Heidi said to Cal,

"I want to buy a pistol just like Rob's."

"Let's see, Rob has a 9mm Berella."

"Yes, that's right, that's what I want."

Cal took one out of his display case. Very carefully Heidi examined it. First thing she did was to point it at a wall, next she ejected the magazine, finally she pulled back the slide. The pistol was safe. She aimed at a few objects, turned to Cal and said,

"I think I can still be a crack shot."

"I know you can Heidi, you're a natural."

"That's also what Rob told me."

"Heidi, I thought Rob was going to buy you a Berella?"

"He was Cal, but I busted up our marriage before he got around to doing it."

Rob was so patient in teaching her how to shoot a pistol and when she started hitting the bull's eye he was thrilled. Ahhh the memory of that hurt.

"Now that you have bought an excellent 9mm, your favorite caliber, why don't you come back to the club and become a part of the women's division again. You're a darn good shot and we certainly could use you."

"Cal, the 9mm Berella I bought is just like Rob's. He had me out at the range many times and you're right, I'm a darn good shot and I don't mean to be bragging."

"I know you are Heidi and that's why I wish you'd come back to the club."

"I'll think about it Cal."

Heidi continued to sit on the stool. She started weeping.

"What's wrong Heidi?"

"Oh Cal, I miss Rob so much, Just talking about all the hours together at the range and thinking about how patient he was with me makes my heart ache."

"If you feel that way Heidi, why don't you go back to him?"

"I can't Cal, I burned all my bridges behind me."

"I'm so sorry to hear that Heidi."

When she got home, Heidi lay her new purchase on the table and looked at it. Then she smiled,

I couldn't kill anyone, not even Sally. Oh well now I have my Berella. Once I get going in my business who knows I just might take Cal up on his offer. I'm a good shot and I could be a real help in the women's division. Rob would be proud of me. She recalled how other members of the team would come over and congratulate her and Rob on their excellent shooting.

Tears came to her eyes. Rob was so proud of her. Heidi sat back and try as she may she couldn't keep other memories from flowing into her conscious awareness. What hit her the hardest was Rob's life and death struggle after being shot. As he lay on the pavement with blood flowing out of his back and chest, he couldn't focus his eyes. He called her name and then with a struggle raised his right arm and stroked her face with the back of his hand. He could speak only in a whisper, he told her for what she believed would be the last time, Remember always Heidi, that I love you. His hand fell onto his chest and for a few moments she thought he had died. Rob took that bullet meant for her.

Dear Alex, if he wouldn't have acted as quickly as he did, there is little doubt Rob would have died. And the many hours she spent by his bedside as he hovered between life and death.

She remembered being told to pray that prayer might well be the only thing that would save him. When she went into the chapel, Clay followed her. What would she have done without his support. He alone was an answer to prayer. And now what had she done, she completely turned her back on God. God gave Rob back to her and then she rejected Him.

Just before he went into his tirade Rob reminded her that both were at a sexual high and he wanted her to ask Susan if there was anyway his hospital room could be their bedroom. Oh, she remembered that well. And what did she say when Rob brought it up, she made light of it and told him it was childish of them.

Juanita told her that she was a far different Heidi than the one she knew when she was working as a call girl, she had changed to the point she no longer knew her.

Heidi laid her head on her arm resting on the table and wept bitter tears. It seemed she couldn't stop weeping. Finally she was able to staunch the flow. Speaking out loud she said,

"Heidi, stop playing games with yourself you still love him, love him so very much. It was you who killed that love. During his tirade he said, And all I wanted to do was love you."

This time it wasn't only tears that came, she cried out loud and her body convulsed with her sobs.

When the sobs stopped, she continued talking to herself out loud.

"How could I have been so blind to my love for Rob, how could I deliberately destroy my marriage? How many men would marry a whore? It is easy to use whore in reference to myself after my talk with Juanita. She is so right, call girl and even prostitute are only euphemisms for whore."

She thought of Rob's explosive outburst, he was livid with anger. He called her a bitch and a whore and he said he hoped her customers would screw her to death. Why didn't he use the F word? Because that wouldn't have been Rob. As angry as he was, he still had some control over his language. Everything he said she had coming. It was a shock when he called her a whore since never once had he used that word around her. It was just a measure of his anger.

Heidi could no longer just sit around the house, she had to get out, had to go somewhere. She decided to drive to Vista Point and gaze at the beauty of Mt. Rainer, to the place where Rob told her that in spite of her past, he loved her.

As she drove toward the overlook, her mind was racing 90 miles an hour with memories of the many, many good times they had together.

When she got to the overlook, she was irresistibly drawn to the picnic table where she sat when Rob walked off to be by himself. He seemed to be gone for such a long time. Then she heard him calling her name and in a moment she was in his arms and he was telling her he loved her in spite of her past and that past was not going to deprive him of that love. He held her tightly and whispered into her ear, I'm not going to give you up Heidi. Somehow we'll work through your past, but I'm not giving you up.

She smiled when she thought of the many questions he asked her. For a man with a Ph.D. he seemed to be rather naïve especially since he was a sex therapist, however, she would never mention that to him. At the same time, most likely any man would have asked the same questions Rob had if he married a whore.

Rob was so sure he would be just another man for her to have sex with. Fondly she remembered him saying, I'll just be number 227. Such a good man such a kind and loving man. How could I have hurt him so much? Heidi, you are an evil woman, a wicked woman and you will be only a whore when you start whoring again. Even hell is too good for you.

Next she walked to the fallen tree upon which both sat when Rob gave her a diamond, a ring she could not bring herself to remove. They sat for a long while just gazing at the beautiful scene down the valley.

It was too much for her. She was weeping as she ran back to her Jaguar. She sat for a moment again at the picnic table, gave a big sigh and said to herself loudly,

"I shouldn't have come here, there are too many memories. I should have stayed home, but I can't stand being alone in that house much longer."

On her drive home, she went past the little restaurant where they ate. Rob told her she would have to be satisfied with it because he couldn't afford the fine restaurants she was used to. He had a hard time accepting the fact she loved him and the kind of restaurant he could afford was just great for her. Why would a mere restaurant matter?

After they married she found the Job with Mr. Simpson, a job she loved. She was good at it, she sold property easily. Mr. Simpson said it was because she was so pretty and she had such a pleasant personality and such an easy going way about her. She was regaining her self respect, she took pride in her ability to relate to customers, she really liked herself.

Mr. Simpson is such a kindly man and she would have to tell him she was leaving her job.

"Heidi," she said out loud, "Ever since you decided to become a call girl again, life has taken a very severe turn for the worse for you."

When she got home, she garaged her car and went into the house. She almost shouted, "Rob, Rob, where are you, and then she had another good cry.

The tile was finished, everything was in place. It was time to call Paul. She thought about that.

I'm going to call Paul and tell him to take my name off the roster and then I'm going to do all I can to meet with Rob and hope and pray we can get back together.

She punched in Paul's number and when he answered, she said

"Paul, this is Heidi."

She hesitated, Paul said,

"Heidi, are you there?"

"Yes Paul, I'm here. I called to tell you I am ready for my first customer. How would the day after tomorrow be?"

"That will be OK Heidi, I wish I could talk you out of it, but I no longer have anything to say."

"Thank you Paul, I'll see you soon."

Heidi sat down. Almost in a state of shock she yelled out,

"What in the hell did I do. When I punched in Paul's number I was going to tell him to take my name off the roster and instead I told him to send me my first customer. Heidi, you're insane. You did just the opposite of what you were going to do."

Suddenly she remembered something Rob had read out of one of the Apostle Paul's epistles, I can't understand myself, the things I want to do I don't, and the things I don't want to do I do. That's was her, that was Heidi Sloan the whore.

The next day Heidi stopped in to see Mr. Simpson. She had asked for a week off and he was most happy to give it to her. When she told him she was leaving her job, he was shocked,

"Heidi, Why? I thought you liked your job. Am I not paying you enough?"

She explained to Mr. Simpson that she wanted to see if she could be successful opening a small business. Another damn lie, she thought to herself. Mr. Simpson expressed his regrets, but did wish her luck in her new venture. He also told her that if she ever wanted her job with him again to come and see him.

When she got home she got out her Berella, turned it over, aimed at a few objects on the wall, laid it on the table and smiled. She said to herself, just think Heidi, you were so angry at Sally that you were ready to kill her. How foolish of me. Like Rob, I am a very gentle person. She couldn't help but smile. Here I spent $550.00 on a new pistol just for the purpose of killing Sally. Maybe I will return to the club and join in on the competition shoots. She enjoyed them immensely, especially since she was such a good shot and Cal wanted her to come back.

There was no reason she couldn't be more social even if she was a call girl. No one had to know. I know what I'll do, something Rob told me a long time ago or at least it seems like a long time ago. I'll print a target, stick it to the wall and dry fire at the target just like Rob showed me. I can't kill Sally and I can't kill myself. I might as well start doing things for myself. I'm so glad I bought the Berella. It's identical to Rob's. It's the same pistol Rob was going to buy for me only I didn't give him a chance to do it.

The pain of Rob not being at the range with her, coaxing her on would be very hard to take, but she had better get used to his absence. She wondered if she could ever fall in love with a man again, if she could ever marry again. Even the thought caused her distress. She concluded that if she could and did, it would be a long, long time in the future and most likely never.

Evening arrived, she was to see her first customer at 7:00 p.m. Paul said he was a nice looking man, a very polite and polished man. Paul even said,

"Well Heidi, if you're going to do it, you might as well start with a nice man.

At 6:00 she found herself getting more and more nervous and anxious. She felt as if a cloud of guilt had settled over her. She was shaking like a leaf. Heidi, she said to herself, what are you doing? You don't want to have sex with a stranger. You are acting like an animal in heat. Juanita was right, if you have sex with just one man other than Rob, you will be committing adultery and if you do that Rob will never want to have anything to do with you again. What should I do?

She had an idea which she had never used before. She would tell the man she had started menstruating shortly before he arrived and it was her policy not to engage in intercourse while menstruating. She would tell him she had cramps in the afternoon and hoped it wasn't the beginning of her period, but unfortunately it was. She would be lying again, but she felt this time it would be a good lie. After she informed the man she would call Paul and ask him to find another girl for him. There always was a girl or two who was free.

Promptly at 7:00, the door bell rang. Heidi had never been so nervous. She answered the door and invited the man to come in. Paul was right, he was a handsome man and impeccably dressed. Heidi asked him to take a seat, she sat across from and begin to talk.

For some reason she felt conspicuous about her appearance. Her breasts were barely covered and her skirt was so short that if she didn't watch how she placed her legs her pubic area would be showing. Ordinarily that's what her customers liked.

"I'm so sorry," she said, "About two hours ago I started menstruating and my policy is not to have intercourse while menstruating."

"Oh that's too bad, you are such an attractive girl."

Heidi thought, he is a nice looking man, he has poise and appears to be dignified, but I just can't go through with it. I don't want to be and I can't be unfaithful to Rob. I don't want to have sex with any man except Rob. I'm so glad and relieved that I decided not to go ahead and have sex with the man, not to go ahead with my plans to be a call girl."

"I'm sorry that it didn't work out for us. Perhaps I can see you another time."

Heidi forced a smile and said,

"Sure, why not.

He was about to leave the house when he turned facing Heidi and said,

"May I ask you a question? First my name is Carl."

Heidi was surprised, thought a moment and then replied,

"You seem like a nice man Carl, what is it you would like to know?"

"Why are you doing this, why are you a prostitute?"

Although she was anxious to see him leave the question was an honest one. She replied,

"Right now, I really don't know why.

"Is it the money?"

"That's part of it, of course."

"Is it the sex? Are all call girls highly sexed?"

"At times it is, yes, but that wouldn't be enough to keep me in this business. The answer to the other part of your question is that not all call girls are highly sexed, however, the setting is so highly charged with sex that often the girl gets turned on herself."

"You have your policy which I respect. You're so petite, so slightly built. Why aren't you married to some nice young man so when you do have sex it will be an act of love and not just the discharge of visceral proddings. You are so pretty, surely there are many nice young men that would fall in love with you and make good husbands."

Tears came to Heidi's eyes.

"I'm sorry, did I say something I shouldn't have?"

"No Carl, "Heidi responded, "I just gave up a wonderful husband to come back here to work."

The man furrowed his brow,

"From the looks of it you are not too happy about your decision."

"It's the worst decision I ever made. That's why I can't give you an answer to your question, why am I doing this?"

"It tears my heart to see you cry. You remind me so much of my daughter. She is pretty and petite like you. I love her very much. She is in her first year of college, she is a good student and I have great hopes for her. I think it would kill me if she went into this kind of business."

"May I ask if your parent's know?"

"No, they don't know and being a prostitute has made me a perpetual liar. I think it would kill my dad if he knew his little girl was a prostitute."

"Can you go back to your husband by any chance?"

"I don't think so."

"You mean you're not sure?"

"Not really."

"Heidi, go back to Rob get out of this business where the only relationship you have with a man is sexual. You seem like such a sensitive young woman. You must have a lot of love to give a man. Heidi is such a pretty name for such a pretty girl."

Heidi sat in shocked amazement.

"Carl, how do you know my name and my husband's name?"

Carl just smiled.

"I don't want you to think I'm just another nameless customer."

Heidi started weeping.

"I'm sorry I made you cry."

"Please don't apologize Carl, I want to go back to Rob in the worst way, but I don't believe he will have me."

"It may take a little doing but Rob will take you back. You are suffering over the rupture in your marriage, so is Rob. Get out of this damn business Heidi and go back to your Rob, ask him to give you another chance. He will."

"I apologize for using such strong language. It hurts me to see you so unhappy."

"Please you don't have to apologize. What you just said is very mild compared to what I have to put up with."

"I'm sure it is."

"Thank you for being so honest in answering my questions. I'll pray for you and Rob Heidi. I'll pray that God will give the two of you another chance. He has already given you two"

"Wha, what do you mean that God has already given us two chances."

"He gave you a chance when Rob was shot. Rob could just as easily have died. He gave the two of you another chance when you almost froze to death. And Heidi, haven't you ever wondered how Rob could carry you so far when he was hurting and bleeding. You may not be aware of it and I don't think Rob is either, but he carried you a full mile."

"A mile. Rob thought it was just ¼ of a mile."

"No Heidi, a mile."

"How could you know that Carl?"

"And haven't you wondered why Rob didn't get an infection in his wound with the two of you being in such a filthy environment with animal droppings and who knows what else scattered around the cabin? Think Heidi, Think. And why do you have such a hard time believing, really believing Rob when he said God brought the two of you together? And Heidi, how do you account for Alex being in exactly the right place at the right time to prevent you from being killed. Was it all coincidental? What do you need to have happen before you start believing?"

Hardly able to contain herself Heidi sobbed,

"To have Rob back again Carl, to have Rob back again. And Carl, I have thought about Rob's survival and Alex's presence at the scene just at the right time and our surviving the storm. And yes, I prayed, prayed so hard that God would not take Rob from me when he was shot. I believed and prayed for a little while then I no longer gave any thought to God's hand in all this."

"I know that Heidi. Believe me you will have Rob back again."

"Carl, please tell me, how could you know about these events in our lives?"

"I know a lot of things Heidi. After Rob's shooting you went into that little chapel and you prayed, you prayed hard. It was a life and death struggle that Rob was in Heidi. If Rob had not found that cabin when he did, there is little doubt the two of you would have froze to death. God wants you and Rob back together again and I will intercede for you, but Heidi, you have to get back to God, start praying again. You have so much to be thankful for."

"Carl, look at my living room, no prayer could get out of this house."

"Take the pictures down Heidi, you don't have to leave them on the wall. And Heidi, go to your book case and retrieve the Bible Clay gave you."

"You know about that too Carl? Carl, you are an angel aren't you, my Guardian Angel?"

Carl smiled but did not respond.

"Get back to God Heidi and get back to Rob. You won't find happiness until you do both."

"I believe you Carl, I do not doubt what you say. I will get right with God and with Rob. And Carl, I want you to know that I've been faithful to Rob. I don't think he believes so, but I am not an adulteress."

"Carl."

"Yes Heidi."

"You didn't come to my house to have sex with me, did you?"

"What do you think Heidi?"

"And Carl, I lied to you, I didn't start menstruating earlier this afternoon. Please forgive me."

"Let's just say that this time it was a good lie. And Heidi, I forgive you."

"I'm ashamed and embarrassed that you found me and my house like this. Look at me so scantily dressed. I'm a fallen woman. Surely God doesn't care for a person such as I."

"Don't be ashamed and embarrassed Heidi, you can remedy all of this. So far as God forgiving a fallen woman, he loves to forgive when forgiveness is asked for."

"I must be going now Heidi, please don't forget what I told you."

Heidi stood, walked over to Carl, threw her arms around him and hugged him.

"How can I ever thank you Carl? You have given me new hope. For the first time in months life seems promising to me."

"Just do what I've asked you to do."

"Carl, I love you."

"And I love you too Heidi. Goodbye."

"Carl will I ever see you again?"

"You never know Heidi, you never know.

"Good bye my Guardian Angel."

"Oh Heidi," Carl said as he turned from the door, "I'm glad that you changed your mind about shooting Sally. That was a very bad idea you had. Vengeance is mine says the Lord"

Heidi smiled and said,

"As soon as I got home, I realized how stupid an idea it was. I sat at the table with my pistol before me just smiling. I said to myself, Heidi you could never shoot Sally nor anyone else. It wasn't a loss though Carl. When Rob and I are back together we will rejoin Cal's club and get back into competition shooting. I'm sure you know both of us enjoy the sport."

"It's a good sport Heidi."

Carl opened the door and in a moment was gone.

Heidi sat down. She was in a state of shock. Was all of this real, she asked herself? I couldn't have been dreaming. No, when I hugged Carl, he was a warm, breathing human being. Carl wouldn't lie to me. He told me he had a daughter in college. He certainly was not a spirit. I know it happened but I'm not going to try to figure it out. Carl said I have work to do, reconcile with Rob and get right with God. I'm going to get started right away.

Heidi picked up the phone and called Paul.

"Paul, did you notice anything different about Carl?"

"Only that he was not the usual kind of customer who comes looking for a girl. I sensed that there was something different about him. When paging through the book as soon as he saw your pictures he said,

"That's the girl, she's the one."

"He looked no further. It almost seemed he knew you."

"I think he did Paul"

"Oh come on Heidi, yes he was not our usual customer, but knew you?"

"Yes Paul, I believe he knew me. Paul, take my name off the roster, permanently this time. I'm through with prostituting myself. Never again will I be a call girl. I am going to get in touch with Rob and beg for his forgiveness. Carl has given me much hope that the two of us will reconcile. I love Rob, Paul and from what Carl said Rob also loves me.

"Is Carl the man's name?"

"Yes Paul.

"Awww, Heidi, I'm so glad to hear that you are getting out of the business for good. You never belonged in this lousy business in the first place. I did my very best to talk you out of it."

"When you first walked in the door, you were the sweetest looking girl I had ever seen. I said to myself, she must have the wrong building. You looked as if you were 16 or 17 years old. I was about to tell you that you weren't allowed inside the building."

"Paul, I love you for the many times you tried to talk me out of being a prostitute. I was just too stubborn, too bull headed to listen to you and I was hungry for money. I've told you before, but I'll say it again, you are my best friend. No matter what, I could always count on you."

"Thank you Heidi. Now let me tell you something personal. Do you Mind?"

"Of course not Paul."

"I fell in love with you the very first day you came through the agency door."

"Why didn't you say something Paul?"

"I wanted to in the worst way, but the fact you were going to be a call girl got in my way. I thought you weren't a very good person if you wanted to be a call girl.

When I took the pictures of you in the nude, the figure of you was seared into my mind. Don't dislike me for what I'm going to say, but I have wanted to have sex with you ever since. I even toyed with the idea of taking on the role of a customer just to do so."

"Paul, I would never dislike you. I know you would never give me reason to do so. You should have given me a call, as I said before the sex would have been on the house."

Paul chuckled.

"Now, of course it's too late for that. Many is the time I wanted to ask you for a date, but just couldn't bring myself to do so. How I regret that. I'm married now to a wonderful girl I love very much. We have one child, a little boy who is the apple of his father's eye."

"Heidi, I never stopped loving you. Do you think it's possible for a man to love two women at the same time?"

"Why not Paul, anything is possible. I'm sorry I broke your heart. I think you and I would have made a happy couple. There aren't many true friends like you in the world. The only other one I know is Rob."

"I'm so glad you are going back to Rob Heidi. I'm getting out of this lousy business. I don't know yet what I will do, but I do know I've had enough of this. I can't take it anymore, I can't see girls ruining their lives, I can't see them selling their bodies to men whose only interest in them is sexual. I have become ashamed of my part in it. I'm out of here Heidi."

Heidi, would you keep in touch with me.?"

"Of course I will Paul, you are my dearest and best friend. You have my phone number, give me yours and we will stay in touch, that's a promise."

"Thank you Heidi, and now go back to Rob."

"Paul, let me ask you something. How could Carl possibly know so much about Rob and I? Carl said Rob will take me back with open arms. I never mentioned Rob's name, but he knew it."

"I don't know Heidi, but it seems awfully strange, doesn't it?"

After Heidi hung up, she sat back and for the first time in months, she felt good about herself.

Chapter Twenty One

Heidi formulated a plan. First she would make an appointment to talk to Clay. Next she would call Lorraine and then depending on what Lorraine has to say, she would call Rob. She had to move fast, too much time had already passed. She would call Clay first thing in the morning. By noon she should be able to call Lorraine and if she's lucky, she could be talking with Rob by mid afternoon. Her plan excited her, excited her enough that again there was no sleep that night. It had been just four weeks since she and Rob broke up.

Maybe that's too soon she thought, however Rob told her that absence instead of making the heart grow fonder makes it grow weaker. She had to act now.

Heidi was up early. She showered, picked out a chic outfit, dressed and fixed breakfast. As she ate and drank coffee, she found herself getting more and more excited. She looked across the table where Rob sat and said to herself. Maybe I'll be extra lucky and soon Rob will be sitting across from me again.

It seemed everyone she came into contact with encouraged her to make an effort to reconcile with Rob. Was it all coincidental? Perhaps yes since those who encouraged her had her best interests at heart.

The one who puzzled her most was Carl. He came out of nowhere, was so very polite and as a complete stranger encouraged her to do whatever she could to get reunited with Rob. He knew her name and

Rob's too. He knew that Rob had been shot and that later they about froze. He told her that Rob was waiting for her, that they would rebuild their marriage. He also said that contrary to what Rob thought, he carried her for a full mile and not just ¼ of a mile. How could he know these small details? He was so sympathetic, even interested in parts of her life that didn't involve Rob. She knew that Carl didn't come to her to have sex. That had to be the last thing on his mind. She recalled that Rob once told her something that his mother passed on to him.

"Let's see, she said out loud, "It had something to do with the visit of angels. It went something like treat strangers with kindness and respect for you never know when you might be visited by an Angel"

Again she had the feeling that Carl was her guardian Angel. Maybe God hasn't abandoned me after all. The thought increased her excitement. And Carl was so determined that she get right with God. Come on Heidi, you are really grasping at straws. Given the kind of person I am, I would be the last person to be visited by an Angel.

She gave a big sigh and said, "anyway, it was a good thought. Now I must find the card Clay gave me, It had both his office and home phone numbers imprinted on it. I know I slipped it into my billfold.

She retrieved her purse, took out her billfold and started thumbing through all of the cards she carried therein. She laid them all on the table, but Clay's card was not among them. She started to panic.

"Clay's card has to be here," she said out loud.

Again she thumbed through the cards and then Clay's card was in her hand.

"Thank God," she continued, "What would I have done if I wouldn't have found the card."

Then she wondered, I certainly seem to be religious this morning. First thinking Carl might be an Angel who came to visit me and now I thanked God. It wouldn't hurt to offer up a prayer that all will turn out well for Rob and I. I told Alex that I no longer knew how to pray. When I was discussing the difficulty I had with praying for Rob, he said Heidi, you talk to God just like you would to a friend. Why? Because he is your friend.

"And God, I did pray after Rob was shot. I prayed well over an hour."

Heidi thought for a moment trying to come up with something that might come to God's attention. She prayed out loud,

"God, this is Heidi Sloan, I keep telling people you don't know me since I have turned my back on you. I even hid my Bible because I didn't want my clients to think I was some kind of religious freak. I'm sorry God that was awful of me. If I did catch your attention, please, I beg of you to make it possible that Rob and I will be reconciled to each other. I know that I'm not worthy of it. Rob once said that you do not with draw from us, rather we with draw from you and that's so true of me. I have with drawn from you God, but I'm trying to get reacquainted. Please God please. I'm going to get back to reading my Bible and that I will do regardless of how things turn out today. If You are close to me, please hear my prayer. And God, I am not trying to butter you up. This has been playing on my mind ever since Rob and I separated."

With her eyes still closed, she sensed that her prayer would be answered. This increased her level of excitement

Promptly at 8:00 she punched in Clay's office number. In a moment she heard' Clay's voice. She was so relieved.

"Reverend Cunningham, I'm so glad I caught you in your office. This is Heidi Sloan. I'm sure you don't remember me, but I haven't forgotten you. About two years ago Rob, my husband, was shot saving my life. It appeared he would not recover. You came into the little chapel while I was trying my best to pray. You were such a help to me. I had given up hope and you restored that hope."

"Of course I remember Mrs. Sloan."

"Please call me Heidi Reverend."

"I will if you call me Clay."

"Would it be possible for you to visit with me either this morning or early afternoon?"

"Let me check my schedule."

There was a moment of silence, then Clay was back on the phone.

"I'm free at 12:30. Would that be too late?"

"That would be wonderful. I'll be knocking at your office door at 12:30."

Heidi was elated that Clay would meet with her. Next it was time to call Lorraine. She punched in Rob's office number. In a moment she heard Lorraine's familiar and friendly voice.

"Hello, Lorraine?"

There was a long moment of silence. Heidi said to herself, I imagine she's not only surprised to hear my voice, but shocked as well.

"Lorraine."

"Heidi is that you."

"Yes Lorraine, believe it or not, it's me."

"You don't sound very chipper."

"Maybe not, but I'm more chipper than when I got up this morning."

"I'm sorry Heidi, I shouldn't have said that."

"And why not? I know there are a lot of things you could say to me that would be harsh and so fitting, much harsher than what chipper means. I'm sure Rob has told you about my insane behavior and decision."

"Well if you want to call it insane, yes he has."

"Not so long ago we were good friends. Now, because of all the bad things I have done, especially the pain inflicted on Rob, I suppose you no longer consider me a friend, how could you?"

"Heidi, I am not fickle."

"I'm so glad to hear that Lorraine, it's good to know not every one is as fickle as I am," replied Heidi.

"Heidi, I don't know what got into you, but you have hurt Rob deeply."

There was silence then Lorraine heard Heidi weeping.

"I know Lorraine, I know. I don't know what got into me. I believe I temporarily lost my mind, but I found it Lorraine and I found it in time."

"What do you mean Heidi?"

"I am not a call girl, I came to my senses just in the nick of time. I have not been unfaithful to Rob. Please don't tell Rob, I want to be the one to do so."

"Of course Heidi."

"Lorraine, I called to see if Rob has taken up with another woman."

"Heidi, it's been only a month since Rob moved out of your house. Although you and he lived together for four months before you separated, you did not do so as husband and wife, not from what Rob has told me. Do you think that as badly hurt as Rob is, that he would take up with another woman in such a short time? You know better than to ask such a question."

"It was stupid of me Lorraine, but you know a man needs a woman to maintain his sense of man hood. Rob has a very strong libido and I really wouldn't have been surprised had you said he was seeing another woman."

"That sounds rather ridiculous coming from a woman who was about to take up with many men other than her husband."

There was silence. Lorraine let it ride. Finally she asked,

"Are you still there Heidi?"

"I'm still here Lorraine. I'm letting what you said sink in. Here I'm worrying about Rob taking up with a woman while, as you said, I was indeed about ready to commence having sex with many, many men. It shows you just how confused I am. Had he taken up with another woman, I wouldn't have blamed him."

"Heidi, perhaps I shouldn't be the one telling you this, but you have to know that Rob still loves you, loves you very much in spite of all the pain you inflicted on him."

Lorraine could hear Heidi sobbing.

"What have I done Lorraine, what have I done?"

"I'll be honest with you Heidi, you have hurt very deeply the most kind and compassionate man I know and from what Rob told me, he did nothing to deserve it. Yes Heidi, I am Rob's confidant, there isn't much he hasn't told me, including intimacies that few men would share with another woman."

"His colleagues can sympathize with him, but it takes a woman to understand what goes on in his heart. It has been very difficult for him to carry on his practice. A number of times I had to encourage him to stay with it, not to give up what it took several years for him to build."

Lorraine was silent for a few moments, then she continued.

"You of all people should know Rob well enough to understand that when he gave his heart to you, he gave it to you for keeps. What I've said has been much more than a yes or no to your question. So let me repeat, so far as I know, up to this time Rob has shown no interest in women, but that isn't to say that women don't continue to show interest in Rob. I know as well as you that he has a strong libido, in fact we discussed that very thing a short time ago, not only his libido, but mine as well"

"Have you and Rob been intimate with each other?"

"Heidi, where are you coming from this morning? Of course I have wanted to and want to be intimate with Rob. Let me tell you, he needs to be intimate with a woman, however I'm married and so is Rob or at least he thinks he's still married."

"He is very much married Lorraine I did not begin divorce proceedings. In fact I don't believe I ever seriously intended to do so."

"I just don't understand you Heidi, how could you so coldly and nonchalantly give up such a man.?"

"I don't understand myself either Lorraine, but one thing I do know, I am going to try to talk to Rob. I'm going to plead with him to come over so we can talk. I'm going to plead with him to give me another chance. I'm not very hopeful, but I must try. I know it sounds hollow Lorraine, I love Rob, I believe I now love him more than ever. It causes me profound agony to think of what I gave up because of a stupid, stupid idea. I have to try Lorraine."

"Well Heidi, it appears that both of you still love each other. I would say that that in itself is in your favor, but I can't say anymore than that. His hurt is very deep. You said some awful things to him. When are you going to call him?"

"Hopefully before mid-afternoon, before he leaves his office. Does he still keep the same hours?"

"Yes he does Heidi."

"Before I call Rob I'm going to see Clay. I have an appointment with him at 12:30. Lorraine, do you remember Clay?"

"I can't say I do."

"Clay is the chaplain who was such a help and comfort to me when Rob lay dying in the hospital,"

Heidi began weeping again.

"From what Rob told me, you treated that sacrifice of his very lightly, as if it no longer meant anything to you."

"Oh God Lorraine, I did, I did. How could I? Lorraine, he took that bullet that was intended for me. He was willing to die for me and look what I've done to him. How can I ever forgive myself Lorraine?"

"I don't know if you will ever be able to. But yes, now I do remember Clay. I remember him as a very sincere chaplain and a wonderful man. It might do you good to visit with him."

"Oh Lord, I hope so. I'm going to hang up now Lorraine, please don't tell Rob I called. I know I can count on you to keep our conversation confidential."

"I won't breathe a word to Rob, Heidi."

"Thank you Lorraine, thank you so very much. You should be getting my call before mid afternoon."

"I'll be waiting for it Heidi."

Promptly at 12:30 Heidi knocked on Clay's door. In a moment it opened. Heidi thought, what a good looking man he is and he is so well built.

"Hello Heidi, It's so good to see you again. Did you say it's been two years since Rob was shot?"

"Yes Clay, it's been two years."

"Please come in and take that chair in front of my desk."

Clay helped seat Heidi and then walked around the desk to his chair.

"Clay, I don't know where to start, but let me say it's so good to see you again. You will never know how much of a help you were to me. Sitting in front of you I feel as if I'm back in familiar territory once again."

"I'm afraid I don't understand you Heidi."

"I think you will in a few minutes Clay. This is going to sound to you as if our meeting is a confessional and maybe it is, but my request will be more specific. I might as well start at the beginning.

"When I was 18 years old, I enrolled in the University of Washington. I did very well with my course work, but I was always broke and getting deeper and deeper into debt. I had a friend, Nancy, who always had money, lots of money. I asked her if she had wealthy parents. She didn't, she said she had become a call girl. My sexual morals were about non-existent. Nancy told me about the agency she worked for and that they were always looking for attractive young women between the ages of 18 and 26. I had been told a number of times that I am attractive and please understand me my intention is not to be bragging about my looks."

"Heidi, you can add my name to those who say you are attractive. In fact to my eyes you are very attractive."

"Thank you Clay. I got to thinking that maybe that's what I should do. I was no longer a virgin and the thought of having sex with many different men didn't really bother me. The very next day I went to the agency in Tacoma. When I walked in a very nice looking young man was sitting behind the desk. He stood up, extended his hand and said, My name is Paul. I told him my name was Heidi. Then he said I assume you know what kind of business we're in? We hire young women to be call girls. I told him that's why I was there, I was interested in becoming a call girl. I told him I was almost 20 so I was in the age group of young women the agency was looking for. Really, he said, you look so young and are so pretty. He rather surprised me when he said, You don't want to get into this business Heidi, believe me. I said I was badly in need of money."

"We chatted a bit about the business then he said, Heidi, please go back to Seattle and give yourself time to think about the step you want to take. That sounded reasonable so that is what I did."

"My financial situation only got worse. I had given considerable thought to what it would mean to be a call girl. I knew I would have to do a lot of lying to my parents and to others however, I was determined to be a call girl."

"To make a long story short, although Paul again appealed to me to drop the idea I told him I had made up my mind. Since call girls work mainly in the evenings and nights I would be able to continue my education at the University during the day time hours. I was majoring in Business Administration. When I mentioned that to Paul he said, why don't you finish your education first then consider being a call girl. I remember I told him it was primarily because I didn't have money to continue my education that I wanted to be a call girl. Although Paul again appealed to me to drop the idea of becoming a call, I told him I had made up my mind."

"He gave up trying to discourage me and then said, Alright Heidi, if that's what you want to do, so be it. Paul then took a number of pictures of me in the nude, pictures of which I was not proud, but I figured that soon many men would see me without my clothes on so what's the big deal. I became an expensive call girl."

"At first I operated out of motel rooms or I met the customer at his home or wherever he wanted us to meet. And it was exciting. I have strong sexual needs and I did enjoy sex with so many different guys, mostly nice, polite, wealthy guys. You will find this hard to believe, but in a relatively short time I was able to put down a large payment on my own house after which I mostly operated out of it."

"I guess I built up a pretty good reputation for I was never wanting for customers. After three years I was burned out and asked for a couple of months off. That was OK with the agency since I was making a lot of money for them."

"It was during my time off that I met Rob. We literally bumped in to each other in a department store in one of the malls. He asked me to have coffee with him and I accepted. He was such a nice looking man, polite and dressed neat as a pin. He was a couple of years older than I. I even amused myself thinking I might proposition him and make an extra couple of hundred dollars for myself. I wasn't serious Clay."

"We visited for two hours. Rob asked me for a date and I accepted. First our dates were weekly and then we were together most of the time. We fell in love Clay, very much in love. I had not been in love before and to be loved like Rob loved me was wonderful. As you know, Rob is a sex and marital therapist. When he asked me what I did, I gave him some cock and bull story of a made up job. He never questioned me."

"I knew that sooner or later I was going to have to tell Rob I was a call girl. Oh how I didn't want to for I knew it would destroy our relationship and my happiness would be over."

"On a Saturday morning we drove to a favorite spot of ours overlooking Mt. Rainier. I told him I had not been honest with him and that I was a call girl. At first he didn't believe me, but I insisted and then when I broke into tears, he knew I wasn't playing games with him."

"Poor Rob, he was shocked. He wanted to be alone and walked down one of the trails for a distance. It was about 45 minutes later I heard him calling me. He came running up to the picnic bench on which I was sitting. He took me in his arms and told me he loved me and was not letting me go. He had many questions, of course, but said we would get to them later."

"Clay, you may find this hard to believe here I was a call girl used to having sex at least three times a week and Rob and I had not yet engaged in intercourse. It was tough on me and I know it was tough on Rob. When we talked about it he just said that he was not yet ready for sex."

"Rob is a man of deep religious convictions. I didn't nor would I have pushed the issue. I just bit my lower lip and bore with my sexual frustration. I knew that sooner or later Rob would be ready. We couldn't be as close as we were and as in love as we were without wanting to experience each other physically."

"I like that Heidi, the idea that you would want to experience each other physically. Is that original with you?"

"No Clay, it is or was original with Rob.

"He gave me a beautiful ring and a short time later we were married. We had 2-1/2 almost three years of wonderful marital bliss. I had never been so happy in my life. I was glad to give up my job as a call girl and so thankful I had a man who loved me in spite of my past. When he was shot that almost killed me. He was ready to give up his life to save mine."

"In the fall of that year, we went hunting grouse and got caught in a terrible blizzard. We headed back to the pickup, but after a time I just couldn't go anymore and collapsed in the snow. Rob had not yet completely healed, yet he picked me up and carried me to a hunter's cabin we had seen earlier. Then he stripped off his jacket and gave that to me in the hopes I would be just a bit warmer. We weren't afraid, we weren't scared, actually we were happy that if we had to die we would die together"

" Then a little more than three months, maybe it was four months ago I met my personal Satan in the form of a call girl who was, and I stress was my friend when I was seeing customers. She was no friend I assure you. She and three other girls I used to hang out with talked me into going back into the call girl business. It was my decision though I can't blame them for that."

"During two of the three months I disengaged from Rob, I was awful to him. I wouldn't communicate with him, I wouldn't let him kiss or hold me, and I rejected his every request to have sex. Clay, Rob is my husband and I did those awful things to him."

"Rob was greatly disturbed and couldn't understand why I had turned on him. Clay, I even made light of the fact that he saved my life by taking that bullet intended for me. I made light of our near death by freezing."

Heidi broke down weeping. When she regained her composure she went on.

"Then I told him I was going to be a call girl again and our marriage was over. Clay, I kicked him out of our house, my own husband, I kicked him out of our house. Oh Clay, I destroyed Rob."

"I doubt that Heidi, Rob is a strong and resilient man."

"I hope you're right Clay. Rob did absolutely nothing to deserve the treatment I handed out to him. I believed I no longer loved him."

"Rob moved out and I got set up to entertain my first customer, only I never did. I got awfully close, but at the last moment, largely as the result of a strange encounter with a man I thought was a customer, I came to my senses. I was overwhelmed by the guilt. It was like a suffocating weight had settled on me. I called my friend Paul at the agency and told him to take my name off the roster, permanently. There was no way I was ever going to be a call girl again. Paul was so happy to do so. Over the years we have become good friends. He has always had my best interests at heart, but I ignored them, however, he never gave up."

"The full impact of what I had done to Rob, and yes to myself as well hit me, and hit me hard. I love Rob, I love him very much. I fully realized I had thrown away the three most happy, wonderful years of marriage, and of my life. In doing so, I destroyed or nearly so, the most wonderful man I have ever known. Clay, I destroyed my husband".

Heidi broke into uncontrollable sobs. Clay let her cry. After she stopped crying she said,

"I'm going to try to get together with Rob so we can talk about what I have done. I'm going to plead with him, beg him to give me another chance, to give our marriage another chance. I love him Clay and I want him back so very bad. Lorraine, his secretary, told me Rob still loves me and that alone gives me a glimmer of hope."

"The reason I'm here Clay is to ask you if you would pray for Rob and I. I can no longer pray, I feel I am not worthy of prayer. I try, but I don't think I'm getting through to God, I abandoned God and I'm sure God has abandoned me. Now I believe my feeble attempts at praying came from the feelings of guilt I had."

"Clay, I did something awful. I kept that beautiful Bible you gave me on the lamp stand. When I was getting ready for customers I took it and hid it behind a row of books on my book shelves. I didn't want my customers to see it and think I had been some kind of religious freak."

"Please pray that God will forgive me .I have so much to be forgiven of. I no longer know how to pray. I try Clay I try. Pray that Rob and I will have a reconciliation. Please pray that Rob will meet with me, that I haven't hurt him so badly that he hates me. Please pray that God may grant me, grant us a second chance. Or as Carl reminded me a fourth chance."

"Who is Carl?"

"The man I mentioned earlier, the man who came to me as a customer, but certainly was not a customer. I call him my Guardian Angel. I'll have to tell you about him later, however that will take considerable time and I want to see Rob this afternoon if he will see me. I'm sure you are curious about that third chance. Carl said God gave us a second chance after Rob was shot. He reminded me that Rob could just as easily have died. The third chance God gave us was when we got caught in that terrible blizzard. How true, it was only by the grace of God that we didn't freeze to death."

"I am very curious about this Carl, Heidi."

"Clay I took my marriage vows before God, Rob, a minister and a few friends and though it was very close, frighteningly close, I did not violate those vows. I remained true to Rob and to my marriage vows. I would appreciate so much if you would pray for us."

Clay was quiet for a long minute and then said,

"That is quite a story Heidi, quite a story indeed. Let me ask you why don't you ask God to forgive you and to give you and Rob another chance?"

"As I said Clay, I can't pray, I try, but I can't get in touch with God. He is too far away from me."

"He seems far away from you Heidi, because you have moved far away from him. He hasn't moved far away from you. I am a man of God I know what I am talking about."

"That is precisely what Rob told me"

"Of course I will pray for you and Rob and I will plead with God to give both of you, as you say, a fourth chance. You seem to be very repentant of what you have done only you have to convey that repentance to God. That I can't do for you. When you do, I promise God will forgive you."

"When are you going to call Rob?"

"This afternoon, I feel that I have to move fast. Too much time has passed already."

"Heidi, may I remind you that we went through this very issue about prayer when Rob lay struggling for his life in the hospital. You made some pretty big promises then."

"Clay among other things that characterize me, I'm the world's greatest liar."

"Heidi, you know what you have to do, I don't have to tell you again."

"I know Clay and I will keep trying."

"And remember I am always as close as your telephone."

Heidi stood up and extended her hand to Clay.

"Thank you Clay, thank you for listening to a fallen woman."

"You know Heidi it's interesting you called yourself a fallen woman. Jesus had a special infinity for fallen women. Yes, even a prostitute and adulteress women."

"Clay, have you any idea how many times I have committed adultery? Most of the men I serviced are married. I have committed adultery many, many times, literally hundreds of times. Rob and I did some figuring and we concluded that in my three active years as a prostitute I had sex with at least 226 men. Now tell me that God will forgive a woman who has committed adultery that many times?"

"Whew," Exclaimed Clay, I must say that is a lot of adultery. Heidi, sit down for just a few minutes. I want to tell you a story. It comes out of the Bible, in the New Testament. A woman was caught in an act of adultery. Under Jewish law she was to be put to death by stoning. Jesus had gotten on his knees and was near the temple in Jerusalem when several men dragged this helpless and very frightened woman to Him. They either stood her before Jesus or threw her at his feet."

"The men reminded Jesus about Jewish law and adulteress women. They said to him, you know the law, what do you say? Jesus was using his finger to write something in the dirt. I don't believe anyone knows what he was writing. The men kept pestering Jesus, Rabbi, this woman was caught in an adulteress act, she is to be stoned to death. The men kept at it until Jesus had enough. He turned to them and said, Alright stone her to death, but let the one among you who is without sin throw the first stone. One by one the men dropped their stones and drifted away."

"After a short time and I like to think her accusers threw her at the feet of Jesus, he most certainly took her by the hand and helped her to her feet. We can also assume that he cut the rope used to drag her to Him. Jesus said to the woman, Woman, where are your accusers? I don't know Lord, they all left. Then Jesus said, Woman, neither do I condemn you, go and sin no more. I believe we can assume that what he had in mind was she should never again commit adultery. It would have been impossible for her to live out her life without committing sin of one kind or another."

Heidi said,

"Clay, what a wonderful story." Then she broke down sobbing. After she quit she said,

"Then there is hope for me too."

"Of course there is Heidi."

"But I have committed adultery so many, many times. God knows that. Surely there is a difference in God's eyes between a woman who commits adultery once and one who has committed adultery many times."

"Heidi, God does not place our sins on a scale and then judge us by the weight of them. Sin is sin regardless if it is committed once or hundreds of times. And all will be forgiven if we confess our sins and ask God's forgiveness. That shouldn't be hard for you to do Heidi. You just told me about these events in your life can't you just as easily tell God about them?"

Heidi was quiet for a time and then said again,

"What a wonderful story Clay. One can only imagine the relief the woman experienced when her accusers dropped their stones and walked away and when Jesus told her He did not condemn her."

"That's right Heidi. And the example I gave you out of the new Testament is not the only time Jesus forgave an adulteress or more specifically a prostitute."

Again Heidi was silent then she said,

"Clay, I must get back to God."

"Yes Heidi, you must. The sin of adultery cannot be forgiven unless the adulterer or adulteress asks God for forgiveness."

Heidi again stood and offered her hand to Clay.

"I wouldn't have missed this talk with you for anything. I want to thank you again so very much. And again please pray for Rob and myself."

"You know I will Heidi. I'll get started on it right away. And Heidi, please keep me informed. I want to know how all of this turns out."

"I will Clay, good or bad I'll keep you informed."

Heidi turned and started for the door then stopped. She turned again and faced Clay.

"Clay, when I first came into your office, I said that what I had to say would sound like it was a confessional. You know, I do believe that is what it turned out to be and much more. I feel as if a very heavy burden has been lifted from my shoulders. I now have faith that when Rob and I meet, we will end up in each other's arms and will began the process of rebuilding our marriage."

"I will pray for that to happen Heidi. Good bye."

"Good bye Clay."

Chapter Twenty Two

A s soon as she got back to her car Heidi called Lorraine's number. Lorraine answered.

"Lorraine, this is Heidi, again, please don't say anything. My visit with Clay went well. Everyone is so encouraging. Its 2:00 p.m. so Rob should be in his office. If he's not tied up with a client, would you please tell him I'm on the phone and would very much like to talk to him."

"He's in his office Heidi and his last client for the day just left. This is a good time for you to be calling him. Hold on a minute and I'll tell him you're on the phone and would like to talk to him."

Lorraine walked into Rob's office,

"Rob, Heidi's on the phone and would like to talk to you."

"Heidi, on the phone?

"Yes."

"Lorraine, you're not playing games with me, are you?"

"What do you think?"

"What do I say? I told her I never wanted to talk to her again."

"You talk to her Rob and above all don't blow your top. Calm down and listen to what she has to say.

"Alright Lorraine I won't blow my top," replied Rob with a smile on his face.

Rob picked up the phone.

"Hello Heidi."

"Hello Rob, do you have a few minutes for me?"

"Sure Heidi, what is it?"

"Rob, I couldn't go through with it. I was wrong about myself. I am no longer 'that person.' Rob, I didn't break my marriage vows to you. I'll admit I came awfully close to it, but I remained faithful to you, I did not commit adultery against you."

The last she spoke very slowly.

"Rob, I know you won't believe me, but I never did fall out of love with you. All the while I was getting ready to be a call girl again, I loved you. I just put a chill on my love."

"You sure are right about that, Heidi."

"The closer I got to seeing my first customer the more I realized I loved you very much. I'm going to be brazen Rob, can we get together? Is there any chance we can get back together? I have been humbled Rob. I am not proud. I made an awful mistake. You were right, I destroyed all that I loved and cherished. I destroyed the four most happy years of my life. Please Rob, can we?"

"Sure we can get together Heidi, but I don't know about us getting back together to rebuild our marriage as husband and wife again. Right now I don't think there is much of a chance of that happening."

Heidi was silent for a moment and then said slowly,

"I understand Rob, could you come over this evening so we can at least talk?"

"Heidi, the last thing I said to you was that I never wanted to see you or talk to you again."

"I, I know Rob, but Please, I beg of you, can't we at least talk?"

"Heidi, I realized shortly after I uttered those words that I didn't mean them. Sure we can get together to talk, how would 7:00 be?"

"I'll be waiting for you Rob. I want you to know I just finished a long visit with Clay. Once again he has been a great source of encouragement. He is praying for us Rob."

Rob sat back in his chair and folded his hands across his chest. It was so good to hear Heidi's voice, especially since there was no sarcasm in it as he last remembered. Can we get back together again as husband and wife? He hadn't thought that would ever be a possibility. In fact, he was sure Heidi had begun divorce proceedings.

Rob walked to the outer office and said to Lorraine,

"Heidi wants us to get together this evening to talk. She wanted to know if I thought we could ever be husband and wife again. She couldn't go through with being a call girl again."

"Rob, I'm so glad to hear that. I never did think Heidi was a bad girl. Someone got to her in a weak moment, of that I'm convinced. Please don't be too hasty and don't tell her there is no chance of a reconciliation. After the two of you broke off your relationship, you told me when you were in tears that you still loved her. You still love her now, don't you?"

"More than I can tell you Lorraine. You are a perceptive woman, how did you know?"

"I'm a woman Rob and I know a man's heart. I have caught you a number of times in deep thought. I just knew you were thinking about Heidi."

"Lorraine, you and Heidi are good friends. Aren't you?"

"Yes Rob we are, I just can't write Heidi off as a friend. There is more to this than meets the eye."

"So you think I should give Heidi another chance?"

"Yes Rob, and I also think you should give yourself another chance no matter how deep the hurt."

Rob nodded his head and gave a deep sigh.

"I'll see you in the morning Lorraine."

"Rob, just a minute."

Lorraine reached for a small book in the top drawer of her desk. She thumbed through it until she found what she was looking for and then began to read,

"Love is patient, love is kind, it does not envy, it does not boast, it is not proud, it is not rude, it is not self seeking, it is not easily angered."

She stopped, looked up at Rob and continued,

"It keeps no record of wrongs, love is not evil, but rejoices with the truth. It always protects, always trusts, always hopes and always perseveres."

Lorraine looked at Rob, there were tears in his eyes.

"First Corinthians 13, the love chapter."

"Yes Rob, and Rob something you repeat often, Forgive us our trespasses as we forgive those who have trespassed against us. There's one more thing Rob and please don't think I'm unfairly piling it on you, but how many times have you encouraged your clients to give one another a second chance?"

Again Rob nodded.

"Many times Lorraine. It's time to take my own advice, isn't it."

"Yes Rob, it is."

Rob cocked his head, narrowed his eyes and smiling said,

"Lorraine, you and Heidi haven't been conspiring against me, have you?

"Of course we have Rob," Lorraine answered with a smile.

"Thank you Lorraine, thank you so very much, I'll see you in the morning."

"Maybe not Rob."

"Lorraine I have a full schedule for tomorrow, I can't very well cancel at this late hour. Heidi will understand"

Rob went to his apartment, closed the drapes and sat on the couch. For the rest of the afternoon his mind was occupied with the 4 years he and Heidi had together. He couldn't think of a single blemish on their marriage. Sure they had problems, all couples do, but it was like they dealt with them in each others arms.

Several memories brought tears to his eyes. Heidi was crying when he had to be by himself after she told him she was a call girl. To tell him took courage on her part. She was sure she would lose him. For a very short time he wasn't sure what he would do. Other than for the past few months she had been a loving and faithful wife, and the over riding factor was that he still loved her very much. Yes, they would give their marriage another try.

Rob had put a few CDs on his player. He wasn't paying much attention to the music. One of the discs was from the sound track of an Island in the Pacific. Suddenly he sat up and listened. Keith Betram was singing;

"Once you have found her never let her go, once you have found her never let her go."

It just couldn't be coincidental, he said to himself. Now I have my answer for sure.

Promptly at 7:00 Rob rang the door bell. In a moment it opened and Heidi was standing before him. She was wearing a rather skimpy outfit knowing that he liked to see her in it and one in which she dressed often. Though her face looked strained and she seemed nervous, she was beautiful, she was his wife. He thought to himself, though she had wounded him deeply, how he loved that woman. He wanted to reach out and take her into his arms. He wanted to feel her soft lips against his. He wanted to hold her and whisper into her ear how much he loved her.

"Hello Heidi."

"Hello Rob, thank you so much for coming. Please come in."

She was inviting him to come into what was for three years also his house. He was going to say something, but thought better of it. Love is kind.

"There is no reason we can't talk Heidi, regardless of what has gone before us."

"Rob, I've made a pot of coffee. Can we go into the kitchen, sit at the table and drink together like we used to?"

Rob thought, oh how that cuts into my heart.

"Sure we can Heidi."

Heidi led the way. Rob took his familiar place at the table. She brought him a cup of coffee just as she always did when they sat down for breakfast. She poured herself a cup and took her familiar place across from Rob.

"Rob, I have much to say. Please listen to me, please let me finish before you respond."

"Alright Heidi, I won't interrupt you."

"About four months ago I met Sally, a former friend and call girl. I met her at Phillips while shopping for a new outfit. I'm sure you don't remember, but I called you at your office and told you I was going shopping and would be late in getting home."

"I remember it very well Heidi."

"Well, from the very start she suggested I come back to the agency and be a call girl again. I told her she was out of her mind. I told her I had a loving husband and a happy marriage. I would never trade them for what I was and did before I met you."

For several weeks she called me every Monday during my lunch break with the same message. Your life is boring, your marriage is boring, your husband is boring and on and on. I told her repeatedly to stop calling me, that she wasn't going to get anywhere with her so called advice.

"When I was a call girl there were five of us who were close friends, Sally, Liz, Betty, Judy and myself. Soon Sally had the other girls calling me with the same message. Come back to where life is exciting and sex is good. I began to weaken and soon I was thinking seriously about becoming a call girl again. Then on a Saturday morning I met the four for breakfast. I can't remember what I told you so I could get away without causing suspicion, but it was a lie. Rob, I never lied to you again after I told you I was a call girl."

"Before that breakfast I had started disengaging from you and I knew that even though you were aware of it, you said nothing. There was no conversation, no kissing, no hugging, no holding and of course no sex. I was so smug and self satisfied with what I was doing. No Rob, I gave no thought to what this was doing to you."

"It was at that breakfast that I decided to become a call girl again. It was only a short while later we had that awful confrontation and I asked you to leave the house. No, that's not right, I kicked you out of the house."

Heidi started crying, while Rob remained silent.

"I redecorated the house so it would look more like a bordello, or to be more frank, so it would look more like a whore house. I also had the bathroom retiled. I bought obscene pictures and hung them on the living room walls. As you can see, I took them down. I also hung them on the bedroom walls. Those I left up so you could see how low I had stooped. I also bought a number of X rated DVDs for those customers who would need to get turned on before we had sex."

With a weak smile forming on her face she said,

"I guess I wasn't sexy enough to get them turned on."

"As I was putting the finishing touches on my preparations, I ran into Juanita or more correctly, she ran into me. Juanita, also a call girl, is a true blue friend. She did about every thing she could to discourage me from returning to the business. They were good arguments, but I just pushed them aside. I must admit however, after the talk with Juanita, I had some serious misgivings.

"She left me by saying I would regret my decision. She took a few steps, turned and said to me, Heidi, do you know what we are? I said yes, we are call girls. No Heidi, we are whores. Juanita, I said, how can you say such a thing? Only because it's true Heidi. One thing I remember from English literature in high school was a statement made by Shakespeare. He said that a rose is a rose, you can call it anything you want, but it still smells like rose. Think about that Heidi."

"Next I called Paul to tell him I was coming back to be a call girl again. Dear Paul he did everything he could to discourage me From coming back to the agency. He threw up some very good arguments telling me why, I shouldn't come back, but just as with Juanita, I ignored them. However, after talking to Juanita and Paul, I now had serious doubts and was getting confused."

"Rob, this will sound strange to you, but what came to mind was something you read one evening from one of Paul's Epistles when he said, I don' t understand myself, the things I don't want to do I do and the things I want to do, I do not. I said to myself, Heidi, that's you but just as with Juanita I ignored Paul's advice and arguments and insisted I was coming back. I was promised I could come back any time I wanted to."

"He begged me not to give you and our marriage up for the sordid life of a call girl. It was then I began to have compelling doubts."

"The next week was a real bad one for me. All I could think of was you and how happy we had been."

Again Heidi broke into tears.

"I'm sorry that this is taking me so long, but I can't stop crying. Rob, I want you to hear the entire story."

"I met Paul when I first contacted the agency. When I told him I had decided to become a call girl he tried his best to discourage me. You don't want to lead that kind of a life; it's darn hard on girls. Most don't last too long and those that do soon lose their looks and their figures and then no man wants them. Most have no skills and find themselves as street hookers. I told him that I didn't intend to be a call girl for very long, just until I got my degree."

"He looked me over and said, you're not a very big girl, some of the men are well endowed. I told him that wouldn't be a problem for me. I also told him Nancy said girls between 18 and 26 were wanted, I'm almost 20. He gave up then. Then pictures were taken of me in the nude, pictures I was not one bit proud of. And when we met, of course I called the agency and quit. I had a standing invitation to return."

"When I was ready to entertain my first customer, I called Paul and asked him to send one over. Again he tried to talk me out of it and again I just swept aside what he was telling me."

"It was arranged that I would have my first customer. That was last evening. He arrived at 7:00 and completely surprised me. He was the nicest man I ever met."

"I got out of it by telling him I had started menstruating that afternoon and it was my policy not to have sex while menstruating. He was very understanding. He took it real well and said he understood where I was coming from"

"He was about to leave when he asked me if I would visit with him for a few minutes. He has a daughter about my age who he loves very much. He asked me why I was in this lousy business? He said if his daughter was a call girl it would break his heart. Like Paul, and Juanita, he encouraged me to get out of it, find a young man who doesn't know my past, get married, have a family and lead the life that a beautiful girl like I should lead."

"Rob, what a nice man, what an understanding man. There was something about him that I just didn't understand. Someone else might have gotten angry with me, but what he had was good advice. I still wonder about him. He knew my name, he knew your name and he assured me that you and I would get back together. He knew that you had been shot and that we almost froze to death. He was much concerned about my spiritual life and told me to get back to God. He would answer my questions with a smile. Just before he left, I asked him if he was God sent. He answered me with a smile. He told me he loved me and God loved me and then he was gone."

"His presence was such an irony. He wasn't interested in having sex with me or any girl. It was after talking to him that I decided whatever the outcome for me would be, I was leaving the business for good. Rob, do you believe in angels? You once told me your mother gave you some very good advice. She said always treat strangers with dignity and respect since you never know when you might be entertaining an angel."

"Yes, mother repeated that often. I believe she based her statement on something that is recorded in the early chapters of Genesis."

"We'll have to study the Bible together, Rob. There is so much I have to learn. I may be way off base Rob, but I think Carl is an angel. Even if I'm wrong I like to think he is my personal angel."

"After he left I was overwhelmed by guilt. I called Paul and told him to take my name off the roster, for good this time, that I didn't want to have sex with any man but you. Paul was ecstatic, so thankful I came to my senses. He told me go back to Rob and rebuild that marriage."

"Paul is really a true blue friend Do you know that Paul was and still is in love with me? He told me so and even though he is happily married and has a son he still loves me. I asked him why he didn't pursue me if he loved me. His answer was that he convinced himself that he would be chasing after a whore. Now I regret that, he said. Then he asked me something interesting. Heidi, he asked, do you think it's possible for a man to love two women at the same time?"

"Poor Paul, I feel so sorry for him. I wanted you to know this Rob. I would not have had sex with any man regardless, but I wanted you to know that this nice gentleman's encouragement, along with Paul's and Juanita's, and the overwhelming feeling of guilt were responsible for me having my name taken off the roster, this time for good."

"Needless to say, I didn't have a very good night. I couldn't sleep and at times I felt I was going to lose my mind. Rob, I didn't have sex with that nice gentleman or with any other man. I didn't violate my marriage vows, I didn't commit adultery."

"I needed to see you so bad. After seeing Clay, I called you. I'm so glad you agreed to visit with me. Rob, please forgive me forever thinking about going back into the business. Forgive me for my stupidity. Forgive me for being so short sighted. Forgive me for saying such awful things to you. I don't know what happened to me Rob, I was like a woman possessed. What has bothered me the most is when I made light of you saving my life and of our near freezing to death. How could I ever do that? Rob forgive me for throwing you out of the house, well, kicking you out really. Forgive me for all the wrongs I did to you. I know it sounds hollow, but Rob I love you, I love you so very much. I thought I had stopped loving you, I was just kidding myself."

"Though I didn't act on it, it was right after you left the house that I realized I never stopped loving you. I actually was blind enough to believe everything would straighten itself out after I got back in the business that my feelings for you would fade. It was just the opposite. Rob, so far as sex is concerned, I am still a faithful wife."

"Rob, I've told you everything, I have held nothing back. Please Rob please, can we give our marriage another chance? Can't I be allowed to make one mistake? More than once you told me you counsel couples to be willing to give the spouse a second chance, another chance. Can't you grant the same to me, your wife?"

"Heidi, you've been talking to Lorraine, haven't you"

"Yes Rob I have, but you told me the same thing I want you back so bad, I want the happiness we once had to be ours again so bad. I guess that's it Rob. Thank you for being so patient and for not interrupting me."

Rob was deep in thought and not aware he had not answered Heidi. Well this is it, he said to himself, she has thrown my very words back in my face.

"Rob," Heidi said, "Have you nothing to say?"

"Heidi, you hurt me deeply and I didn't know why you were doing so until you told me you were going to be a call girl again. The things you said to me were just plain mean. Your intention was to hurt me deeply. All I wanted to do was love you. That is except for the past few months. I too thought my love for you had faded. You made fun of my pain and as you mentioned, the worst was when you so nonchalantly dismissed the fact that I almost died from that bullet wound. And you treated our near freezing to death like it was nothing at all. I was told not to strain myself in anyway and yet I picked you up and carried you to the cabin."

"Rob. Please excuse me for interrupting you. You thought you carried me ¼ of a mile. Carl told me that you carried me a full mile. How did you do it Rob? How could you do it?"

"You say I carried you for a full mile? That can't be. I didn't have the strength to do so. With every step I thought I would collapse."

"I know why you could do it, God gave you the strength. He didn't want us to die."

"You know Heidi, I believe you are right. A full mile, that seems impossible. Every step I took was an agony and I could feel that I was bleeding. I gave you my jacket in hopes if some one had to freeze it would be me."

Heidi was weeping.

"I know Rob, I said that to hurt you."

There was an uncomfortable silence. Rob was staring at the floor. Then with tears welling up in her eyes Heidi spoke

"Rob, Have you nothing to say. I've told you everything and you have told me how badly I hurt you. Does your silence mean you do not believe we can rebuild our marriage?"

Rob looked up into Heidi's tear streaked face and his heart melted.,

"No Heidi, no." Sobbing, Rob continued, "That's not what my silence means, I was trying to get control of my emotions."

He stood, walked behind Heidi's chair, put his hands on her shoulders and gently lifted her to her feet, then turned her to face him. He took out his handkerchief and wiped the tears away.

"No Heidi, that is not the message I mean to convey. It's been a rough time for both of us. You asked for forgiveness and I forgive you. We don't have to start anew. We will start where we left off. We were so happy, so much in love and that love never really faded for either of us. We know how to make our lives happy. That's where we will begin Heidi. We will never be able to completely forget the past four month, but in no way are they going to interfere with regaining the kind of marriage we had before all this happened. We're going to rebuild our marriage and it's going to be better than ever. God how I love you Heidi Girl, how I missed you!"

Heidi broke into deep sobs and buried her face on Rob's Chest.

"Oh Rob, you called me Heidi Girl. How I yearned to hear that from you."

Rob's sobbing continued. Through a strained voice he whispered into Heidi's ear,

"Why is it that we ended up hurting each other so bad when we love each other so much?"

Both were weeping, Heidi with her head on Rob's chest and Rob with his head resting on Heidi's. Heidi could feel Rob shaking, she looked up and saw Rob weeping.

"Go ahead and cry Sweetheart. I think you're more of a man for doing so. You must know that I feel there is nothing unmanly about shedding tears. My father is a bull of a man, strong as an ox and yet he is very emotional. When I left to come out here to college and just before I boarded the plane, he took me into his arms and wept bitterly. My Little Girl he said, I don't want you to leave, but I know I have to let you go. Please take care of yourself, never lie and remember the things your mother and I have taught you"

Heidi could not stop weeping.

"Please hold me tight Rob and never let me go."

Rob leaned back from Heidi, took his index finger and tilted her head upward ever so slightly then he lowered his head and kissed her.

"Oh how wonderful," he said "I have been deprived of this for four long months."

"I'm so sorry Rob, just hold me"

After a minute Heidi looked into Rob's face and said,

"Thank you Darling, thank you for giving us another chance."

"You don't have to thank me Sweetheart, it's something we both want."

"Rob, I thought I would never again hear the name Sweetheart cross your lips. It sounds so good. Let's go sit on the couch."

Heidi sat on Rob's lap and put her arms around his neck.

"Heidi, you are not the only one who needs forgiveness. What I said to you, what I called you still haunts me. I said terrible things to you, I cursed and swore at you, I called you a bitch and told you to shut up. Once when I stepped towards you, you put your arms up to your face fearing I was going to hit you. You were trembling with fear. Heidi, I couldn't have and I wouldn't have struck you. The memory of you holding your hands up to your face to protect it is etched in my memory. At that moment Heidi, I hated you, hated you with a passion, but I couldn't have hit you. I kept telling myself, she's my wife, she's my wife."

"Rob, do you still hate me just a little?"

"Hate you, I never really did hate you. I told myself I did, but that came from the rage I was in. Heidi, I love you, I never stopped loving you and that's what hurt so bad."

"And Heidi I used a word that I did not use once in our three years of marriage, I called you a whore, not once but several times. Then I said something vulgar, I said I hoped your customers would screw you to death. I didn't know what I was saying, I was livid with anger, but I can't give that as an excuse. I said and did all those things to you, my wife. You can't know how that has been eating away at me."

Rob lowered his head and Heidi could see he was weeping again.

"I'm so sorry Darling, I assume all the blame for your outbursts. I taunted you, I set out to make you angry so you would not want me back again, so you could leave without any sense of remorse. It was all my fault."

"No Heidi, that does not excuse my out of mind behavior. As I have forgiven you, I ask you to forgive me."

"Rob, I don't think you need to ask for my forgiveness, but if that's what you want, of course you are forgiven, you are forgiven, seven times seventy."

"Heidi, you remember that?"

"I do Rob, I surprised even myself.

"You are forgiven Darling again and again. Rob, the last few days what I learned from you about religion, about faith and all that, has been creeping into my conscious awareness. I just said I forgive you seventy times seven. I even called on God to please make it possible for us to get back together again. And Rob, Clay was such a help. He assured me that in spite of my sordid past, God loves me and will forgive me if I seek his forgiveness. He related a story to me from the New Testament. A story of Jesus' forgiveness of a woman just like I, an adulteress. I believed I was hopelessly lost. I'm not Rob, there is hope for me."

"Of course there is Heidi."

"It all started when Carl visited with me. There was something about him that I just can't explain. There are thousands of men out there looking for call girls every day, but it was Carl who came to me. Why? I couldn't get him and what he said during our visit out of my mind. That's when I remembered what your mother told you about angels."

"When she told me that I didn't pay much attention to it, but why couldn't it be so. You certainly experienced something during your visit with Carl."

"Right or wrong, it thrills me."

They were quiet, just content to be in each other's arms. Heidi spoke up,

"Rob Darling, I prided myself on being honest. I may have forgotten or ignored many of the things mom and dad taught me, but whenever I was tempted to lie I remembered dad's words, Never lie for if you do one lie will lead to another and eventually they will catch up with you. Rob, I have become a liar."

"After I met Sally, I lied to you many times. I lied when I told that nice man I was menstruating, I lied to who ever I told I no longer loved you, I lied when I said I was eager to be a call girl again. It got to the point that I no longer knew the truth from the lies. You must help me to get over lying. Dad would be heart broken if he knew how often his Little Girl lied. Not only heartbroken, but ashamed of me and disappointed in me. I have neglected them so much. I used to call regularly. I can't remember when I last called them. As you know mother wrote often and asked about my schooling, my job, etc. When I did answer I lied to them. Mother finally gave up on writing because there was no response from me. I am sure they must think the worst of me."

"That can and must be remedied. Once we get things squared away, you must invite them for a visit."

"But Rob, won't that only lead to more lies?"

"Yes Heidi, I imagine so but maybe lies would be less painful to your dad than the truth."

Heidi shed tears again.

"What if they found out their Little Girl was a call girl for three years, a prostitute?"

"We must see to it that your parents never find out about it."

"I know Rob we must. Dad is not a prude, but when I reached pubescence he told me to guard myself carefully. Sex, he said, is a wonderful thing to be experienced by a husband and wife who love each other. And look what I've done Rob. I lost my virginity before I was out of high school and now I have had sex with at least 226 men many of them married. Dad and mom's little girl is not a good girl."

"Heidi, you and I have forgiven each other, now you need to seek God's forgiveness for all you have been talking about."

"I know Rob, that's also what Clay said, but I have fallen by the wayside. I didn't want my customers to see my Bible, the one Clay gave me, so what did I do, I stuck it behind a row of books so no one would see it. I no longer know how to pray. Rob, I don't think there is much use for me to try, I am hopelessly lost."

"No you're not Heidi, but you do have a lot of brushing up to do. We can do that together."

"Will you help me Rob?"

"Of course I will."

"Rob Darling, please don't go back to your apartment for the night. I don't want you to leave me."

"I have no intention of returning to my apartment Sweetheart. This is where I belong and this is where I'm going to stay."

"Thank you Rob, thank you. That sounds so good. Rob Darling, the timing may not be right, but I want you to make love to me."

"And I want to make love to you Heidi, however, I think we might have a problem"

"What is that Rob?"

"I believe I'm impotent."

"No Rob, I did that to you too?"

"I'm afraid so Heidi. I want to have sex with you in the worst way, however, as you suggested, I don't think the timing is right. It has been a very emotional evening for both of us, I'm tired and I'm sure you are. Why don't we wait till morning before we give it a try?"

"You're right Rob, I am tired and if you are impotent, being emotionally spent and tired would not be a good time for us to commence having sex. Let's wait till morning. Oh gosh, I forgot, you will have to go to work."

"You're right I have clients scheduled till 3:00 P.M. At this late hour it wouldn't be fair to Lorraine if she had to postpone those appointments so we will have to wait till tomorrow evening. That might be better"

"We're back together now Sweetheart and that is where we will stay till death do us part."

"Yes Darling, till death do us part."

"You know Heidi, you have a very strong ally in Lorraine. In spite of everything that has happened she considers you her friend."

"She and I must go out for lunch real soon. And Rob, I must stop at James' real estate office to see if there is any chance of getting my job back. I guess I have my work cut out for me."

"Alright Rob, no sex tonight, however, we can still shower together. And Rob, I threw that stupid night gown in the trash. I'm sorry about that too."

Rob laughed,

"For two people who want to postpone sex until morning, showering together is the last thing we should be doing. Last one in the shower has to make breakfast."

Heidi was last, on purpose. The shower was highly arousing, however once in bed they were so tired that sleep was their primary drive. Dreamily Rob asked Heidi, "Heidi would you like to go on a second honeymoon?"

"I'd just love to Rob and I want to go just as soon as possible."

"How about next weekend?"

"Great Rob and I would like to go to Vista Point for our second honeymoon. I want to go to Vista Point and nowhere else."

"That wouldn't be much of a honeymoon destination, but if you want to go to Vista Point, that's where we're going. We can spend Saturday night in Packwood."

"Why Packwood?"

"Wouldn't you like to spend a little time at Paradise and Sunrise?"

"I'd love to. I'll have to dig my camera out of mothballs. I have woefully neglected it. You're going to have to teach me all over again"

"Tomorrow call Packwood and make motel reservations. You can pack a lunch for Saturday noon, then Saturday morning, early we can be on our way and spend the day at Vista point and if we feel like it, after Sunrise, we can go back to Vista Point and spend more time there."

"That sounds wonderful Rob, that's all I want."

They snuggled close together and soon both were sleeping.

Chapter Twenty Three

H eidi was the first to awaken. She went into the bathroom, washed, brushed her hair, put on a bit of make up and then went back to the bed. She bent over Rob and whispered into his ear,

"Wake up sleepy head, this is the day we start our second honeymoon."

"Rob groaned and asked

"So early,? What time is it anyway?"

"It's 6:00, and time for us to get going."

He looked up at Heidi and said,

"Good morning Sweetheart, bend over so I can give you a kiss."

Heidi threw herself over Rob, he held her and kissed her passionately.

"What say we make love first? I'm eager to know if I'm still impotent."

"Not here big boy, part of our honeymoon is to have sex at our favorite spot, Vistapoint."

"Ah ha woman, there is madness in your motive."

"Well if you want to call it that, yes there is madness in my motive. Now hurry it up a bit."

Rob quickly washed and shaved, grabbed the cooler containing their lunch and drinks and headed out the door to his Chrysler

"Not the Chrysler Rob, we're taking the Jaguar."

"We can take the Chrysler."

"Nope, the Jaguar. Don't argue, we could be on our way. Back it out of the garage and let's get going."

With Rob behind the wheel, they headed for Vista Point. Heidi sat as close to Rob as she could. Rob glanced at Heidi and said,

"Sweetheart, there are two things we need to talk about."

With alarm, Heidi asked,

"Oh Rob, it isn't something about our separation, is it?"

"No Heidi, I'm trying very hard to put the entire past month behind me, trying to tuck them into the furthest reaches of my mind."

"I am too, Rob. It's going to take time, isn't it."

"It will Heidi, I don't know about you, but I have made a good start already."

"So have I Rob."

"What I want to talk about is very much in the present and we need to deal with both, now. Heidi Darling, I know that earlier I said it would be best if we kept your prostitution from your parents. I don't believe that would be right. We would have to lie and you remember what your dad told you, one lie will lead to another, to another until it becomes hard to distinguish truth from fiction. Now here is my plan. We will invite your parents to come and see us. We will get two airline tickets and have them fly out. I don't know about Sioux City, but I know United has a flight out of Sioux Falls. If necessary, your folks could drive to Sioux Falls. They will have to go either to Denver or Salt Lake City, but eventually they will get to Tacoma. There is much to show them out here and when the time is right we can tell them about your prostitution."

"Oh, I don't know Rob, knowing I was a prostitute for three years would devastate them."

"Yes it might, but do you want to live a lie for the rest of your life. Your folks will have no choice but to accept the fact. Once it is out in the open normal relations with them can be established again. Don't you want that?"

"More than you can ever know Rob."

"I'm not going to try to force this on you Heidi, it has to be your decision, but now you know what my thinking is on the issue."

Heidi was silent. They covered several miles before Heidi spoke up.

"You're right Rob, I don't want to live a lie for the rest of my life and I'm so eager to see mom and dad. Rob, it's been more than six years since I last saw them. And I haven't written for nearly as long. They may think I am no longer living. They may disown me Rob."

"No Heidi, from what you have told me about your parents that will hardly be the case. You remember Jesus' parable about the prodigal son, well there can also be a prodigal daughter. Your parents will forgive you then once again they can be your parents and you can be their daughter."

Again Heidi was silent for a couple of miles, then spoke up.

"You're right Rob, it must be done and the sooner the better. My gosh Rob, they don't even know their little girl is married and I so want them to get to know you. We'll do it Rob, but when?"

"Just as soon as we can Heidi. This evening if there is time you can call them and if not tomorrow evening."

"I'll do it Rob, as surely as I'm sitting beside you, I'll do it. That is going to be a great burden lifted off my heart. But Rob, they might still reject me.

"Very small chance of that Heidi."

"OK, it's settled, but wouldn't it be better if I called them from home?"

"It's your choice Heidi."

"Now what's the second issue?"

"Heidi Girl, I want Clay to read the marriage ceremony for us again. I want for us to go through the entire ceremony."

"Rob, that's a wonderful idea. We may be putting the cart before the horse in that this is our second honeymoon, but that makes no difference. Oh my gosh, I promised Clay I would let him know how our get together last week went. I'm going to call him right now."

"Good idea Heidi and while you're on the phone with him you might ask him if he would marry us again."

When they reached a high point, using her cell phone Heidi punched in Clay's number. In a few moments he was on the phone.

"Hello, Clay."

"Don't tell me it's you Heidi? I almost hate to ask, but how did it go with you and Rob. Are you together?"

"It went wonderful Clay. We had a joyous reconciliation. We are very much in love and are working hard to put the past behind us"

"I'm so happy to hear that Heidi. My prayers and I'm sure yours and Robs have been answered."

"Yes Clay, our prayers and your prayers have been answered in a marvelous way. Right now we are on our way to Vista Point. Rob asked me if I wanted a second honeymoon. I told him, yes, I want to go to Vista Point and I can't think of a better place for a honeymoon. We always find much to do there and the views are spectacular. Some months back Rob bought me a good camera and I have really been taken with photography. Of course I have an excellent teacher."

"Heidi, my day is made. By the way Heidi, where is Vista Point?"

"There is no Vista Point as such, it's an overlook that gives us a wonderful view of Mt. Rainier. Rob gave it the name of Vista Point."

"You and Rob enjoy yourself at the point"

"I assure you we will Clay. And Clay by the way, would you be kind enough to take us through the wedding ceremony again. We both feel as if we should be remarried."

"I'd be most happy to Heidi, just let me know when it suites you and Rob. Again Heidi, I am so thankful and happy for you and Rob."

"Thank you Clay, Goodbye."

"Goodbye Heidi, greet Rob."

"Clay is so happy we have reconciled our differences and are back together. I don't believe either of us thought that a few days after our reconciliation we would be on our way to Vista Point. It's wonderful Rob, absolutely wonderful. Clay also said he would be most happy to take us through the marriage ceremony again. Now Rob, we must not put it off. Let's make sure we have Clay perform the ceremony in no more than two weeks from now."

"That suites me fine Heidi."

"Rob, Clay said our being together again when it seemed all was lost is God's answer to prayer. Although I may not be much good at praying yet, there is no question in my mind that God wanted us back together again. Oh, by the way, Clay said to greet you."

"You and Clay have become good friends."

"We have Rob. He has been such a help and comfort to me. I couldn't ask for a better friend. It's miraculous the way everything has come together."

"Heidi Girl, have you forgotten that we haven't eaten breakfast?"

"I have Rob. I knew something was wrong, I haven't eaten for quite some time. Rob Sweetheart, would you mind if we ate at the little restaurant we did coming back from our first time at Vista Point?"

"Of course not Heidi, I was thinking the same thing."

When they entered the Restaurant, Heidi stopped and looked around.

"This place holds many pleasant memories for me. I drove to Vista Point twice while we were separated. One was a good experience and the other was not so good. I also stopped here for a cup of coffee. I guess I was trying to recapture the good times we had together. There was no way I could do it alone, but now we are together and the good times are ours again. Oh Rob, I'm so thankful."

"No more than I am Sweetheart."

It was only a short drive from the restaurant to Vista Point. When they stopped, Heidi jumped out of the car and called to Rob.

"Hurry slowpoke, get out of the car. Just smell and feel the wonderful cool air. I love this place Rob, it's our place. So much has happened here."

"Yes, and I'm expecting something of great importance to happen here today."

Heidi laughed and asked,

"Rob, is sex all you think of?"

"Right now lady it is."

"Don't you think it's a bit cool to be stretched out on the forest floor?"

"Sweetheart, you weren't listening, I said sometime today, not right now."

"Well I know you, with just a wee bit of coaxing it would be right now."

"Well, go ahead and coax."

"How about just a bit later?"

"By then the Point may be crawling with people"

"Not today Sweetheart, today Vista point is ours. Rob, why don't we grab our cameras and hike a couple of the trails. The sun isn't too high, we should be able to get some good pictures."

"Rob I'm ashamed to admit that I haven't used my camera since our last trip to Mt Rainier and Mt Saint Helens. I even came up here without it. I knew it would remind me of the time we went shopping for it. I was so excited and so thrilled when you bought it for me. Isn't it strange that I did such awful things and then did all I could to avoid thinking about the wonderful times we had together and the wonderful things we did together?"

Tears were streaming down Heidi's cheeks. Rob took her in his arms and just held her. Heidi rested her head against Rob's chest.

"Sweetheart, this is our special weekend, don't torment yourself with such thoughts."

"I'm afraid I'm going to be tormented by them for awhile. Try as I may I can't put them out of my mind."

"I guess we both will and when it happens we have to help each other. OK now, which trail do you want to hike first?"

"It doesn't make any difference, they all lead to great views of Rainier."

As they headed down the trail, Rob said to Heidi,

"Some weekend we are going to pack the tent and other camping equipment in the Chrysler and we're going to spend Saturday night up here. There is a rather rare phenomenon that takes place and we just might be lucky enough to witness it."

"What is it Rob?"

"It's called alpenglow. When it occurs, the whole mountain is bathed in the most beautiful rose color. I have seen it only a couple of times and though I had my camera with me, because of the heavy traffic there was no place for me to pull off the road. It was darn frustrating. You know Heidi, one of these days we are going to leave Tacoma and move to a smaller city with less traffic and less people. How does that appeal to you?"

"Both of us were raised in small towns and there are times I yearn to live in such a place."

"It can't be too small since there has to be a rather sizeable population if I am to continue my practice. But this city is getting on my nerves."

"Mine too."

"Now, back to alpenglow. It is the photographer's dream to be at a place where he gets an unobstructed view of whatever mountain he wants to photograph."

"It doesn't only happen at Mt. Rainier then."

"No, it can happen at any mountain range. If we can get up here before dark so we can set up camp, it will give us two mornings when we just might luck out."

"Why just two mornings? Why not spend a week of our vacation time here. I would love to do that."

"As you can see, camping up here would be pretty primitive. Could you tolerate a week without a shower, cooking on a camp stove, sleeping in a tent in a sleeping bag?"

"I believe I could. When I was a child we often camped. Dad loves to fish. My brothers and I were young then and we loved it. We would pack up the pickup or car and head for one of the nearby lakes. Of course I was a child then, a time when mother would literally have to drag me into the shower before I would take one."

"There is running water up here, in streams that is. We could heat some water on the camp stove and while you slowly poured it over me, I could scrub myself. I could at least get a reasonably facsimile of a shower."

"We'll have to keep that in mind but even giving ourselves a week we would have no guarantee we would witness the alpenglow."

"Well, I guess we would just have to take a chance that it would happen."

"Your right, that is about all we could do.

"So yes, I believe I could handle it, how about you?"

"Heidi Girl, I grew up camping. I often yearn to get back to it."

"OK then Rob, let's plan to do it, but we will have to arrange our vacation time accordingly. I don't yet have a job with Mr. Simpson, and I may not get back my old job. So for the moment anyway, the time would not be a problem."

"I hope you will make an effort to contact Mr. Simpson soon. You like him and he likes you. Further, if you don't find a job you are going to get bored to death just sitting around the house."

"I plan to see him Monday morning Rob. I'm keeping my fingers crossed that he will take me back. Not every one is good at selling real estate and from what Mr. Simpson told me, I was doing a very good job.

"Now it's time to take some pictures after which we will have sex and then lunch."

Heidi squinted her eyes as she looked at Rob and said,

"How about the other way around? First we'll eat lunch and then have sex."

"Oh no you don't, sex first then lunch."

Heidi laughed.

"I knew that would get a rise out of you."

Heidi raised her camera and was about to take a picture when Rob said,

"Whoa, aren't you forgetting something?"

"I don't think so."

"If I remember correctly, your teacher, that's me' instructed you to look for something like a tree branch, a stream, just anything that will lead the viewer's eye to your main subject."

"I shouldn't have forgotten that Rob. It just shows you how long it has been since I last used my camera.

After taking a number of pictures, Heidi started looking around.

"What are you looking for Heidi?"

"A nice soft place where we can make love without being interrupted and I think I've found a place. We've been up here a couple of hours and so far we are the only ones here."

Heidi pointed to a small depression covered with grass, no small trees growing in it, no branches just a nice grassy spot.

"Come on big boy, it's been almost four months since we last had sex. We have a lot of catching up to do"

Heidi undressed and stretched out in the grassy depression. Rob was hesitant and moved slowly.

"What's wrong Rob, I thought you were eager to have sex?"

"More than you know Heidi. OK, let's give it a try."

"Give it a try, what do you mean?"

Rob stretched out beside Heidi and pulled her on top of him. After a short time and speaking quietly he said,

"It's no use Heidi, I still can't get it up. I was hoping a few days would make a difference. I'm impotent."

Heidi cried out,

"Oh no Rob I was hoping it was temporary, just a passing thing. It's my fault."

Heidi started crying

"I deliberately set out to make you impotent Rob. I figured I could accomplish it by telling you repeatedly that I was tired of having sex with the same man, with you over and over again, that I needed variety, I needed a change. All along I denied you sex and kept telling you I was no longer interested in you sexually. And then I started wearing that stupid night gown. Oh Rob, what have I done to you. You can't want me now."

Heidi rolled on her side with her back to Rob. She continued sobbing. Rob put his arm under her shoulders and raised her to a sitting position.

"Heidi Sweetheart, I'm not heart broken. I feared this would continue for a while. As far as not wanting you I want you more than ever."

"He pulled her to him and kissed her, kissed her passionately.

"At least I can kiss you passionately, right?"

"Your kisses always turned me on Rob, until four months ago that is. I want to be turned on now, but how can I knowing I made you impotent?"

"I'll tell you how, by helping me overcome it. I can't do it alone Heidi."

"I'll do anything to help you Rob, You know that."

Then Heidi smiled weekly and said,

"Don't forget that I too am about climbing the wall. Forgive me for this awful thing I've done to you Rob. How could a woman who loves her man set out to deliberately make him impotent? I'm an evil woman Rob, evil, evil, evil."

"Heidi, you were a confused woman, you succumbed to a very strong willed group of women. That doesn't make you evil."

Heidi looked at Rob with tear filled eyes,

"Oh Rob, how can you be so understanding? I love you so much."

"I love you too Heidi and I never want to lose that love and I never want to lose your love for me."

Heidi replied,

"There is nothing you can do or say to make me give up my love for you. The last four months are too deeply rooted in my mind."

Rob pulled her close and kissed her again.

"Let's go home Rob." "

"No way Heidi, this is our second honeymoon. We got a bit of a jolt, but for us this day is just beginning."

"I don't know if I want to continue."

"You will. There's something I want to tell you. Not far from this fallen tree is the faint outline of a path, of a trail. It must be a tough one, but we're both tough. I have a hunch it leads to a terrific view of Mt. Rainier. I've got my compass and GPS in the car. We'll take a reading and become bush whackers. How does that sound to you? I see fantastic pictures in the making."

The excitement showed in Heidi's eyes and voice.

"Let's do it Rob, I'm more than game."

"OK, you sit on the fallen tree, I'll run back to the car and get the compass and GPS and we will be on our way. Are you sure you don't mind a few scratches and maybe a tear or two in your top?"

"Not in the least."

"Be sure because we are going to be eating in a restaurant this evening."

"We are?"

"Yes, this evening the sky is the limit."

"That will be fun Rob, I can hardly wait. If the tears are too many I can wear my light jacket. Scratches, well the restaurant people will just have to put up with them."

"You'll have to wait, we're far from through with Vista Point for the day"

"OK, I'll take the lead and you follow behind."

And bush whacking they did. At times they were about ready to turn back, but perseverance won out.

After about an hour they began to see Rainier through the thinning trees. Then they stepped out in the open and as Rob surmised the view was nothing short of fantastic. A short distance ahead of them was a precipitous drop of hundreds of feet. Both were silent as they gazed at the beauty before them.

"Oh my," said Rob, "I knew there had to be something special at the end of the trail. From the looks of it few people have seen Rainier from this wonderful point of view. It's just plain beautiful. Now imagine, if you can, the entire mountain bathed in the most delicate of pink hues. That, Heidi my dear would be alpenglow."

"Both took a number of pictures and then just sat back and enjoyed the beauty of their surroundings.

It was late afternoon when Rob said to Heidi,

"Sweetheart, I hate to leave this place, but we do have dinner reservations at a lodge between here and Packwood."

"Look at us Rob, I have scratches on my legs, and my top is torn. I'm dirty and in need of a shower, we'll never be allowed into the lodge."

"Oh yes we will. I talked to the manager and told him that most likely we would look pretty rough having spent a day in the mountains. No problem, he said, we advertise come as you are. People show up in jeans, sneakers, unshaven, hair unruly, you name it. This is tourist and vacation country. We are inclusive in that we cater to anyone. The crowd might not look the best but our food is."

"That sounds like a fun place, let's go. Rob, do you think we can find our way back to Vista Point?"

"With the aid of the GPS, we shouldn't have any trouble."

"OK, there will be more scratches, more tears in my top and more sweating, but if we will be accepted as we are, let's get going."

"Me too Heidi, so what. If others look cruddy, we will be in good company."

Going back was easier since their bush whacking had left more of a distinct trail.

"Rob, we have to come back here real soon."

"We will sweetheart, I too love this place."

As they drove from Vista Point to the lodge, Heidi put her head on Rob's shoulder and began sobbing.

"I made you impotent Rob and I did it on purpose. How can you forgive me, how can I forgive myself."

"Heidi, you must put it out of your mind. I want you to remember this day with fondness. I don't want you to regret it. Further, aren't you forgetting something?"

"What is that Rob?"

"Didn't you once tell me that as a prostitute you learned every trick of the trade and were instrumental in helping men overcome their impotency? If you were successful with strangers, surely you can be successful with your husband."

"Rob, what ails me. I didn't give that a thought. Maybe they shouldn't even be called skills."

"As long as they work you can call them anything you want."

"Rob, I can promise you, we'll have you up and functioning in no time. Why didn't you remind me sooner?"

"I guess I was expecting you to come up with it."

"I feel much better now, step on it, I'm hungry."

It was twilight when they got to the lodge and as Rob was told, they did not feel out of place. As they looked around they saw people who looked far worse than they did.

Rob ordered a bottle of wine which they sipped while their meal was being prepared.

"Rob Sweetheart, this is like old times. I am very tired but so happy."

As they visited they did a good job of staying away from events of the past four months.

Although she was still uncertain about her parent's visit, at the same time just the thought of it excited Heidi. She wondered if they had changed much in appearance. She knew she had, after all when she left home she was just a kid, now she was a fully matured woman.

"Rob, when my parent's see me they will think I've become an old woman."

"Why do you say that?"

"Because my appearance has changed so much."

"Oh no it hasn't, and if it has it is for the better. You were just a kid when you left home, now you are a woman."

Heidi laughed.

"That is just what I got through telling myself."

They ate their dinner leisurely, often reaching under the table to hold hands.

It was late when they arrived at their motel in Packwood. There was a coffee maker in their room. Heidi made two cups. They sat at the little table drinking their coffee and visiting.

"Well Sweetheart, how has your second honeymoon been so far, has it been satisfactory?"

"Rob Darling, it has been wonderful. There is no need to drive many miles to have a wonderful time. The only blemish on what otherwise was a perfect day is your impotency, but since I am confident my skills can overcome it, even that one blemish has faded. We can even give it a try tonight if you want to."

"Let's shower together and go to bed "

"Your rubbing it in aren't you. You know what showering together does to me and I am helpless to do anything about it."

"I know but let's do it anyway. A shower will feel so good. I feel absolutely filthy. If you're up to it we can try having sex again."

After their shower and both were lying in bed, Heidi said.

"Do you want to give it another try Rob?"

"I'd like to but honestly Heidi. I'm too tired and that alone might bring about failure. I'd just as soon not face that twice in one day."

"Your right Rob, we'll give it a try tomorrow evening."

Lying in bed Heidi snuggled up close to Rob and said,

"Thank you for a wonderful day Sweetheart, our second honeymoon. We did so many great things. I'll never forget that fantastic view of Mt. Rainier, I'm ready to bushwhack again tomorrow."

"You'll get filthy again."

"So what we can shower when we get home."

"And Heidi, thank you for a wonderful day. God certainly has blessed us. Now lets get to sleep, we have another day ahead of us to look forward to."

"Goodnight Sweetheart,"

"Goodnight Darling."

Having decided to go to Sunrise instead of Paradise they were up early and on the way by 7:30.

After they arrived they took a trail leading to the rim overlooking Rainier. The day was clear, no haze as often is the case. With a map in hand they were able to locate most of the glaciers on the north side. They had arrived early enough to get some good pictures. Rob had Heidi take most of them while he gave her instructions on framing and using something natural pointing to the mountain, streams, and glaciers.

Again Rob reminded her that if it's done right, one who looks at the pictures will start from where the branch, or whatever, leads to the primary subject which was Rainier.

"Rob you drilled that into me to the point that that's the first thing I do, look for a natural pointer."

"Just a reminder," replied Rob.

Next they hiked the trail to the north of the visitor's center. The air was so clear they could see Mt. Baker off in the distance. When they got back to the visitor's center, Rob looked at his watch and ,said,

"Heidi, it's 11:00 already. If we want to go back to Vista Point we have to get started."

"Let's go Rob, it shouldn't take us more than an hour and a half to get there from here."

It was after noon before Heidi and Rob reached Vista point. It was another beautiful day. The sky was perfect for pictures with white cumulus clouds floating by. They had picked up rolls and pop at a grocery store and that was to be there lunch.

"Not much of a lunch is it?" said Rob.

"After the big dinner we had last evening and the continental breakfast we had this morning who needs a big lunch? I certainly don't," answered Heidi.

"That goes for me too," replied Rob.

They sat at the table, the one where all the adventure took place, which was now in shade. When they finished, Heidi said to Rob,

"I still have a lot to learn about my camera and photography.

If it's OK with you, I'm going down one or two of the trails which will give me good views of Mt. Rainier. Want to come along?"

"If it's OK with you Heidi, I'm going to stretch out and take a nap. These late hours are catching up with me."

"You do that and when I come back and if you're still sleeping I'll awaken you."

"Don't forget to look for something natural to lead to your main subject."

"How could I you've reminded me to do it so many times."

"I just want you to come back with pictures that satisfy you."

"When I get back it should be time to start for home."

Heidi gave Rob a kiss and then took off down one of the trails.

Rob looked at his watch it was just 2:30. He stretched out on the picnic bench and was soon sleeping soundly. When he awoke he looked at his watch and said,

"My gosh it's 6:30. I've been sleeping for four hours. Heidi was supposed to wake me."

He sat up and looked around. Heidi was no where in sight. He called out her name, but there was no answer. He called out again only louder this time. Still no answer. At that point he began to get concerned. She should have been back a couple hours ago.

He jumped off the table and ran to the Jaguar, opened the trunk and took out a first aid kit and a large rechargeable spot light.

"Thank Heavens," he said, I remembered to charge it Friday evening."

Then he started down the trail that Heidi had taken. As he went along he called out Heidi's name at regular intervals. No answer. When he reached the end of the trail he ran back to the picnic table and took another trail. He also ran down that trail calling out Heidi's name. There was no answer. Now his concern was beginning to turn into panic. Whoa, he said to himself. I must keep my cool. She's got to be somewhere near. The trails leading to views of Mt. Rainier aren't that long.

Maybe she fell and injured herself. Good Lord, there are some pretty sharp precipices at the end of a couple of the trails. Immediately a feeling of panic swept over him again. Easy Rob, you mustn't let the panic get to you. I have to find Heidi and if I fail I'll have to call 911 and get a search and rescue team up here. There are two more trails branching off. I'll go down one and come back up the other.

His efforts proved to be fruitless. He said to himself, I've been down all the trails and nothing. Am I missing something? Nothing came to mind. He stifled a sob. Where could she be? It's almost dark. Soon visibility will be nil and then I will have to search with the help of the spotlight. Being all alone and lost Heidi will be terrified.

"Wait a minute," he said slowly and deliberately out loud. "There's the trail we had to bushwhack through. But no, she wouldn't try that alone and yet she said she wanted to take that trail again just to take in the breath taking view and if conditions were right to take a few more pictures. Oh no, she wouldn't be that foolish. She had to hang onto me to make it through the first time we broke through the brush. It's time to call 911."

He reached for his phone then put it back into it's holster.

Before I make that call, Rob said to himself, I'm going to try and find the trail and bust my way through it.

Rob walked to the east. He came to the dead tree upon which they sat so often. The trail wasn't too far from the tree. He walked more slowly moving the spotlight back and forth. He thought he saw where brush had been trampled, however, it was too close to the tree. He continued walking.

"I've missed it," he said out loud, "I must retrace my steps."

When he came to the place where the brush appeared to be trampled

he said,

"This has to be the place."

Throwing the beam of light ahead of him he began pushing through the brush. He called out Heidi's name, no answer. It seemed to him that someone had gone through the brush not too long ago. He moved forward and called Heidi' name again. No answer. I have to be about halfway through the trail he said to himself. If she's anywhere near here, she has to hear my voice. He walked on again, calling as he went.

Suddenly he stopped. Had he heard his name being called?

"Heidi," he called out with all the volume he could muster.

There it was, a faint answer. But where was it coming from. He took out his knife and cut off a number of branches from the brush and made a pile on the trail. If moving ahead didn't bring him closer to Heidi he could return. For the first time he noticed that the air was damp and chilly. He walked ahead a few hundred feet, stopped and called again,

"Heidi, where are you?"

This time Heidi's voice was more distinct.

"Heidi, call my name again. I can't get the direction your voice is coming from."

Although it was dim he heard her voice. He pushed through the tangled brush. He was hardly dressed to do so, but that made no difference.

He began angling to the west since Heidi's voice was coming from that direction. He continued calling Heidi's name as he went, progress was slow. Her answer came clearer to him. He was moving in the right direction. He called out,

"Heidi, whatever you do, don't move."

At times the brush was almost impassable. Then he had to make a detour.

"Heidi," he called.

Now her voice was clear, he was close. He believed he could pin point about from where her voice was coming from.

"Keep talking Heidi, sing do anything but keep talking."

Heidi did as she was told. Now it wasn't hard to follow her voice. He walked a short distance then stopped.

"Heidi, I'm going to point the spotlight straight up. You should be able to see it."

"I see it Rob, I see it."

" Am I to the right or left of you."

"You are to the left just a little ways."

Rob turned ever so slightly and then moved forward.

"Keep talking Heidi."

When she started speaking Rob was almost on top of her. He moved the spotlight back and forth. Then he saw Heidi.

"Heidi," he cried.

He dropped to his knees beside her, took her into his arms and began sobbing.

"I imagined the worst had happened to you. That you had been raped or even killed, that you might have been attacked by a mountain lion or fallen over one of the cliffs. Why did you try the trail by yourself? It was tough enough for the two of us."

"Oh Rob," Heidi sobbed, "I am so glad to see you. I was so frightened. I thought you would never find me. I remembered you telling me that if I ever got lost in the mountains to sit down and stay in one place, don't move. It was awful hard to just sit. Please forgive me for causing you so much anguish. I knew you would be worried to death. I'm so cold."

He pulled Heidi tightly against his body while she put her arms around him. Both wept, wept openly and so hard neither could talk. Finally Rob shown the light on Heidi. Her clothes were about torn from her body. She had deep scratches everywhere. Her face was badly scratched and was bleeding

"I knew you would come, I just knew it. I had that assurance. Rob, it was like a voice spoke to me. It said don't be afraid Heidi, Rob will find you. Oh Rob, Rob God led you to me. I know he did."

"Can you stand?"

"Yes, I think so. I'm cold and so hungry."

Rob took off his jacket and put it around Heidi's shoulders he reached Into one of the pockets and took out a candy bar.

"This will have to do for now."

"Rob Darling, isn't this the second act of the same story. Once before you draped your jacket over me when I was so cold. The situation seemed hopeless. For a while it seemed that way to me again, but then I received the assurance you would find me. I was praying hard and often. It kept playing over and over in my head, "Rob will find you. Don't be afraid, Heidi, Rob will find you. This is right where I fell."

Rob helped Heidi to her feet.

"If we go real slow, do you think you can walk out of here."

"I can Rob, I know I can."

"Grab my belt and don't let go. If I can see it, I'll try to follow my trail in here."

With the powerful beam aiming ahead of him, slowly Rob made his way back to the trail he and Heidi had bush whacked.

"Darling, we haven't much farther to go. Hold on."

"I am Rob and I won't let go."

And then they broke out into the clearing. Heidi said,

"Rob, I don't think I can walk any farther. I hurt all over and I'm exhausted."

Rob handed Heidi the spotlight, picked her up and headed up the trail to the picnic bench and the Jaguar.

"I'm too heavy for you, aren't I?"

"Hardly Sweetheart, I'll have us back to the car in a few minutes."

The Jaguar came into view and they knew the ordeal was over.

"The two blankets we usually carry in the trunk are still there. I'll drape one over the seat and cover you with the other. Keep it on until the heater is throwing out heat."

After Rob arranged Heidi, he crawled under the steering wheel and they started for home.

"Rob, Darling, I want you to know that I still have my camera. I draped it over my neck so it hung by my left side. I wasn't going to leave that behind."

"Well Sweetheart, did you get some good pictures?"

"Yes, for just a moment it was almost like alpenglow and I shot off a lot of pictures."

"Heidi, why didn't you wake me when you went by the picnic table? If you had we could have avoided all this. I was about in a state of panic. I went down all the trails leading from the table. When I couldn't find you I feared the worst. I didn't know what to do. I was about to call 911 when I remembered the trail we made through the brush. At first I thought you wouldn't be foolish enough to try that by yourself. Then I told myself, Yes she would be."

With tears streaming down her cheeks, Heidi said,

"Rob Darling, I'm so sorry I put you through such anguish. It was foolish of me. I realized that when I turned around and saw it was almost too dark for me to follow the slight trail. I started out and then knew I had gotten off the trail. That's when I fell and just waited.

"You did the right thing Sweetheart and now other than for a few bruises and deep scratches and cuts, you are OK."

"Rob, I'm going to unfasten my seatbelt and slide over to you so I can rest my head on your shoulder. I'm so tired."

"Go ahead and do it Heidi. Go to sleep and when you awaken we will be home. When we get there, the first thing you will do is take a good hot shower. I'm going to have to soap you all over we need to get soap into all those cuts and scratches. Then I will dress the worst ones."

"Rob Sweetheart, may I remind you that that isn't the reason we usually shower together."

"Tell you what, tonight we will make an exception."

"Are you sure, is that a promise?" Heidi said tauntingly.

"Darling, I have a hunch that tonight even you wouldn't be able to perform."

"Do you want to bet on it?" said Heidi sleepily."

"No because I don't want to take your money. Now go to sleep."

Chapter Twenty Four

≡ ·|||· ≡

All day Heidi was nervous as a cat. What would she say? What would her mom and dad say? How would she explain her failure to keep in touch with them? It had been at least five years since she wrote, called or made any effort to contact her parents. Rob suggested that she tell them she will explain why when they come to Tacoma. That will make them very curious, but she could hardly tell them she had been a call girl over the phone. What would their reaction be when she told them she had been married for more than three years? Most parents want to be involved, especially in a daughter's marriage. But I didn't even tell them, she said to herself. I have really created a dilemma for myself and for Rob too, but especially for myself.

She and Rob agreed that their earlier breakup is something they would not bring up. There would be more than enough to explain without bringing that into her confessions. She finally decided she would just let it play out as it will She couldn't remember if she had told Rob the name of her parents. She called into the living room.

"Rob, have I ever told you my parent's names?"

"No Heidi, I can't recall that you did."

"How awful of me, I'm sorry Rob, I should have done so a long time ago. Dad's name is Trevor and mother's is Naomi, Trevor and Naomi Faust."

"What nice names," Rob responded.

With hands shaking Heidi picked up the phone and punched in her parent's number. She could feel her pulse beating in her ears. There was a slight pause then Heidi's mother was on the phone.

"Hello."

"Hello mom, this is Heidi."

There was a short pause, and then Heidi heard her mother say,

"Quick Trevor, pick up the other phone, it's Heidi."

"Heidi, her Father said, "My Little Girl. Oh Lord how wonderful."

"Mom and dad first let me say I love you."

In a moment all three were weeping. Heidi couldn't go on with her conversation. Rob gently took the phone from Heidi's hand,

"Hello Mr. and Mrs. Faust, my name is Robert Sloan and I'm Heidi's husband. At the moment all Heidi can do is weep. She'll calm down soon and then she can take the phone again. Heidi is alright, she is well, she is not ill in any way. We have been married for a bit more than three years. I wanted Heidi to tell you since we first married, however she was having problems that prevented her from doing so. She has not been in trouble with the law, has not been on drugs or any such thing."

"Trevor and Naomi, I want you to know that your little girl and I are very much in love and ours is a very happy marriage. Heidi is a good wife. My only complaint is she should have made this phone call ages ago. Even though we have never met, Heidi has told me much about you. I feel that I know you. I hope you don't mind if I call you Naomi and Trevor? Please call me Rob."

"You haven't seen your little girl in more than six years. That is far too long. Heidi and I are going to send you two tickets on United Airlines. Since we haven't checked, we don't know if you can catch a flight out of Sioux City, however, I believe there are a couple flights out of Sioux Falls each day."

"You may be wondering where I got my information from. I was born and grew up in South Eastern South Dakota and attended the University in Vermillion before moving to Tacoma."

Mr. Faust broke in,

"Heidi has been living in Tacoma and not in Seattle?"

"No she hasn't, we met in Tacoma."

"And you are from South Dakota? From what part?"

"Do you know where Yankton is?"

"Of course I do."

"My parental home is just 35 miles from Yankton."

"Fancy that, Heidi from Western Iowa and you from South Dakota. Why you were practically next door neighbors and you both had to go to Tacoma to meet."

"Yes that is something, Heidi and I have talked about the coincidence. Mr. Faust, Do you think you and Mrs. Faust could find time to fly out here to Tacoma?"

"Even though we haven't met, you are my son-in law, it is OK if you call me Trevor and my wife Naomi."

"I'll do that Trevor if you'll call me Rob. Do you think you could find time to fly out here to Tacoma? I would love to meet you and I know you very much want to see Heidi."

Rob could hear sobbing in the background and then Heidi's mother spoke up.

"Mr. Sloan , "

"Rob, please."

"Why hasn't Heidi been in touch with us for such a long time? We feared she was no longer living. It has been awful not knowing if our daughter was alive or dead."

"She is very much alive Naomi and she will have to tell you why she avoided staying in touch with you and that will have to wait until we are all together. Do you think you could fly to Tacoma ?"

"Nothing could keep us from doing so," answered Treavor. "You don't have to buy us tickets, that will not be necessary."

"Both Heidi and I want to send you tickets so please let us do that."

"We won't argue. Fancy that, we are talking with our son-in-law when we didn't know if Heidi was alive."

"She is very much alive Trevor. I do believe Heidi has regained her composure and hopefully can talk without breaking down"

Trevor said, "Before putting Heidi on the phone, when would you like us to fly to Tacoma?"

"Just as soon as possible Trevor. Here's Heidi."

"Mom and dad, it's so good to hear your voices. How have the two of you been?"

"Other than living with constant anxiety wondering what happened to you, we've been well Heidi. My leg healed completely and there is nothing around the farm that I can't do."

"How are the boys?"

This time Naomi spoke up,

"Charles and Jerry are married, but Alfred is not. He says he has not yet found the right girl. Dad and I are grandparents three times. I guess that means were getting old Heidi."

"No way Mom, people become grandparents at young ages these days."

Heidi could hear her mother weeping.

"Heidi, why did you stop communicating with us? All of my letters went unanswered and suddenly your phone calls stopped. For a time we thought we may have said something or I may have written something to offend you."

"You didn't offend me in any way mom and dad. I stopped communicating because of something I was doing. I want to tell you what it was, but that will have to wait until we're together."

"My goodness Heidi," said Naomi, "What terrible thing could you have been doing to cut us off from all communication?"

"It was pretty terrible mom. Dad, What I was doing would not make you proud of your little girl."

Trevor was silent and then said,

"It couldn't have been that bad Heidi."

"It was worse dad, but that is now behind me, behind Rob and me."

"Alright Heidi, we won't pressure you to tell us now. We are just so happy you are alright and happy. Your husband Rob, appears to be a nice man"

"He is mom and dad, he is a therapist who helps troubled people. He is a good therapist. He has helped me so much and he has a very good practice. I just can't tell you how much I love him.

"For that we are real happy Heidi," said her mother.

"And what are you doing? Did you finish college? What did you major in?" asked Trevor.

"Yes dad, I finished college and I majored in Business Administration. At the moment I don't have a job, but I will be seeing my previous employer in a day or two."

"When do you think you can fly out? I'm just dying to see both of you." Trevor chuckled and said,

"Don't do that Heidi, we thought you were dead, now we don't want you to die before we see you."

"You still have your sense of humor dad that makes me happy. Mother, are you still there?"

"I am Heidi, but I'm afraid I am in a near state of shock I'll get over it and before we fly to Tacoma, I'll be doing a lot of calling. Give us your phone number, and we will check the calendar and plan to fly out just as soon as we can."

"I can hardly wait to see you, please hurry. I love you both so very much."

"And we love you Heidi. How we wish we could take you into our arms."

"You will mom and dad, and very soon I hope."

"Please tell Rob goodbye from us and also tell him we are so anxious to meet him."

"I will mom and dad. I'll call you again in a day or two just to keep in touch. Let me know just as soon as possible when we can expect your visit. We have so much to show you. Goodbye mom and dad. I love you very much."

"Goodbye Heidi and we love you. Tonight when we have devotions we will thank God for answered prayer. And Heidi, for the first time in years, we will sleep extra good, knowing you are safe."

"Goodbye my Little Girl." Trevor said

Heidi put the phone down, rested her head on her arm which was on the table and wept and wept some more. Rob put his arms around her shoulder, but said nothing. Finally the weeping stopped. Heidi raised her head and looked at Rob.

"And to think, if you wouldn't have encouraged me to call home, I may not have done so for another six years. How awful of me to neglect them so. Mom said that tonight when they have devotions they are going to thank God for answered prayer. Mom also said they would sleep extra good tonight knowing I am safe and well. Oh Rob, what would I do without you, and, and to think I threw you away."

Again Heidi started weeping.

Rob raised her to her feet, held her close and said,

"Now, Heidi, no more of that."

"I can't help it Rob, you came to me when I believed God wouldn't hear my prayer asking Him to bring us back together."

"He did Heidi even though you said you no longer knew how to pray, He heard you and He heard my prayer also. You have made contact with your parents. They will be out here soon and then there will be more rejoicing."

"Yes Rob, but the tough part still lies ahead of me. You know, I too am a prodigal, a prodigal daughter. I just hope the ending will be as joyous as it was when the father embraced his son when he returned home after spending his inheritance on prostitutes and riotous living."

"Heidi, you surprise me, I didn't know you knew the parable of the prodigal son."

"Rob, I have been reading from the New Testament. I find Jesus' parables so very interesting. It is so interesting how he could weave a story to make his point understood."

"I didn't know you had been reading your Bible."

"I had time on my hands. One day I remembered that I had stuck my Bible behind a row of books so my customers wouldn't see it and think I was some kind of religious freak. I now feel so humiliated at what I did. I promised Clay I would read and study the Bible he gave me when you lay dying in the hospital."

"I not only let God down, I let Clay down and Rob, I also let you down."

Heidi looked at Rob and the tears began to flow.

"Oh Rob, do you think there is any hope for me?"

"I know there is hope for you Heidi, and I think you have made a good beginning in understanding what the Bible is all about."

"There are things which leave me completely stumped. Do you think we could sit down together and you could help me to understand?"

"Of course, I have been waiting for you to ask to read and study the Bible together. Haven't you read enough to know that there is always hope for a prodigal, if the prodigal recognizes her sins and asks for forgiveness and repents?"

"Rob, if repentance means turning away from a sinful life style, I have done that. I will never, never again become a prostitute."

"You're right on Heidi, that's precisely what repentance is." There is hope for me then."

"Always Heidi, always."

"Hold me Rob, hold me tight and never let me go."

After a time, Heidi said,

"I will tell mom and dad what I did for three years and like the prodigal son, ask them for forgiveness."

"And you will get it Heidi. It most likely will be a bit stormy at first, but I have faith your folks, once they get over the shock of what you had been doing, will forgive you with open arms. Then a new era in the relationship between you and your parents will begin, just like our second honeymoon was symbolic of the new era in our relationship."

"Rob Darling, you have such a good way of putting things. Hold me Darling, kiss me."

Chapter Twenty Five

≡ ⫿⫿⫿ ≡

It was time for Heidi to start looking for a job. Since it had been more than six years since she graduated and held no job relative to her degree in business administration, there wasn't much for her to look for. Worse than that, she had only Mr. Simpson and Paul to give her a reference. Mr. Simpson's would be good, that she knew and so would Paul's, however, any potential employer wouldn't be too impressed with a reference telling him or her how good she was as a prostitute. She smiled as she thought about Paul. Wouldn't that be something if she put him down as a reference. He would give her one for sure, but wouldn't it be an eye opener. If she would be looking for a reference for another call girl agency, Paul's would be a gem.

There was one other possibility, remote as it might be, Mr. Simpson's last words to her were, If your business doesn't pan out and you're looking for work, be sure to check with me first, I just might have an opening. It bothered her that she had lied to Mr. Simpson. He had been so good to her.

Then she thought, well in a way, I guess being a call girl operating out of my own home could be called a business of sorts. She smiled, Come on Heidi, you are only rationalizing. But she could say that the business didn't pan out. If she was lucky, he wouldn't pursue the issue, but what if he did? Then her only way out would be to lie. Well hopefully that was behind her now. She did not want to lie again especially to Mr. Simpson. No more lying.

On the Monday following Rob's and her second honeymoon weekend, she decided that was the day to see Mr. Simpson. He opened his office at 9:00 a.m., so 10:00 would be a good time to drop in. Previously when she opened the office the first thing she did was make a pot of coffee for Mr. Simpson of course, but for herself as well. She knew she drank too much coffee, but try as she may, she could not cut back. She told Rob coffee was far better than alcohol. He agreed of course and promised to help her as she made an effort to cut back. He suggested tea, but tea held no appeal for her. He cautioned her against soft drinks since they too were potentially addictive and could cause health problems.

About 11:00 Mr. Simpson would call out to her to bring in two cups of coffee while they visited. He had done very well with his real estate business and at this point in life he didn't have to work, but he did so because he was very gregarious and loved working with people. Before he hired Heidi his was pretty much a one man operation. He had decided it was time to hire someone to take people to land and homes that were potential sales. That had been Heidi's job and she loved it. Maybe it was because she was so petite and pretty that clients took to her easily. In addition being a call girl honed her skills working with men to a fine edge. She knew how to interact with people, especially men. She spoke out loud.

"Why did I ever quit my job with Mr. Simpson? Why did I ever think I wanted to be a call girl again? Why oh why had I treated Rob so unmercifully bad? I was either out of my mind or possessed by some kind of evil spirit. It had to be one or the other."

What a grand weekend she and Rob had at Vista Point. She felt so sorry for him as he struggled with his impotency. He could say it was nothing and he would get over it, but she knew it bothered him. And why not? In their four years of being together and married not once had he failed to achieve an erection when they had sex. She was the one who deliberately set out to make him feel less than a man by turning herself off to him, by letting him know she no longer desired to have sex with him. And she succeeded. Now it was up to her to remedy the problem for if Rob suffered from months of sexual deprivation she did too.

My dear Rob, she thought, how could I, how could I? That damn Sally, why did we have to meet at Phillips? Had we not met, the breakdown of Rob's and my relationship for the past four months would never have happened. I'd like to knock her over the head with something hard. She almost ruined my life, completely and forever. Heidi wept.

Heidi had parked about 2 blocks from Mr. Simpson's office. She was an hour early, but it gave her the opportunity she needed to go over many things that were bothering her. As she thought about the weekend at Vista Point, she was aware of just how hard up she was. She wanted to have sex with Rob so bad, and that was just around the corner. Rob's impotency was psychological in nature. She didn't have to be a psychiatrist to know that. Rob had diagnosed his condition accurately. She caused it and she would have to remedy it.

Promptly at 10:00 she left her Jaguar and walked to Mr. Simpson's office. She had to go by a construction site. Some guy hollered out,

"Hey babe, what would you charge for a good lay? You sure are a pretty thing."

Heidi ignored him and continued on her way. What the man said did not offend her since she heard similar comments from her customers many times. In fact it rather pleased her. Men found her attractive and wanted to have sex with her. It was crude, but that's the only approach some men are capable of using.

When Heidi got to Mr. Simpson's office she opened the door and stepped inside. Mr. Simpson was on the phone with his back toward her. He put his hand over the mouth piece and without turning said,

"I'll be with you in a minute," then continued his conversation.

Heidi looked around at the familiar surroundings. She looked at the coffee pot. Two things she noticed. It was dirty and it was empty. She really believed that Mr. Simpson didn't know how to make coffee.

Mr. Simpson was on the phone a couple of minutes longer, hung up and swung his chair around to face Heidi.

He looked at Heidi in obvious surprise and said nothing for a moment or two.

"Heidi, Heidi, is it really you? It's so good to see you. I really never expected to see you again."

"It's I Mr. Simpson, all of me."

"Heidi, have you forgotten, it's James?

"How many times have I told you, you are such a pretty girl, so petit, not skinny, but for a girl of your height, proportioned just right."

"Many times James."

"I hope you still accept it as a compliment and not find it offensive."

"Does any girl find a compliment offensive when it is given sincerely?"

"Heidi, you know me, I couldn't be more sincere. Now I'm going to my inner office. Would you make a pot of coffee and bring two cups so we can visit?"

"I would be most happy to James."

Heidi felt so good it was like she had never left James. Fix a pot of coffee and bring two cups into my office so we can visit. How many times had she heard that? She picked up a cup and noticed it was filthy. All of the cups were unclean. She wondered when they had been last washed. The coffee pot was equally filthy. With a smile on her face and cups and coffee pot in hand, she walked to a back room that had a sink and running water.

When a pot had perked, Heidi poured two cups, walked in to his office and took her chair. James had been following her with his eyes.

"Heidi, it's so good to see you, I missed you when you left."

Heidi smiled and said,

"Mr. Simpson, you should wash the coffee pot and cups at the end of each day. If you don't mind my saying so, they were filthy."

"I know Heidi, but I forget to do it and I tell myself they will be OK for one more day. As you noticed, it's always one more day and I never get to it. Tell me, how is your business going?"

"It isn't James. I gave up the idea before I started."

"What kind of business were you going to go into?"

"The service business, but after looking through the Yellow Pages I realized the field was more than crowded, and I didn't have the money to do the kind of necessary advertising."

Another lie, however it was half true since prostitution was certainly a service business.

"I'm sorry to hear that."

Raising his left arm he said,

"Look I've got my fingers crossed. You wouldn't be here to see if the job you left is available, would you?"

"James, that's why I'm here."

"Well Heidi, I'm very happy to tell you that it is open and it's yours if you want it."

"Oh James, I want it. I need a job and though I thought the chances would be very slim, I decided I would see you first"

"Heidi, you don't know how happy that makes me. Let's see you've been gone six or 7 weeks, right?"

"Six weeks."

"Well in those six weeks I tried two girls. One left after her very first day, she said she wasn't cut out to be a sales person. The other had a drinking problem and was unreliable. Most mornings she was late and smelled of alcohol, I had no choice but to let her go. You don't know how glad I am that you want your job back."

"James, you're happy I'm available. I'm overjoyed you want me back."

"You have proved your dependability and your talent at making sales. You can start whenever you are ready?"

"Please give me a couple of days to get things in order, can you do that?"

"Take all the time you need."

"Thank you, let's see this is Monday, how would Thursday A.M. be?"

"Are you sure that's enough time?"

"Three days will be all I need, Thursday it will be."

"What a relief Heidi, I didn't want to advertise again. Girls who are dependable, who are go getters like you, are hard to find these days. Oh, and by the way, you will have a new mini van to take people around to look at land and houses. I bought it shortly after you left me."

"That's great James, I will sit extra tall in a new van."

"And Heidi, I like to hear you call me James. Mr. Simpson will still be OK when there is a client in the office, otherwise it will be James."

"Alright, James I won't forget. Oh by the way, Rob and I are expecting my parents, who live in Iowa, to come to Tacoma to visit us one of these days. I don't know how long they will stay, but Rob and I would like to take them to Seaside, Oregon and to Mt. St. Helens and Rainier. Would it be possible for me to have some time off? I would be gone one or two days, then I would be back on the job and then gone for a couple of days again."

"Of course Heidi, when they arrive and you make out a schedule, just let me know."

"I will James."

Heidi stood up as did James. Heidi took the few steps to where James was standing and hugged him. She could see that he was obviously pleased.

"Heidi, have you any idea how it makes me feel to be hugged by a young woman, other than my daughters, and by such an attractive young woman at that. I don't believe a man ever reaches the point that when a young woman hugs him his heart doesn't quicken just a bit. I hope you don't mind my saying so.

"Not at all James, I take that as a compliment and James, I want you to know that it feels so good to have my job back and to be able to go to work for you again."

James' face was beaming.

"You still know how to make a good cup of coffee Heidi, I'm glad you haven't forgotten how. As you know, I'm still not good at making it."

"You don't have to remind me, just looking at your dirty cups and coffee pot reminded me how awful your coffee is.

I'll see you Thursday morning James."

"Goodbye Heidi. I am looking forward to your return. Please greet Rob for me."

As Heidi walked back to her car, she said to herself, I don't know why you are so good to me God for I certainly don't deserve it. Rob and I are together and more in love than ever. I've called mom and dad and we had a good conversation and now I have my old job again. Thank You, I promise I will get to know you better."

That evening Heidi had good news to tell Rob.

"It was so good to see James again."

"James."

"Yes James. Only when there are clients in the office am I to address him as Mr. Simpson. We had a good visit and the first thing he asked me to do was to make a pot of coffee, fill two cups and join him in his office so we could visit. I wish you could have seen the coffee pot and cups, they were filthy. It's a good thing he gave up perking coffee since no client would want to drink it. I washed the pot and cups and told James he should keep them clean. He said he procrastinated and no one would drink the coffee he made anyway. And best of all, he didn't pursue the business I was going to start when I left my job. I had to tell a bit of a lie, but I didn't think it would be lying to tell him I was going to start a business since prostitution is certainly a business."

"I told him it was to be a helping service and certainly prostitution is a service and as we have already discussed, I've helped many men."

"Well, that's stretching it a bit, don't you think?"

"Anyway, from then on I'm afraid I fibbed a bit"

"When do you start working?"

"Thursday AM and it will be good to be back at my old job. It's going to take a bit of time to get used to calling him James again, but that's what he wants. Oh yes, James bought a new mini van for me to ferry people around who are looking for land or houses."

"I'm very happy for you Heidi. I know you weren't very hopeful."

"Rob, God continues to move in our lives. I want to go to church every Sunday and I'm hoping you will be willing to join a Bible study group with me."

"Of course I will Heidi. It's just so good to hear you are anxious to deepen your spiritual life. Now, no more talk of not knowing how or of not being able to pray."

"I pray often now Rob, not out loud or on my knees. I just talk to God when I feel I have something to say to Him."

"Now Mr. Sloan, we have some urgent business to attend to."

"I'm sure you are too tired to try anything this evening Heidi."

"That Mr. Sloan, is just an excuse, it's yours not mine. Into the bedroom with you, we'll take a nice hot shower together and then it's time for me to go to work. You are going to have to cooperate however, and you will have to yield to me one hundred percent. You will have to do exactly as I say, is that understood?"

"Yes doctor, I understand fully."

The shower alone was enough to arouse both to a feverish pitch. When they jumped into bed Heidi began by giving Rob a complete body massage, all the while encouraging him to relax. She was highly erotic in her speech reminding Rob what they would do once he achieved erection. Rob began to feel the change coming over him. Then Heidi said,

"Well Sweetheart, I believe you have arrived. Anything else I do will be redundant. Your impotence wasn't as deep or as serious as you thought so come on I'm waiting for you.

Rob had complete success. He had no trouble maintaining an erection. Heidi, as usual climaxed quickly which was followed by two more. Afterwards as Heidi lay next to Rob who had his arm around her Rob said,

"I'm jealous, here you had three orgasms and I had only one. Do you call that fair?"

"Well Dr. Sloan, all I can tell you is that is one big advantage women have over men , however, when ever you are ready to have sex just let me know and we'll do it again, but don' be surprised if I outdo you again.

"When it comes to sex nothing about you surprises me."

"Aren't you glad? Because of my vast knowledge about sex you are no longer impotent?"

"Tell you what Heidi, let's divide my practice, I'll do the marital therapy and you do the sexual therapy."

"You really don't mean that," Heidi chided Rob. "Would you want me to do to your impotent male clients what I just did to you?"

Rob smiled,

"I never thought of that. The answer is an emphatic, Hell No."

"Rob you swore."

"Yes I swore, what you just did is for me and me alone, understood?"

"Understood master," Heidi replied.

"Heidi, I do have a bit of a confession to make however. I must say that when you and I were having sex I got some of those feelings again, you know, the kind I got when you told me you had sex with so many men. I just can't keep them from creeping into my mind. I want so much to know that what you and I just had is always and has been always just for you and I alone."

"Heidi raised up on one elbow,

"I'm sorry Sweetheart, however, we can't remove the past. I wonder if it might not be due in part to the way I treated you over the past four months and if that's so, eventually, as you have said, you'll tuck them way back in the recesses of your mind."

"I think you might be right Heidi, that could be the reason and now that I know you are mine and mine alone forever, I shouldn't have much trouble shoving the feelings way back in my mind."

"And Rob, you are mine and mine alone forever, what I have is for you and you alone. I never again want to go through anything like the past four months."

"We won't Heidi, I know we won't."

"I still think you should take over the sexual therapy with my customers, minus the full body massage, of course."

Heidi broke out in laughter,

"No way Robert."

With both being sexually satisfied for the first time in almost four months, in a few minutes they were sleeping soundly.

Chapter Twenty Six

⸺ ◜◟◝ ⸺

It had been several months since Heidi and Rob had their reconciliation. Lorraine again mentioned that the two of them should spend a day shopping, dining, visiting and maybe even take in a movie or doing whatever else they desired. Rob told Lorraine she could take off any day she wanted.

"I guess Heidi and I could cut our outing to half a day that way you wouldn't be left with all the work."

"Lorraine, I said the whole day. If I would say half a day I would catch it from Heidi and further you are entitled to several days off, not just one"

"OK boss, I won't argue with you I'll take the whole day."

Lorraine called Heidi to tell her she could take off about any day she wanted to.

"Your kind husband said I can take off for the entire day."

"He'd better give you an entire day you certainly are entitled to it."

"I do get very liberal vacation time and further I love my work. As a rule I can't wait to get to the office and part of that is due to a wonderful boss."

"You and Rob get along very well don't you?"

"Yes Heidi we do. I have been Rob's confidant on a number of occasions and especially when the two of you were separated.

"After the way I cut him off, I really wouldn't have been surprised if the relationship between you and Rob went further than friendship. You're a very attractive woman Lorraine."

"Thank you Heidi. You don't think for a moment that we didn't think and talk about it do you?"

"No, you are attractive and Rob is such a good looking man."

"You can say that again."

"I wouldn't have been surprised nor would it have bothered me too much. Given my past I could hardly fault him."

"Heidi, there were temptations. However, Ted and I are very happily married. Do you think for one moment that I want to go through what you and Rob did? I type up the notes from his sessions and I can tell you that few marriages can survive the knowledge of infidelity. I have some thoughts on this which I will share with you when we have our day off."

"The next step is for me to talk to James and see if he will give me a day off."

"Do you think you'll have a problem?"

"No, James and I get along very well, I'm sure he will be more than happy to let me take a day off. It's interesting Lorraine, I'm much like you, I enjoy my work and am eager to get to the office each morning."

At 11:00 James called Heidi and asked her if she would please bring him a cup of coffee. It had been a busy morning with many phone calls. The real estate business was booming. Heidi had just fixed a fresh pot of coffee. She knew just how much sugar and cream James liked. James looked up and said,

"Thank you Heidi. You have been working too hard lately. This is your first day in the office for over a week. Take a day off and enjoy yourself."

Heidi laughed and said,

"James I was just about to ask you if I could take Friday off. Lorraine and I would like to spend the day together."

"You sure can and enjoy yourself. By the way Heidi whenever you would like a day off don't hesitate to ask."

"Thank you James do you have a moment to give me?"

"Of course I do"

"May I share something with you that I haven't even shared with Rob, at least not recently? I want to have a baby. Do you remember the talk you gave me before I foolishly quit working for you?"

"I sure do Heidi. That's been some time ago."

"I believe my maternal or mothering instincts have kicked in. The last time I brought it up Rob said the timing just wasn't right. That could go on forever. I could trick him by not taking my pills, but I don't want to do that."

"You know Heidi you're such a pretty girl with such an attractive figure. It may be that Rob is stalling because he doesn't want you to lose your figure."

"You know James, that thought has crossed my mind. I have a hunch Rob fears I will lose my sex appeal as my figure begins to change shape. He has a very strong sex drive and I don't think he wants a damper to be put on it."

"Well yes, a pregnant woman does lose her shapely figure and along with that might go her sex appeal, but it's only for a short time."

"Rob knows that. Maybe he doesn't want to share me with a baby."

"That's also a possibility Heidi, but whatever, he'll survive."

As if speaking to herself, Heidi said,

"There are times when I think Rob has not fully grown up."

"Couldn't that be said of all of us Heidi?"

Heidi smiled and the thought ran through her mind that picking prostitution as a lifestyle at the age of 20 certainly was not a sign of maturity on her part. Then she replied.

"Of course it could be James, Rob certainly would be no exception."

"Stick to your guns Heidi and have that baby."

Heidi smiled and looked at James coyly.

"If I do will I still have my job after I leave the baby with a day care service?"

"When we had our initial talk about babies, when I encouraged you to get pregnant I assured you, you would have your job. I haven't changed my mind. Now go ahead and have that baby and don't worry about your job."

"James, I want you to know that a girl couldn't have a better boss. Lorraine calls Rob her confidant. You are more like a father than a boss. With most men I would never feel free or comfortable discussing such an intimate subject. You are my confidant."

"James beamed and replied,

"Thank you Heidi that makes me feel real good. Any time you need some fatherly advice, my door is always open. Now you take Friday off and you and Lorraine have a great time.

"I know we will James and again thank you."

As Heidi went back to her desk she sat for a moment deep in thought, then she said to herself, how wonderful it is to feel good about myself, how wonderful it is to have self respect and how wonderful it is to have an employer who has my best interests at heart. How wonderful to have a trusted friend like Lorraine who could easily have scratched me off her list of friends when I put Rob through Hell. And best of all, how wonderful to have a husband who loves me, who never brings up my past and who seldom says any thing about the events leading up to the rupture in our relationship.

Heidi you have been blessed and to think at one time you almost traded all this to be a call girl again. As Rob has said, Heidi you certainly must have loved money. Now money is no longer important. It is love and friendship and good self feelings that are important, very important.

She gave a big sigh then called Lorraine and told her that James had given her Friday off and Friday is the day they will spend together.

"Great," said Lorraine, "I'm really looking forward to it."

"So am I Lorraine, in fact I wish tomorrow were Friday. We'll have breakfast out, then do some shopping, have lunch and after that if we feel like it we can take in a movie. And all the while we can be visiting."

"That sounds great Heidi."

"If you tell me how to get to your place I will pick you up around 8:00. I'm eager to show you my Jaguar. I no longer can call it new, but I just love that sport car."

"I have a better idea, meet me at the office."

"Are you sure you want to drive to the office. From what Rob has said, you have quite a long drive every morning."

"I've driven it so often it doesn't seem long to me and at no time do I have to encounter heavy traffic."

"OK then Lorraine, Friday at 8:00."

With a feeling of contentment Heidi hung up the phone and went back to work.

When Heidi and Lorraine walked back to her Jaguar from Rob's office, Lorraine walked around the convertible looking it over then crawled into the passenger seat.

"Heidi, you really do have a snazzy sport car. How in the world could you afford it?"

"You know the answer to that Lorraine."

"For a moment I forgot and that's good. Out here you don't get to use it much with the top down."

"Not as often as I would like, but often enough. And of course, when we go places we often take Rob's Chrysler."

"Unless you have some specific restaurant in mind, I know of a very nice, small restaurant not too far from here. It's one I used to frequent quite often."

"That sounds good to me, let's hurry I'm hungry."

After they had been served, Heidi said to Lorraine,

"How long have you and Ted been married?"

"Well, let me see. I'm 28 so Ted and I have been married eight years."

"You did marry young didn't you?"

"Yes I did, but you know Heidi I have no regrets. I have a wonderful husband and a wonderful marriage."

Heidi was quiet for a moment and then said rather wistfully,

"I too had a wonderful marriage until I lost my mind, then I destroyed it."

"Yes you did for four months or so, but I can tell from Rob's demeanor that the two of you have a wonderful marriage again."

"We do Lorraine thanks to a wonderful and forgiving husband. I understand you played no little part in Rob's willingness to forgive me."

"I can't take much credit, but I helped where and when I could."

"That's not what Rob says. I don't know how to thank you enough for your part in bringing us back together.

"I'm just so glad you and Rob are back together. Rob said the two of you are happier than ever."

"We are Lorraine. I still suffer from guilt and from bouts of anxiety when I think of what I did to my marriage. More importantly what I did to Rob. After he walked out of our house I really thought I would never see or talk to him again. My life was a shambles and as you know I was about ready to become a call girl again, but I came to my senses in time. It was then I called you. The anxiety was over the possibility Rob would have simply said, no, I don't want to see her again."

"I noticed you said our house. Rob said when you told him to leave you said leave my house."

"Please Lorraine, don't remind me of that. It just goes to show you how crazy I had become.

"Well that's not the way it turned out Heidi."

"No it isn't. I believe your wisdom in reading the 13th chapter of 1st Corinthians and reminding him of the phrase of forgiveness in the Lord's Prayer, and of course, calling to his attention the many times he has encouraged a wounded spouse to give his or her partner another chance made all the difference in the world."

"Remember Heidi, Rob was still very much in love with you. Had he not been all the encouragement in the world would have done no good. However, you are back together and both of you are happy. Stop punishing yourself."

"You're right Lorraine, I should let go of it."

"We were talking about age, you're 28 and I'm 27. Can I ask you a very personal question?"

"Working for your husband he has asked me many personal questions so go ahead, what is it.?"

"How come you have no children?"

Lorraine was quiet for a minute and then replied,

"Because, Ted doesn't want children. If only I could convey to you just how much I want to have a baby."

"What's Ted's problem?"

"I don't think he wants to share me, not even with his own child."

"Lorraine, it appears both of our husbands are showing streaks of immaturity. I too want a baby, but Rob is reluctant, he keeps putting it off. As I told James, my maternal instincts, my mothering instincts have kicked in. I believe Rob's problem is he doesn't want me to lose my figure."

"I think that's also a concern of Ted's."

"Lorraine, I'm going to talk to Rob one more time about my desire to have a baby and if he puts me off again I'm going to stop taking my pills. I know that would be kind of mean of me, but after all, I'm a woman and I should have just as much of a say so about a pregnancy as Rob. When I think about it, it is always Rob who says the time is not right and not I. Knowing Rob, once I'm pregnant he will accept it without too much of a fuss."

"Wouldn't that be deceitful Heidi? You could tell him no more sex until it is with the intent of getting you pregnant."

"I will never deny Rob sex again Lorraine. I hurt him immensely and my turning cold on him is one of the reasons he ended up impotent. It still hurts inside when I think about it. Further, that would be using sex as a weapon. I think that's plain mean. Rob has told me about women he has counseled who use sex not only as a weapon, but as a bargaining tool. In all honesty Lorraine, that's exactly what I did to Rob, I used sex as a weapon and in such a way that he would no longer desire to have sex with me, so it would drive a wedge between us and it worked. Do you use sex as a weapon or bargaining tool against Ted?"

"Perish the thought Heidi. I love Ted too much to ever do that. Further my sex needs are strong. What if he would retaliate by using it as a weapon against me? I don't know what I was thinking about when I mentioned it."

"Going off the pill without Rob's knowledge, for me at least, would be a far better choice. Would it be kind of deceitful? Yes it would, but what about us, do our husbands have the right to deprive us of the joys of motherhood?"

"No they don't Heidi, but remember that motherhood is not all Joy."

"I know that Lorraine, but I believe I'm mature enough to take the negative along with the positive.

"I too have thought about not taking my pills."

"Tell you what, if Rob gives me a hard time again let's both get pregnant at the same time."

"That would be something wouldn't it?"

"In a few weeks Rob and I are going to spend a week at Vista Point. At that time I'm going to bring up my desire for a baby one more time. If he still stalls, off the pills I go."

"OK Heidi, let me know when you leave for Vista Point. During the weekend you talk to Rob, I'll bring it up to Ted one more time also and if he stalls, we'll both go off our pills at the same time, agreed?"

"Agreed," said Heidi Let's shake on it."

Both reached across the table and shook hands.

"Further," said Lorraine, "I have been on pills for more than five years. After five years a woman is supposed to lay off them."

"It's been longer than that for me Lorraine it's time I also laid off the pills."

Heidi looked at her watch.

"Lorraine if we are going to accomplish everything we planned to do, we had better get going."

"OK Heidi, where would you like to start?"

"At Phillips Department Store in the mall if it's OK with you? I want to show you where Rob and I first met."

"Let's go."

When they entered Phillips Heidi walked directly to the counter where she and Rob bumped into each other.

"This is where we met Lorraine. I knocked a bottle of shaving lotion out of Rob's hand and wanted to pay for it. We both bent over at the same time and while we were down our eyes met. Something clicked in me as it did in Rob. He told me to forget about the lotion, however, he would be most happy if I stepped across the walkway to have a cup of coffee with him. I figured that is the least I could do."

"Something I never told Rob, I was going to take a few sips of coffee and then excuse myself. There was something about Rob that was so compelling, I decided to finish my coffee and then leave, but you know once we started visiting I discovered that Rob was so open. He told me he had just started his therapy business. That was before he hired you."

"We discovered we grew up and lived a bit more than 100 miles from each other. That was back in Iowa and South Dakota. We just talked and talked for two and a half hours. I told Rob I just had to leave. I can distinctly remember what he said. Heidi, I don't want to seem forward, but when a fellow meets a pretty girl he has to move fast. Would you have a date with me?"

"Of course I accepted believing it would be our first and last date. As it turned out it was the beginning of our relationship which quickly turned into love. As it is said, the rest is history."

"Oh yes I must tell you, on our second date Rob again walked me to the door. We talked about the wonderful evening we had and then he asked, Heidi, may I kiss you?

"You mean he actually asked you if he could kiss you?"

"Yes I told him that a fellow doesn't ask a girl if he can kiss her, he tries and if she resists he has his answer. If she yields to him he also has his answer."

Rob said,

"Heidi, I guess I'm just old fashioned but imbued with the culture of the Midwest where we treated a date as something special. Then we kissed and it was like a seal on our relationship which quickly blossomed into love."

"It was kind of an irony the way you met wasn't it?"

"Yes, especially since I was in the middle of a break from my work as a call girl."

"When you left Rob and he was feeling so down and depressed, one day he asked me, Lorraine, why couldn't you and I have met before you met Ted and before I met Heidi? We are so compatible. My answer was, it just wasn't meant to be Rob. It is true, Rob and I are very compatible and often intimate in our discussions."

"I know Lorraine, Rob has told me. I do believe that in good measure it was your closeness that enabled him to survive the first couple of weeks after I left him."

"Although he may have given up on me you didn't. That in itself had to give him encouragement. Before I left him, that's putting it mildly. Lorraine if you don't mind my strong language, it was a hell of a lot more than that, I kicked him out of the house."

"If you and Rob were so close, how in the world did you keep from having sex with each other?"

"It was Rob, Heidi. I felt vulnerable and available. I never came right out and said, Rob I want to have sex with you. Instead I asked him if he thought it was wrong for a woman to desire to have sex with a man other than her husband? As difficult as it must have been for him he pointed out what the negative implications of us having sex would be. And he was right. I could never have forgiven myself and I would have been unfaithful to Ted, something I vowed never to be. You have to understand Heidi that Rob and I are not only close but often the atmosphere in the office becomes highly sexually charged as we talk about sexual problems couples bring to him."

"Heidi, had Rob and I had sex, in all likelihood I would no longer be his secretary. He pointed out that our relationship would change in a way that would make it difficult for us to work together. Heidi, you have a wonderful, intelligent and knowledgeable husband and I want to be quick to add, a husband who has tremendous discipline and will power."

"Do you know it isn't unusual for some women in therapy to try to seduce him especially those who have been unfaithful to their husbands. Rob said their reasoning goes something like this. If I can get the therapist to fall then I'm really not so bad after all. And let me tell you some of those women are very attractive. I had no problem like theirs, but I could have fallen only Rob wouldn't let me fall."

There was a moment of silence then Lorraine spoke up.

"Heidi, I just said that even though I was telling myself don't do it, don't do it, I was trying to seduce your husband. Doesn't that make you jealous? Doesn't that make you angry with me?"

"No Lorraine, it doesn't make me jealous nor does it make me angry with you. You were one of my few, loyal friends."

Heidi smiled and said,

"Still are one of my loyal friends."

"We all have our weak moments. I should know. For one thing I trust Rob implicitly. He didn't know if I had started divorce proceedings and yet he said he could not commit adultery against me. Look what you just said? Do you think for a moment that Rob didn't want to have sex with you? You are a very attractive woman and as sexy as can be and in a round about way you tried to seduce him and yet though I'm sure he very much desired to have sex with you, he didn't. From what you have said, I would say he had your best interests in mind rather than his own. In addition, how could I ever fault Rob if he did have sex with another woman?"

"I was setting myself up to have sex with many men. I was prepared to commit adultery against Rob over and over again. No Lorraine, I hold no jealousy and no animosity towards you. Rob is a very handsome man who is complemented by his sense of responsibility and compassion. We are friends Lorraine and I want it to remain that way."

"So do I Heidi."

"Lorraine if you don't mind my strong language it was a hell of a lot more than just my leaving him."

"I know Heidi, Rob told me about the confrontation you two had. You have no idea how he suffered over what he said to you. Poor Rob, he said, Lorraine, I called my wife a bitch and worst of all a two-bit whore. He broke down in tears."

Lorraine looked at Heidi's face, tears were running down her cheeks and she was quiet.

"I angered and enraged him Lorraine. What he said to me was my fault and not his. I have never fully forgiven myself for having done so. Yes Loraine, poor Rob."

"Well Lorraine, if we are going to get any shopping done we had better move. We'll come back here for lunch. Hopefully "our" table will be empty.

Although they did a lot of browsing they made few purchases. Both bought a rather short skirt, the kind both of their men liked.

Heidi asked Lorraine,

"Do we buy our clothes for ourselves or our men?"

"Both," replied Lorraine. "I love the compliments I get from Ted it makes me feel real good. I feel that if Ted finds me attractive and sexy in my outfits so will other men. And let's face it we are more interested in what men see in us than in what women see in us."

"That's a very good answer Lorraine I couldn't have come up with one as good."

"Well Heidi, don't forget I have a great teacher in the office. I am learning so much from Rob and from typing his interviews into the computer."

They went into the dressing room and started to undress.

"You know Lorraine, I sometimes wonder why we even bother to wear panties they are usually so skimpy."

"As you notice mine are as skimpy as yours. Heidi, would you take off your blouse?"

"LORRAINE."

"Oh come on Heidi, you know better."

Heidi removed her blouse. Both were standing wearing only their panties and bras. Lorraine stepped beside Heidi and said,

"Now turn around and face the mirror."

They both turned around and gazed at the two mages.

"My gosh Lorraine, we are so much alike that we could be twins. Same dark hair worn the same way, same height and I would be willing to bet same weight, same hips, same bust line and same nicely shaped legs. Isn't it amazing there is even a slight resemblance in our faces?"

"Now, when I see us standing side by side, had I taken my clothes off for Rob, in effect he would have been looking at you."

"I'm sure there are some subtle differences."

"I agree, after all we aren't completely naked. Shall we find out? I'm only kidding."

"Heidi are you like I, it seems I'm hard up most of the time even though Ted and I have sex often, very often."

"Lorraine in the hard up department we are as much alike as we are standing here looking in the mirror."

"Well, I'd sooner be that way than cold and unresponsive."

"So would I. If I were cold and unresponsive I wouldn't have been a call girl."

"Good point."

"Take a good look at us once again. We both have very nice figures. Do you realize what would happen to them if we got pregnant? I shudder to think of it. No wonder our husbands keep saying the timing is never right."

There was silence as both were deep in thought.

"Yes Lorraine, we would lose our nice figures, but not to have a baby because, temporarily at least, we would become distorted and bloated would show immaturity on our part. If you had to choose between your figure and a baby what would it be?" Again there was silence finally broken by Lorraine.

"A baby, of course. I want a baby and there's another reason, as we get older we are going to lose our figures anyway. In ten years from now if we came back here and stripped and stood in front of this mirror, I'm afraid we would look quite a bit different."

"I don't like to think of that, responded Heidi. I don't like to think of getting old, period. Let's try on our outfits and get out of here before we both end up depressed."

At noon they went back to the small restaurant where Rob and Heidi had coffee. The table was empty. Heidi said,

"Lunch is on me. I'm going to have a Reuben sandwich and coffee, how about you Lorraine?"

"I'll have the same,"

Heidi went to the counter and placed her order then walked back to the table.

"The young fellow behind the counter said he would bring us our sandwiches."

As they were eating and visiting and after a brief pause, Lorraine spoke,

"Heidi, I once asked you what it was like to have sex with a couple hundred different men. You said that once we got together you would tell me. I'm still curious."

"Lorraine, it is a mixed bag. At first I was nervous and anxious, however, when I discovered it was no problem for me I got into it. It wasn't long before I was looking forward to servicing customers. I saw three different men a week. More was not necessary since I was making plenty of money with three. I was making money and it was so easy. It got to the place where I could hardly wait for my next customer."

"For a time I considered being available for five days a week. It wasn't just the money, I enjoy sex. And I enjoyed it with my customers."

"Were you able to respond to them?"

"In what way?"

"Were you able to have orgasms?"

"Almost always Lorraine and that I guess is one thing that made me so popular. It gives men a lot of pride if their partner has an orgasm. It's kind of a dirty little secret among call girls, but men don't give me an orgasm, I allow myself to have them. If I were to tell my customers that it would certainly deflate their egos. It might even make them impotent during the encounter. I won't say that my partner's didn't play their part, but had I not allowed it to happen it wouldn't have happened. It's amazing what kind of control we women have."

"Once a man gets started there is no quitting until he is done."

Lorraine was quiet then said,

"So it was exciting."

"Yes it was."

"Weren't there some men you couldn't handle?"

"You mean too big for me?"

"Yes that's what I mean."

"Yes there were some, but most men who were well endowed were very gentle with me. And, Lorraine let me be quick to add that most men are average. It is the exceptional one who is well endowed. Did the fact they were well endowed make sex with them more pleasurable, more exciting?"

"No Lorraine, as a rule not. I can truthfully say that it didn't, size was never an issue with me."

"It didn't, are you being truthful?"

"I wouldn't tell you size made no difference if it did. Oh, as I told Rob, if the man was extremely good looking and well endowed, yes it might have made a difference."

"I too enjoy sex very much and often fantasize I'm having sex with a man I can hardly handle. I get so hot I about blow a fuse."

"There are some call girls for whom size does make a difference. They hoped that their next customer would be well endowed. You just might be one of those girls."

"I guess I'll never know, but gosh, I sure would like to try out such a man. Heidi, do you think it's fair that a married girl has to confine her sexual relationships to one man?"

"Lorraine ..."

"I'm curious Heidi, that's all and I admit there are times I feel I am missing out on some real pleasure."

"Don't you and Ted have a satisfying sexual relationship?"

"Oh yes Heidi, we do, Ted is the best and what makes it the best is knowing he loves me and I love him."

"Don't you ever think Ted wonders what it would be like to have sex with women other than you?"

"Of course I think he does and he knows I wonder what it would be like to have sex with other men. This bothered me for some time. When Rob was going through the difficult time I asked him if he thought it was wrong for me to desire to have sex with a man other than Ted. Again he gave me an answer I won't forget. He looked at me with desire in his eyes and said, No Lorraine, I don't think it would be wrong to desire sex with a man other than Ted, that is temptation which is not a sin. It's when you yield to that temptation that it becomes wrong. Rob has been such a help to me. That man has tremendous will power, a darn side more than I have."

"So having sex with a couple hundred men was exciting, enjoyable and satisfying."

"I don't know if in that order, but yes Lorraine it was most of the time, but let me tell you that can't compare with having sex with the same man repeatedly when you love him and you know he loves you. It is much more so with Rob."

"I learned my lesson the hard way Lorraine I have absolutely no desire to be a call girl again. Sex with Rob is wonderful, just being held tightly by him and knowing I'm a party to his satisfaction gives me a feeling I can't explain. Do I have orgasms with Rob? Every time Lorraine. Does Rob feel the same way? Oh yes. Do you have orgasms with Ted?"

"Like you Heidi every time. My gosh, I can't get over how much alike we are. It's more than amazing. Let me say it's astounding."

"You want to know something, first Rob always thanked me after we had sex. I told him, Rob you don't have to thank me. His answer was and is, I'll thank you if I want to. And now after we have had sex I whisper into his ear, thank you."

"You two really have a wonderful relationship since your reconciliation."

"We do Lorraine, I couldn't ask for more and at times I feel so undeserving. You see, we both have been on the other side and that is never going to happen again. In spite of the awful things I did to Rob, God wants us to love each other and to have a wonderful relationship. At one time I would have scoffed at that, but no more. Lorraine, I have learned a lot and a lot of it has come from Rob."

"Thank you Heidi I suppose I will still wonder what it would be like to have sex with many different men and I suppose I will still fantasize about it, but after listening to you and to Rob, I love Ted more than ever and am so thankful we have a good sexual relationship."

"Well if we're going to take in a movie we had better get moving."

The movie was a love story, a fitting finish to their discussion about love and sex. Both found it enjoyable. As they drove back to Lorraine's car parked close to Rob's office it was close to 5:00 pm.

"Lorraine," Heidi said, Its been a wonderful day. We'll have to do it again real soon. And Lorraine, Rob and I are going to have you and Ted over for dinner."

"Heidi, I don't know when I've spent such a wonderful day. You have wisdom in an area that few women have. First Rob has been a great help to me and now you. Ted and I will also have you and Rob over for dinner. Now Heidi, having had the talk we did over lunch and then the movie, I am at the boiling point. I must dash home to Ted or I will for sure burn out a fuse."

Heidi laughed,

"I was wondering if you felt the same way I do. Isn't it wonderful that we can both go home to loving husbands who will be more than happy to satisfy our burning sexual desire?"

"We are fortunate, aren't we Heidi? Good bye Heidi, you and Rob have a good weekend."

"We will and you and Ted also. Good bye Lorraine."

Chapter Twenty Seven

=⫶⫶⫶=

Heidi and Rob had spent an evening out. They ate late and finished with a bottle of good wine so by the time they started for home they were slightly inebriated. When they got home it was in the wee hours of the morning. As usual, they showered together and with the affects of the wine were exceedingly amorous. Heidi said to Rob,

"A perfect ending to this wonderful evening is to make love."

"I am in total agreement," said Rob.

And so they made love. It seemed that with them every time they had sex it was the best. Rob took note of this and said to Heidi,

"Each time we make love and when we are finished it is always the best ever. Is it really or do we have short memories?"

"Isn't it always the best Rob?"

"That's a good way of putting it Sweetheart, even when it is kind of mediocre and there are such times, we always say it was the best ever and that is good. But many times it really is the best, like this morning which was no exception."

"Why do you think some times are better than others?"

"There are many reasons and I don't want to get into a lengthy discussion this morning. Sometimes a steak is better than at other times. The meat may always be the best and the preparation always the best, but upon eating it, we conclude it wasn't as good as last week or it wasn't as good as the one we ate at Lonnie's But many times it really is the best. Sex is the same way, sometimes it is unusually high key, even though it may not have been, but it is always good, right?"

"Right you are darling. Where do you come up with these analogies?"

"Oh well, that's because I'm a smart guy and it just seems to make sense."

"Oh sure," said Heidi, "I'll accept the making sense part, but I question the smart guy part."

"OK," said Rob, "Have it your way. Come over here so I can kiss you."

It was a long kiss and when they broke, Heidi said,

"Whew, much more of that and we'll be having sex again. I have a different idea, let's s drink a cup of coffee instead."

It was 3:30 when they finally went to bed. Sex is usually followed by a cup of coffee and visiting. Rob said to Heidi,

"We don't have to get up in the morning so we can sleep in just as long as we desire."

"Isn't that good," responded Heidi.

Promptly at 7:30 the phone rang, Heidi picked it up,

"Hello," she said sleepily.

"Thank heavens it's you Heidi."

Heidi had come alive and pushed herself up against the wall as she answered.

"Damn it Sally, I told you never to call me again. I have absolutely nothing to say to you. You are an evil woman and I want nothing further to do with you. I never again want to be in your presence."

"I know Heidi, I deserve everything you said and I apologize to you and Rob for the way I have sinned against you."

For a moment Heidi was quiet,

"Sinned against Rob and I, you know because of you our marriage was almost destroyed. You and your stupid idea of how great it would be to be a call girl again. I should never have listened to a word you said. You weren't concerned about me joining the happy five again your objective was to destroy my marriage and my love for Rob. Sally, you were envious of my marriage and my happiness. You almost succeeded, but you failed in your attempt. If Rob were not the kind of man he is, right now I would be the most miserable woman in the world instead of the happiest."

"That's all I have to say to you Sally, good bye and don't even think about calling me again, ever."

"Heidi, please," Sally broke in before Heidi had a chance to hang up.

"I'm getting out of the call girl business. Something happened to me that caused me to make that decision. Earlier I intended to stay with it until age forced me to quit. Not any longer, that all has changed. And Heidi, there is no longer a happy four, there is no longer a happy anything. The other girls and I have nothing to do with each other. Heidi, are you still there?"

"I'm here Sally."

"Heidi, I had an experience that shook me to the very foundation of my self. Paul told me that you too had an experience with a customer which caused you to conclude you would never again have anything to do with prostitution. Heidi, please hear me, I desperately need to visit with you."

"Sally, I don't trust you, I don't trust you one bit. So far as I'm concerned you have another cockeyed idea about me and prostitution. You talked to Paul and he told you about my experience with Carl, so you decided to make up a story to get us together so you could start out on me again."

Heidi could hear Sally sobbing and strangely, felt sorry for her.

"Please Heidi, I need your help."

"Just a minute, I'm going to talk to Rob about this. Rob, it's Sally, my personal demon, she quit the call girl business primarily because she had an experience like the one I had with Carl. Paul told her about it. Now she wants to get together with me, she said she just has to visit with me. Rob, I despise that woman."

Heidi started sobbing.

"She almost destroyed us, why should I care about her?"

Rob was silent for a long moment. Heidi put the receiver to her ear and said,

"Sally, I'm still here. Rob, what am I going to tell her, I really don't want to see her. I see her as a woman with a set of horns growing out of her head."

"Heidi Sweetheart, listen to me. Do you remember when I asked you for forgiveness for the terrible things I said to you, the awful names I called you and the vulgarity I used when I said, I hoped your customers would screw you to death."

"You couldn't use the F word, could you?" Rob nodded his head.

"I begged you to forgive me even though you said there was nothing to forgive. Finally you said, seven times seventy I forgive you. Now it sounds like Sally is asking you to do the same thing with her, to forgive her."

"Do you think I should visit with her?"

"I do Sweetheart, from what I have heard from your conversation and from what you have told me so far, it sounds like Sally is desperate."

"I want to tell you something Sally, Rob, my wonderful husband, the man you set out to destroy, just said I should visit with you. Do you hear me Sally? Rob said I should visit with you."

Sally sobbed,

"I really didn't know what I was doing. I see that now. Heidi. I know you don't trust me and for good reason, but if you are fearful of what my motive is, bring Rob with you."

"Hold on Sally, she said I could bring you with me."

"That shouldn't be necessary. Heidi. You will be able to handle yourself very well."

"Maybe you have too much confidence in me Rob."

"Lord Heidi, I hope not and I don't believe so. Heidi, I love you and I trust you. See what Sally wants."

"You listen to me Sally June Kuski. The man whose life you put into shambles says I should meet with you. If Rob has that kind of trust and faith in me then I will meet with you. I am back at my old job now and I love it. I love everything about my life now and I will not allow you to make one tiny dent in that love. When we meet, it will have to be in the evening. Hold on again Sally."

"Rob, I can't take time off from my job, so we will have to meet some evening. I am going to suggest the mall eatery where you and I had the first tingling of love."

Rob was grinning from ear to ear,

"Are you sure it was tingling of love and not lust"

"Alright, tinglings of lust if you like that better." Suddenly both broke out in laughter.

"Rob, you always come up with a wonderful way of defusing a situation. Tingling of lust, I like that. Now for sure I am confident I can meet Sally without one iota of fear of what she might have on her mind."

"I'm glad of that Sweetheart, You will do great."

"Rob, Will you at least come with me and while Sally and I visit you can go through the photo shops again."

"Sure Sweetheart, if that would make you feel more secure."

"It will Rob, I know it will. Sally, we will have to meet some evening and we will meet at the eatery where Rob and I initially fell in love, the one where you and I had coffee, near fatal coffee for me. And since I can't bring myself to trust you Sally, I'm bringing Rob with me. While you and I visit, Rob will be nearby going through the photo shops."

"That's wonderful Heidi, how soon can we get together?"

"Let's see, this is Sunday, how about Wednesday evening at 7:30? We will meet at Rex's eatery. Is that good enough for you?"

"Yes Heidi, anything is good enough so long as you will visit with me."

"And Sally, you can take it for what it's worth I know what you're going through. Good bye and I'll see you Wednesday evening at 7:30.

"Rob, I hope you don't mind the commitment I made for you on Wednesday evening? I don't want to be alone"

"I'll be happy to accompany you Heidi and the truth is I want to stop in at a couple of photo shops in the mall."

"What a strange turn of events. I can't believe I will see Sally Wednesday evening."

"Obviously something is going on with Sally, Heidi. I would at least like to meet her."

"I want you to meet her Rob."

On Monday Heidi had to take a couple to Bremerton to show them what James had listed as a starter house. They were a young couple with no children. The young man was attending The University of Washington. Heidi asked him what his major was.

"Business Administration," was his reply.

"Isn't that a coincidence," said Heidi, "My major at the U was Business Administration and this is how I am using it."

"It seems like it would be interesting work."

"It is, believe me. It's the kind of job where I can hardly wait to get to work"

As they continued conversing they discovered they had taken course work from some of the same professors. By the time they reached Bremerton, they were more than relaxed with each other. Heidi showed them the house and commented on its size.

"Not big, but big enough for a starter home."

The young wife chimed in,

"First you called it a house and now a home, what is it?"

"Both, you are now looking at a house. If you decide to buy it, it will quickly become a home since home is an atmosphere, it's the love between the people living in the house, it's the care and concern each has for the other and I could go on."

"That's interesting, I never thought of it that way. So Brad and I will buy a house but it will quickly become a home."

"You've got it," said Heidi."

That morning Heidi made a sale. She had made quite a few for James since she started working for him again. One customer told

James that she had charmed him and his wife into buying the house. It felt so good for Heidi to feel good about herself. She and James were so compatible with each other. The routine established before she left James continued. When he got to the office, after greeting Heidi, the first thing he said was, "Make a pot of coffee, fill two cups, bring them in and let's visit."

Often the visit consisted of Heidi's assignment for the day, either looking at a house to determine it's status or taking an individual, a couple or a family to look at a house or piece of land. Regardless of who the people were, in no time Heidi had them relaxed and once they reached the house it seemed to her that questions about it never stopped coming. Heidi told herself often that she was so at ease with potential buyers and was able to put them at ease because of three years during which a good part of her efforts were directed at putting customers at ease so they could perform.

Speaking out loud she said to herself,

"I would never have thought that being a call girl was good preparation for selling houses."

Just the thought of it made her chuckle.

One morning when she and James were visiting, James said,

"Heidi, would you be offended if I once again asked you a personal question?"

"Not at all because I know your questions are reasonable ones."

"When are you and Rob going to have that baby that we talked about earlier? You know you aren't getting any younger. You may want to have more than one child."

"According to Rob, the timing has to be right."

"Is timing ever right Heidi?"

"I guess not James. I have about made up my mind to discontinue taking my pills. I want to get pregnant and if Rob doesn't like it, well, he is just going to have to get used to the idea that he is going to be a father."

"That is the spirit Heidi"

"Before you leave for your first assignment, I want you to know that sales have increased markedly since you've been back on the job. Clients of yours often comment on how much of a pleasure it is to work with you. One even asked, what's your secret Mr. Simpson, how can an old man, young man like you attract a beautiful young woman like Heidi to be your sales person? My answer was because I'm so darn good looking, that beautiful women just can't resist me. Then we had a good laugh."

"First of all, thank you for the compliment James. I'm sure you are aware there is a lot of truth in what you said, I don't know how old you are, but you are a very handsome grandfather."

James beamed.

"Thank you Heidi."

Wednesday dawned as a beautiful early fall day. Heidi was aching to go to Vista Point, but that would have to wait till the weekend. The day went well for her but she couldn't keep the anxiety level down. Why would Sally want to see her and what would she have to say to Sally, nothing. She disliked her with a vengeance. Rob told her that forgiveness has to be more than words it has to be a change of heart.

At 7:00 p.m., she and Rob set out for the mall.

"Rob, could we go to the counter where we met. That few feet of floor has meaning to me."

"Sure we can Heidi, they have meaning to me also."

"In spite of what I did to you?"

"In spite of what you did to me and now young lady, I want you to remember, that is behind us."

"I know Rob, but it's impossible for me to completely put it behind me."

"I understand Heidi, I feel the same way, but we must use those memories to strengthen our relationship and our love for each other."

As they walked to the counter at Phillips, Heidi said,

"It was right here."

"How do you know this is the exact spot?"

Heidi squatted down and pointed to a very slight depression in the floor.

"This is where your bottle of cologne hit the floor."

"I believe your right Heidi. Now we must go across the hall, somebody is waiting for you."

They stepped across the hall and immediately Heidi could see Sally sitting at a table.

"Rob, I hate that woman."

"Sweetheart, you will get nowhere with her if you are filled with hate."

"I know Rob I'll keep it under control. Come with me, I want you to meet Sally."

Sally saw them coming and stood to greet them. Heidi was the first to speak,

"Sally, I want you to meet my husband Dr. Robert Sloan, but I and his friends call him Rob."

Sally looked at Rob whose face was completely relaxed and thought, what a good looking man, so slim and trim and so well built and to think I tried to destroy his marriage and his love for Heidi.

Rob smiled and said,

"I'm glad to meet you Sally. You and Heidi have something to talk about and I want to visit a few photo shops so I will be on my way. See you later. "

"How much later Rob?"

"Would two hours give the two of you enough time?"

"More than enough," answered Heidi.

"OK then, how about an hour and a half?"

"That will be enough time, Rob. Enjoy your window shopping."

"It's good to see you again Heidi. My, what a handsome man is your husband."

"And a kind, gentle loving man who can't do enough to show his love for me. That's the man you set out to destroy Sally. I really can't say it's good to see you. Just the sight of you angers me and brings up the most unpleasant memories. However, I see no reason why we can't visit."

"I understand Heidi. I really didn't think you would meet with me."

"You can thank Rob for that. He's a very forgiving man."

"Now what is this about a customer of yours whose visit made you decide to get out of the business?"

"It was the strangest thing Heidi. He was not a young man. I would say he is in his late 40s early fifties, about the age of many of our customers. Immediately I sensed there was something different about him. He was darn handsome, had mostly dark hair with quite a bit of grey at the temples which made him look very dignified. He spoke quietly and in perfect English. All I was wearing was a brief smock with no under clothing. I just let it flop open since he would soon be seeing me in the buff anyway. I figured we would get right to the sex business, he would be on his way and I would be through for the night. But you know Heidi, he paid no attention to my near nudity. He told me his name was John and wondered if we could have a cup of coffee before we had sex.

I started feeling uncomfortable about the way I was dressed and pulled my smock rather tight around me to cover my breasts and pubic area. He was my only customer for the evening. He paid enough for me so I thought why not. As we drank coffee he wanted to know where I grew up, how old I was, how long I had been in the business.

Given that he was a customer, I thought his next question was rather weird. He wanted to know if I had any regrets being a call girl. I told him yes I do. Then he said, If that's the case why do you stay in the business. I told him what all of us usually say, money and sex. He wanted to know if I could get another job which would pay enough to support me. I was going to say, you sure are full of questions, but I didn't. He wanted to know if I had a boy friend. I told him I had many. He just smiled and my answer made me feel pretty foolish.

"Then he said, you are such a pretty girl, there must be many young men who would make good husbands and who could provide you with all the sex you want and need. I responded to his question by saying yes, I guess so, but I like variety."

"He asked me if that really was an honest answer. I told him I had been in the business for five years and in all truthfulness, I was about burned out and that the variety of men had nothing to do with my staying in the business. He wanted to know if my parents knew I was a call girl. Heavens no, I told him. Why? he asked. They would be devastated if they knew what I was doing. Then he said, then get out of the business Sally."

"I was shocked, he knew my name. I didn't give it to him and I know Paul didn't give him my real name. I had this strange feeling come over me. I wondered who he was and if he was interested in having sex, why were we sitting at the table and talking about me"

"Then he said, find a good job Sally and live a good, respectable life style. You're pretty enough. I guarantee you will have no trouble finding a good and satisfying job. Then he asked me a question which really floored me, he asked me if my being a call girl affected my spiritual life? I said heavens no, I have no spiritual life. He smiled and said, We all have a spiritual life. What makes a difference is the direction it takes. I asked him what he meant. His answer was, Have you ever asked God to help you get out of this business? Rather sarcastically I answered that I didn't know God, He didn't know me and I wasn't even sure there was a God. He answered me in his soft spoken way saying, There is Sally, believe me there is and whereas you may not know Him He knows you very intimately. It hurts Him that you are in this kind of business. You can be sure He didn't plan this for you. I told him that I guess not, I just kind of fell into it. Then he said, Sally, look after your spiritual life, it can work a profound change in you. You are much too young to be throwing your life away in this manner."

"He stood and said, Sally, I now know you too well to have sex with you. I feel I would be violating the trust we have established in each other. You have told me many personal things and there is no way I want to contribute to your involvement in this business. Please think about what I have said Sally, you have such great potential."

"Then he said, you will get whatever your share of the money is for entertaining a customer. In fact I left a bonus for you. I said, but why would you do that, you didn't even know who I was until you walked in my door. He said, I knew your name, didn't I? I'll be praying for you."

"He walked out the door and was gone. Heidi, I just sat in that chair in a daze. I felt guilty, real guilty and suddenly it dawned on me I had literally wasted five years of my life. I did not sleep that night and first thing in the morning I went to see Paul and told him to take my name off the roster, I was quitting. I thought he would try to talk me into staying. Instead he said, I'm so glad to hear that Sally, you don't belong in this sordid business. You have so much potential."

"It was then he told me he knew there was bad blood between us, but it was because of an experience similar to mine that determined for you that you were leaving the business for good and going back to Rob if he would have you. Then he said, Heidi and Rob are back together and once again she is a very happy woman, very much in love with Rob and so content to be Rob's wife."

"Paul said to me being in love is so wonderful."

"That Paul, I didn't know he was such a great guy. Did you know he is looking for a different job?"

Heidi sat transfixed. Had she heard Sally correctly? Their experiences were so similar. And the description she gave of the man, beyond doubt it was Carl, but Sally said his name is John. The same wonderful man, Carl to me and John to Sally.

"Yes Sally, your experience was very similar to mine."

As she looked at Sally who seemed so perplexed, she could feel the hatred she felt for her diminishing.

"Sally, because of what Carl did for and to me I call him my personal angel. It was his visit that determined for me that I was out of the business for good. He encouraged me to go back to Rob. I told him Rob will never take me back. Carl just smiled and in his quiet voice said, He will. That gave me the hope I needed."

"A short time ago you met Rob so you know Carl was right. When Carl left, for the first time I really believed that Rob and I had a chance at reconciliation. And it was a wonderful reconciliation. We are more in love than ever. We even had a one weekend second honeymoon at our favorite spot."

"Heidi, as you know I'm not a religious person, at least I haven't been up till now, but ironically I felt just like you did, I felt John was my personal angel who came to visit me. Everything he said encouraged me and like you it was John who determined for me that I was going to leave the business for good. But why would I have a personal Angel? God doesn't know me. John said He does, but given the kind of life I have been living I find that very hard to believe. How could God have interest in one who has been a call girl for five years and committed adultery perhaps hundreds of times?"

"Sally, there were also doubts and questions I had, but it was Rob who helped me see the light."

Heidi looked up and saw Rob approaching. He pulled out a chair next to Heidi, put his arm around her shoulder, and pulled her close. Heidi raised her face to him and they kissed. Sally witnessed this and thought, Oh how I wish I had a man who loved me as much as Rob loves Heidi.

"Rob, you may find this hard to believe, but Sally had an experience similar to the one I had that was instrumental in her getting out of the call girl business. And like I she is confused. Maybe you can help her out, after all you are Dr. Robert Sloan, therapist."

"You are a doctor?"

"Well, I guess you could say that."

"What do you mean by you guess you could say that? You are a doctor," chimed in Heidi. "Don't be so darn reluctant to admit it."

Rob just smiled.

"Rob, I don't feel right in asking you anything after what I tried to do and did to Heidi's and your marriage, after I almost succeeded in destroying your love for each other."

"Sally, what you did to Heidi and I is inexcusable and almost unforgivable, however, Heidi and I have adopted an incident in the New

Testament that we use as a guideline. On one occasion Jesus' disciples asked him how often they had to forgive one who offended them. His disciples asked Him if seven times was enough? His answer was, No, seven times seventy. In other words, there is no limit. Heidi and I try to live by that, but at times it's very hard to do. I must admit Sally, what you did to Heidi makes it very difficult to forgive you. You tried and almost succeeded in destroying an immense love that two people had for each other. And what you tried to get Heidi to do had nothing to do with wanting her be a call girl again and everything to do with destroying her marriage and her love for me".

"Having said that, I forgive you. It is more difficult for Heidi to do so, but I believe she is now close to it. Words are easy to come by Sally, but true forgiveness comes from the heart and not the mouth. The mere fact that the two of you could sit here and converse without one or the other getting up and walking away, tells me that Heidi's heart is softening. Am I right Sweetheart?"

"Yes Rob, you are right."

"Now what are your questions?"

"First, thank you for your forgiveness Rob and Heidi, thank you for working on it. Before you returned, Heidi and I were talking about the customer we both had who had a profound impact on our decision to get out of the call girl business. Heidi believes Carl might have been an Angel. I know nothing about Angels so I am confused. John was not an ordinary man. When he walked into my house a sense of peace came over me. Here my walls were decorated with erotic pictures and I was almost naked and yet he made no mention of either. Instead he talked about me and the potential I had and how I was wasting my life. Not once did he raise his voice and a number of times his answer to my questions was just a smile, no words and yet those smiles spoke volumes."

"When I told him I knew nothing about religion and God and that if there was a God He certainly didn't know me. He just smiled and then said softly, you're wrong Sally God not only knows you, He knows all about you. Rob, he knew my name, I never gave it to him nor did Paul. How did he know it was Sally? I said, then He knows what a wicked woman I have been, surely He has no use for me. Oh you're wrong Sally, God has much use for you, but if you want to know what it is you must first find Him and then get right with Him. Rob, was I visited by an Angel or do I just have an over active mind. If John isn't an Angel, who is he?"

Rob was silent for a time and then said,

"I don't know if Carl or John is an angel. If you believe there are angels, he could be. From what both you and Heidi have said, I am assuming the visitor the two of you had is the same person It's possible that he is very human. I'm going to say he is very human. Why? Because he told Heidi he had a daughter in college. I don't believe angels have daughters. If he is, he must be a good man and a man of great and unwavering faith. If I am correct, it is possible God singled him out to visit both of you. Why he picked the two of you, I don't know. Will he visit other call girls or has he done so already? It could be his calling is to visit call girls. I wouldn't be one bit surprised if he visits prostitutes often."

"He apparently is a wealthy man. It is possible he has people working for him, people who dug into the pasts of both you and Heidi. If I'm right and I might be way out in left field, but if I'm right then he came to the two of you knowing about as much about you as you know about yourselves."

"What I do know is his visit had a profound impact on both of you. Sally, I would say that since you were singled out, God must have great plans for you, but as John said, you must come to know Him first."

"But how Rob?"

"It's not difficult Sally, but you must make a beginning. You need to ask for forgiveness and repent. What that means is that you must never again be a call girl."

"Heidi," Sally asked, "Is that what you have done?"

"Yes Sally, but I have just made a beginning and have a long ways to go. But with Rob's help I know I will get there."

"I have no one to help me."

Heidi spoke up suddenly,

"Oh yes you do. He is Reverend Clay Cunningham."

"Who is he?"

"A very dear friend who has been of immense help and comfort to me. I just know Clay would be more than happy to be your guide and mentor. Are you willing to meet with a man of deep faith, a man of the cloth"

"Ten days ago I would have said no, but today I say yes, yes."

"Alright, I'll call Clay to make sure he has time to see you and I'm almost positive he will. I will set up an appointment for you to meet him, but you must keep it."

"I will Heidi, I will."

"Do you own a Bible Sally?"

"No Heidi, I don't."

"The first thing you want to do is go to a book store, look over the various translations and buy what you like and be sure you take it with you when you see Clay."

"Would it be OK if I started reading it before I saw Clay?"

"Of course, but don't be surprised if you find yourself stumped and confused. Clay will help straighten it out for you."

"I'll buy a Bible tomorrow Heidi and start reading it right away. Well, I'm sure both of you are more than ready to return home. Thank you so much Heidi for agreeing to visit with me and both of you for forgiving me. I needed that so badly, and Rob, thank you for your views on who John or Carl is. That really gives me something to think about."

"Sally, give me your phone number, I'll call Clay and get back to you after I visit with him."

"That would be great Heidi. I am so anxious to meet this Clay."

All three stood, Sally turned to Heidi and asked,

"May I hug you Heidi?"

"Of course Sally," and they hugged.

When they broke both were shedding tears.

"Once you meet with Clay, we must keep in touch Sally"

"Are you sure you want to Heidi?"

"Heidi took Rob's hand and replied,

"As Rob says so often, that is now behind us and now we must move ahead. We are moving ahead Sally and we will continue to do so."

"You wonderful people, I never dreamed it would end like this."

"I didn't either Sally, but God did."

That night as Heidi and Rob lay in bed with Rob's arm under Heidi's head and Heidi snuggled up close, Rob said,

"Heidi, God has a purpose in everything he does. He rescued you and now you are helping Sally to see the light. In addition to saving our marriage and our love for each other, Carl's purpose was to prepare you to meet with and forgive Sally and to get her on her way to believing in and establishing faith in God."

"Rob, you handled Sally's question so well."

"I wish I could have said more to reassure her, but I too have my limitations you know," he said with a smile.

"Maybe so Rob, but surely you see how God has been using you?"

"Yes Heidi, I do. I'll say one thing Heidi, you certainly were right when you said Sally is an attractive woman. She must have been very popular with her customers."

"She was Rob. Is she prettier than I?"

"No way Sweetheart."

It was with feelings of contentment that both were sleeping in short order.

The next day Heidi called Clay and explained the situation with Sally.

"Clay, Sally needs guidance and is ready for it."

"Heidi, I would be most happy to meet with Sally and to do so on a regular basis until she feels she can move forward on her own."

"Wonderful Clay, that will mean much to Sally. And Clay, Rob and I still want you to remarry us and real soon."

"Just let me know Heidi and we will set a date."

"Clay, Sally is a very attractive girl. When you see her you might wonder if all call girls are attractive. Yes, they are, but some are more so than others and Sally is one."

"And Heidi is two."

"Thank you for the compliment Clay."

"I like to compliment when it is deserved. Now don't forget about that wedding date."

"You'll hear from us within the next week or two. Thank you so much Clay for agreeing to help Sally."

"Well Heidi, isn't that what I'm all about?"

"Of course Clay."

That evening Heidi called Sally and gave her the good news.

"Clay will be most happy to meet with you on a regular basis. Now Sally, don't you dare drop out."

"I promise I won't Heidi. And Heidi, I bought the most beautiful Bible today bound in leather."

"That's wonderful Sally, but it's what's inside that is important. Please call me often and let me know how you are progressing with your meetings with Clay."

"I will Heidi, and that's another promise."

"And Sally, just let me say that Clay is a very handsome man, tall and rugged looking and with the most disarming smile. Now I don't want you to go getting any ideas," said Heidi laughingly.

"Well now Heidi, that is one thing I won't promise," Sally responded with a laugh. "Oh yes Heidi, I want you to know that tomorrow I go job hunting, wish me luck."

"I'll do more than that Sally, I'll pray that God will lead you to a job that will be both challenging and satisfying."

"Heidi, I want you to know how good it is to have you as a friend again. I didn't think it was possible for it to happen."

When Heidi hung up she went into the living room where Rob was going through some therapy notes.

"I don't particularly care to bring this kind of work home, but I must make the notes legible so Lorraine can read them."

"You really don't have a very good handwriting do you Rob?"

"About the worst there is Heidi. How did your conversation with Sally go?"

"Rob, you were so right as usual, I feel so good having forgiven Sally. It wasn't easy to do."

"And you think your folks won't forgive you?"

"That really concerns me Rob. Sally is Sally, but we are talking about my parents."

There was silence. Finally Rob spoke up.

"We've looked at about every possible reaction from your parents. I'm optimistic. Heidi, if you have doubts, remember I said whether or not to tell your parents is up to you."

"I know Rob, but to be honest with you, right now I don't know what to do, I don't know what the right thing is to do."

"Come over here Sweetheart and sit on my lap."

Heidi went over to Rob, sat on his lap and laid her head against his chest.

"You don't have to make the decision now, we still don't know when it will suit your parents to come to Tacoma, and it just might be that your decision will be a spur of the moment one. You have plenty time to turn it over in your mind."

"If I wouldn't have been so stupid in the first place I wouldn't be faced with this hard decision."

"You're not stupid Heidi, you didn't use your head, but you're not stupid."

Chapter Twenty Eight

≡ ⫿⫿ ≡

Trevor and Naomi's plane would arrive at 3:30 p.m. Lorraine scheduled clients for only the morning hours. Rob would be with Heidi when she needed him. She hadn't slept and when she got up, she was not only tired, but also a nervous wreck. Would they recognize her? Would she recognize them? Rob told her, her anxieties were for naught since of course they would recognize one another. James told her that her two weeks leave would begin the day after her parents arrived and would end one day after they left.

"And Heidi," he said to her, "Any sales which are made with clients with whom you have been working with, you will continue to get your commission."

What a good man he is she thought. It still bothered her that she had lied to him when she told him she was starting a business of her own. What would it do to her if she continued to lie to her parents, if she failed to tell them she had been a call girl?

Just before Rob left for the office she told him she didn't know if she would survive the next two weeks. Rob's response was,

"You'll survive Heidi, of that I have no doubt. I will always be by your side."

Just to hear him say that was a source of comfort.

Promptly at 1:00 Rob arrived home. They would take his Chrysler to meet Trevor and Naomi. At 1:30 they left for the airport arriving at 2:00. They would have an hour to wait if the plane was on time.

"Rob, I'm going to crawl out of my skin."

"Let's get a cup of coffee perhaps that will calm you down."

At 2:45 an announcement came over the loud speaker that Trevor and Naomi's plane would be on time. They left the dining area and walked to the waiting area. The voice over the loud speaker announced that the plane was arriving. Heidi could hardly contain herself. She was bombarded with a host of feelings leaving her totally confused.

And then she saw her parents coming down the steps. She recognized them at once. They had aged in six years, her mother had more grey hair and her father had less. They looked around and Heidi called out,

"Dad, Mom over here."

They turned, saw Heidi and just stood still. Heidi ran up to them and they all embraced. There were so many tears that no one could speak. Finally Trevor said,

"My Little Girl, you're no longer a Little Girl you are a very mature, beautiful young woman."

"No dad, I'll always be your little girl."

"Heidi, Heidi why did you make us wait so long for this reunion?" said her mother.

Rob noticed a moment of hesitation and then Heidi spoke up,

"I will tell you about it, but that will have to wait awhile."

Again they all embraced and wept.

"Heidi," her mother said, "We were sure something awful had happened to you, so awful that no one was aware and couldn't inform us."

"Mom and Dad, I am so very, very sorry. It was awful of me not to keep in touch and not to come home for a visit. A bit later you will understand."

Rob said to himself, she is going to tell them. He coughed and said,

"Heidi Girl, I'm here too."

Heidi turned around and said,

"Oh Rob, please forgive me, I'm afraid I forgot for a moment that you were with me. Mom and Dad, I've been neglecting my husband. I want you to meet the joy of my life. This is my husband, Dr. Robert Sloan, Rob my parents Trevor and Naomi. Naomi hugged Rob and Trevor shook his hand.

"My goodness Dr. Sloan, we didn't even know Heidi was married, much less that she married a doctor." Rob smiled and said,

"Let's get something straight here and now. I am Rob, I hardly know Dr. Robert Sloan. I'm a therapist, I work with people's problems and with their minds and not with their bodies."

Trevor had remained silent. It was clear to Rob that he was looking him over. Finally he spoke up.

"You are a fine specimen of a man and you are a professional man. That's good. You married my Little Girl and my biggest concern is that you love her as I do."

"Trevor, Heidi is the light of my life. I couldn't love her more."

Heidi slipped over to Rob and raised her face to him, Rob bent down and kissed her.

"Dad, if you had spent 10 years of your life searching for a husband for me you couldn't have done as well as Rob and I finding each other."

"I'm glad," Trevor replied, "I want only happiness for you Heidi. Step back Heidi and let me take a good look at you. What happened to my Little Girl. I knew that when you matured more you would develop into a beautiful woman. Am I right Rob?"

"Totally right Treavor. She was beautiful when we first met and she's even more beautiful now. I want you to know I couldn't love your little girl more. She is in good hands."

"I can see that Rob and it makes Naomi and I very happy."

Rob slapped his hands together and said,

"I don't know about the rest of you, but I'm hungry, what say we eat."

"That sounds good Rob, just as soon as we get our luggage."

Rob and Treavor walked over to where the luggage was coming in on a conveyor belt. While they were waiting, Naomi said,

"Heidi how could you be so lucky to marry such a handsome and well groomed young man."

"Well Mom." Heidi said with a laugh, "I guess beautiful women attract handsome men. More seriously Mom, Rob and I have concluded that God brought us together."

"Have you gotten religious Heidi? When you left home you wanted nothing to do with your church."

"Mom, I'll be honest, for most of the time since I left home, I have had nothing to do with religion. Some of my teachers convinced me it was a bunch of hokus pokus. It was Rob and a number of terrifying incidents that steered me back to religion. I am now a believer although I have a long ways to go. Rob is my teacher and I feel I am learning by leaps and bounds."

"I am so glad to hear that Heidi and I know your dad will be too."

Soon Trevor and Rob had the luggage and walked out to the car. When the luggage was stowed in the trunk and they were in the car, Rob turned and said,

"Heidi and I have decided we are going to eat Italian food this afternoon. Is that alright with you?"

"We haven't eaten much, but I'm sure we will enjoy it. Let's get to that restaurant," replied Naomi.

The food was great, but the visiting, the reunion was better. Rob sat next to Heidi, Heidi sat next to Trevor and Naomi sat next to Rob. Trevor said,

"Rob, how did you know that United had flights out of Sioux Falls?"

"I was born and grew up in a small town just 35 miles from Yankton and 50 miles Southwest of Sioux Falls."

"What a coincidence that you two should meet. The two of you grew up just a bit more than 100 miles apart."

"Trevor, there have been many coincidences in our lives together and apart. We will have plenty of time to tell you about them. I'm sure you will see they were more than happenings."

"Now, I have a hunch both of you are tired. What say we go home? The two of you take a hot shower, Heidi will perk a pot of coffee and we will sit around the table and do some more visiting."

"That sounds good Rob, I am tired and I'm sure so is Naomi."

"OK, home it is."

When they arrived home Trevor and Naomi were more than a little surprised by the house. Naomi said,

"My goodness you have such a lovely house. The rooms are so large and spacious. Are you renting it?"

"No mom, we aren't"

"You must have a very good paying job Heidi, and Rob, you must be doing real well with your therapy."

"Well we certainly can't complain, Rob is a marriage and sex therapist and has built up a very good practice. I work for a kind, elderly gentleman selling real estate. He is very good to me and gives me a good share of the sales I make."

The visiting around the table was lively and animated. At 9:30 Trevor said,

"Naomi and I are very tired, would it be alright if we turned in for the night."

"Of course, I'm sure you both are very tired, I will be leaving for my office quite early. The two of you sleep in. I'll do my level best to be home shortly after noon."

"Mom & Dad, James has given me a two week leave to spend time with you so I won't be going anywhere in the morning."

When Trevor and Naomi came into the kitchen Heidi had breakfast ready for them. What she had fixed was her dad's favorite breakfast. As they started to eat Trevor put down his fork and looking at Heidi and said,

"Little Girl, you certainly haven't forgotten how to cook. This is delicious and you remembered this is my favorite breakfast dish."

"You didn't think I would forget, did you dad? I love to cook and Rob loves to eat my cooking."

After a brief visit, Naomi said to Heidi,

"Just what is a sex therapist? I have heard of marriage counselors but never a sex therapist."

"Mom, there was a time when people who had an unsatisfactory and disappointing sexual relationship in their marriage would just grin and bear it. That is no longer the case. People want to be happy in their sexual lives. If Rob were here he would tell you that where there is a marital problem there is a sexual problem and where there is a sexual problem there is a marital problem. The two go hand in hand. I can assure you he is correct. I have read some of the notes he has taken at his therapy sessions."

"My times have changed. When you're dad and I married sex just wasn't that important."

"Mom, are you being fully honest with me?"

"No I'm not Heidi, you're dad and I had our problems but there were no sex therapists available to us."

"Would you have gone to one?"

"I certainly would have," answered Trevor.

"Your Rob is a wise man, he is so right sexual problems and marital problems go hand in hand. But I must say you're mother and I did a good job of working out our differences, without help I may add."

Rob arrived home shortly after noon. After a quick lunch He and Heidi took Trevor and Naomi to Bremerton on the other side of the bay. They also stopped at a number of small towns. What impressed Trevor most was the traffic.

"I have never seen the likes. How in the world can you stand it, day after day without let up?"

"It's not easy Trevor, but we have no choice. My business has to be where there are many people. I would never survive in a small town."

They drove as far as Townsend, where Trevor and Naomi bought a few souvenirs."

"Now," said Rob, "We can either stay here a bit longer and eat in one of the restaurants that serves fresh fish, or we can go home and Heidi can fix us some fresh salmon."

Naomi and Trevor answered as if in one voice,

"Let's go home I want to eat more of Heidi's good cooking."

"Alright home we will go."

That night as Heidi and Rob cuddled, Heidi said to Rob,

"Do you think you can come home around noon again tomorrow?"

"When I left yesterday nothing was scheduled for tomorrow afternoon. Let me call Lorraine to see if she has scheduled anyone."

Rob called Lorraine at home. Ted answered.

"Hi Ted, this is Rob, I hope I didn't get you out of bed?"

"We are just getting ready to go to bed, but no, you didn't awaken us. I suppose you want to talk with Lorraine."

"I do Ted."

"Hi Rob, what's up?"

"How heavy is my schedule for tomorrow afternoon?"

"You have one appointment from 12:30 to 1:30 and that's it. I'm trying to keep your afternoons light."

"Good girl Lorraine, I can't keep this up much longer, but a day or two more won't hurt. I'll be leaving the office after 1:30."

"OK Rob."

"Thanks Lorraine."

"Enjoy yourselves. Has Heidi dropped the bombshell yet?"

"Not yet, but that is just around the corner."

"Poor Heidi, I feel for her."

"She's going to need our support," answered Rob.

"She has mine."

"Good night Lorraine."

"Goodnight Rob."

"The afternoon is largely free Sweetheart, what do you have in mind?"

"Let's take mom and dad to Vista Point. If it gets a bit late we can eat out."

"That suits me fine Sweetheart. Have a lunch ready when I get home and we'll take off."

After crawling into bed, Heidi pressed close to Rob and said,
"Rob, Sweetheart, I love you, you know."
"I know Darling and I love you."
They cuddled closer and soon were sleeping soundly.

Chapter Twenty Nine

= ⑴⑴⑴ =

At noon Rob came home. Heidi had fixed a big lunch and was waiting for him.

"Lunch is ready Sweetheart, let's eat and be on our way. I've been telling mom and dad about our favorite overlook and they are anxious to see it"

"Let me get into something more casual, we'll eat and then be on our way."

As they drove toward Vista Point, Trevor and Naomi got glimpses of Mt. Rainier.

"Can't you stop so we can get a good look?" asked Trevor.

"There's too much traffic and no place to pull off the highway."

"How do you put up with this traffic?"

"Barely Trevor, just barely,"

"I'll take Iowa any day."

"Whoa Trevor, you haven't seen anything of Washington yet. Yes, I hate the traffic and the congestion, but I love the beauty of the country. I could never be happy back in the Midwest."

"How about you Heidi, do you feel the same way?"

"Dad, Iowa will always be my home, my parental home, but like Rob, after living here for seven years, I could never be happy back in Iowa. It isn't only the mountains we love, it's also the ocean. We have a place we go to several times a year. It's at the Northwest tip of Oregon, a town called Seaside. We plan to take you there."

"Have you ever seen the ocean, Naomi, Trevor?"

"Never have," replied Trevor "And I look forward to seeing it."

When they reached Vista Point, Heidi and Rob took them down a couple of trails that led to unobstructed views of Mt. Rainier.

"How beautiful," Naomi said. "I can see why you wouldn't want to leave country that has this kind of beauty. Are we anywhere near Mt. St. Helens?"

"On a clear day, when there isn't so much haze in the air, you can see it from here."

"Is there any chance we could go there?"

"Of course, Heidi and I are anxious to get back to St. Helens."

At the end of one of the trails they sat for an hour and drank in the beauty. When they got back to the car they sat at "their" picnic table and visited.

"Dad, mom, it was here that Rob gave me a diamond and asked me to marry him. We also had an experience here that wasn't so pleasant."

"What was it Heidi?"

"That is also something we will tell you about later."

"What is the big secret the two of you are keeping from us? You mentioned it at the airport and at least one other time and now you mention it again."

"Very soon I will tell you mom and dad."

On the drive home Rob asked,

"OK, where will it be this evening? Do we eat out or at home?"

"At home of course, we can always eat out."

"Home it will be."

When they hit the traffic, Trevor again said,

"I'll take Iowa any day."

Rob and Heidi looked at each other and smiled.

The next day Rob had a full schedule. He told Trevor and Naomi he would see them around 5:30. Heidi took them to Phillips and Heidi showed them the spot where she and Rob met.

"Mom and dad, it was no mere coincidence Rob and I met, it

was meant to be. Other than for a brief interlude, we have been so happy."

When they returned home Heidi fixed another of her dad's favorite dishes.

When Rob got to the office Lorraine wanted to know how they were all getting along.

"So far so good Lorraine, however, Heidi has not yet told them she was a call girl for three years. Trevor, her father, is very opinionated about a lot of things. I fear we will have trouble with him. Naomi is different and I don't think she will be as difficult to deal with as Trevor."

"How soon is Heidi going to tell them?"

"She has to very soon. Trevor is getting suspicious about Heidi's silence. They are very curious about this thing she will share with them later. She has told them several times that it would be later or soon."

"Poor Heidi, now when she and her parents have been reunited, she is about to drop a bombshell in their laps."

"Yes Lorraine, I agree. Poor Heidi, I'll let you know Trevor and Naomi's reaction once Heidi tells them she was a call girl."

"I'll keep my fingers crossed for all of you and pray that in the end her past will be resolved without any rupture in Heidi's family."

"And how goes it with you and Heidi?"

"Wonderful Lorraine, just wonderful. We are doing a good job of putting the past behind us. Heidi still goes through periods of remorse, but we just hold each other and I let her cry. You know Lorraine, crying can be good therapy."

"I know Rob, I have put that in client's records many times. And Rob, may I ask you something personal?"

"You know you can Lorraine."

"Is Heidi satisfied with having sex with but one man?"

"Lorraine, as I've said before, you know you and I can be personal with each other any time. Did I tell you that initially I was impotent? That about broke Heidi up since she accepted full responsibility for it. She sobbed, now I know for sure you don't want me back. I reminded her that she once told me she was able to help many of her customers who couldn't achieve an erection although most of the time it was only temporary to begin with. None the less without her skilled intervention, both she and her customer would have wound up frustrated. The customer because he wasn't able to have sex and Heidi because she couldn't be helpful. I told her that if she could help strangers overcome episodic impotence she surely could help her husband. And she did."

"What in the world is episodic impotence?"

"I'm sorry Lorraine, I shouldn't have used episodic. It means that whereas a man is usually able to perform, something happens that causes him to fail to have an erection. It's simply an episode of impotence, and not an ongoing problem."

"Lorraine frowned, was quiet for a moment and then said,

"Why didn't you say that in the first place?"

Rob laughed,

"Lorraine, there are times I forget I'm not in my office with a client. That three month period before we broke up devastated my self confidence as you well know. But as Heidi said, she had a few tricks up her sleeve only they weren't up her sleeve," Rob said with a smile.

"I see," said Lorraine, "In certain respects female anatomy has certain advantages that are beneficial to men. You know that, don't you?"

"I sure do. Did you say certain respects, certain advantages?"

"Oh, you know what I mean"

"Now it's time for you to get to your office, your first client will be here shortly."

"OK Lorraine and by the way, I never did answer your question. If Heidi isn't satisfied with having sex with one man, her husband, she certainly hasn't said anything to me about it."

"That's wonderful Rob."

Rob arrived home at 5:30. Heidi suggested he shower, put on something comfortable.

"By the time you finish dinner will be ready."

The dinner was delicious and the conversation light and easy. Trevor couldn't believe the size of the mall and all the people milling about. Again he asked,

"How in the world do you put up with it?"

After dinner, Heidi and Naomi cleared dishes from the table, put them in the dish washer, then joined Trevor and Rob in the living room. Rob was on the couch while Trevor occupied one of the recliners. Naomi took the other recliner.

They had just seated themselves when Trevor said,

"Now what is the big secret you two have been keeping from us?"

The time has arrived, thought Rob. Heidi started right out.

"Dad, mom the expenses involved in getting a college education are almost unbelievable. The help you gave me dad was most appreciated and it helped, but was not nearly enough. I took a job at a fast food restaurant, but was paid only the minimum wage. I went further and further in debt. I had a friend who always seemed to have money. She paid for her education and had plenty left over. I thought her family was wealthy. They weren't."

"Nancy, a very attractive young woman and good friend made her money as a call girl. She told me I didn't always have to be broke instead I could be rolling in money in a very short time. She told me that with my looks and figure I would be a shoo in. She gave me the name of the agency she worked for and I thought I would check it out. The agency was looking for girls between the ages of 18 and 26 willing to be call girls. At first I put the idea out of my mind, but my debts kept increasing. I went back to the agency and told a nice young man that I would give it a try."

"What kind of agency is it, and what kind of work did they have for young women?"

"The agency was recruiting young women to be call girls."

"Call girls, what are call girls?" asked Trevor.

"Call girls are very high priced prostitutes."

There was a shocked silence.

"You, you mean you were a prostitute?" gasped Trevor.

"Yes dad I was, for three years. I made a lot of money and was able to eliminate my debt and put a good part of my earnings in the bank. I bought this house with some of the money."

"You mean making money was so important to you that you would sell your body for it?"

"Yes dad, that's a good way of putting it."

Trevor had turned pale.

"My daughter, my Little Girl a common whore for three years?"

Rob quickly broke in,

"Please "Trevor, we don't use that word around here."

"Why not, that's what she was. I can't believe it. Your mother and I thought we raised you to be a decent, respectable young woman. We failed."

"No dad, don't look at it that way."

"There is no other way to look at it. So that is why you drummed your mother and I out of your life, that is why you totally ignored us because you were a common whore."

Again Rob broke in,

"Trevor, I asked you not to use that word again. It is my wife that you are calling such a vulgar name."

"When you married this prostitute, did you know she was a prostitute?"

"Yes Trevor I did."

"What kind of morals do you live by man?"

Heidi was in tears and was sobbing heavily as was her mother.

"I believe I lead a good and moral life. I fell in love with Heidi, she told me about her past, I had a struggle with it, but I believe God wanted me to love Heidi and to take her for my wife."

"Were you out of your mind man, knowing she was a prostitute you can honestly say God wanted you to love and marry her?"

"Yes Trevor, I firmly believe so."

"Boy, you are some screwball."

Up till now Naomi had said nothing, suddenly she spoke up.

"That's about enough of that Trevor. What right do you have questioning Rob's morals and questioning his belief that God wanted him to love and marry our daughter?"

"You keep out of this."

"No, I will no longer remain silent."

"Well, let me tell you something, she may be your daughter, but she isn't mine."

"Dad," Heidi cried out.

"I no longer have a little girl, I no longer have a daughter."

Rob took Heidi into his arms and pulled her head close to his chest.

"I suppose next you will tell me you entertained your johns in this house."

"Yes dad, I did," Heidi sobbed.

"Why did we ever come out here? It would have been better had some accident taken your life. That would have been easier to handle than knowing you spent three years as a whor--, as a prostitute."

"Dad, Heidi cried out, you would have sooner been told I had died?"

Trevor was silent.

"I could have told you a bunch of lies, is that what you would have me do?"

Again Trevor was silent. Then he rose and said to Naomi,

"Let's pack Naomi, we're leaving for home tomorrow."

"Maybe you are Trevor, but I'm going to stay with my daughter."

"Alright then, I'll leave alone."

Rob stood and looking at Trevor said,

"Sit down Trevor, now it's my turn. Yes Heidi was a prostitute. Telling you was a very difficult decision for her to make. She knew your reaction would be strong and even suggested you might disown her, yet she didn't want to lie the rest of her life."

"Lie, that would have been mild compared to being a prostitute."

"Have it your way. Have you never heard of forgiveness? Heidi made an awful mistake she made a very bad decision. All of us have made mistakes of one kind or another. None of us is perfect none of us is without sin. I don't care what you say, Heidi is your daughter. She is flesh of your flesh and blood of your blood. Trevor, I want to read something to you."

Rob walked to his book shelves and took out a Bible.

"Ha," said Trevor, "What are you going to do, preach to me?"

Naomi shouted out,

"Trevor, that is enough of that, what on earth is wrong with you, have you lost your mind?"

"No, I'm not going to preach to you Trevor, but I'm going to read something I want you to hear. It is found in the book of Luke, chapter 15 starting with verse 11."

Rob proceeded to read Jesus' parable of the prodigal son. Before he finished he closed the Bible and laid it on the coffee table.

"I want to finish the parable without reading it. It may vary from the story as it is presented in the Bible, but I believe it will be close enough."

"Every day this wealthy man, this father, walked to the end of the road and gazed in the direction that his son had vanished. Day after day he kept his vigil. Then one day, far in the distance he saw a figure approaching. With a heart full of hope he said, Could it be? He watched intently as the figure approached. When the figure was a short distance off he recognized him as his son."

"He ran forward and embraced him and kissed him and weeping said, my son, my son. The young man slipped to the ground and wrapped his arms around his father's legs. Looking up at him he said, Father, I have sinned against heaven and you. Please forgive me and take me back as only a servant."

"The father who was weeping profusely called to a servant. Go kill and prepare the fatted calf, bring a gold ring for my son's finger and a robe with which to cover him. We are going to have a banquet. For once this my son was lost, but now I have found him."

When Rob finished, he looked at Trevor and said,

"Jesus could just as easily have substituted daughter for son. Heidi is a prodigal daughter who has returned home and has been completely forgiven by her husband and I believe by God. And you can't find it in your heart to forgive your only daughter, your Little Girl? She made a terrible decision as did the prodigal son. But when he confessed the error of his ways, his father forgave him and welcomed him with open arms."

There was a long period of silence. Trevor's chin fell to his chest, his shoulders began to shake and then he began to weep and soon was sobbing almost uncontrollably. He stood and cried out,

"Heidi, Heidi, my Little Girl, forgive me, oh please forgive me. Oh God, what have I done? What have I said? Come to me my Little Girl."

Heidi, who was shedding copious tears stood and went to her father. He embraced Heidi all the time asking her to forgive him.

"Dad, dad," she said, "I love you like the little girl I once was. Of course I forgive you dad and I pray that you will forgive me for my many sins, for my abandonment of you and mother, for disappointing you so, for abandoning those values you instilled in me, for every way in which I betrayed and hurt you, please, please forgive me."

"Heidi, Heidi my Little Girl. I forgive you seven times seventy. I'm afraid I lost my mind there for awhile. And my Little Girl, please forgive me for all the horrible things I said about you, for the awful name I called you. How could I, you are my daughter, my Little Girl. I love you Heidi, I have always and will always love you. How could I speak to you as I did while inside I have nothing but love for you?"

"Dad, you know you are forgiven. I can only imagine how you must have felt when I said I was a prostitute for three years. Deep down I was ashamed of myself, so very ashamed of myself and of what I was doing and that is the reason I cut off communication with you and mom."

They continued to cling to each other as they wept. When the weeping subsided, Trevor looked at Rob and said,

"You're a good man Rob, I'm proud to have you as a son-in-law. Few men would marry a girl knowing she was a prostitute yet you loved her and were willing to take her as your wife."

"Trevor, love does wonderful things to people. After we broke through that thick exterior of yours and got to your heart, the love you had for Heidi all along came pouring out."

Trevor again pulled Heidi close and with that big rough hand pushed the hair from her face and stroked it. It was then Rob remembered Heidi telling him her father was a bull of a man and yet highly emotional.

"Dad, I must go to mother."

"Of course you must Heidi."

Heidi went to her mother who also was standing. With tears in her eyes she embraced her.

"Please mother, forgive me for all the ways in which I have wronged you. I can imagine your concern and fear when month after month went by without hearing from me. The business I was in made me a different woman, but love changes things. When I fell in love with Rob, I was the old Heidi and mother I want you to know if it weren't for Rob, I wouldn't have made that first phone call. It was Rob who told me it would be best if I told you and dad the truth. He asked me if I wanted to live the rest of my life living on lies."

"At first I didn't know what to do. Rob told me the decision was mine. Earlier when dad asked what the big secret was, I knew I could not go on lying. I knew I was taking a chance of losing both you and dad, but it was a chance I had to take."

Naomi was sobbing.

"When you and I fixed supper this evening, I could see that little girl standing on a stool next to me helping me and asking so many questions. And that little girl, now a bit older taking over the household responsibilities while I worked until your dad's injury had healed. You don't know how much those memories seared into my heart when we didn't hear from you. We thought you had died through some accident and even that you might have been murdered. It was awful. We didn't know where you were or who to contact. And so we just waited and waited and waited. And when you called six or seven weeks ago, your dad and I agreed it was a gift from heaven."

"I'm so sorry mom that I put you through so much. Now I ask myself how could I have treated you so terribly. Here is the man you can thank. The most kind, considerate and loving husband any woman could have and I wasn't always kind to him either, but our love for each other weathered the storm."

Neither Naomi nor Trevor asked her what the storm was about. Heidi thought to herself, Thank heavens they didn't ask me about the storm, I don't believe I could have handled going through that awful time again.

After all had dried their tears, Rob said,

"I don't know about the rest of you, but I could feel the spirit of God in our midst. I don't think it would have turned out this way if it were not for that."

"I agree with you Rob. When you read and told the parable of the prodigal son, suddenly something came over me and I realized how wrong I was. I had such a lump in my throat I could hardly swallow."

Heidi kissed her mom, went to her dad and kissed him and then went to Rob and kissed him.

"Oh how I love you. Without you and your ability to keep your cool, I don't believe it would have turned out this way. You knew what to do and say at precisely the right time.

"Sweetheart," Rob said, "I haven't always kept my cool."

"And Rob Darling, that was my fault."

Again, neither Trevor nor Naomi asked any questions. Heidi said, "I'm going to make a pot of fresh coffee, we'll gather around the table and when we finish with our coffee, I think all of us need to get to bed.

As they walked to the kitchen, Trevor sided up next to Rob and said,

"Rob, I am so glad you are Heidi's husband. You are a man of great understanding."

"How about a man with an ability to love and to keep that love going."

"I like that Robert."

"It's Rob, Trevor."

"And why not Doctor?"

"That's OK around my office in the presence of clients, but not among family and friends."

"You are a humble man, aren't you."

"Trevor, if I am, I must give my mother credit for that."

When they had finished with their coffee there was hugging all around, Heidi kissed her mother and dad and then all went to bed.

Heidi and Rob lay awake for awhile.

"Sweetheart," Heidi said, "I'm emotionally drained. I was so afraid that my relationship with mom and dad had come to an end. You were wonderful Darling. Your use of the parable of the prodigal son was a stroke of genius."

"Hardly genius Sweetheart, maybe a good idea, but hardly genius."

"There's no arguing with you, is there," Heidi said with a smile.

"Anyway, as you read, I could just see the change come over dad. Rob Sweetheart, I love you so much that if we weren't both so tired I would suggest we make love."

"Ahhh, Heidi Girl that sounds so good. I'll remind you of that when we aren't so tired."

"Sweetheart, that's one thing you won't have to do."

In a short time both were asleep in their favorite position with Rob's arm under Heidi's neck and Heidi pressed as close against him as she could get.

The remainder of Trevor's and Naomi's stay was a pleasure for them all. Never again was Heidi's prostitution mentioned. Rob and Heidi took them to Seaside, Oregon and to Mt. St Helens. For Naomi it was a highlight of their trip.

It was with reluctance they left for home and it was with reluctance that Heidi and Rob saw them leave. However, promises were made all around that they would frequently keep in touch and that they would also visit back and forth. When they said their goodbyes at the airport, it was a far different scene from that which transpired in the living room two weeks earlier. Seldom did Trevor refer to Heidi by her name. It was almost always, my Little Girl.

As they headed home, Heidi gave a big sigh and said,

"Well, that's over. No more secrets and no more lies to mom and dad."

"It was a spur of the moment decision, wasn't it Heidi?"

"Yes Rob, it was. I just couldn't see mom and dad leaving for home without knowing the truth. The lies would have had to continue. That person who lived on lies for so long no longer exists. How would I ever reconcile a life of lies with God? I would be a hypocrite."

Rob reached over and took Heidi's hand.

"You've come a long way Sweetheart."

"Yes Rob I have, but one thing is sure, I have not stopped growing in my spiritual life."

"Even with a concerted effort, I don't think any of us ever stops growing Sweetheart."

When they arrived home, garaged the car and were seated around the kitchen table drinking coffee and going over the past 2-1/2 weeks, Rob said to Heidi,

"Seems to me that about two weeks ago while lying in bed you told me that if you weren't so tired, you would ask me to make love to you.? Are you still too tired?"

"Much too tired," Heidi said to Rob somberly.

Then she broke into laughter, got up, took Rob by the hand and said,

"Come on lover boy, let's make love."

Chapter Thirty

=≡ ⑾⑾ ≡=

It had been a busy day for Heidi. She got home before Rob and took a hot shower. The moment she turned the shower off she said,

"Oh, oh, Rob isn't going to be happy with me. He wants us to shower together. Oh well, I won't tell him I showered and I can take another."

She put on something sexy, but comfortable. Since her and Rob's marriage had been "reborn" as she called it, Rob didn't seem to be able to get his libido under control. That suited her just fine. After what she did to Rob he would have been more than justified in having an affair, however not Rob. He just suffered through the "draught" as he called it. She had feared that they would not be able to respond sexually to each other as they had before she broke with Rob and decided to be a call girl once again. For a very short time Rob was impotent but only for a short time.

She had wondered how a man could become impotent so easily and so quickly. Rob had explained why, however, when she considered her own ability to respond fully, orgasm and all after their reconciliation, she still wondered about it. If a man's ego is so sensitive she said to herself, then it's amazing there are so many people on the globe.

Heidi's reverie was interrupted by the ringing of the phone. She picked it up and said,

"Hello,"

"Hello, Heidi?"

"Yes, this is Heidi, who am I talking to?"

"Heidi, this is Juanita. Paul told me you made a quick decision not to go back into business. He said you and Rob, that's his name isn't it? He said you two are back together once again and you are the happy girl you were before you got that stupid idea to be a call girl again."

"Juanita, it's so good to hear your voice. You know you were one of the people who helped me to come to my senses. You gave me the kind of dressing down that I needed. What you said about being a whore really troubled me."

"Heidi, I'm so glad I played even a small part in getting you to change your mind."

"Juanita, I hesitate to ask you, but have you been able to leave the business?"

There was silence, then through tears Juanita replied,

"No Heidi, I am still in the business. I have been looking for a different job long before we met at the mall. I have had no luck I just don't have any saleable skills."

"I pray that you and Jeremy are still together."

"We are Heidi, but I don't know for how much longer. It is getting more and more difficult for Jeremy to have sex with me and I must admit I am a lousy, non-responsive wife."

"Juanita, that's because you have been denying your own sexual needs."

"It's hopeless for me Heidi, hopeless."

"No it isn't Juanita, Rob has told me about patients he worked with who had become estranged, got back together, had a difficult time getting connected again sexually and after a bit of counseling redeveloped a meaningful sexual relationship."

"But Heidi, how am I going to be able to hang onto Jeremy?"

Again there was silence. Heidi could hear Juanita sobbing on the other end. Suddenly she got an idea. Rob had many friends in one business or another. Maybe he could help.

"Juanita, don't give up and do your best to hang on to Jeremy. I have an idea. It's just an idea mind you, but that's better than nothing. I still have your phone number and I'll get back to you very soon. And Juanita, thank you for calling it means very much to me. I'll go to work on my idea right away."

It was only a wild idea with only a glimmer of a chance of succeeding. Now she was anxious for Rob to get home.

She didn't have to wait long. She met him at the door. Rob put his briefcase on the floor, gathered Heidi up in his arms and said,

"I love you, you know."

"I know Rob and you know how much I love you. Rob, I have something on my mind that's been bothering me. It's past time that we have Clay renew our marriage vows. It's been a month, maybe two since we asked him to do so. He will think we are no longer interested."

"You're right Heidi, after all our marriage has been reborn. Why have we been procrastinating?"

"Is there a particular date you have in mind Rob?"

"No so long as it isn't on a work day."

"Alright, I'll call Clay and if he is free and still willing, I'll have him set it up for this coming Sunday."

"So soon?"

"This coming Sunday Rob."

"OK, if it suits Clay this coming Sunday afternoon it will be. I really think we should be in church Sunday morning."

"Have you forgotten that Clay also pastors a church? It would have to be an afternoon or evening ceremony. It will be just the three of us, Clay, You and I."

Rob looked at the top of Heidi's head and said,

"Your hair is wet, have you been exercising?"

"No, but haven't you noticed how hot it is?"

"I really haven't been paying too much attention to the temperature on the outside, but I know that on the inside it's about boiling."

"Well," said Heidi, "We're going to have to take care of that."

Rob pushed a few hairs out of Heidi's face and kissed her.

"Now Heidi Girl, how about supper?"

"All I have to do is put it on the table."

"Good," said Rob, I'm starving."

After they had eaten they went into the living room. Rob picked up a book he had been reading and Heidi picked up the newspaper. After about 15 minutes Heidi put down the paper, turned to Rob and said,

"Rob, Sweetheart, could we talk?"

Rob put down his book and said,

"When Sweetheart follows Rob, I know it must be something important."

"That's not fair I often call you Rob Sweetheart."

"I know you do, I was just having fun with you. Come over here sit beside me and tell me what you want to talk about."

Heidi scooted over to Rob and sat close beside him.

"Now tell me what it is you want to talk about."

"Please just listen till I finish."

"Will do," answered Rob.

"I have a friend who is a call girl. Juanita is a good friend and hers was one of the voices that caused me to think seriously about the wisdom of going back into the call girl business. Juanita wants to get out of the business in the worst way. Her husband Jeremy has been very patient and understanding with her but both are running out. Juanita is very fearful that her marriage is going to end. That would be a tragedy since they are very much in love, but Jeremy is about at the end of his rope. He finds it more and more difficult to have sex with Juanita. He feels much like he is just another customer.

What makes it worse is that Juanita has become unresponsive in their sexual relations which makes Jeremy feel like he is a failure. Juanita has been looking for a job, but she has no marketable skills and they could never make it financially if she quit the business and worked at a fast food restaurant which, she said, is about all she is qualified to do."

Heidi was quiet for a moment then continued.

"Juanita is a good typist and was an 'A' student in high school which means she has ability. With her typing skill I have a hunch she could master a computer in a short time. Rob, you have many friends who are business men. Perhaps one of them is looking for an employee and if one would be real benevolent and patient might be willing to take Juanita on."

"If Jeremy leaves her she will be devastated. Did I say they have a little boy about three years old? I am real concerned about Juanita and much like I she went into the business because she and Jeremy were badly in need of money. It was supposed to be for a very short time, however Jeremy simply cannot make enough money to support them. Well, that's about it. Now you know what I wanted to talk to you about."

With a smile on his face Rob responded,

"I'll tell you one thing Heidi, it sure was a one sided conversation, but your heart certainly is in the right place. Pucker up I want to kiss you. Now my Dear, let me say something. Lorraine and I had a good talk the other day. My business has grown to the point where the work load is almost too much for her. She has been working after hours just to keep up and that she shouldn't have to do. It would mean that in addition to her work she would have to train Juanita. She's a tough cookie, but I just don't know if she has the stamina or time to train a girl who has no experience."

"Lorraine is also a very compassionate girl, but I can't say whether or not she would be willing to take on that kind of a task. However, I'll certainly discuss it with her"

"Rob, you are a wonderful man. I had no idea you were looking for someone to help Lorraine."

Again Rob tilted Heidi's head with his index finger and kissed her.

"I'll do what I can Sweetheart and I'll do it tomorrow. If Lorraine agrees you will have a job for Juanita.

"Rob Sweetheart, I can hardly wait until tomorrow evening. Now you wonderful husband didn't you say you were about to boil over inside. We had better go and take care of it right now before you blow a fuse. Here, give me your hand."

Heidi took Rob's hand and led him into the bedroom.

Later they were lying in each other's arms when Rob said,

"Is it my imagination or does sex keep getting better and better?"

Heidi broke out laughing.

"Dr. Robert, Sloan, just how many times are you going to say that sex is getting better and better? It isn't your imagination Darling. It is getting better and better. It sure was great this evening. Could it also be because you were ready to blow a fuse?"

"It could be that that had something to do with it, but only something. It's getting better and better because, if it's possible, our love for each other just keeps growing At any rate Darling, once again thank you."

"Rob, I've told you many times you don't have to thank me. I get as much pleasure and enjoyment as you do and it's all because of you."

"And as I've said, if I want to thank you I'm going to thank you."

"It's early yet," said Heidi, "What say we take a shower and go to bed. I want to be in your arms."

"And I want you in my arms. We'll take that shower together of course."

"By all means," responded Heidi.

The next day it was hard for Heidi to keep her mind on her work. She wanted to pick up the phone and call Rob to find out if Lorraine was willing to train Juanita along with all of her other work. She decided it would be best if she waited till Rob got home.

Heidi kept going from the kitchen to the living room window looking for Rob coming down the street. Finally Rob was parked in front of the house. Heidi closed her eyes and prayed.

"Please Lord make it work out for Juanita."

Rob came into the house and called out,

"Sweetheart, I'm home."

Heidi came running from the kitchen, they kissed and embraced.

"How was your day?" asked Rob.

"Terrible," replied Heidi.

"I'm sure it was. Come over here and sit beside me on the couch."

Oh no, she thought, the news isn't good.

"Mrs. Sloan, I talked to Lorraine and she is more than willing to give Juanita a chance. It will be a real challenge for Lorraine, but as I told you she is a very compassionate and caring woman. I told her you would come in and tell her what you told me about Juanita. She will be waiting for you sometime tomorrow. Give her a call and let her know what time you will be showing up. Lorraine knows that Juanita is a call girl, which will not be an issue with her."

"I would guess not since you are married to one, to an ex call girl that is and Lorraine is fully aware of that."

"Lorraine is just glad if she can get Juanita out of that sordid business."

Heidi was in tears and sobbing loudly.

"You wonderful people you and Lorraine. You are all so compassionate. God has answered my prayer. I'm going to call Juanita immediately. How soon can she start and though I hate to bring it up, what will her salary be."

"I haven't decided on that yet, but you tell Juanita that with Jeremy working it will be a salary she and her family can live on."

Heidi had the card Juanita gave her when they had coffee in the mall. She got it out and immediately punched in Juanita's number. Jeremy answered,

"Jeremy, this is Heidi Sloan. We haven't met, but Juanita and I are friends. Although we haven't met I feel like I know you. Juanita mentioned you often."

"I guess in a way you and Juanita had and have similar problems," replied Jeremy.

"That's a good way of putting it Jeremy?"

"Is Juanita home?"

"Yes she is Heidi I'll put her on the phone."

"Heidi, is that you?"

"Yes Juanita your days of being a call girl are just about over."

"What do you mean Heidi?"

"Rob, my husband and Lorraine his secretary have been talking about hiring another girl to help Lorraine. They know that you have few developed skills, however I told Rob about your high school record, about your ability to type and both are certain you will learn quickly. Although Rob hasn't decided on what your salary will be, Rob said to tell you it will most certainly be a salary, along with Jeremy's, on which you can live comfortably."

There was silence and then Heidi could hear Juanita weeping.

"Oh Heidi, I can't believe it are you sure?"

"Of course I am Juanita."

"Does Lorraine know I'm a call girl?"

"Lorraine knows it and that makes no difference. It shouldn't her boss has been married to one for better then three years. Both Lorraine and Rob want to see you out of the business. So tell Jeremy that it's over. No more will he have to kiss you goodbye as you go off to be a prostitute. No more will he have to agonize over you having sex with multiple men."

"Heidi, you've saved my marriage, you've saved my life."

"Juanita, it is an answer to prayer."

"Yes Heidi, it's an answer to prayer. "

"When do I start?"

"I'm going to talk to Lorraine tomorrow, after that you will start. Don't entertain any more customers."

"Oh Heidi, how can I ever thank you? I didn't have the slightest inkling this is what you had in mind, finding me a job."

"You don't have to thank me Juanita, thank God."

"I will Heidi, I will."

"I'll call you tomorrow evening. Call Paul and tell him you are through with the call girl business"

"He will be happy to hear that Heidi."

"I know he will, Juanita. He wants to help as many girls leave the business as possible. Should it be found out what he is doing he will lose his job for sure, however he told me he was looking for a different job so it wouldn't be a disaster. Until tomorrow evening then Juanita, Goodbye."

"Goodbye Heidi and again thank you so very, very much."

The next morning which was Tuesday Heidi asked James if she could leave about two hours early.

"I have important business with Rob's secretary."

"Take the entire afternoon off if you would like Heidi."

"Thank you James, but that won't be necessary."

"You know Heidi, I would like to have a long visit with Rob. I would like to get to know him better."

"I want you and Rob to have that long visit. Do you think you and Doris could come to our house for dinner one of these early evenings?"

"I would like to do that very much Heidi and I know Doris would also like to visit with you and Rob."

"That's settled then, let me check my calendar at home and then we will set a date. I know you and Rob will have much to talk about. As you know I was raised on a farm in N.E. Iowa. Mother taught me early how to cook. During harvest I did all the cooking while mother attended her ladies organizations. I do believe she belonged to every organization within a radius of 100 miles. That's stretching it a bit, but it seems she was always on the go."

"Then when dad was injured in a farm accident, mother had to go to work and all household chores fell to me. I have three brothers but not one is house broken. Further dad has a large acreage and they were needed outside. I'm a pretty good cook James."

"I know the baked goodies you have brought to the office are proof of that."

"Didn't spending so much time looking after the family limit your social life?"

"Very much so James. I didn't do much dating and I had the reputation of being a wall flower."

"That must have hurt."

"It did and I must say I could hardly wait for graduation so I could go off somewhere to college. Don't get me wrong James, I love my parents and brothers very much, but my social life was almost nil."

"Let's see, you attended the University of Washington, right?"

"Yes."

"Wasn't it a bit traumatic making the shift from a high school in a small rural town to such a big university as Washington?"

"Very much so. At first I didn't think I was going to make it, but after making a few friends things got better."

"Do you and Rob go back to Iowa often?"

"Not nearly often enough. Oh yes James, as you know Rob and I were raised about 100 mikes apart. At first I was going to go to college in Vermillion, but then I changed my mind. Who knows, had I gone to Vermillion Rob and I might have met much earlier."

"Yes Heidi you told me about your earlier plans and where both you and Rob were brought up. Don't forget I was raised near Omaha."

"I'm sorry James, I have a way of repeating myself."

"Heidi you don't have to apologize."

Rob went to lunch early, he felt he needed to talk to Lorraine. Not knowing just when Heidi would show up at the office Lorraine had brought her lunch. After hanging his jacket in his inner office he walked out and pulled up a chair beside Lorraine's desk.

"Lorraine there is something you and I need to talk about. When Juanita is here, how are we going to continue our intimate discussions?"

"Interesting you should bring that up now Rob, I was wondering about the same thing on my drive into the office this morning. I don't want to have to give them up. After all I am your confidant and you are mine."

"I have an idea Lorraine there is always the privacy of my inner office. If you start coming in the very first day Juanita is here and close the door behind you and keep it up she will soon get the idea that when you close the door I have something confidential to talk over with you."

"That sounds like a good idea Rob. Since your office is sound proof we won't have to whisper. Doesn't just talking about our private moment's sort of make you feel like we are planning an affair?"

Rob threw his head back and laughed,

"It sure does. Would you like to talk about one now?"

"Sure, where do we meet?"

"Right here in the office. Once Juanita leaves for the day it will be just you and I." Lorraine smiled and asked,

"Do you suppose this is the way arrangements are made between a boss and his secretary?"

"Could be, but I think it would be more likely they would make the arrangements over lunch and a couple of stiff drinks."

"It's joking with each other just like this that I don't want to give up," said Lorraine.

"Neither do I and we don't have to give it up," replied Rob.

Lorraine looked at her watch and said to Rob,

"Oh my gosh, it's time for your first clients. Are you ready for them?"

"Not exactly, our talk about arranging an affair has gotten me rather steamed up."

"I was wondering if you felt like I do."

"Now, into your inner office."

Promptly at 3:00 Heidi bid James goodbye and drove to Rob's office. She was anxious to see Lorraine again. Lorraine and she were not only friends, but very good friends. When she walked into the outer office Lorraine was sitting at her desk. Heidi was again impressed with how attractive she was. She would have to ask her if Rob had trouble keeping his hands off her since they last had lunch.

Lorraine looked up from her work and turned to face Heidi.

"Hi Heidi, how goes the real estate business?"

"It's booming Lorraine. So far as my job is concerned that is a good thing, but I don't like to see so many people pouring into the area."

"I don't either Heidi. Say when are we going to take another day off so we can continue talking about your call girl days?"

"Any time, but lets make it sooner than later."

"Lorraine I'm here so we can talk about Juanita. Rob has given you some information I hope to fill you in on the rest. Juanita and I were fellow call girls, I guess I should say sister call girls for three years. We became close friends. After I quit our friendship drifted somewhat apart. I ran into her at the lunch shop across from Phillips in the mall. She told me about the difficulty Jeremy, her husband, was having staying with her. He just couldn't have sex with her for two or three days after she saw her last customer. They were drifting apart. She loves Jeremy and doesn't want to lose him."

"I asked her why she didn't get out of the business. It was then she told me she had no skills other than being a call girl. She also told me she was the fastest typist in her class and also graduated at the top of her class. She has talent and ability."

"She called me the other evening to express her thankfulness that Rob and I were back together. She was still at the business and had no prospect of leaving. She could get a job at a fast food restaurant, but that wouldn't be nearly enough to keep a roof over their heads much less food on the table. "

"Poor girl, she was in tears much of the time. She and Jeremy were drifting further apart and the thought of him leaving her was agonizing. It was then I had the idea that perhaps one of Rob's business friends might be able to take her on, have his secretary train her and get her out of that lousy business. When he told me you and he had discussed the need for additional help for you, it was like an answer to prayer. You will like Juanita. She is not as outgoing as either you or I, but she is no great introvert either. I believe her ethnic background has something to do with it. She is a very attractive woman about our age, has a gift of speech, is quick to learn and it seems to me has a native ability to do things right."

"I know that doing all the work Rob gives you and training a new girl isn't going to be easy, but I have a hunch you will find Juanita an eager student and quick learner especially with her typing skills. If I may be a Pollyanna, when it looks as if it's getting too tough, just think about what your generosity and compassion has done for Juanita. You and Rob got her out of that lousy business of being a call girl. Most likely you saved her marriage"

"Whoa, saving marriages is your husband's business, not mine."

"You know what I mean."

"Does she have any children?"

"Yes, a small boy. She and Jeremy wanted more, but she contacted Gonorrhea and before she sought treatment her tubes had become infected. She will have no more children. That weighs heavily upon her. Do you have any specific questions for me Lorraine?"

"Not now Heidi, but maybe later. Tell Juanita she can start in the morning. Let's all show up at the office at 7:00. That will give me time to show her around and at least tell her what her responsibilities are going to be."

"Lorraine, you are a wonderful person. You came to Rob's rescue when he needed you most and now you have come to Juanita's rescue. I wish I could have a record like that.

"Heidi, I see one thing for you to do, love Rob always. I just know you will never put him through such an ordeal again."

"I won't Lorraine. I promise you I will never do anything like that again. I still think that for a time I was possessed by the devil. Rob and I are more deeply in love now than before our breakup. I will do nothing to willingly hurt him again, ever.

"Well, I must be going. I have some grocery shopping to do."

"How do you like your real estate job.?"

"I love it. James is such a dear to work for."

"James?"

"Yes, he doesn't like me to call him Mr. Simpson. He is James to me and I am Heidi to him. I just love selling real estate and if you can take a bit of bragging, I'm pretty darn good at it.

"Lorraine, remember, very soon you and I must get together for an afternoon of shopping, lunch, or whatever we would like to do and let's make it soon."

"I'm all for it Heidi."

That evening Heidi called Juanita with the good news. Juanita was elated as was Jeremy. She had called Paul as Heidi expected. Paul was very happy for her and wished her the best. Heidi asked,

"Could you be up early enough so we can be at Rob's office by 7:00?"

"If need be I'll be up early enough to be at the office by 2:00 a.m."

It was decided that Juanita would drive to Heidi's and Rob's house, leave her car there and drive with Heidi to Rob's office. Heidi would make the introductions then in the evening she would ride back to the house with Rob, pick up her car and go on home.

"Heidi, how should I dress?"

"Not like a call girl, that's for sure although I have a hunch Rob wouldn't mind it one bit."

Juanita laughed.

"Don't dress too conservatively either. Rob likes women to be in skirts. You will notice that Lorraine will be dressed in a skirt and blouse. Your skirt doesn't have to be too long either. Rob admires beauty and a good figure in women and you have both."

"Not really Heidi, I'm rather common in both departments."

"Whoever told you that?"

"I'm afraid I heard too much of that when I was growing up."

"You will like Lorraine. You and she are the same age."

"I thought I would be working with a woman considerably older than I."

"No way, Rob likes young women around him. I'm just joking. I believe he would have hired Lorraine regardless of her age."

In the evening Heidi again called Juanita just to visit with her.

"I'm looking forward to meeting both Rob and Lorraine. I'm so excited and you should see Jeremy he is on cloud nine. No more will he have to send his wife off to have sex with nameless men."

"Heidi, you and I are really going to have to work on Jeremy's and my relationship. It is not the best right now, but with me out of the business I am so hoping it will improve. I'll be coming to you for advice."

"Juanita, there is someone much better than I for doing that. Didn't I tell you that Rob is a marriage and sex therapist? You just ask him anything you want. He is a very understanding and compassionate man. With Rob and Lorraine around you will be in good hands."

Promptly at 7:00 a.m. Heidi and Juanita walked into Rob's outer office. Lorraine was waiting for them. Juanita looked striking with her dark hair and dark eyes. She was dressed just right to enhance her good looks and figure. She knew Rob would be pleasantly surprised when he met her. Lorraine took Juanita into Rob's inner office and explained what he did.

"How does one counsel a couple that is having marriage problems, what does he say to them and what do they say to him?"

"In due time you'll find out as you type up Rob's notes."

"You call him Rob, shouldn't it be Dr. Sloan?"

"Not with Rob. The only time we use Doctor is when there are clients in the outer office. When it is just the three of us it is Rob."

"He must be a very humble man."

"He is Juanita. I assure you, you, will like him."

Next Lorraine showed Juanita where patient files were kept and said a few words about her filing system.

"It won't take you long to catch on."

"Oh yes, if you arrive before I do, be sure to make a pot of coffee. I'm assuming you can make a good cup of coffee?"

"I have never had any complaints."

Rob will be calling both of us into his office just to talk or to plan the day. That always takes place with coffee in hand. For awhile there was quite a bit of leisure time, but his business has picked up to a point where he is kept busy until 3:00 p.m."

"Isn't that a bit early to be quitting for the day?"

"Not for Rob. He may leave for home, may do a bit of shopping or may call us into the office just to visit."

"He certainly sounds like the kind of man a girl would like to work for."

Heidi piped up,

"He is Juanita, of that I can assure you."

"You will have to learn to use the computer, but with your typing skills I don't believe it will take long for you to catch on. Whenever you have a question or questions do not hesitate to call me. I'll drop what I'm doing, if I can, and give you a hand. Now, do you have any questions?"

Heidi was surprised at the kind of questions Juanita asked.

"That girl is smart," she said to herself."

When Rob arrived at the office, Heidi went to him, kissed him and said,

"Good morning Sweetheart this is one morning I got up before you did."

"Good morning Darling, you sure did beat me out of bed. For a moment I forgot you and Juanita had this early morning appointment with Lorraine and I wondered where you had gone."

Heidi then made the introductions. Juanita was very gracious and Rob the perfect gentleman doing all he could to put Juanita at ease and make her feel welcome.

"With two beautiful women just an arm's length away, how am I going to get any counseling done?"

"Just like you did when there was only one beautiful woman just an arm's length away." piped up Lorraine.

That brought laughter to all of them.

"Well," Heidi said, "I have to be going. James also likes to have a cup of coffee waiting for him when he arrives at the office."

She walked up to Rob, threw her arms around his neck, kissed him and said,

"See you this evening Sweetheart."

"At about 4:00 Darling," replied Rob. "Will you be home by then?"

"I'll make it a point to be home. It appears it's going to be another hot day and I don't want you to blow a fuse."

Rob blushed and disappeared into his office and closed the door.

"Those two sure love each other," said Juanita.

"They do," answered Lorraine, "But it wasn't always that way around here."

"I know," replied Juanita, "That was a very sad situation."

As Heidi drove to work, she felt so good. She just knew it wouldn't fail.

In the evening when Rob arrived home Heidi met him at the door.

"Well," she said,

"Well What?" replied Rob.

"Rob, please don't keep me in suspense. What do you think of Juanita and is she going to work out?"

"Heidi, I find her a very attractive girl, she is friendly and outgoing. She will be a real asset around the office."

"And I thought she was rather reticent," said Heidi.

"Best of all Lorraine is very impressed with her. She catches on very quickly, has a sharp mind and if she has a question or problem, she does not hesitate to call Lorraine. It will take a little while of course, but Lorraine said there is no doubt in her mind that she will work out, she will prove to be a real asset to us. And one more thing, already she and Lorraine are good friends."

"Sweetheart, you have done a very good thing. You got Juanita out of the trap of prostitution and I just feel it won't be too long before her self esteem shoots way up."

"And you dear girl get all the credit."

"No Rob, no I don't. There are a number of players in this success story. Jeremy with his great love for and patience with Juanita. Paul, who encouraged her and then praised her for leaving the call girl business, Lorraine who so willingly agreed to train Juanita and you Rob, you who said you would do all you could to see that Juanita and her family got another chance at life."

Heidi gave a big sigh and said,

"OK, I'll accept the role of conductor with the rest of you all members of the orchestra. Rob Sweetheart, I feel so good."

"Darling, you have every right to feel good, so very good. Come here so I can kiss you and hold you to my breast. I love you, you know."

"I know Rob and you know how very much I love you."

They kissed for what seemed a long time. Then they embraced and just stayed that way for awhile.

Chapter Thirty One

≡ ⑈ ≡

A month had gone by since Heidi had last talked to Clay. Since she told him she and Rob wanted him to marry them within a week or two she felt guilty. She got on the phone. When Clay answered she apologized several times.

"That's alright Heidi, however I am assuming this call is about setting a time when I can remarry you and Rob"

"You're right Clay. Let's see, this is Thursday. Would you marry us on a Sunday afternoon?"

"Of course and Sunday seems very appropriate."

"Well then how about this coming Sunday?"

"Just a minute while I take a look at my schedule. The afternoon of this coming Sunday will be fine. Do you have any special place and time in mind?"

"Could we possibly be remarried in the hospital chapel? That would be so meaningful to me"

"I see no reason why not. I'm assuming you don't want a long ceremony."

"No Clay, just a brief ceremony and it will only be Rob and I since we need no witnesses."

"You have church services so would 3:00 be too early?"

"Three O'clock would be just fine. I usually get home around 1:00."

"That's great Clay. Rob and I will be taking a sort of 2nd, 2nd honeymoon. We will soon be going to Vista point for three days of camping.

"You too certainly like that place."

"We love it Clay. Rob and I will see you on Sunday afternoon at 3:00. Oh by the way Clay, how are the meetings with Sally coming?"

"Very well Heidi. She is an eager learner and some of the questions she asks even stump me. She shows considerable depth of thought. She has found a small community church close to where she lives and says she attends regularly. There is still much she questions, but we work through these slowly until she is satisfied. Then we move on. I enjoy working with her. For a man my age it's a pleasure to sit next to such an attractive young woman."

"Oh come on Clay you're not that old. Why you can't be 4 or 5 years older than Rob and I.

"Maybe not, but that's 5 years. And like you Heidi, she struggles with her past. Although she is getting over it, at first she believed that God has no use for her. The Gospels are a real eye opener for her. She's going to be alright. And Heidi, keep in touch with her. She feels pretty lonely at times."

"I have been negligent Clay, but I will remedy that very quickly

"Heidi, you did a wonderful thing steering Sally to me. We get along very well. We are now good friends as well as teacher and student."

"Sally is a very attractive girl with a large wardrobe. I'll bet she comes to the sessions dressed fit to kill."

"Not fit to kill Heidi, fit to arouse a man. There are times when I have to remind myself that I'm a minister. She is kind of a flirt you know"

"I know and why wouldn't she be, after all she was a call girl for five years."

"Heidi, you and I are more than mere friends. We are very close. I want to share something with you. Sally and I are also more than friends. We are dating regularly and both of us have expressed our love for each other. I have never been in love before that is not with someone other than family members. I have realized how much I have missed living the single life. When I told Sally I was falling in love with her she wanted to know how that could be possible given she had been a prostitute and I'm a minister. I told her that she had said it, she HAD been a prostitute. I told her, Sally that is now behind you and I certainly don't see you as a prostitute. I see you as a beautiful and fine young woman with whom I have fallen in love. She broke into tears Heidi, and then she told me that she too had fallen in love with me. She said, I just couldn't help it Clay, you are such a wonderful man, so handsome, so understanding, and so strong. I needed to love a man and God has brought us together. You know Heidi, I told her that I needed to love a woman, that something had been missing in my life that she was filling."

Clay chuckled and said,

"I told her to go easy on that wonderful handsome and strong man bit, that I was a man with a great capacity to love."

"Both you and Rob, Clay."

Clay continued,

"Yes, God brought us together, of that I have no doubt, but he did it through you Heidi and for that I will be forever grateful to you."

"Oh Clay, I'm so happy for both of you. Isn't being in love wonderful?"

"I never imagined how wonderful, Heidi."

"Both Rob and I wish you and Sally the very best. Please convey my message to her."

"You will be hearing from us Heidi. I believe that not too far down the road wedding bells will be ringing for Sally and I and when they do we want you and Rob to be present."

"We wouldn't miss it Clay."

It was a good six weeks after Heidi and Lorraine had their last days outing. The weather forecast for the coming weekend called for clear skies and warm temperatures. Sunday evening after Heidi and Rob had crawled into bed Heidi said,

"Rob Sweetheart, I have a suggestion.

"Oh oh," Rob replied, "When Sweetheart follows Rob I know you have something important on your mind."

"There you go again and as I reminded you, there are more times when I have said Rob Sweetheart than just Rob."

"You know I think you're right. Come over here as close as you can and tell me what's on your mind."

"Let's go to Vista Point for the coming weekend. It's been at least a month since we were last there. It's past time for our 2nd, 2nd honeymoon. Let's take our camping equipment and spend both Friday and Saturday nights at our favorite overlook."

"Are you ready to tramp through all that brush again wearing a backpack?"

"Don't you think we've been there often enough that we have made a pretty good trail?"

"Not too good I hope, we don't want hoards of people discovering our private overlook. Do you think you're up to it?"

"I've done it before and I can do it again. I would like for us to be alone."

"OK Sweetheart, this Friday afternoon we are leaving for Vista Point. I too am anxious to spend a weekend at our private overlook. Perhaps during the week you can work out a menu and then we can go shopping for the items we need."

"Sounds good to me," replied Heidi, "I'm really looking forward to the weekend."

Monday morning Rob asked Lorraine not to schedule patients Friday afternoon.

"Heidi and I are going to spend the weekend at Vista Point."

"Rob,"

"Yes Lorraine,"

"When are you going to ask Ted and I to go with you?"

"I had no idea you would like to go camping with us. You are more than welcome to come with us this weekend."

"I guess a weekend would be too much for us, it would have to be a day's outing since we have no camping equipment."

"Do you have access to a tent and sleeping bags?"

"No, but I suppose we could either buy or rent them."

"Have you and Ted ever camped Lorraine? If you haven't, I would suggest renting since camping may not be for you."

"No, we have never camped, but you've talked so much about it I think I would love it so long as we don't freeze or get caught in a two day rain."

"If we can believe the forecasters, this coming weekend is supposed to be warm with clear skies. I don't think we have to worry about either cold temperatures or rain."

"Let me talk to Ted this evening and I'll let you know if it will work out for us to go with you."

Cocking her head to the side and narrowing her eyes, Lorraine continued,

"That is if you give me the afternoon off."

"Lorraine, you don't have to ask, you've hurt my feelings."

"Yes, I'm sure I did," replied Lorraine with a big smile on her face. "Since Ted works four 10 hour days it won't be a problem for him."

That evening Rob told Heidi that Lorraine and Ted would like to go with them to Vista Point.

"Lorraine asked me why I have never asked them to go with us. She thought we would be gone just for the day. When I told her we would be camping the entire weekend she really got excited."

"Why not, she's my twin."

"What are you talking about?"

"I meant to tell you this before, but it slipped my mind. Some time ago Lorraine and I spent the day together shopping, eating and visiting, we both picked out a nice chic outfit. We were in the dressing room trying on the skirts. We were about nude when Lorraine asked me to turn around and face the mirror. We both did at the same time. Rob, we are so much alike that we could be twins."

Heidi hesitated for a moment then continued. Laughingly she said,

"Lorraine and I agreed that if we took our clothes off and covered our heads neither you nor Ted would know which of us is his wife."

"There's one way to find out, up at Vista Point you and Lorraine can strip in the tents, cover your heads, stand side by side and we will see if I can distinguish between you and Lorraine."

"Oh, you'd just love that wouldn't you?"

"I sure would, I've wanted to see Lorraine without her clothes on for a long time. This would give me the opportunity to do so."

"OK now, let's get serious."

"In other words you don't like my idea do you?"

"No, and must I say more."

Rob laughed, then said,

"If they can find a tent and bags to rent that's all they will need. We have all the other necessary equipment."

"It will be fun to have Lorraine and Ted along, but I was hoping we could be alone this weekend. Oh well, it really makes no difference. I never thought Lorraine and Ted would like to go camping with us."

"Lorraine will clear with Ted this evening and let me know tomorrow if it will work out for them."

"Now that there is that possibility I hope it does work out for Lorraine and Ted."

Ted had no trouble locating camping equipment and rented a tent, two sleeping bags and two back packs for the coming weekend.

"Will we have to back pack far?" Asked Lorraine.

"I'd say at most about 1 ½ miles. Think you can make that? I would like to say it's an easy hike, but we will have to do a bit of bush whacking to get to our favorite spot. It's really not that bad. Heidi and I have been there often enough that we have made something that resembles a trail."

"If Heidi can make it I'm sure I can. After all we are twins."

"So I hear."

"Did Heidi tell you about the comparison we made in the dressing room?"

"Yes she did. I had concluded quite some time ago that the two of you could be twins other than for your faces, that is. And even they bear resemblance. Now I suggest you give Heidi a call, the two of you can plan meals."

"I'll do that this evening. Tell Heidi to stay close to the phone."

It didn't take long for the two women to plan meals for the weekend. Lorraine suggested items they could not take since everything would have to be carried in on back packs.

"Just goes to show you what I know about camping," she said.

When they finished with the menu Heidi said,

"Lorraine, I'm going to be in the office alone tomorrow. James will be gone for the day. Give me a call when Rob starts with a patient so we can talk without being interrupted."

"OK Heidi will do."

At 10:00 Lorraine called Heidi.

"OK Heidi what is it you want to tell me?"

"This weekend I'm going to tell Rob I want a baby. I'm not going to ask him if the time for a baby is right because I know what he will say. I'm going to tell him that if he stalls for more time again that I'll get pregnant by someone else. I know plenty of men who would be more than willing to get the job done."

"Heidi you wouldn't?."

"Yes, but of course, I wouldn't mean it. But I will tell him that in 9 or 10 months I want to have a baby and that I won't accept any more stalling. Have you told Ted about your desire for a baby since we had our shopping and visiting day?"

"No I haven't Heidi."

"Well, why don't you join me? I know the two of you are going to enjoy yourselves if you know what I mean. It would be the perfect time to tell him you want a baby."

"Heidi, that's a wonderful idea. I've been going to have a talk with

Ted ever since our day together, but every time I feel I'm ready I chicken out. If you're going to put the bite on Rob I'll put the bite on Ted."

"One thing more Lorraine, Rob and I usually make love when we camp. If Ted is any thing like Rob, being outdoors for two days really gets his hormones to raging. When that happens he is like putty in my hands. Further it would give us a chance to get started on our get pregnant project."

"I know I won't have any trouble with Ted he likes to make love in places other than the bedroom. And I have a hunch a day outdoors will also get his hormones raging."

"I must warn you the fresh air will get our hormones raging also. A perfect set up, don't you think? We'll have to wear jeans to get to the camping spot, but after we're there we can just about go naked."

"We really won't be naked, will we Heidi?"

"Does the idea bother you Lorraine?"

"Well, I guess not really. It would be different wouldn't it and if we can get the men to strip we would have a regular nudist camp."

"No Lorraine, we won't be naked. If we were I'm afraid Rob would start looking at you with sex on his mind."

Lorraine laughed and said,

"And I'm afraid Ted would be looking at you with sex on his mind."

"That would never do. We want to get pregnant, but not by each other's husband."

"Heidi you're a card, but it isn't a bad idea. It sure would be erotic, wouldn't it?"

"I'm afraid it might turn out to be something more than erotic. Just bring something skimpy and sexy along so we can give Mother Nature a bit of a boost."

The four of them left for Vista Point at 2:00 P.M. By 3:30 they reached Vista Point and by 4:30 they had barged through the brush and were in the clearing that Rob and Heidi called their favorite place. Lorraine and Ted were awed by the beauty, by the unobstructed view of Mt. Rainier. Lorraine said,

"And back packing is the only way we can spend two days here."
"It was a bit tough navigating your so-called trail, but let me say, every scratch, every bruise is worth it."

While the men set up the camp the women prepared the evening meal. After they ate Heidi sat next to Rob with Rob's arm around her waist. They stayed that way until darkness blotted out their view of Mt. Rainier. Then they retreated to their tent. Rob and Heidi's sleeping bags zipped together and as they cuddled Rob said to Heidi,

"Lorraine sure has a great figure and does she ever look sexy in that skimpy outfit."

"Down boy, remember what you told Lorraine when we were separated, we can look but we can't touch the merchandise. Further Darling, you told me that when you look at Lorraine you see me and when you look at me you see Lorraine."

"Well, whatever, let's make love."

"Rob, it's been a busy and hard day, pushing through the brush with a back pack really left me tired. Could we wait until tomorrow evening?"

"Well, OK, but I can't guarantee you I'm going to be able to fall asleep."

"You don't want to admit it, but you too are tired."

"Yeah, I guess I am."

Heidi was still awake while Rob was sleeping soundly. At 5:30 Rob pulled on his trousers and shoes, grabbed his camera and telephoto lens and was about to step out the tent door when Heidi awakened.

"Where in the world are you going, it's only 5:30?"

"I'm going to set up my camera and hope there will be some alpenglow this morning."

"You don't mind if I don't join you, do You?"

"You go back to sleep Sweetheart. If the magic hour passes and there is no alpenglow I'll crawl back in bed with you."

At 6:30 Rob was back in the sleeping bags with Heidi. By 8:00 they were all up. The men shaved while the women put on a bit of makeup and of course they were wearing their brief and sexy outfits. As Lorraine and Heidi were fixing breakfast Heidi said to Lorraine,

"Today's the day Lorraine and tonight's the night. Be as sexy and seductive as you can be."

"Ted wanted to have sex last night, but I put him off by telling him that I was too tired. You know what he said? This is the first time you've turned me down because you're too tired. I said, Ted, I'm not used to carrying a back pack and pushing my way through a tangle of brush. We can make double time tomorrow night. Is that OK? Sure, he said and in a few minutes was sleeping soundly."

Heidi laughed quietly,

"It was the same with Rob. I feel a bit guilty that you and I have conspired against our husbands, but I'm assuming it's all for the good. By this evening they will be climbing the wall. Now remember, no sex until you talk baby."

"Don't worry Heidi, baby comes first and then sex. Oh, by the way, Ted said when he looked at you in your skimpy outfit you really turned him on."

Again Heidi laughed quietly,

"Rob said the same thing about you."

"What gives with our husbands Heidi?"

"You should know Lorraine, they're men."

Lorraine nodded her head and said,

"You sure are right there Heidi. Now if we can just keep our husbands from rushing us to bed before tonight."

"Lorraine, we really don't have to wait until tonight so long as its baby talk before sex, agreed?"

"Agreed?"

"What are you gals whispering about," Asked Ted."

"Oh, just women's talk that's all."

"I'm hungry, how long will it be before breakfast's ready?"

"It will be coming up in a few minutes," Replied Lorraine."

Rob said,

"You know you two gals don't have to wear much makeup to look great in the mornings. Don't you agree Ted?"

"Agreed," Replied Ted.

The day was spent in a leisurely fashion. They all hiked a mile in each direction from their camp. They agreed that the best view of Mt Rainier was the one where they were camped. After lunch they all took a nap. It was 4:00 before they awoke and the first thing Rob said was,

"Let's eat early, I'm hungry."

Ted joined in and said,

"This mountain air and the leisure sure does things to a person. It sure increases my appetites."

Heidi caught Lorraine's eye and winked.

Lorraine said,

"You guys are going to have to wait about half an hour. Heidi and I want to take a short walk along the rim. We won't be able to do that tomorrow evening, we'll all be back in crazy Cityville."

"OK," replied Ted, "But don't be gone too long and don't get too close to the edge of the rim."

After the two women had walked about 100 yards, Heidi said to Lorraine,

"Tonight's the night Lorraine. Tonight we lay it on them. Get me pregnant or I'll find someone else to do it. You're in agreement, aren't you?"

"I sure am, Ted is in an amorous mood and so am I. I think it's this wonderful mountain air and all the relaxing we have been doing."

Heidi laughed,

"I am more than hard up and I won't have to do any coaxing with Rob. Remember, we may not get pregnant tonight so we are going to have to keep after them. Do you see that as a problem Lorraine?"

"Heavens no, my concern is we may wear them out before we are pregnant."

"Not a chance with Rob."

"And I'm quite sure I will have no problem with Ted."

"Don't you feel a bit sinister with all this plotting behind our husbands backs?" Asked Heidi.

"You bet I do and I'm enjoying it," Replied Lorraine.

"Heidi, have you noticed how much like little boys our husbands are? The moment they woke up from their nap they complained they were hungry. What they were really saying was, Hey you gals, time to get started with dinner. They could have gotten the food together and started dinner without us."

"Of course I have Lorraine, but aren't they two wonderful little boys? Well we had better get back before they throw a temper tantrum."

After the evening meal they visited about numerous things, hunting, fishing, but mostly politics. Showing no interest in politics the women spent much time talking about recipes and cooking. The men built a cozy camp fire and all gathered around it.

"One of the nice things about this spot is that the evenings are always cool", said Heidi. "Lorraine don't you feel like you need a light jacket?"

"I sure do Heidi, let's get one."

It was obvious to the women that the men were in an amorous mood. At 9:30 Heidi said,

"I'm tired let's roll in early."

"Suits me," chimed in Lorraine. Heidi and I want to wash up first. Would you men mind taking a walk along the rim? Just be careful you don't fall over it."

"No thanks, we'll stay, said Rob, we'd like to watch. Both of you have nothing that Ted and I haven't seen many times over."

"Alright busters, get a move on, spoke up Lorraine."

"OK," grumbled Rob, "How much time do you need?"

"Give us 20 minutes."

"Alright," said Ted, "But no longer than 20 minutes."

It was exactly 20 minutes later when the men came walking back into camp. The women had just finished washing.

"It hardly pays for us to dress Lorraine," said Heidi, "We're going from here into the tent and into bed."

"That's OK with Rob and I" said Ted."

"What gives with you guys?" asked Lorraine.

"I'll give you one guess," replied Rob.

"I don't have to guess I know, let's turn in," said Lorraine.

When Rob and Heidi were comfortably situated in their sleeping bags, Heidi said to Rob.

"There is something I want to talk to you about, Rob."

"How about after we've made love for the first time?" Replied Rob."

"No Rob, not until we've had our talk."

"Heidi, what are you trying to do to me?"

"After our talk Rob."

"OK looks like I have no choice."

"You're right Rob, you have no choice."

"Rob, Sweetheart, I want a baby and I want it now. What I mean is in nine or ten months or a bit longer."

"Slide over here Sweetheart," Rob said as he pulled Heidi close. "Heidi Girl, you have been very patient with me and my stalling, always coming up with some reason or other why having a baby should be postponed. There will be no more stalling and no more postponements. You shall have you're baby or I should say, it's time we start a family."

"Rob Sweetheart, do you mean it?"

"Of course I mean it. Lately I've been feeling guilty over putting off getting you pregnant while you have wanted to have a baby so badly."

"Rob, I guess my mothering instincts have kicked in and I'm not getting any younger. I've waited until now to tell you that I saw Dr. Swanson. She ran some tests on me and she sees no reason why I can't conceive. My tubes are open. I must tell you, when I walked into her office she recognized me immediately, she said Heidi, it's so good to see you. I'm keeping my fingers crossed, you aren't here to see me because you are having trouble with your cervix. I told her no Dr Swanson, I took your advice, I quit prostitution about three years ago, found and fell deeply in love with that loving young man you said I should be looking for and since our last meeting he is the only man I've had sex with and the only man I will ever have six with. But I must tell you he is a sexual dynamo and I hope that frequency of sex wont damage my cervix because if it does I'm going to be in trouble. Laughing Dr. Swanson said, when you first came to see me Heidi, you were not much more than a girl. That was a dangerous time for you as a prostitute since the tissue on your cervix was not yet fully developed. Under any circumstances you should not have been having intercourse frequently and not with a variety of men, especially un-circumcised men. You are no longer that young girl, you are now a fully matured woman. I'm assuming from the beginning your husband has been gentle with you. I said, Dr. Swanson, if there is anything Rob was concerned with it was with not hurting me. I really expect you to find my cervix completely healed and will be able to give me a clean bill of health. She did. I told her I was going to get pregnant even if I had to deceive you by discontinuing my pills. She laughed and said, you wouldn't be the first woman who pulled that trick on her husband. Further, it will be good for you to get pregnant. I said, expect to see me in a month or two. As I was about to leave she said, you were such a pretty girl when I first saw you. I replied, no longer, right? Now Heidi, you are a very attractive young woman. It's obvious you have taken care of yourself. Dr. Swanson, I replied, that's what a good marriage and marriage to a wonderful man has done to me. I told her you are a doctor and have a successful practice in marriage and sexual therapy. She said to greet you and she is looking forward to meeting you. Then she said, I think your husband and I will have much to talk about."

"You recall a long time ago I told you she had some concern that the Chlamydia might have affected my tubes. Well it didn't."

"I'm happy to hear that Heidi."

"Now darling there was something we postponed from last night to tonight."

"I stopped taking my pills Thursday evening. Maybe that wasn't soon enough and I don't know if this is the right time of the month, but I'm hoping that tonight is the night I get pregnant. Enough talk let's get started on making a baby. You realize of course, if I don't conceive right away that when it's time for me to ovulate we may have to have sex at least two or three times a day for about 10 days."

Rob was silent, then with a chuckle he replied,

"Heidi girl, now you're getting into my field. There is approximately a 36 hour window of opportunity for you to conceive each month. You have been charting your periods so I'm sure you know about when you ovulate. Granted, because of the slight irregularity of your periods, we'll have to back off a few days and go beyond the expected time of ovulation for a few days, but as good as it sounds to me, intercourse once a day for those 10 days should be sufficient. If by chance we could have sex two or three times a day for 10 days, I would say that after about two days my sperm count would be so low, sex or no sex you wouldn't get pregnant."

"Shucks, I should have known I couldn't fool you on that two or three times a day business. I also thought it would sound good to you."

"Heidi Sweetheart, I may have a raging libido as you often say, but I am not a sexual athlete, I couldn't measure up to that many times a day for 10 days."

"You mean you're admitting you have limitations?"

"I'm afraid so Sweetheart."

"Want to know something, if we had to have sex two or three times a day, I would have to quit my job and I would get nothing done around the house. So just let me say, thank heavens for limitations."

"Now that you understand clearly, it's time we try at least twice tonight and hope that you have an egg in one of your tubes."

"Want to know something Rob, I'm so darn hard up that I could climb a wall and that's a good sign."

"Oh I rather think it's all the fresh air and being outdoors that inflames your libido."

"Rob. Now you're pulling my leg, but just let me say that I have noticed that about the time when I should be ovulating I especially desire having sex. So maybe, just maybe tonight's the night."

"Mark it on your calendar."

"Now let's get started before we both fall asleep," said Heidi.

Afterwards when they were in each others arms Heidi said to Rob,

"Darling I believe that was the best ever."

"Of course it was Sweetheart. Now I feel deliciously tired, let's sleep.

"That's a good way of putting it Rob, deliciously tired. Let's sleep," replied Heidi.

It was 5:00 Sunday morning when Rob got up pulled on his trousers, put on his shoes and was about to step outside the tent. His movements awoke Heidi, she rose up on one elbow and put her head in her hand and looked at Rob.

"You just won't give up will you?"

"No Sweetheart, I won't"

"Rob, thank you for last night. I can't think of another time when we've had sex that it has been so deliciously wonderful."

"Heidi Girl, you don't have to thank me."

"Aren't you the one who said I'll thank you if I want to?"

"You've got me there Sweetheart. As long as we are throwing out thank yous, let me thank you. It was deliciously wonderful, so much so that I wouldn't be surprised if sperm and egg aren't just about to meet."

Heidi laughed,

"There are times when you can be a funny guy."

"Funny guy, who me? Never. Now go back to sleep."

Rob walked to the edge of the rim and once again set up his camera. When finished he sat down and waited. Twenty minutes later he was back in the tent.

"Heidi, grab your camera and come quick. Rainier is bathed in alpenglow. It's beautiful, it's fantastic. Such a delicate rose color I have never seen before."

Heidi slipped on her shorts and a sweater, grabbed her camera and joined Rob who was taking picture after picture. When she stepped out of the tent she looked at Rainier and gasped.

"Oh Rob, it's so beautiful. This has to be a sacred moment."

"That's a wonderful way of putting it Heidi. I must awaken Lorraine and Ted it would be sinful if they missed this."

Rob stepped to the entrance of their tent and called,

"Lorraine, Ted, quick get up. Put on anything that is handy there is a phenomenon out here that you just can't miss. This very well may be a once in a life time experience."

In a moment Lorraine and Ted stepped out of the tent. Lorraine gasped. Ted said,

"Oh my God, what is it?"

"It's called alpenglow Ted."

"God has blessed us to allow us to see such a sight, such beauty. I feel like I'm standing on sacred ground, like I should take off my slippers," said Lorraine

"What a wonderful way of putting it Lorraine. Heidi called it a 'sacred moment.' You women surely have the right words that I guess we men just can't come up with. We must remember what both of you said."

Many pictures were taken. Then as the sun continued on its journey to the horizon the beautiful rose color began to fade and soon it was over.

"Let's go back to bed for another hour or two before we get up," said Ted.

"We are already up Ted," answered Lorraine.

"You know what I mean."

"I know Darling I was just having fun with you."

Heidi and Lorraine got behind their men and when Ted and Rob entered the tents, they tarried for a moment. Heidi looked at Lorraine who was about 10 feet away. Both had big smiles on their faces. Heidi made a circle with her thumb and fore finger and raised her hand so

Lorraine could see it. Lorraine also formed a ring with her thumb and fore finger and waved it at Heidi. Heidi stepped closer to Lorraine and whispered,

"Mission accomplished Lorraine."

"Mission accomplished Heidi."

Both returned to their tent, crawled into the sleeping bags, snuggled up against their husbands and soon all four were sleeping soundly.